Praise for
Ellington Boulev...

"Inventive, funny, and touching . . . the real joy comes from the humor that Langer injects into almost every page . . . It's all a delight, ingeniously plotted and expertly written." —*St. Louis Post-Dispatch*

"When a character finds a good parking space in the first sentence, you know you've encountered a New York novel that's full of hope . . . Langer has written an original and humorous urban novel, a theatrical musical of a novel (with an appendix of songs), a chain of love stories set during the city's real estate boom." —*The Jewish Week*

"Langer writes beautifully about the city and how it is stunning and crushing at the same time." —*St. Petersburg Times*

"In Adam Langer's *Ellington Boulevard*, a cast of thrillingly nuanced characters spin around one another in pursuit of happiness, love and, above all, real estate." —*New York Observer*

"A New York City novel par excellence." —*Kirkus Reviews* (starred)

"*Ellington Boulevard* captures all of Manhattan's quirky insanity with great style and a huge amount of fun." —Barbara Corcoran, founder of the Corcoran Group

"Adam Langer, who is either a genius or a schizophrenic, inhabits his characters—from a pregnant woman to a pigeon—with brilliant stealth and loveable insouciance. Finally a book has come along that has gotten me excited about reading and even New York again." —Jennifer Belle, author of *High Maintenance* and *Little Stalker*

"Adam Langer took me on a wonderful trip all over the Upper West Side of Manhattan. The reader will meet musicians, actors and even a dog named Herbie Mann—open the cover, read, and enjoy! This is his best book yet." —Eli Wallach

"An apartment on West 106th Street (aka Ellington Boulevard) links a disparate group of New Yorkers in this intricate tale of life, love, and real estate . . . Langer takes his time in developing the characters and the depths of their interconnectedness, rendering the twists, doubts, and heartbreaks that afflict the milieu highly affecting. For readers who turn first on Sunday morning to the real estate section, it doesn't get much better." —*Publishers Weekly*

"I loved this book, but then I've always been a sucker for quality. Adam Langer lifts the lid off the top of New York City and lets us see, close up, and terribly personally, the cosmopolitan complexity of the city that never sleeps alone. In his fugue-like charting of their lives—lives that cross, lives that double-cross—he reveals his love of all things New York: its people, its dogs, and even more remarkably, its pigeons. The composition and orchestration that Mr. Langer has gifted us with would have delighted the Duke himself." —Larry Gelbart, creator of *M*A*S*H*, co-screenwriter of *Tootsie*, and Tony Award–winning author of *City of Angels* and *A Funny Thing Happened on the Way to the Forum*

"I laughed out loud throughout this simultaneously cynical and sentimental New York fairy tale with a love for off-Broadway musicals and the seventeen-key clarinet and a profound understanding of the importance of dogs." —Stephen Schwartz, Academy Award–winning lyricist and composer for *Wicked, Godspell, Pippin,* and *The Prince of Egypt*

"Langer excels at digging into the nitty gritty of his setting . . . He chronicles the loss of local bodegas and local characters, replaced by yuppies, breakfast nooks, and nail salons." —*New York Post*

"The gentrifying Upper West Side provides a complex and ideal backdrop for a *la ronde* involving a musician on the verge of eviction, his rescued dog, the people who are buying his apartment, a family of pigeons, and an editor . . . There is also an unexpected charm in the way Langer choreographs these people's destinies." —*Time Out New York*

ELLINGTON BOULEVARD

{ *A Novel in A-Flat* }

Adam Langer

SPIEGEL & GRAU

New York

2009

2009 Spiegel & Grau Trade Paperback Edition

Published in the United States by Spiegel & Grau, an imprint of
The Random House Publishing Group, a division of
Random House, Inc., New York.

Originally published in hardcover in the United States by Spiegel & Grau,
an imprint of The Random House Publishing Group,
a division of Random House, Inc., in 2008.

SPIEGEL & GRAU is a trademark of Random House, Inc.

Library of Congress Cataloging-in-Publication Data
Langer, Adam.
Ellington Boulevard : a novel in a-flat / Adam Langer
p.   cm.
ISBN: 978-0-385-52206-9
1. Musicians—Fiction. 2. Manhattan (New York, N.Y.)—Fiction. I. Title.

PS3612.A57E45 2008
813'.6—dc22
2007016207

PRINTED IN THE UNITED STATES OF AMERICA

www.spiegelandgrau.com

1 3 5 7 9 10 8 6 4 2

First Paperback Edition

BOOK DESIGN BY AMANDA DEWEY

This book is dedicated to
my wife, Beate; my daughter, Nora;
my parents, Esther and Seymour;
and my dog, Kazoo[1]

---

[1]And all the dogs we have known and befriended, who include Prince, Lucy, Zoe, Maddie, Charlie, Moona, Princess, Buddy, Georgia, Jazz, Fig, Liz, Lola, Rosie, Otto, Higgs, Sadie, Onyx, Otis, Barkie, Klondike, Buber, Schnitzel, Jackson, Francine, Oscar, Chloe, Griffin, László, Humphrey, Alice, Shadow, Gracie, Duncan, Duffy, Dinky, Gizmo, Sachi, Ginny, Guinness, Jessie, Peanut, My Girl, Dante, et al.

Wouldn't you like to have a smart little place of your own?

From the song "Wouldn't You Like to Be on Broadway?"

FROM THE MUSICAL STREET SCENE

Book by Elmer Rice, lyrics by Langston Hughes, music by Kurt Weill

CONTENTS

ELLINGTON
BOULEVARD

OVERTURE

Curtain rises on Duke Ellington Boulevard, also known as West 106th Street, six blocks that slice through the rapidly gentrifying neighborhood of Manhattan Valley on New York's Upper West Side. Barbershops and bodegas, storefront churches and pizza joints, soaring new condo developments, tenements in the process of being renovated—workmen have applied fresh mortar between their white, tan, and red bricks and new coats of paint on their black and green fire escapes. Men wearing knit hats, down coats, and gloves are seated on milk crates in front of a corner grocery, listening to salsa music on a beat-up radio. Truckers are unloading cases of beer and soda in front of the Parkside Mini Supermarket as customers exit the store with lottery tickets and bags of groceries. Dog walkers lead their animals east toward Central Park or west toward Riverside Park. Kids returning from school leap off the M7 bus and race for home.

Over the doorway of the Roberto Clemente Building, a renovated five-story, redbrick, prewar tenement with a gray stone façade, a banner is flying: OPEN HOUSE TONIGHT!

Most of the people who are heading down the boulevard bound for this condominium building weren't born in this city. And years ago, when they first came to New York, they lived in walk-ups or railroad flats, sharing rooms with strangers above restaurants, taverns, and corner delis. They had left their hometowns for this city because of a bold, romantic song they knew by heart, because of a story a father or teacher had told them about growing up here. They had come to this place because of a novel they had read where Manhattan was all fast-paced, snappy dialogue and gritty, honest romance; because of a black-and-white movie they had watched over and over where New York was all glimmering neon, opening parties, and a night lit up by skyscrapers. To them, all those years ago, the city was a clarinet trilling Gershwin, a tenor belting out Sondheim; the city was a kiss on a bench under a moonlit bridge, a chorus girl becoming a star; the city was the book they would finish writing here, the melody they would hear, the role they would finally get to play, the person they would meet, the person they would become.

But now that they've been here for some time, they have begun to forget the city they had come to find. They have boxed away their manuscripts, sold their books and musical instruments to secondhand shops. They have become bankers, traders, corporate writers, marketing directors, website content providers. There are only a few dreamers in the mix today—look, there's a young editor and her husband, a graduate student in English literature, walking toward the Roberto Clemente Building. But as they head up the steps of the building with the rest of the crowd, there is little need for a profession to define them; all that is needed is the checkbook in their pocket. Tonight, everyone is a tenant or a landlord, a buyer or a seller, a customer or a client. They have all come here to meet a broker and to look at a piece of property.

Outside, on Duke Ellington Boulevard, snow is beginning to fall, and a man and his dog are on their way home.

Lights up full.

From Ellington Boulevard (M. Dimmelow, G. Malinowski), the musical based on the following true-life events.

{ 1 }

AN OFFER
IS MADE

I've been down in New York City, brother,
and that ain't no place to be down.

GIL SCOTT-HERON,
"Blue Collar"

THE TENANT

On the evening when he will learn that his apartment is being sold out from under him, Ike Ambrose Morphy finds a good parking space on Central Park West, then walks north toward home beside his dog, Herbie, through the early-December snow. Though he has just spent the better part of seven and a half long months in Chicago at his mother's bedside, Ike can already feel the crisp New York air instilling in him nearly the same energy and sense of purpose he felt twenty years ago when he dropped out of college, left his mom's house and his hometown, and moved to this city that, for him, always represented freedom and possibility. Man, he can barely wait to get to his street, return to his building, climb the stairs to the second floor, enter his apartment, lock his door, drop his suitcases, take his clarinet out of its case, and play once again just as he promised his mother, Ella Mae Morphy, he would on the morning earlier this week when she closed her eyes for the last time.

At the corner of Central Park West and 106th, Ike turns to cross the street. He is bound for the Roberto Clemente Building, where he has lived for just about all of the two decades he has spent here in Manhattan

Valley. But the moment the traffic light changes to green, Ike's unleashed seventy-pound black retriever-chow mix bounds up the steps of the park's Strangers' Gate entrance. Ike now recognizes just how stifled Herbie must have felt in Ike's ailing mom's drab, run-down house on Colfax Avenue on the South Side of Chicago. "Wait up, Herb," he tells his dog, and then he jogs the half block back to his maroon Dodge pickup truck. He puts his suitcases on the floor of the car, locks and closes the door, and returns to Strangers' Gate with an old tennis ball. He flips the ball to Herbie and soon the man and his dog are running up the steps side by side.

The steps here at Strangers' Gate are divided into eight segments, and as Ike follows Herbie up toward the Great Hill, he counts them—ten steps, ten steps, ten again, eleven, eight, eleven, another ten, then seven. To Ike, who has always found inspiration for his music in the sights and sounds of this city, the arrangement of steps seems suggestive of a progression of notes, unpredictable yet part of some pattern, vaguely reminiscent of A Love Supreme, but he is trying too hard to keep pace with his dog to discern any specific melody. After they have climbed the steps, Ike and Herbie briefly continue to run, but when they reach the temporary black fence surrounding the lawn on the hill, the animal stops. Now, Herbie begins to whine. He crouches down and he jumps up; he puts up his paws and barks at a sign on the fence: CLOSED FOR THE SEASON. NO TRESPASSING.

Ike Morphy can remember when he first came to this part of Central Park. Then, he was just some poor, gangly, bespectacled nineteen-year-old kid only trying to make enough dough playing music or working construction so that he wouldn't have to turn around and head home, so that he wouldn't have to go back to Chicago, where he'd found himself finally unable to study or play his clarinet since he always had to mediate the incessant arguments about money and boyfriends and God-knows-what-else between his sister, Naima, and their widowed mother, Ella Mae. During Ike's first days in New York in the late 1980s, nobody seemed to give a damn about the park lawns this far north. Ike slept for three straight nights amid overgrown weeds and broken glass, and never even saw a cop. But now that every inch of Central Park seems to have become as pristine as the rehabbed buildings that surround it, the city says Ike and his dog can't even walk on the lawn.

Herbie at his side, Ike walks around the fence, searching for the usual opening. Failing to find it, Ike heads back to his pickup again with Herbie, this time to retrieve a long pair of shears from the gardening kit that once belonged to his mother; the kit is the only item that Ike has brought back to New York from his childhood home. Ella Mae Morphy had been a horticulturist at Chicago's Garfield Park Conservatory, a verdant oasis in the midst of one of the city's most neglected neighborhoods, while his father, Bill, who died when Ike was in high school, had worked as a painter and set designer for the few theaters that remained on Chicago's South Side. From his parents, Ike inherited both a love of the beautiful and a gnawing sense that others would never fully appreciate it, and his worldview, like Bill's and Ella Mae's, could be both cynical and naïve at the same time. Ike's expectations were often so lofty that he felt unbearably frustrated when, inevitably, they were not met.

Now, Ike and the dog return to the Great Hill, where Ike looks to see if anyone else is around before he uses his mother's shears to cut open the fence. Soon Herbie is romping gleefully through the clean white fluff. As Ike watches the dog, he isn't sure who feels happier—Herbie for being able to run again, or himself for being able to see his animal so excited and free. Ike hums to himself as Herbie drops his ball, chases it, buries it in the snow, digs it out, then chases it again—nearly an hour of this until a squad car pulls up.

At one time, Ike knew all the beat cops, and in the winter they would always let dog owners open up the fence here so that their pets could play. But Ike doesn't recognize this cop—he's a hostile dude with a buzz cut, "Cahill" on his nameplate. The cop leans out his window as he drives over the asphalt path, through the opening Ike cut in the fence, then onto the lawn, asking Ike, what does he think he's doing here, neighbor? Ike explains with a confident smile that all the cops around here know him and Herbie, but Cahill doesn't respond, just picks up his ticket book and starts writing; to him, Ike isn't Ike Morphy the virtuoso clarinet player, onetime member of the R & B outfit the Funkshuns, and longtime resident of

Manhattan Valley anymore. Apparently he's just some thug, some tall, menacing, thirty-nine-year-old black dude with a shaved head, a gold stud in one ear, a pair of thick glasses, and a set of garden shears ready to do some damage. Cahill doesn't even look up at Ike, keeps asking for ID, muttering about trespassing and violation 161.05 in the New York City health code. Hey, man, Ike tells Cahill, this has always been a tight-knit community where everybody looks out for one another. He offers his hand and begins to introduce himself to the officer, but Cahill still doesn't make eye contact, not even when Ike points out the treads the squad car made in the snow, and remarks that Cahill has probably already done more damage to the lawn by driving over it than Herbie ever did by playing.

You know what, Ike says—he'll bet that Cahill will be the laughing-stock of his precinct if he bothers writing him up for letting his dog play on the lawn. This is his and Herbie's turf, Ike thinks; the cop must be new on the job—doesn't know how things work up here. When Cahill snorts and keeps writing, Ike snaps his fingers in front of Herbie's snoot. "Follow," he commands. Man and dog quickly walk away from the cop, then start running again, Ike feeling certain that no officer around here would chase him over a lousy seventy-five-buck trespassing ticket. Over the path they go, down the steps, out the park at Strangers' Gate, across the street, west on 106th past Manhattan Avenue until they reach Ike's block and the Roberto Clemente Building.

Ike stands outside at the top of the Clemente's steps underneath the banner that reads OPEN HOUSE TONIGHT! and tries to catch his breath. He looks up and down the street to make sure Cahill hasn't followed. As he reaches into his blue-jeans pocket for his keys, he notices a moon-faced, ruddy-cheeked young white guy in a dark gray suit worn underneath a full-length black leather duster opening the door from the inside to leave the building. When Ike reaches for the handle, the man firmly closes the door behind him, then takes his iPod earbuds out of his ears and stares Ike down.

"Uh, do you live here, sir?" the man asks.

The question smacks Ike like a snowball to the face.

Does he live here, sir?

Well, yes, he does, sir, he thinks, longer than just about anyone else in this building. Ike has lived here long enough to remember his first days on this street when some of the apartment buildings looked like bombed-out ruins—warped boards up on all the windows; toughs in Starter jackets loitering by Amsterdam Avenue in front of the Round the Clock Deli; crack packets on the sidewalk and in the gutters, color-coded to differentiate which gang had sold them; rats jumping out of trash bags, so bold they didn't even bother to scurry out of people's way. Ike has lived here long enough to remember when he, Ricardo Melendez, and some other dudes started helping to renovate the Clemente and a crackhead from the rehab clinic down the street wandered in and started banging on everybody's doors; Ike and Ricardo took the brother over to the A&P on Columbus and made him drink a whole bottle of orange soda to settle him down. Ike can remember when he and Ricardo joined the other members of the neighborhood block association to protest that youth hostel down the street because, back then, it was a whorehouse with royal blue shower curtains in every bathroom and a sign in the lobby that read: $25 FOR FOUR HOURS. NO LUGGAGE ALLOWED. Tough neighborhood in those days, some said, but Ike was always street smart; he kept to himself and rarely had any trouble. Sometimes, though, he and Ricardo made up stories about how dangerous the street was just so jackasses like this guy wouldn't move in and start raising the cost of living for everybody in the community.

Does he live here, sir?

Ike can still remember when he began playing clarinet with the Funkshuns and their tunes were just starting to get airplay on some FM stations at the right end of the dial, and supers and store owners would greet him as he walked by: "Hey, Ike." "S'up, Ike?" "Soundin' good, Ike." Ike can still remember when that condo building over there on 106th and Manhattan was a community garden called the Common Ground where on summer nights he and his old on-again, off-again girlfriend Muriel Ostrow would get drunk and watch 16-millimeter movies on a collapsible screen. Ike can recite the name of every liquor store owner on Amsterdam, every numbers runner who patrolled the bodegas of Manhattan Avenue, every fix-it man in every Columbus Avenue hardware store where Ike has shopped ever since he quit the band nearly seven years ago, returning to work construction gigs in the city until he could decide whether he wanted to keep playing music or not. He's lived here long enough to remember when Columbus Avenue didn't have any gumbo restaurants or tapas bars or creperies, long enough, in fact, to remember when practically the only white guys around were the ones who drove in from Jersey looking to buy reefer.

Does he live here, sir?

Ike pulls out his keys and inserts one in the lock. "That answer your question, sir?" he asks, gesturing to the key. The man mumbles "Sorry" and walks quickly past Ike and down the front stairs as Ike and Herbie enter, Ike counting steps all the way, searching for some melody, some pattern upon which he can improvise the moment after he takes his clarinet out of his hall closet. But when he reaches apartment 2B, the pattern he was starting to hear fades and disappears as Ike notices that his door is already half open.

Standing before the door, Ike flinches and tries to shake off the nagging sense that, in his long absence, something as yet indefinable has changed in his city. He thinks of the cop in the park, the yuppie in the leather duster downstairs. He breathes deeply, takes a tighter hold of Herbie's leash. Warily, he pushes the door open the rest of the way. Could he have been so damn absentminded as to have forgotten to lock up half a year ago before leaving town to tend to his mother? he is wondering, when his eyes settle upon three strangers, thieves perhaps, who are walking through his apartment.

No, they don't look like typical thieves, Ike knows, but he still thinks he can recognize them as such, the men at least, just as record execs and talent scouts have always looked like thieves to him; he can't imagine why, though, they would bother pillaging the meager contents of this shabby two-bedroom apartment for which Ike still pays the same $350 monthly rent to Jerry Masler as when he first moved in. After all, Ike hasn't ever repainted his place, has never fully furnished it. The floors need waxing, and the pigeons on the air conditioner make a mess of Ike's bedroom window; he has never had the heart to remove their nest. Still, as long as Ike has been able to sleep with the living room windows open, listening to the music of sirens, traffic, boom boxes, and mah-jongg tiles on the boulevard, the apartment has felt like home to him.

Ike takes off the leash and Herbie lopes suspiciously through the apartment, sniffing the baseboards and growling at the new scents, Ike puts his garden shears in the hall closet and tries to make sense of the present scene. In his bedroom, a scruffy-looking white guy, maybe about thirty years old, wears a frayed army jacket, a bucket hat, and scuffed black Doc Martens. The guy—he's still a guy, not quite a man—snorts as he surveys Ike's air-conditioning unit, then makes a snide remark to his wife about the pigeons roosting upon it ("Air-rifle those mofos"). It's clear that this woman—long red hair; no makeup; gullible green eyes; big, flat, brown shoes; actually kind of lovely in a gawky, doesn't-think-she-is way—is the guy's wife, even though she doesn't wear a wedding ring. She's six feet easy, a good deal taller than her husband, just a few inches shorter than Ike. After she scribbles something in a notebook, she turns to face the hallway; she smiles at Ike as if she recognizes him, apparently decides that she doesn't or that recognizing him might be rude, and returns to her notebook.

The woman seems so much at home here, Ike thinks as he gazes at her, so at home in Ike's home—could he have wandered into the wrong apartment? On the road back in his band days when he drank nearly every night to stave off the loneliness and the persistent memories of those endless family fights that helped convince him to leave Chicago, he often made just that sort of mistake—*Sorry, my fault, no need to call the cops, I'll run along to my room now*—but ever since he walked out on the Funkshuns right in the middle of a concert at the Arie Crown Theater and never came back, he has barely touched liquor or anything else. Maybe he should knock on Ricardo and Marlena's door across the hall to see if his old buddies have any inkling of why these people are in his apartment. But their dog, Buster, didn't bark when he and Herbie returned, so they obviously aren't home.

Ike is opening his mouth to speak, trying to formulate the proper way in which to ask these yuppies exactly what they think they're doing here, when Herbie takes matters into his own paws; the mutt wags his fluffy tail at the woman, but then—*grrrrrr!*—darts toward her husband, who shouts, "Hey, what the fuck!" and edges backward. The man holds his hands out in front of him, uttering clipped commands of "No!" to the approaching dog ("No! No, you son of a bitch!"), then spews forth a litany of foreign curses: *"Non, espèce de salope de merde. Nein, du fricking Scheisshund, nein!"* Ike follows Herbie into the room and grabs him by the collar. He orders the dog into a down-stay while the third intruder, a short, slim young man in a black overcoat, with slicked-back, sandy-blond hair, apple cheeks, and earnest blue eyes, charges toward Ike. The man wears pleated wool slacks, shiny black shoes, and a fake gold watch, the kind Ike remembers seeing hustlers sell to tourists on the subway. He asks Ike if he can help him.

"Can you what, now?" asks Ike.

"Help you, sir," the man says.

"I live here, brother," says Ike.

The man in the black overcoat nods, then furrows his brow meaningfully.

"Oh, Mr. Morphy," he says, and adds that they won't be here much longer. He asks the red-haired woman if she and Darrell need a few more minutes. No, she says, they can just study the floor plan and watch the virtual tour again at home. Perfect, the man says. And, he continues as he picks up a black folder from Ike's kitchen counter and walks toward Ike's door, if they want to see the apartment again, they should call him on his cell and he'll sign out the keys.

"Keys to what?" asks Ike. The man smiles and holds out his hand. "Josh Dybnick," he says. "From Overman." He pulls a card out of his wallet: "Joshua Dybnick, Associate Broker, The Overman Group." Dybnick grins vacantly at Ike, reminding him of that officious, clean-cut guy who appears in Overman Group commercials before the movie trailers at Lincoln Plaza Cinemas ("Isn't it time you moved up to Overman?"). Dybnick says that "Mr. Masler" tried to call Ike several times, but Ike's phone was disconnected; Ike should call Masler for an explanation.

Josh tries to lead the couple out, but Ike is still standing in the doorway. His apartment isn't for sale, brother, Ike tells him. Josh opens his black

folder and pulls out a double-sided sheet of paper: on one side is a break-
down of estimated mortgage and maintenance payments, on the other are
color snapshots of Ike's apartment beneath a double-decker headline: TWO
BEDROOMS ON ELLINGTON BOULEVARD: AN UPPER UPPER WEST SIDE STEAL!
Ike takes a moment before realizing that the apartment being depicted is
his. *Ellington Boulevard?* Hardly anyone around here calls it that, just
tourists and prospectors. *Upper Upper West Side?* Who came up with that
name? This is Manhattan Valley.

"I said my place isn't for sale," Ike says. He doesn't know why in the
world Josh and his "backup singers" think his apartment is on the block,
he says, but for their information, he has a goddamn lease.

But as he mentions the lease, Ike remembers that he doesn't actually
have one, not on paper. Even though he laid these floors himself, built this
kitchen, helped install the tubs, toilets, and sinks in every apartment in the
Roberto Clemente Building, all he has is a spoken sweat-equity agreement
with Jerry Masler—in exchange for his labor, he could keep the apartment
for $350 a month for as long as he wanted to live here. *Jesus*, Ike thinks. Now
he can remember when Jerry urged him to buy this apartment for $80K, and
even though the Funkshuns had their first Top 40 single out then and he
could have swung the dough, he couldn't believe anyone would pay that
much just for a place to live. He has a goddamn lease, Ike repeats now, hoping that if he makes this assertion confidently enough, these people will
leave him alone so he can call Jerry and find out what's going on.

Sure enough, Josh quickly maneuvers his customers past Ike and out
the front door, the woman smiling apologetically, Darrell looking back at
the dog. Once they have left, Ike can hear the three commiserating in the
hallway as if he'd just tried to bum-rush them. He hears a man laughing,
footsteps heading downstairs, the front door opening, closing. He walks to
the window, Herbie following behind.

Herbie places his paws on the windowsill beside Ike's hands, and Ike
puts an arm around Herbie and holds him close, bending down to feel the
dog's warm ear twitch against his cheek. Through the window, Ike and
Herbie watch Darrell and his wife walk out into the cold, snowy night
while Josh, folded OPEN HOUSE TONIGHT! banner under his arm, runs

across the slick boulevard to flag down a cab. Ike walks to the bedroom and picks up his phone to call Jerry Masler but can't get a dial tone. He knocks on Ricardo and Marlena's door across the hall but nobody answers, and Buster doesn't bark. So Ike calls Herbie, attaches the leash, and as the two head back out to get Ike's luggage out of his truck, Ike notices that Ricardo and Marlena's names are no longer on their mailbox. And as he is weighing this particular bit of information, he has already forgotten the music he was beginning to hear; at this moment, he doesn't even remember that he was thinking of any melody at all. Snow is falling down harder, and as he walks east, Ike Morphy can't escape the sensation that he has returned home only to learn that he has become a stranger here, that this city is no longer his.

THE SELLER

Mark Masler, current owner of apartment 2B in the Roberto Clemente Building, may not yet have learned all he needs to know about his late father Jerry Masler's business and personal affairs, but he knows enough to have a pretty good hunch that, during the twenty years Ike Morphy has lived in apartment 2B at 64 West 106th Street, Jerry Masler never had him sign any sort of legal document. Had there been a lease, Mark surely would have found it in his father's old files by now. And this is precisely what Mark will tell his broker, Josh Dybnick, when he calls him at eight this morning, a time Mark finds unreasonably late for anyone to be starting the workday.

Not long ago, Mark Masler would never have been awake at this hour, unless he hadn't gone to sleep at all—in which case he would have been nursing some hangover, returning bleary-eyed and cotton-mouthed from a party he had catered, arguing with or making love to some freak he had met at a concert or dance club. But this morning, as he sits behind the desk in the Union Square office suite that once belonged to his dad, he has already *davened* at shul, worked out at the gym, read the *Wall Street Journal* and the business section of the *Post*, responded to all his e-mails, and cycled through his voice messages—two from his attorney, Alan Ziegler; three from an increasingly agitated Ike Morphy; a half-dozen from commercial real estate brokers with properties to show him; even one from a young woman named Allie Scheinblum, who has called to say she recently saw Mark at a Shabbat service at the B'nai Akiva Synagogue in Riverdale and wants to invite him to deliver a speech to the temple's Young Leaders Committee.

Allie's is the only female voice Mark has heard on his voice mail since June, when he returned home early from a men's-only anger-management retreat to attend his father's funeral and listened to the condolences of his first wife. But right now, the only urgent message is the one from Josh Dybnick regarding the most recent open house at the Clemente, where Josh reports that he met Rebecca Sugarman and Darrell Schiff, a couple who showed up at the end of the night and seemed very interested in Mark's apartment until Ike Morphy entered with his dog, claiming to have a lease.

Eight o'clock finally arrives. Mark Masler picks up the desk phone and calls Josh. The apartment is his, free and clear, Mark says, he's sure of it. Late last year when he inherited all his father's remaining properties and began selling them off, he actually did try, against his lawyer's advice, to contact Ike to work out an arrangement, even waited to list the property with the Overman Group on the off chance that Ike might want to buy it. But at this late date, Mark will not allow Ike to cock up the plans he will finally put into action once the apartment has been sold. Let the guy find whatever agreement he thinks he has and show it to a lawyer, Mark tells Josh, then directs the broker to call back his potential buyers; the property has been on the block long enough and it's time to move.

The conventional wisdom about the men in the Masler family has always been that Jerry Masler was the mensch of all mensches, and this boy of his, this Mark, is the consummate schmuck. Mark knows this characterization is unfair and simplistic, but today, at the age of forty-two, as he speaks on the phone with Josh Dybnick, he understands how it came to gain currency; Jerry Masler's act was a tough one to follow. In any city smaller than New York, Jerry would have had streets and buildings named after him, not just one small wing of St. Luke's Hospital.

Mark Masler spent his earliest years in Sunnyside, Queens, back in the days when his dad, a Manhattan real estate attorney, was still preaching thrift while saving for his family's future. Then, the Maslers lived in a three-bedroom split-level with couches and armchairs wrapped in plastic, tablecloths used as slipcovers, and paper plates at the table in the kitchen, where Mark would help his mom, a full-time homemaker who idolized Mark and treated him as her favorite. Together, Luann Masler and her son would take leftovers and turn them into casseroles, loaves, pot pies, and tetrazzinis. But shortly after Mark's mother died while he was in fourth grade, his two older sisters, Miriam and Bess, moved out, and Mark's father married his longtime secretary, Carla Grilli. Realizing he had spent his professional life saving money for an idyllic future that would never arrive, Jerry Masler moved with Carla and Mark to the Upper West Side, retired early, and embraced a life of profligate spending. Take-out meals replaced Mark's mom's scrumptious home-cooked dinners; short rides in taxis and limos replaced long drives in the clunky Buick Century. Soon there was a summer home in Southampton, along with ski vacations in Aspen and monthlong trips to Europe, until Carla OD'd on cocaine, after which Jerry went back to work, turning his attention to housing activism, rededicating his life to providing for families other than his own.

Up until the day he was killed by a hit-and-run driver while power walking to Central Park, Jerry Masler worked closely with the state attorney general's office and New York's Department of Housing Preservation and Development; he took advantage of the city's Interim Lease and Dollar Sale programs, acquiring and developing delinquent and condemned properties, such as the abandoned five-story tenement at 64 West 106th Street, which he rehabbed with the help of several community leaders and Ike Morphy, an eager young black musician who had learned carpentry from his late father. Together, they converted 64 West into a condo building and named it after the Puerto Rico–born baseball star Roberto Clemente.

Jerry's wealth was always strangely demoralizing to his son Mark, who, until he discovered that his trust fund was not sufficiently generous to fully fund all his dream projects, had been under the impression he would never really have to work. If he had an innate sense of ambition that might have motivated him, after losing his mother he never developed it. And Jerry Masler was hardly a disciplinarian; he generally ignored his son's poor grades, his truancy, and his other forms of bad behavior.

At Wadleigh, a public high school Mark attended after flunking out of Dwight, he became a hell-raiser; he played football but was cut from the varsity team for making too many late hits, for engaging in too much horseplay in the showers, and for once tricking a field-goal kicker into performing blindfolded atomic sit-ups beneath the members of the defensive line. After graduating, he dropped out of two SUNY schools and City College; then he attended the Culinary Institute in Hyde Park with the vague idea that he might open his own restaurant someday, though he never knew what kind. He married Holly Kovacs at twenty-two but divorced her soon afterward, then married Tessa Minkoff and divorced her even more quickly. He drank too much, got fired by one restaurant, dried out at a clinic, did too much coke, got fired by another restaurant, dried out at a more expensive clinic, spent two weeks at a sex-addiction clinic but was asked to leave for his excessive boasting during group sessions.

On the day of Jerry Masler's funeral in the late spring, Mark hadn't seen his father in half a year. He had finally forgiven his dad for marrying so quickly after his first wife had died, but still had grown to feel ashamed in the man's presence, didn't know how someone more than fifty years older than him could have so much drive. He didn't like the old man's unquestioning nature, vaguely resented that whenever he asked his dad for more cash to invest in some business—a skateboard and heavy-metal CD store, a mobile karaoke recording studio in the back of a stretch limo, a chain of roadside bathing and toilet facilities named S&S (Shit and a Shower)— Jerry Masler always indulged him. Mark had looked forward to a day when his father would tell him no, so that he wouldn't feel so paralyzed by possibility. But Jerry would only grasp Mark's knee or clutch his shoulder, then say, "Well, you tried your best, kid o' mine."

After the funeral, however, Mark began to approach his life with new sobriety. It was time for him to take his place as an upstanding member of his community, his first wife, Holly, told him. On her advice, he cut his hair short, eighty-sixing the mullet he sported with pride long after it had fallen out of fashion. No more Grecian Formula; he kept the sideburns gray. He lost the necklaces and the bracelets, avoided all clubs and tit bars, swore off cheap sex with club girls and sous-chefs, vowed he would not travel to Vegas or Atlantic City anymore unless he had business to conduct there. He threw out most of his old headbanger CDs and began listening to U2, Bruce Springsteen, John Mayer, and Dave Matthews, because chicks his age dug those artists—most women over forty wouldn't screw to Black Sabbath or Dokken unless they were freaks, and, sadly, mensches with reputations as pillars of their community weren't supposed to date freaks.

Now, Mark works out every day either in the basement gym of his high-rise building, the Landmark Apartments at 455 Central Park West, or at the West Side JCC; he jogs; he lifts weights; he watches MSNBC and the Financial Network while he's on the StairMaster. He donates to the United Jewish Appeal, frequents forties-and-up singles' events, and attends motivational talks given by Rudy Giuliani, Larry King, and Benjamin Netanyahu. He reads biographies of military men, inspirational books about mission-based leadership, life coaching, and human potential training. He subscribes to *Money* magazine, *Commentary*, and *The American Standard*. He has sold all his old gangster and porn videos on eBay and, to inspire his personal makeover, watches bodybuilding DVDs and motivational movies—*Breaking Away*, *Pumping Iron*, *Exodus*, *Taxi zum Klo*, *The Raid on Entebbe*, *Rocky II–IV* (not the original *Rocky*, though, because he could never feel inspired by a palooka who went the distance but got his ass kicked by Apollo Creed anyway). Recently, he has also begun accepting speaking invitations initially directed to his father, and lecturing not-for-profits and housing advocacy groups about keeping focused, maximizing effective leadership skills, and staying true to your mission, which, for Mark, is a business enterprise called "Rolls Restaurant & Wash."

Mark invented both the idea and the name while standing in the viewing corridor of the Riverdale White Glove, where he was having his yellow Hummer washed before *shiva* at his sister Miriam's house. He had always liked the multiple implications of the name "Rolls"—dinner rolls with pats of butter on them, the rolling wheels of the Buick in which his mother had driven him to school, the rollmops and roll-ups she served at the Sunny-side dinner parties she hosted. Watching men in red jumpsuits buffing out his SUV, Mark wondered why they were working so slowly. Old Mark would lurk behind car wash employees, point out dings to his bumper and finish, then threaten to stiff them. New Mark felt no urge to watch, but there was no place to sit, nothing good to eat. Then came the idea: a car wash–cum–restaurant with pop tunes thumping out of a kick-ass sound system, hunky waiters in swimsuits and flip-flops serving the casseroles and pot pies Mark had enjoyed in Sunnyside. The business would pay tribute to the life he'd left behind before he moved with his father and stepmom to Manhattan. Start-up costs would be massive, though, and Mark knew that before he could secure the right lot on which to build the first Rolls Restaurant & Wash, he would need every penny he gained from the properties he was inheriting. Today, Roberto Clemente Building, #2B, is the only one that remains.

Mark has finished his call with Josh Dybnick and is just preparing to dial Allie Scheinblum's number to accept her invitation to speak at B'nai Akiva when his secretary, Maria Aquino, instant-messages to say that Ike Morphy is standing in their reception area and says he won't leave until he has spoken with Mark. Maria says she has told Ike that Jerry Masler passed away months ago, but Ike still won't go. She asks if she should call security. But Mark is a mature man now, always ready to face conflict head-on by utilizing the interpersonal skills he has honed during all-day motivational seminars at the Jacob K. Javits Convention Center. After he peers through his office window and gets a good look at the smooth-scalped, bespectacled jazzman slouching in his reception area—the man is undoubtedly another one of his father's well-intentioned but misguided do-gooder projects— Mark, a former defensive tackle, becomes confident that, though Ike is a good deal taller than he is, he himself is stockier, has a lower center of gravity, and could whomp the man in a street fight should the need arise. He directs Maria to send Mr. Morphy into his office.

Ike enters the office uneasily, almost as if he's still looking for Jerry Masler, then realizing too late that he is not here. He shakes Mark's hand and sits in the chair across from him. He says he is truly sorry to hear that

Mark's father has passed away—had he not been in Chicago with his mom, who also passed away recently, he certainly would have attended the funeral; losing any parent is rough, and Jerry was one of the most decent men he ever knew. Mark acknowledges Ike's good wishes with a nod and a mouthed thank-you; he says he feels sorry for Ike's loss, offers Ike a brief Jewish blessing for the bereaved ("No more sorrows; only good days"), then gets down to business. He asks if Ike has come to discuss the apartment. Mark says he tried to contact Ike before putting it on the market, but the phone was disconnected, and Ike's new neighbor across the hall said he thought #2B was vacant.

Ike recognizes Mark's glib, ingratiating tone—it calls to mind the voices of record-company lawyers telling the band why royalty checks would be slow in coming, of slick PR guys explaining why he would have to hang around a photo shoot for another three hours. Still, he maintains his composure. He tells Mark he doesn't know about all that, but he's back home now and he's planning to start working on his music again. He informs Mark of the sweat-equity agreement he made with Jerry Masler some twenty years ago—if Mark needs him to do some work on one of his apartments, he'll oblige, but he won't be moving out anytime soon.

Yep, Mark says, Jerry Masler was truly a mensch, but sometimes more mensch than businessman. His father made many agreements in his life, but with the real estate market booming and an exciting business opportunity beckoning, now is the time to sell. In any event, he says, no buyer has made an offer yet, and even when he receives a signed contract, closing will probably take at least ninety days; Ike won't have to move immediately.

"But that's not the agreement I made with your father," says Ike.

Maybe not, Mark says, but that's the agreement now. Look, he says, the best situation for everybody would be for the two of them to reach their own agreement, if Ike could find the money to buy the apartment himself. Given that Ike had a relationship with his dad, he might even be able to cut the broker out of the deal, save Ike 6 percent.

Ike waits to see if Mark is joking, but the man doesn't crack a smile. Ike takes a breath—he hates nothing so much as being put in the position of having to ask for things. Does Mark think he has six hundred large just lying around? Ike asks. He reminds Mark that he has come here because of the agreement he made with Mark's father; he still has, for all intents and purposes, a goddamn lease.

Sure, says Mark, he's heard about that lease, but where is it? Does it exist on paper?

What difference does that make, brother? Ike asks. Mark's father never gave a damn about paper.

"But I do, 'brother,' " says Mark, now knowing he was right: no lease ever existed—Ike cannot stand in his way. Mark removes his glasses, rubs his eyes, then reminds Ike that he is in charge now, and though he feels bad about Ike's predicament, he really doesn't have more time to discuss it. If Ike's needs had been so important to Jerry Masler, he would have put their agreement on paper and Ike and Mark wouldn't be having this discussion. Now, if Ike will excuse him, he has a busy day ahead of him.

Ike looks at Mark long and hard but can't think of anything to say that's not either a petty, cutting remark or a pathetic, desperate plea. He could come off as some self-righteous hothead or some poor beggar; better to say nothing at all. As Mark advises him to "go in good health," Ike walks out the door.

Mark watches from his desk to make sure Ike exits the reception area without causing any trouble. Then he picks up the phone and dials Allie Scheinblum's number. Why, of course he'll speak to her and her young colleagues at shul, he says, adding that he'll even waive his standard honorarium. He says he thinks that the topic on which he'd like to speak will be mastering people skills to achieve your mission—when you see something you want, you've got to know how to go for it, he says. He then calls Josh Dybnick one more time to tell his broker that he was right about that lease all along.

THE BUYER

The morning *American Standard* editorial meeting has ended and Rebecca Sugarman walks briskly back to her cubicle, where her telephone's red voice-mail alert is blinking. Her first message as assistant literary editor—she feels almost embarrassingly giddy about it. After spending so many years sequestered in grad school, barely ever getting out of grim, isolated Morningside Heights, she is ecstatic to have a job in which she has contact with the outside world, to be working right in the nerve center of New York City with serious responsibilities at a publication she has long admired. Though the age of the average reader of *The American Standard* is still only slightly less than that of the magazine itself (sixty-two), and the readership has declined markedly in the past decade, Rebecca has been reading the magazine since age eleven, even longer if one counts the times when her father, Phil, would read the *Standard*'s short stories, essays, and jazz reviews aloud while feeding her from a bottle. Aside from *Harper's*, *The New Yorker*, the *New York Review of Books*, *The Atlantic Monthly*, *Foreign Affairs*, *The Economist*, *The New Republic*, the *Times Literary Supplement*, *In These Times*, *The American Prospect*, *The Nation*, *Mother Jones*, and the *Utne Reader*, it is the only print periodical that Rebecca reads religiously.

Rebecca has always loved how the *Standard* has maintained its wry sense of humor in its lengthy essays about politics and high culture; she has always appreciated how the monthly magazine has introduced new writers straight from the Ivy League in freshly pressed shirts and their fathers' ties alongside rumpled, old-guard lefties who have written for the *Standard* since the Vietnam era. On the autumn day that she first interviewed here with longtime literary editor Elizabeth Fogelson, the vibe of the Garment District office seemed delightfully scrappy, energetic, retro, classic Manhattan, a scene right out of the boyhood of Rebecca's father, who grew up in a working-class Hell's Kitchen family, went to Harvard, and later became president of the Sugarman & Krayvitz jingle house in Boston. The view from the *Standard*'s dirty windows gave out onto an Eighth Avenue that was positively pulsing with life—button and fabric shops filled with customers sifting through the contents of dented cardboard boxes, twenty-four-hour Pakistani fast-food restaurants, kosher pizza and falafel joints, commuters and tourists shoving their way in and out of the Port Authority Bus Terminal.

Inside the *Standard* office, Rebecca saw the musty lending library that was staffed Monday to Thursday from nine to one by Myrna Lanzmann, who had begun working here as a teenager in 1954; she saw the portable black-and-white TV that sat on the top shelf of a hall closet, to be taken down only to monitor key political events; she saw the rickety liquor trolley that was called into service every Friday at two. On a warped red Ping-Pong table, dutiful bloggers, such as the Evening Noose's Nick Renfield, author of the *Standard*'s "Under the Radar" media column, were trading volleys with art and theater critics who still submitted their scrawl to the copy desk for transcription. Rebecca could not have imagined another place where she would have preferred to work—here, she could call herself something she had always dreamed of becoming: a New York editor.

This morning, she had crowded into a southbound No. 1 subway car with a brand-new black leather bag crammed with reference books and style manuals. She'd carried a double espresso from Oren's Daily Roast and a copy of the *Times*. Emerging from the train at Forty-second Street, she'd bounded breathlessly up the stairs with her coat unbuttoned, then walked—nearly glided—down icy Eighth Avenue, moving to the sounds of idling buses and taxis stuck in traffic, past pawnshops, electronics stores, and barbershops, past cramped, makeshift storefronts where African and Eastern European immigrants hawked knockoff handbags, until she reached the *Standard*'s offices on Thirty-seventh Street and sprinted up to the sixth floor.

From her pristine cubicle, Rebecca now dials her voice-mail number and listens to a message from Darrell; she smiles at the novelty of her husband's calling her at her new office. Darrell sounds uncharacteristically confident and professional, his voice deep, his speech fast, his vocabulary refreshingly devoid of swearwords. "We oughta move on this apartment," he says, and he tells Rebecca to call him at home before he leaves for the library so they can discuss placing a bid on the condo in the Roberto Clemente Building. As Rebecca listens to this message a second time, she feels oddly thrilled that Darrell is displaying so much initiative. To her, his message is a sign of happier days to come—Darrell is finally expressing enthusiasm not only for an apartment, but for their future together.

After deciding that they should move out of their cramped, Columbia University–owned, one-bedroom walk-up on Amsterdam Avenue and Seminary Row and buy a place with room for an as-yet-unconceived child, Rebecca asked Darrell to take charge of their real estate search, not because she necessarily trusts his judgment more than her own, and not because Darrell, a veteran teaching assistant in Columbia's English and Comp Lit Department who has long since completed coursework and preliminary exams for his Ph.D., has the more flexible schedule. It is more because she senses that if she chooses the apartment, uses her parents' money for the down payment with the real estate company that employed her dad's firm to write its signature jingle ("Time to move up, move up, move up to Overman"), then Darrell might say the apartment isn't really his. Which would be, of course, ridiculous. But, ever since their marriage four years ago in the Conservatory Garden of Central Park, followed by a reception at the Yale Club, Darrell has made the difference in their upbringings a frustratingly recurrent theme in their conversations.

Darrell hardly hails from humble, bootstrapping origins—his parents, Peter Schiff and Margaret Finneran, are both English profs at the University of Wisconsin, which, granted, pays nowhere near as well as either Rebecca's mother's Boston obstetric practice or her father's ad business. Rebecca did grow up in Cambridge, while Darrell's family moved from one college town to another because, until they arrived in Madison, only his mother could ever achieve tenure. And yes, Darrell's frugal folks, though well into their sixties, still live like pack rat grad students, driving a 1970 Volvo that Darrell calls the "crunk car" and living in an overstuffed ranch house in Madison, while the Sugarmans own a gorgeous four-bedroom colonial in Cambridge, a pied-à-terre in SoHo that Phil Sugarman uses when he's in the city on business, and a nineteenth-century vacation home in Maine. But Phil volunteers on weekends teaching jazz composition to teenagers in Roxbury and has written and produced free jingles for Greenpeace and the Sierra Club, and Rebecca's mom, Judith Mintz-Sugarman, puts in three afternoons a week at Planned Parenthood. If anything, Rebecca suspects that her father, who had given up his dream of playing music professionally and always urged his children to act more radically than he ever dared to, was disappointed that she chose to marry someone as familiarly white, overeducated, and middle-class as Darrell. Rebecca has never cared even slightly about money, never considers the topic unless Darrell forces her to do so, as on their first honeymoon night in the Grosvenor Hotel in London, when Darrell asked her to estimate the difference between the amounts his parents and hers had spent on the wedding. She told him she had no idea, only to wake up the next day and find on the pillow next to her a hand-drawn chart on which Darrell estimated the cost differential at $67,000.

Now, whenever Rebecca suggests they dine out, Darrell insists on Sal & Carmine's on Broadway for pizza slices, the 125th Street McDonald's for burgers and shakes, or his favorite Tiemann Place pharmacy for turkey hoagies. And when Rebecca points out that she just doesn't enjoy eating fast food on trays, Darrell says, "That's 'cause you've never had to work for a living," never mind that Darrell has only ever worked one real job aside from his teaching assistantship: three weeks at the downtown Madison Starbucks the summer before his senior year at Penn (he was fired when he refused to stop asking customers whether they "felt like taking a big crappuccino today").

What initially made Rebecca fall in love with Darrell when they met at Columbia, where both were being interviewed for the graduate English program, was just how little he seemed to care about money or appearances, how refreshingly frank and honest he appeared to be; his caustic and irreverent sense of humor seemed so much more genuine than the studied witticisms delivered by the earnest yet passionless Lit majors and teaching assistants who typically expressed interest in her. The other prospective male students at the catered reception in Columbia's faculty lounge wore suits, ties, and polished shoes, but Darrell wore jeans, an untucked Kurt Cobain flannel shirt, an anorak, hiking boots, and a bucket hat. Later, during a cocktail reception at La Terrace, Darrell surveyed the other students in attendance, mumbled "What a bunch of fricking ass-kissing puds," and then asked if Rebecca wanted to "blow this popsicle stand" and head out to the West End Tavern for some booze. And afterward, when they were drunk on gin and tonics, they had sex outside on an Arctic-themed mosaic bench on the site of the General Grant National Memorial—the first and only time Rebecca ever made love to a stranger. When Rebecca was back in school in New Haven and Darrell was in Philly, they talked on the phone for hours, and he always made her laugh. She liked the fact that Darrell was rough around the edges and seemed to be a work in progress; she knew her parents had made life easy for her and she longed to work hard for something she wanted, to make this relationship as successful as she knew it could become.

Darrell and Rebecca decided that both would attend Columbia, even though Rebecca had received better offers from Berkeley, Yale, and Tufts, the latter of which Darrell, who had been accepted only by Columbia, told her to reject simply because the university's name sounded "too pubic." Nonetheless, Rebecca was elated to go to Columbia with Darrell; though she knew this was hopelessly dorky, whenever she thought about taking classes in the same halls where Allen Ginsberg and Jack Kerouac had sat, speaking from the same lecterns that Lionel Trilling and Jacques Barzun had used, she got actual goose bumps. In New York, Darrell was the one who immediately began to grouse about graduate study—the absurdity of writing rarified essays and articles that fewer than two dozen people would read, the appropriateness of the fact that the university had been built on the site of a former lunatic asylum. He would bemoan the fact that he was turning into his pop, who had spent fifteen years writing an eight-hundred-page dissertation analyzing a mere six poems by Wordsworth that was turned down by more than twenty publishers before finding a home at a third-tier academic press.

Darrell would bitch incessantly to Rebecca about ruining his eyesight and potentially contracting black lung disease by poring over brittle documents in this or that rare-books reading room or in the Butler Library "piles"—he never referred to them as "the stacks," always "the piles." Unlike Rebecca, who spoke fluent French and Hebrew, he had never had the attention span to master any foreign language, but he cursed in a variety of tongues, labeling fellow students *culos, Arschlocher, bojis, jajis, chahts, langers,* "pot-wallopers," *couillons,* and *salauds,* and opining of his onerous teaching load that he had *die Arschkarte gezogen* (drawn the ass-card). As both student and teaching assistant, Darrell swore liberally in class, and he once informed a professor in a Renaissance poetry seminar that "seminar" and "semen" derived from the same root, which meant that seminars mostly concerned jerking off. As a T.A., he rarely remembered his students' names, and in conversations with Rebecca referred to them only by the names of the Dr. Seuss characters he thought they resembled—the Bofa on the Sofa, Gertrude McFuzz, Gerald McBoing-Boing, the Wickersham Brothers. While discussing his professors, he would offer disparaging quotations from old-school hip-hop artists, such as Tupac Shakur, LL Cool J, and Ice Cube, frequently asserting that his dissertation chair, Bernard Ostrow, who had attended grad school in Minnesota with Darrell's parents, could either "eat a dick straight up" or "autograph my nutsack."

But though Rebecca always attended cocktail parties and dinners with her students, her classmates, and her professors, while Darrell didn't have any friends among his fellow graduate students, Rebecca was the one to leave the program, admitting to herself that "Something of Great Constancy," her stalled dissertation on the wide gulf between the physical representations of love and the idealized descriptions of it in Shakespeare's comedies, offered nothing new to her discipline. She suspected that Darrell had been right when he called her draft chapters "sappy," and she wondered whether Darrell's growing frustration with grad school resulted from the fact that he thought he had to compete with her. She justified dropping out to herself by deciding that she would prefer a career that would allow her to express her love for literature rather than spend her life overanalyzing and arguing about it. What was the point of living in the literature capital of the country when it seemed that her only contact with books came in libraries or classrooms that could have been anywhere in the world?

Meanwhile, Darrell continued to hole up every night in "the piles," procrastinating working on his own dissertation by writing increasingly preposterous articles about such topics as the unintended ribaldry in the work of nineteenth-century scribes ("But the Worm Shall Revive: The Strange Swinburnian Obsession with Erectile Tissue"; "The Sunbeams Are My Shafts: Shelley's Problematic, Self-Aggrandizing Priapism"). Rebecca took an entry-level PR job at Spofford & Quimby Publishers, where her uncle worked as an editor; she spent two not particularly fulfilling or edifying years there before returning to Columbia for a journalism degree, then nabbed the assistant literary editor position at *The American Standard*.

The entire *Standard* staff had attended this morning's editorial meeting, save for Elizabeth Fogelson, who had hired Rebecca. Fogelson was such a tough critic that all but the most desperate or naïve publishers had ceased sending books to her. One of her regular columns, "Books Not Worth Reviewing," employed a system of literary analysis that she called "Page Sixty-seven, Paragraph Three." She would open a book, turn to the sixty-seventh page, and if the third paragraph failed to inspire her, she would deem the book "not worth reviewing." A collection of her criticism was published in 1967 in response to Susan Sontag's *Against Interpretation*. The title of Fogelson's collection was *Against Everything*.

In truth, Rebecca had felt slightly relieved when she arrived this morning and saw that the lights were out in Fogelson's office. Her sole interview with the literary editor had been harrowing, like a pop quiz in a subject she had never studied. Which early Bellow was worse, *The Victim* or *Dangling Man*? Wasn't *The Naked and the Dead* overrated he-man agitprop? Which Alfred Kazin essay was most self-indulgent? Had anyone ever really finished reading *Gravity's Rainbow*? Really? Who? Liar! Could anything be more preposterous than the sex scenes in John Updike's Rabbit novels? And could Rebecca explain to her exactly why "Call me Ishmael" was supposed to be such a great opening line anyway? It was only three words long. Rebecca couldn't recall saying anything coherent for the entire forty-five minutes, and spent weeks afterward lamenting her distressingly eager and wide-eyed performance, torturing herself with all the sharp, insightful answers she should have given but didn't. Which was why she was so surprised to receive the call from Fogelson two months later; she half-wondered if the woman was confusing her with another job applicant.

"No, my talented child," Liz Fogelson said. "I have the right number, all right."

Now, Rebecca dials her husband at home. "Yeah?" Darrell asks. Lately, he sounds harried and peeved whenever he answers the phone, a fact that Rebecca ascribes to the impermanence of their living situation. Once they settle on an apartment and stop paying rent, Darrell can concentrate on what is most important, i.e., finishing his dissertation and starting a family.

"So, I think we should move on this joint on 'Duke Ellington Boulevard,'" Darrell tells Rebecca. He adds that the "unit" is "aggressively priced" and has "a lot of upside" to it. He continues, using more words that sound unnatural coming from him, words from which Rebecca's parents have sheltered her for most of her life. Darrell suggests they make a bid that "comes within five percent of asking," and that they research "option adjustable-rate mortgages" and lock in those "sweet rates" as soon as they can.

Rebecca wonders at her husband's newfound interest in the apartment on West 106th; she'd thought that, as was the case with all the other apartments they had seen, only she had liked it. On the taxi ride home, she re-marked upon the vitality of the neighborhood, the thrill her father would get from her living on the street that had once been home to Duke Ellington and Billy Strayhorn, while Darrell only complained about the "fricking out-of-control crack addict squatter gangsta" and his "rabid-ass dog." Still, Darrell was a contrarian, and when Rebecca observed that buying an apartment and displacing its tenant seemed both rude and hegemonic, Darrell scoffed at her "white liberal guilt trip," then started enumerating the positive aspects of the place. And now, here he is on the phone, telling Rebecca he wants to call Joshua Dybnick and the lawyer and the "whip-smart mortgage broker" Josh has recommended. Rebecca doesn't want to temper Darrell's excitement; still, she reminds him that the apartment has been on the market for more than a month and they needn't rush—perhaps her dad could see it before they make an offer, and in the meanwhile Darrell can look at some other apartments.

At this proposal, Darrell turns irritable. Why, he asks, because "Daddy Warbucks" doesn't trust them to make their own decisions? He says he hates receiving gifts with strings attached, then proceeds to quote race-car driver Willy T. Ribbs, declaring that he does not appreciate the idea of being "somebody's boy," that he will not say "Yes, suh" or "No, suh" to any man. Rebecca says another set of eyes is always helpful, but when she sees *American Standard* publisher and editorial director Chloe Linton approaching her cubicle, wearing an off-white business suit and a pale orange scarf that matches her pantyhose, Rebecca apologizes for questioning Darrell, quickly tells him she has to go, then advises him to do whatever he feels is right. If the Clemente apartment is the one he wants, they'll bid on it.

Rebecca looks up and smiles nervously at Chloe, who stands outside her cubicle, smelling strongly of Jean Naté perfume. Rebecca wonders if Chloe will chastise her for making a personal call during business hours. But when Rebecca hangs up the phone, Chloe instead tells her that the two of them need to meet immediately to discuss Rebecca's new responsibilities as the *Standard*'s acting literary editor because Elizabeth Fogelson has just resigned.

THE BROKER

Josh Dybnick pushes open the rear exit doors of the M4 bus and steps out at 114th Street. He has begun walking down Broadway toward 109th Street, where the newest uptown office of the Overman Group is located, when he hears his cell phone chime the six opening notes of "Our Time" from the musical *Merrily We Roll Along*. He looks down at his cell phone display: "Darrell Schiff." He's surprised to see that Darrell is returning his most recent call; people return his calls only when they want to make an offer on an apartment, and Josh is fairly certain that Ike Morphy scared off Darrell and Rebecca, and that the high price Mark Masler has set for the unit has scared off everyone else. He'd figured he'd have to wait until the new year to schedule another open house, then talk Masler down.

With the glaring exception of his social life, which has always been a disaster, Joshua has sharp instincts about people. As an actor, he can sense the exact moment when a director decides not to cast him, and as a real estate broker, he can say with 99 percent certainty whether or not a potential buyer will make a serious offer—a good skill in a business where more than half of everyone's yesses usually turn out to be noes. He has become all too familiar with this sort of yes-to-no ratio in the worlds of film, television, and theater, where he has made callbacks for shows that didn't find funding, gotten cast in pilots that were never picked up, rehearsed a three-character drama whose author wrote him out of the script when he realized his production could afford only two actors.

Though Josh has worked as a real estate salesperson for just over two years, he still sees himself as an actor. Acting is what he came to this city to do; it has been his goal for nearly a decade, ever since he defied his father by switching his major at Oberlin College from economics to drama. At Oberlin, Joshua was president of the Dramatic Association; he played all the roles in his own solo adaptation of *Candide* and won a statewide directing award for his production of August Wilson's *Two Trains Running*, in which he cast himself against type in the role of Hambone, gaining plaudits for his impassioned delivery of the line "He gonna gimme my ham!" Every morning, as he biked from his dorm to class, he blasted "Conquering the City" from *Wonderful Town* on his Discman, putting from his mind the fear that his true theme from that show would turn out to be the lyric, "Why did I ever leave Ohiiiiiio?"

But upon arriving here in New York after spending six dreadful months clerking in his father's Shaker Heights law office, Joshua found himself surrounded by thousands of actors, many equally talented, most seemingly better connected. The question wasn't whether he'd win a role but whether he would get to audition at all. He would wait on hold for hours only to learn that every slot for the Oregon Shakespeare Festival had already been filled. He spent his dad's money on headshots, acting classes, seminars with casting directors who shoveled down their catered poached-salmon lunches while telling him that even with a beard he'd look too clean-cut, which was why they'd never consider casting him as "atmosphere" on *Law & Order*.

Joshua began his transition into real estate after Overman Group CEO Bradley Overman saw him performing one of his only paying roles: a broker in a thirty-second spot for the Overman Group. "Isn't it time you moved up to Overman?" Joshua asked, shaking hands with a customer, then turning to face the camera. Watching the commercial, Bradley Overman realized that not one of the salespeople in any of his branch offices appeared as trustworthy as Joshua seemed in the ad—none, with the possible exception of Bradley Overman himself. But ever since his divorce from Chloe Linton, to whom he rarely spoke but with whom he still split a Riverside Drive duplex because they had agreed not to sell until the real estate market peaked, he was devoting most of his work hours to planning for the long-term future of his company so that he could eventually retire.

Like Joshua, Bradley Overman had never intended to work in real estate. A smooth, street-smart journeyman carpenter and a late-night weekend progressive rock deejay who in the mid-1970s spun album sides by King Crimson; Emerson, Lake & Palmer; and Procul Harum for a low-watt FM station in the Hudson Valley, he picked up side work selling houses for Dubman Realty, one of his show's sponsors for whom he read advertising copy, and quickly realized that the rapacious real estate industry could benefit from more down-to-earth and community-oriented tactics.

Bradley opened his first Manhattan office on Madison Avenue and Seventy-seventh Street, right on the ground floor, with giant windows that gave out onto the street; a front door that was always open during business hours, weather permitting; and free coffee, chamomile tea, and brownies for the neighborhood's up-and-coming bankers, attorneys, and other young professionals, who strolled by on weekends with their families en route to the Met or the park. This was before the metastasis of slick, boutique real estate brokerages, before the era of billboards and bus-shelter placards advertising Halstead Property, the Corcoran Group, and Prudential Douglas Elliman. Overman provided a hip alternative in the world of high-dollar apartment sales that was still largely the provenance of gray men in gray Brooks Brothers suits, white Arrow shirts, and club ties.

Bradley popularized the practice of co-brokering, in which salespeople from competing agencies worked together to make deals. Although just about every other firm in the state treated salespeople as independent contractors, Overman gave associate brokers who proved themselves to be particularly skillful and loyal the additional title of vice president, which carried with it a base salary and medical benefits. Bradley's approach was so successful that, within a decade, he had opened offices in every borough, and soon the only evidence of his deejaying career was the Yes and Mahavishnu Orchestra music that played through the speakers in all his offices.

But by the time Bradley Overman treated Joshua Dybnick to lunch at Le Monde on Broadway and offered to pay for the young man's real estate licensing class, then give him a desk and a phone after he passed his exams, Bradley was acutely aware of disturbing trends among his employees and his salespeople. Some thirty years earlier, when he started his business, he had wanted to promote the image of real estate as a cool but noble pursuit, providing for a very basic need. During his first decade, a surprisingly large number of his salespeople lived in New York because they had artistic passions they needed to support; some were folksingers, painters, choreographers. Now, most everyone he interviewed saw the industry as a means to wealth for its own sake. They were here in the city only because this was where the real money was. They paid mere lip service to the Realtors Code of Ethics, viewed it not as a standard to meet but an obstacle to overcome. They spewed lingo that Bradley loathed and that made some of his highly educated and cultured Manhattan clients uncomfortable; they bragged about conversion rates and complained about floor time and unfair distribution of "ups." They spoke of lead farming and fought over turf. And when Bradley refused to pay the obscene commission splits they demanded, they quit to work for other brokers or opened their own shops, leaving him with offices overpopulated by slick, opportunistic secondraters.

Overman could not dispute his remaining agents' success, he told Joshua at that first lunch; mortgage money was historically cheap, the average prices of condos and co-ops had been rising at an average of 25 percent every year, the median price of a Manhattan appartment was now well over $1 million. After the Twin Towers fell, the industry had seen a brief lull but then it had returned with unprecedented frenzy, almost as if people needed something permanent to hang on to and would pay any amount to get it. If the price of an apartment doubled in the space of a year, Overman's bonus-laden investment-banker, commodities-trader, and hedge-fund-manager clients wouldn't blink; they would even write on real estate blogs about how much they'd overpaid. Sometimes he felt himself becoming as cynical as his brokers, Bradley Overman said, and felt cheered by bad news on CNN when it meant greater profits for his company. Still, when prices returned to earth, the liabilities of this new breed of salesperson would reveal themselves, and qualities such as creativity, trustworthiness, and dedication would once again come into play. Bradley said he met a lot of men in this industry, but Joshua could become someone truly special. So, he asked with a smile and an outstretched hand, wasn't it time to move up?

Joshua felt an immediate, visceral reaction to Bradley Overman's proposal, as if the hand of Satan himself, or perhaps that of his father, Paul Dybnick, a personal-injury lawyer with political aspirations ("Didja fall? Call Paul!"), was being offered to him. Joshua was no salesman; he was an actor, an artist, a man of conviction. When he wasn't auditioning or taking classes or waiting tables to make his rent, he was volunteering for right-minded causes; he had worked for a month at a phone bank on 106th and Broadway, cold-calling registered voters, asking them to write their senators and urge them to support gay marriage and to protect a woman's right to choose. But at Le Monde, as he greedily consumed his plate of monkfish medallions, the best meal he'd eaten in the city all year, he contemplated Brad Overman's pitch and realized the grim truth: banning gay marriage wouldn't really affect him, seeing as he hadn't had a second date in months and could rarely afford to pay for any of his dates' meals, and as far as abortion was concerned, he certainly would never need one for himself. By now, the office of that last nonprofit for which he had volunteered was gone anyway—a new business had opened with a chocolate-colored canopy out front: THE HOME STORE.

Plus, Joshua was so tired of eating Pop-Tarts and ramen noodles, so tired of wearing the fake gold watch he'd purchased from a hustler on the A train, so tired of working until one in the morning then waking up four hours later to wait on line at open audition calls, so tired of planning imaginary shows for theaters that would probably never deign to return his calls. But he shook Bradley Overman's hand only when he realized he wouldn't really have to become a salesperson after all; he could simply act the role.

Broadway had always been his future, and prophetically, that's where the Overman Group's newest office was located. And if he could make the kind of money Overman said was possible while he was playing his role, well, then maybe he could finally get out of debt; maybe he could move out of his ant-infested Washington Heights ground-floor apartment; maybe he could answer some of the personal ads that listed salary requirements on howdypartner.net; maybe he could rent out Soho Rep or the Manhattan Theater Project and produce a season of shows, casting himself in the roles for which directors usually said he was too bland-looking or just too short.

In college, Joshua had always approached every directing and acting gig, no matter how seemingly trivial, with a focus and an attention to detail so intense that many actors and designers refused to work with him afterward. His approach to real estate was equally obsessive. He read the *Post's* real estate section on Thursday, *Newsday's* and the *Times's* on the weekend; he pored over every word of *Crain's New York Business*, *Real Estate Weekly*, *The Real Deal*, and *curbed.com*. He attended open houses five days a week. He arrived early and stayed late at every class and tutoring session offered by the Manhattan Real Estate Professional School on Thirty-second Street, listened to every broker's recruitment pitch, ultimately declining six job offers because he had committed to work for Brad Overman.

At Overman, he began by handling rentals and, on his fourth day there, collected his first commission check, nearly $2,600 for a dingy ground-floor one-bedroom on 108th Street that no one else at the agency had been able to unload. One month into his new career, he had successfully engineered six apartment rentals, and was already so addicted to the checks he was banking that he was working fifty-hour weeks. On average, a talented and motivated Overman full-timer made his first sale about a third of the way through the first year, but Joshua did it by week four.

Quickly he assembled a reliable network of business contacts for putting together deals; it was composed largely of alluring, hyperprofessional women whose hard-luck stories, he thought, would make potential customers feel that much guiltier about pulling out—mortgage broker Megan Yu, a South Korean immigrant working long hours to support her family;

real estate attorney Gretchen Gruetke, a former actress whom he'd known in college and who was now a single mother of triplets. If a customer was only partially hooked, Josh's team could usually reel him in the rest of the way.

Now that Josh has passed his second round of exams and graduated to the title of associate broker, his phone seems to be ringing all the time. Sometimes he feels as if this whole city's for sale; there is an urgency, an energy that he has felt only on open calls for major Hollywood feature films. He spends weekends in crowds of men and women clutching color-Xerox pages and folded copies of the *Times* Real Estate section tattooed with thick black Xs and red circles as they scramble from one open house to the next. Every Sunday, Josh's picture appears on page 16 in the right-hand corner of the Overman Group ad. Bradley Overman feeds Josh great leads, but unlike the other salespeople at his office, Josh generates most of his own by tracking down people who might be inclined to sell. He rides slow-moving crosstown buses during rush hour and eavesdrops on cell phone conversations; when he hears someone talking about buying or selling, about getting married or divorced, he whips out a business card. He takes the subway down to the city's Deeds office on John Street where he chats up attorneys and contractors. He gets haircuts every other week on Amsterdam or Columbus Avenue, makes sure that each barber has at least three of his cards in both English and Spanish. He greases supers, scours the daily papers for obituaries, swoops down upon recent crime victims— if living in the city is getting too tough for them, he says, now would be a perfect time to sell.

Most of Overman's salespeople seem to feel that, given the current boom climate, they needn't do anything to promote their listings other than advertise them on Craigslist or in the *Times*. If an apartment isn't selling, they'll shoot three minutes of shoddy digital video, upload it to the Overman website, and call it a virtual tour. But Josh uses the state-of-the-art editing software he asked Brad Overman to buy to create rousing, inspirational videos for his listings, complete with crystalline narration, perfectly executed fade-ins and fade-outs, scoring his sound tracks with snatches from his favorite show tunes.

In person at open houses or private showings, Joshua relies on his theatrical training; actors are good at the short, intense relationships real estate requires. As a stage actor playing Hamlet or Cyrano, Joshua would sometimes have to question his motivation: Why was he saying this line? Why was he moving here or there? As a broker, he never asks these questions, because the motivation is always the same: to sell. A skilled memorizer, Joshua remembers everyone's name after he hears it once. Moments after he has visited an apartment, he can draw its layout from memory as if it were a set he had designed; he can speak with authority about every neighboring apartment listed on the *New York Times* website. He knows just how to convincingly deliver his lines in the dialogue he engages in on a near-daily basis. This neighborhood in which Josh makes most of his sales isn't simply "Manhattan Valley," it's "the last frontier of Central Park West." West 109th Street isn't "dicey," it's "in transition." Buyers here aren't "speculating," they're "pioneering." "West 110th" and "West 106th" sound too gritty to him; he always calls them "Cathedral Parkway" and "Ellington Boulevard." Those guys in Knicks and Wizards jerseys, North Face jackets, and Philadelphia 76ers caps hanging out in front of Mama's Pizzeria, showing off their neck tattoos as they blast Nas, 50 Cent, and the Game out of the speakers of their parked SUVs aren't gangbangers, they're the folks who give this neighborhood its character. No, that apartment isn't the gnarliest one on Manhattan Avenue; it's a rare opportunity to live affordably in a historic district. Whenever an apartment is in disrepair, Josh recommends rehabbing it; his favorite phrase has become "See, if I were living here, I'd take down these walls." And if anybody complains that a property is less appealing than expected, he says curtly, "Well, that's why we priced it this way."

One of the best parts of the job is just how useful it has already become for his craft—for designing sets, developing plots, and most of all for creating characters. It rarely takes Joshua more than an instant to recognize his audience, his customers, and to modify his pitch to suit them: the just-out-of-business-school slicksters who'll offer to pay 50 percent down in cash; the anxious first-timers who'll never bid on anything and are just wasting everyone's time; the Wall Street bankers and traders who'll tell Josh they're working only with him but are already bidding on a half-dozen other properties; the Ivy League grads with prestigious, low-paying jobs and bank accounts filled with family money; the eager young couples who'll spend three more years in the city at most.

Sure, you can meet a lot of types while tending bar or waiting tables, but you only ever really see their external personae—not bad for developing arch sitcom types, but woefully insufficient for serious character work. As a broker, Josh meets people at key moments: getting married or divorced, starting new jobs or quitting them, arriving in New York full of hope or leaving it defeated. He sees buyers' and sellers' lives both onstage and off, sees where his clients and customers live, how much they make, who they think they are and who they aspire to be. Each sale is its own miniature play: a wry Neil Simon comedy about a couple selling the walkup where they first fell in love, a bleak Arthur Miller family drama about siblings feuding over inherited property, an August Wilson tragedy about a man forced to sell because he can't keep pace with the rising cost of living. Each deal condenses a lifetime's worth of theater into an easily defined period from open house to closing. An empty apartment is as rife with possibility as a bare stage.

Nevertheless, to maintain his sanity and his self-image, Joshua has lately been pretending that he has been divided into two different people: Joshua and Josh. At the office, on his cell phone, and at apartment showings, he is smooth Josh, salesman Josh. Joshua, on the other hand, still walks home alone every night from the 178th Street bus stop, then calls his mother to tell her about his day. Joshua sends greeting cards on holidays to every member of his extended family, and still cries when his father doesn't call to thank him. Joshua has rented every Laurence Olivier and Robert Donat movie from Netflix, has watched them with the two cats he named after his favorite playwrights, Pinter and Gray, because he still can't seem to find a date. As it turns out, Joshua hasn't auditioned for a show in more than a year; Josh hasn't been able to give him the time. Now, Josh's plan is to work full-time at Overman for about two more years; he'll repair his credit history, show evidence of a steady, reliable income so he can put a down payment on an apartment and get out of Washington Heights, then start working half-time while producing and starring in one-man shows.

Crossing 113th Street as he walks down Broadway, Josh pushes the "OK" button on his cell phone. "Hey, Darrell—how're you doing, buddy?" he asks as he passes the sadly crumbling Manhattan Theater Project, a relic of the neighborhood's artistic past and its last remaining operational legitimate theater.

"It looks like a go," says Darrell, who sounds more assertive than when Josh met him. Josh wonders why Darrell's wife has asked him to handle their real estate search; clearly, Rebecca has the better business sense. He remembers his parents behaving this way before their divorce—his mother assigning his father easy household chores to fool him into thinking he was a decent husband.

Darrell says he and his wife have decided to make an offer on the Clemente apartment once his father-in-law has seen the place. He provides the information that asking for Phil Sugarman's opinion was his idea, intended to make Rebecca feel more comfortable with the purchase. He adds that "Daddy-O" will take the train in from Boston to view the apartment.

"Shouldn't be a problem," Josh says. He would prefer to avoid another interaction with Ike Morphy and his dog, so he says he'll call Mark Masler and set an appointment for a time when Darrell and Rebecca won't have to contend with the tenant or his pet. Darrell says the dog won't pose a problem—Rebecca and her dad will go alone, and they like dogs; as for himself, he'll be at the library working on his dissertation anyway.

Josh reaches Mark Masler on his cell phone and asks if Mark can clear some time with Ike. But Masler, who is too busy rewriting the speech he'll soon be delivering at B'nai Akiva, asks Josh to make the call. Happily reminding himself that, as agent for both buyer and seller in this potential $650K direct deal, he can collect a full 6 percent commission at closing, an amount roughly equivalent to three months' rent at the Manhattan Theater Project, Josh Dybnick leaves a brief, stern message for Ike telling him that he'll have to clear some time for Josh's clients. As Josh continues striding down Broadway toward his office, he is humming Leonard Bernstein.

THE BUYER'S HUSBAND

Darrell Finneran Schiff hangs up his phone, then places a call to Rebecca at *The American Standard* to report on his conversation with Josh Dybnick. Christ, he thinks, what a coward he is; at this moment, in this city, in the prime of his life, with no particular place to be, he could be doing just about anything. Instead, he leaves a message on Rebecca's voice mail telling her to pick a time to meet Josh so her folks can buy them an apartment he can't admit he doesn't really want. Instead, he takes one final look at his last condom package, then fastballs it into the bathroom wastebasket to prepare for the imminent Schiff-Sugarman baby-creation project that he has put off long enough. Instead, he packs up his laptop and book bag so he can work on the dissertation he has never given a damn about. Darrell knows he doesn't have to perform any of these activities, but he will; he has spent his adult life taking the easiest and most obvious paths, then complaining only when it seems too late to change course.

Darrell puts on his coat and saunters down five flights of stairs and out onto slushy Amsterdam Avenue, bound for Kent Hall and Columbia's East Asian Library. He shares an office on the sixth floor of Philosophy Hall with three other grad students who hate his guts; but even if they didn't, he would still prefer the East Asian Library, because only there can he spend all day listening to music and staring into space without the risk of anyone from his own department noticing he's still not doing any work.

Since grade school in Lincoln, Nebraska, where Darrell picked wild-flowers for his mother on the day he first received straight As but the next day kicked his dad in the shins after grounding into a double play during a JCC T-ball game, Darrell has had an intensely reactive personality. When his research is going well (it hasn't been for some time), when Bernard Ostrow writes him an encouraging note (that hasn't happened since he passed his exams five years ago), he can be a model husband—buys Rebecca *tzatzkehs* from toy stores and card shops, makes sure dinner is waiting for her when she comes home, makes love to her and always makes sure she climaxes first. But when writer's block thwacks him once again, when Bernard Ostrow refers to him as "my superannuated grad student," when Rebecca patronizes him by suggesting he view more apartments to buy with her parents' money, when some creepy, black-clad prospective college student named Caleb busts him in an introductory lit lecture for not having read the material he is supposed to be teaching ("No, man, Don Quixote was chill; he never murdered nobody—you must be confusing him with Aeneas or Ulysses or some other dude," the teenager had said), Darrell turns sullen, starts arguments with strangers on the No. 1 train, suggests placing a bid on an apartment just because he doesn't like the tenant's sense of entitlement or the looks of his dog, and spends hours in the library lusting after girls (but never getting up the gumption to talk to them).

There's one girl in particular whom he always sees sitting by a south-facing window at one of the upstairs tables. She appears to be in her early twenties and has fierce slate-colored eyes, pale skin, a perpetually amused smile, freckles, and short dyed-orange hair that, to Darrell's eyes, make her resemble a tantalizingly slutty Raggedy Ann. Though Darrell has never spoken to her, as he enters the library he transfers his wedding band from his ring finger to his index. He feels little guilt as he makes this switch be-cause Rebecca doesn't wear a wedding ring (and the seventy-five-cent-model engagement ring Darrell bought her at a San Francisco Woolworth's didn't fit). And he's barely ever committed adultery anyway, unless one wants to count such activities as going down on Millie Werling at the Radisson in Sheboygan, Wisconsin, during the annual Victorian scholars conference. This had been an act committed merely out of boredom and habit, one he had performed with Millie on numerous earlier occasions, one that could be considered infidelity only by those wedded to the concept of linear time, which Rebecca, the only person who could ever explain the tenets of postmodernism to Darrell in a way he could understand, is not.

Darrell is not so much seeking an affair. He loves Rebecca, loves her at least as much as he has allowed himself to love anybody since Jessica Bosman dumped him near the end of high school then hightailed it back to Kenya, has loved Rebecca even more ever since she dropped out of grad school—her doing so allows him to feel slightly less inferior to her, even though he is certain that the reason she didn't persevere was her perfectionism, whereas he's muddled through with laughably uninspired and cynical work, too afraid to admit failure by leaving while ABD (All But Dissertation, in common parlance; All But Dick in Darrell's patois).

Still, Rebecca has always been at least one step ahead of Darrell. She's the woman for whom gravity does not exist, Darrell often says: even when she seems to fall, she winds up rising anyway. Rebecca is one year younger than Darrell, almost to the day; she's five inches taller; she's kicked his ass in every sport or game they've ever tried, even mini-golf; he was a third-string catcher on the last-place Madison High baseball team, while Rebecca was a Massachusetts state record holder in cross-country who quit her team when she discovered that she enjoyed winning far less than she hated seeing other people lose. Rebecca seems at home here in New York; she makes him feel like some bucktoothed hick on *Hee Haw* whenever she tells him that only tourists say "Avenue of the Americas" instead of "Sixth Avenue" or "Duke Ellington Boulevard" instead of "West 106th Street." The woman knows all the things about the city that only New Yorkers are supposed to know—good places for dim sum and smoked sturgeon, weird-ass clothing boutiques that keep weird-ass hours, the gleaming white apartment building on Eighty-first Street off West End Avenue where Mick

Jagger once lived. She's always pointing out sights—this used to be Rumpelmayer's, where her grandpa took her and her brother for ice-cream sundaes; this was Bonwit's, where her mother purchased her wedding dress—while Darrell treats Manhattan as if it were any other college town, one where the cheeseburgers just happen to be more expensive.

But the disparities don't end there. For Rebecca got her B.A. from Yale, while Darrell graduated from Penn; Rebecca has a teardrop tattooed on her left ankle, while Darrell chickened out of getting Pepé Le Pew tattooed on his ass; she's sampled Ecstasy and mushrooms, he's never tried anything harder than pot; Rebecca's parents are Jewish and she was bat mitzvahed, while Darrell, raised by one Jewish agnostic and one Catholic atheist, feels a kinship only with Floyd Ellis, the janitor of his freshman-year dorm who once told him, "White boy, you're goin' places; this black man's got no place to go." That's him, he sometimes feels when he's with Rebecca; he's Floyd Ellis, the man with no fricking place to go.

And, perhaps most important of all these inequities, Rebecca has said that she has had five sexual partners, while Darrell, though he told her he'd had six, has had only four, and one of those four was a hard-faced hooker named Larissa in Piccadilly Circus, where he'd trolled for streetwalkers instead of attending a session of a research conference about D. H. Lawrence's gender orientation. Particularly troubling to Darrell is the fact that anyone seeing the two of them together would probably think that well-spoken, seemingly prim Rebecca lacked sexual experience. Early in their relationship, he quizzed Rebecca, asked if any of her previous partners had been abusive, if the sex had been consensual, but she always spoke fondly of her ex-lovers and showed him pictures—a Rainbow Coalition of studs, all of whom could have made a living as male models, save for Sabine Buresch, maid of honor at Darrell and Rebecca's wedding.

Just one time, he'd like to be Rebecca's equal. He wants one final bachelor fling, one more experience to even the score at five partners apiece, and then he'll learn how to be a perfectly respectable professor and father. Time is running out; he's thirty-one years old; he's preparing for condomless sex; he's bidding on a condo; soon he'll be organizing a file for a mortgage broker; at the Columbia gym, the towel boy has started calling him

"sir." "This is a dead man talkin' to me," he tells himself frequently, quoting the movie *The Untouchables*. "I'm talkin' to a dead man." And besides,
the girl in the East Asian Library is hot.

She's there as Darrell tromps up the stairs. He drops his book bag on
her table, takes a seat across from her, removes his laptop, and presses the
power button on it. She looks up, but only briefly, then starts writing fever-
ishly in a purple notebook while Darrell shudders at the drivel posing as a
dissertation on his computer screen—"Strong Pulling: Meredith, Mastur-
batory Metaphor, and the Victorian Imagination." The title, much like
everything else he has written in his academic career, began as parody, a
vicious mockery of both the impenetrable postmodern hooey that made
his mother, Margaret Finneran, a leading lit-crit scholar and the hopelessly
outdated and sycophantic suck-offs of nineteenth-century poets that make
the jaded grad students of his father, Peter Schiff, love and pity the poor,
earnest mope in spite of themselves. For his part, Darrell often passes time
by proposing absurd paper topics, such as "Bagshot, Popenjoy, and the
Newcomes: Lewd Punning and Thackeray's Homosocial Nomenclature,"
"Ejaculations and Penetralia: Self-Revelation and Self-Abuse in James's
The Bostonians," or "Cursed Be Thy Stones: Genital Humiliation Among
Peter Quince's All-Too-Rude Mechanicals," fully expecting to be hurled
out of academia. To his surprise, his papers are accepted by journals, and
his mailbox fills with invitations to conferences, where he has to stifle giggles while appearing with other windbag presenters offering insight into
such topics as "Representations of Pubic Hair in Early Lithography," "Vul-
vular Ornamentation and *The Golden Bowl*," "Recent Letters to *Penthouse*
Forum and the Queering of the American Tall Tale," "Heterosexual Subtext in John Ford's Westerns," or whatever the hell. For twenty-page academic articles, he can conceal the admittedly vapid and sophomoric
nature of his own observations beneath a surfeit of convoluted verbiage.
But at the length of a dissertation, unless he can hoodwink Bernie Ostrow
and his committee with a greatest-hits package of only tangentially related
articles, he assuredly will be outed as a fraud.

He never should have gone to graduate school, he thinks as he watches
the young woman write with more passion than he has ever brought to his

academic work. He should have been a film critic, a music writer, a pop culture expert on the talk show circuit. He possesses boundless enthusiasm for just about any topic unrelated to his discipline—comic strips, gangsta rap, dime-store romances, *Mad* magazine, Dr. Seuss, the books of Beverly Cleary, Wallace & Gromit cartoons, movies directed by Sam Fuller, Gordon Parks, John Boorman, and Michael Mann. Under such pseudonyms as "Caspar Goodwood" and "Henrietta Stackpole," he writes blistering critiques on the Internet Movie Database that are sharper than any of his scholarship. He can't remember the names of characters or the basic plots of *To the Lighthouse* or *Sons and Lovers*, but he knows every single moment in the shootout scene in *Heat* and every line of dialogue in *Office Space*. He can quote by heart LL Cool J songs, *Simpsons* episodes, blaxploitation flicks, Patrick McGoohan shows, Sean Connery movies, *Conan the Barbarian* ("Contemplate this on the tree of woe!"). He aced every question in auditions for *Who Wants to Be a Millionaire*, and assumes that he was disqualified just because he didn't shave or wear a tie to the callback. And yet only Rebecca still seems to believe he is the rebel he has always pretended to be. He is, when it comes right down to it, a married graduate student, soon to be a professor and father, mindlessly following his parents' career path because in the college towns where he was raised, he saw few other options for a smart, argumentative kid who didn't want to work nine to five. Never has Darrell met any man as conventional as himself; every day when he passes the statue of Alma Mater on the Columbia campus, he imagines that the seated, scepter-wielding figure is flipping him off.

Darrell pulls a pair of headphones and a Gil Scott-Heron CD out of his computer bag. He often tries feebly to inspire himself by listening to aggressive, antiestablishment music, by blasting N.W.A.'s *Straight Outta Compton*, Tupac's *Resurrection*, and early bootleg Rovner! CDs. He taps his thumbs on his table and quietly sings "Angola, Louisiana" along with Heron, whose music he recently discovered via the MP3 downloading service Stealware, illegal music downloading being only one of many methods he employs to avoid writing his dissertation. Lately Darrell has been downloading British deejays' mash-ups: Barry Manilow vs. Busta Rhymes,

Moby vs. Peter Frampton, "Fuck da Police" vs. "Mr. Roboto" ("Fuck Mr. Roboto"). These inspire him to spend hours imagining the mash-ups he could create to juice up his conference presentations: Nirvana vs. Samuel Taylor Coleridge ("Smells Like Teen Albatross"); *Star Trek II* vs. Coleridge ("The Wrath of Kubla Khan"), Virginia Woolf vs. The Prodigy ("Smack Mrs. Dalloway Up"); John Keats vs. Snoop Dogg ("Drop It Like It's a Grecian Urn").

But after Darrell has listened to his CD all the way through, he hasn't added one word to his thesis, while the young woman is still writing intensely in the same purple notebook, and Darrell half-wonders if she might be autistic. He can't imagine how anyone could be so committed to her work; something must be wrong with her. He's been hoping that she'll glare at him, tell him to stop daydreaming and singing; any acknowledgment of his existence would be fine. Darrell takes off his headphones and asks if he can borrow a pen.

She looks up and smirks—a haughty yet mischievous smirk, almost as if she's trying to stop herself from laughing at Darrell. Now, why the hell would he need a pen? she asks. He already has a laptop and, once again, he hasn't written anything all day; he's only hummed off-key to Gil Scott-Heron. Darrell shrugs and flashes an "all right, you got me" smile, then says they've both been working too hard and need a break; can he buy her some lunch? He waits for her to say no, just so he can forget about her and return to his so-called work, but her smile broadens and her eyes sparkle. If she needed food, she would already have purchased some, she says. Darrell can't tell if he's irritating her or if she's testing him. Oh, what the hell, he thinks, he's married, he has nothing to lose, he never has to see this Raggedy Ann–looking shorty again. Come on, he says, some protein will give her energy. Silently, she stands up, grabs her coat and notebook, and starts walking toward the stairs, and when Darrell follows her down, she doesn't tell him to stop. As they step out of the library, she turns to Darrell and asks if he's some sort of stalker. Darrell shakes his head ruefully; he would be, he says, but he's writing his dissertation and doesn't have the time. At this, she actually laughs, and even though Darrell rarely eats at restaurants with waiters or silverware, he suggests a stroll to Taqueria y

Fonda on Amsterdam Avenue. Once again, amazingly, the woman doesn't
say no.

Along their walk, they introduce themselves. She says her name is Jane
Earhart and she's taking a writing class at Columbia, and the only reason
she works at the East Asian Library is that she's always losing her ID, and
there nobody ever asks for it. Darrell has the oddly captivating sensation
that he could ask this Jane anything and she wouldn't care, that he could
invite her to do whatever crossed his mind and she would say yes, but also
that she wouldn't give a damn if he never spoke to her again. Her responses
to his questions and statements are rarely the ones he desires or intends;
her sporadic laughter comes only at his expense. When he actually cracks
a joke, she just scribbles in her notebook, and when he casually dismisses
his dissertation adviser as "the type of guy that likes to drink Olde English,"
she crinkles her nose and asks why the hell he's still quoting LL Cool J;
how old is Darrell anyway?

At the crowded taco joint, while a waiter fills their water glasses, Jane
fixes her intense stare on Darrell's left hand and asks if liberated husbands
now wear their wedding bands on their index fingers as a political statement. This show's over, Darrell tells himself. *Move along, people, there's
nothing to see here*. He stammers, then admits that he's married, whereupon Jane laughs harder than she has at any of his jokes. But later, after
they have parted, and Darrell has caught up with her at the Strangers' Gate
entrance to Central Park to return the wallet she inadvertently left on their
table, just for the hell of it he asks if she'd like to go out some time. Jane
tells Darrell she is usually free on Saturday nights.

THE TENANT'S DOG

Herbie Mann is standing impatiently in his apartment, waiting to go out. Herbie Mann is usually outside long before the sun has started to set. He has spent the past half hour watching exasperatedly as Ike Morphy stood atop a ladder in their living room with a can of black paint and a brush, writing I'VE GOT A GODDAMN LEASE! on his ceiling. "It isn't right," Ike said, half to himself, half to his dog. "If a man gives his word, his son should honor it." Herbie has not understood the specific words that Ike has been saying in reference to Mark Masler; to the dog, they sound like one word all run together—*ItisntrightItjustisntright*. Still, Herbie can sense both Ike's anxiety and the disruption of routine. The dog understands that ladders should not be in living rooms. Ike tells Herbie to "rest," but the animal can lie still for only a half minute, after which he gets up, trots to the window, then to the door, sneezes nervously at the ladder, then rests, then gets up again.

Herbie Mann is the full name of the mutt that has inhabited apartment 2B for more than six years. Save for the few white sprinkles on his paws and the tuft of his tail, and the new splash of gray around his muzzle, he is all black, even the spots on his tongue. With the exception of Ike Morphy's late mother's house on South Colfax, and Ricardo and Marlena's former place across the hall, Ike's apartment is the only home the animal has known since Ike adopted him from the East 110th Street shelter.

Herbie Mann is standing at his usual post, looking out the window toward the Parkside Mini Supermarket, when the doorbell rings. Doorbells are exciting; doorbells mean visitors; doorbells mean friends; this doorbell might mean that Ricardo, Marlena, and Buster have finally come home. Herbie dashes to the door, wagging and whining, but then Ike descends from the ladder, puts on his coat, fetches the leash, and leads him downstairs past Josh Dybnick, Rebecca Sugarman, and her leather-jacketed, ponytailed father, Phil. As Ike and Herbie head outside, the dog, ears tilted, hears Rebecca, Josh, and Phil's conversation fading into the distance: *AreyousurehewontmindusgoinginJoshAbsolutelywecleardthistimeHey-Dadwouldyoustopstaring?*

Ike named Herbie Mann after one of his favorite jazz performers, the jazz flutist who, like Ike, gained acclaim for playing an instrument outside its traditional context. But Herbie wasn't the dog's first name. Born on a construction site behind the Cathedral of St. John the Divine, amid Dumpsters, pallets, wheelbarrows, and tarps, he was the one member of his litter with the presence of mind to wriggle out of a hole in the church fence the moment after a city animal-control van arrived. For two weeks, he lived in the hills of Morningside Park, subsisting on picnic scraps and Dumpster food until his incessant whining caught the attention of a passerby, who named him Lucky and brought him back to his duplex on Riverside Drive.

Herbie remembers his life in that duplex as a mosaic of images and scents—Jean Naté perfume, sharp and tingling in his nose; the rough scrape of the Riverside Park jogging path against his paws; the taste of carpet and of shoes; the satisfying crunch of a piano leg; unintelligible shouts; a hand on his neck; a phone call; silence. He still remembers what happened when he was removed from his home for reasons he could never have begun to understand—he remembers the muzzle placed over his snoot; the tug of the leash; the long, bumpy, stop-and-start ride up a potholed avenue; the sidewalk outside the shelter littered with glass; the cold, cracked, green linoleum floor in a fluorescent-lit room full of cages; the grim sight of other frightened dogs being led in by men in khaki jumpsuits; the lonely sound of doors clanging shut. He remembers sitting in his cage, listening to plaintive wails and angry barks, then whining to drown out the other dogs' voices; he remembers dreaming of squirrels, then waking up when his nose bumped into the cage; he remembers seeing dusty boots walking back and forth in front of the cages; he remembers the frayed cuffs of Ike's faded jeans; he remembers Ike calling him Herbie and leading him out of the shelter into a bright September afternoon. He remembers arriving at this apartment where he felt so safe he never wanted to leave.

HeymanyoullbeallrightwithmeYouvegotmywordonthat, Herbie heard Ike say.

The music was what attracted Ike Morphy. He had never owned a pet; his parents never wanted one and his lifestyle as a musician on the road had never allowed him to consider the possibility. But when he walked past the 110th Street shelter and heard the clusters of tones—the dissonant choruses of yips, yelps, and yaps; the threatening crescendos and the plaintive diminuendos; the hopeful cadenzas; the resigned caesuras; and then, the mournful sound of a low A-flat being emitted by one particular animal— he didn't know how he'd lived so long without one.

Although Ike, who knew the difficulties of having to leave a home behind, would have treated any dog that had been abandoned at the shelter with sympathy and respect, he immediately felt a special connection to this one, a dog of sometimes shockingly astute powers of discernment, a dog with opinions he never concealed, a dog who never suffered fools gladly, a dog who seemed to carry within him a profoundly troubled and mysterious history, a dog who, Ike sometimes thought, was almost an outward expression of his own repressed subconscious, displaying the emotions Ike could not with an honesty few humans would dare employ. The animal has always reminded the man of a musical instrument, one that never plays a false note, his barks, whines, growls, and groans as heartfelt and meaningful as any solo by Miles or Coltrane.

"Come on, Herb," Ike says now as he leads his dog west toward Riverside

Park for his late-afternoon walk. In the Ana Beauty Salon, a caged parrot is squawking away. "Come on, Herb," the parrot says. *ComeonHerbComeon-Herb*. Herbie happily crosses Columbus, wagging at "the *compañeros*," four retired men wearing parkas who sit on folding chairs and Clover Farms dairy crates outside the Felipe Grocery. They are playing Patato Valdez music on a silver boombox. "Hey, Blackie," one of them shouts at Herbie. *Hey-blackdogblackdog*.

Herbie pulls Ike down Columbus, taking in every sight and smell—the warm gust of fabric softener from the Laundromat, churros and disinfectant from the Felipe Grocery, doughnuts and slices from Jimmy's Pizza & Coffee Shop, stale beer from last night's debauchery at the Ding Dong Lounge. As they walk, Herbie hears church bells, fire engine sirens, car radios, bus motors, stroller wheels rolling over pavement; he hears dominoes clacking, clothes twirling in washer-driers, the *New World* Symphony playing from a speaker mounted atop a mechanical horse outside a barbershop. He trots past billboard advertisements: LIVE WHO YOU ARE. ISN'T IT TIME YOU MOVED UP? He smells bouquets of roses, roasted chicken, falafel, shawarma, fresh bread, coffee, trash, the 103rd Street subway station. Herbie picks up his pace; he can smell Riverside Park and the 106th Street dog run just ahead.

Past icy, leaf-strewn paths, behind a chest-high, black iron fence, dog owners and dog walkers sit on park benches beneath London plane trees and work the *Times* crossword or stand on the dirt, holding cups of coffee or cans of soda. The younger dogs run laps, play with Kongs and tennis balls, tackle one another, then get back up in clouds of beige dust. Older dogs sun themselves on grassy patches or seek out blotches of shade underneath the benches and trees. In a corner of the run, a few small dogs are gathered around a blue plastic swimming pool, sipping melted ice and gray-brown slush, something that Herbie has learned not to do, associating that water with waking up every hour one night, begging Ike to take him out, leading the way to Strangers' Gate so that he could relieve his bowels on the cobblestones.

After Ike brought Herbie home and vowed to provide the animal with a safe, healthy life, the man and the dog became well known at this dog run. Here Ike—an omnivorous reader who would stay up late poring over every book about canine care he'd found at the Bloomingdale Branch Library—spoke with authority on home remedies for animals: kelp to aid digestion, witch hazel for joint pain, slippery elm for gastric distress, yogurt and egg yolks to keep a dog's coat shiny, beef soup bones to clean his teeth. Although Ike chose his words carefully on most topics, where Herbie was concerned he was always an enthusiastic fount of knowledge. But since their return from Chicago, Ike hasn't recognized many animals here. Gone are the tough Manhattan Valley mutts with names like Diego, Jazz, and Buddha; in their place are expensive purebreds, many of them named for specialty food items or Upper West Side food emporia—Zabar, Fairway, Camembert, and a pair of Swiss mountain dogs named Bagel and Schmear.

Herbie patrols the run, searching for familiar faces or scents, then resignedly settles atop a picnic table until—*yessss*—he gets a whiff of Ricardo Melendez and his yellow Lab mix, Buster. Herbie scrambles to his feet and stands on the picnic table, tail wagging like the arm of a metronome. And when Buster and Ricardo enter the dog run, Herbie leaps off the table and gallops to the front gate. He sniffs Buster, dive-bombs into Ricardo's protuberant belly, drops his wet tennis ball at the man's feet, barks and wags until Ricardo laughs and throws the ball for him. Herbie zooms after the wet ball and brings it back to Ricardo, who laughs and throws it again.

Ricardo Melendez, a man with a salt-and-pepper brush mustache, a black bolero, and a considerable paunch, all of which give him the aspect of some oil magnate on his day off, had been the first president of the condo board at the Clemente. Born in the Dominican Republic in the small coastal village of Cabrera, he arrived in New York in 1965; attended City College; moved to Manhattan Valley while studying at Columbia, where he completed a Ph.D.; then eventually found a job teaching economics at Rutgers. Ricardo was instrumental in helping to clean up the Roberto Clemente Building and the block, winning the trust of both dealers and beat cops. While his wife, Marlena, took care of their three children and sometimes those of her neighbors in the day-care center she operated in their second-floor apartment, Ricardo spent nights and week-

ends at Jerry Masler's Union Square office helping to draft letters petition-
ing the city to decrease the tax burden on the first-time unit owners in the
Clemente. At night, when Ike wasn't out on tour with the Funkshuns, gigging in some uptown club, or passed out with his old girlfriend, the caustic and dissolute fashion model and actress Muriel Ostrow, Ricardo would
invite him over and the men would stay up until dawn drinking Genesee
and passionately discussing movies, music, politics, art. Now, in the dog
run, Ike slaps Ricardo on the back and says *damn*, he's so glad to see a familiar face; he was beginning to think he didn't know anyone left in the
city. Where has Ricardo been keeping himself?

"I sold out, man," Ricardo tells Ike with a laugh, then plays a bongo solo
on his stomach and strikes a pantomime cymbal. "I've become fat, rich,
and happy." Ike asks what Ricardo means and the laugh turns bitter. Yeah,
he finally broke down and sold his place, Ricardo admits. He'd had a good
run, but after Jerry Masler's funeral, he realized that their twenty-year civic
improvement project in Manhattan Valley was nearing its conclusion.
When he and Marlena moved in, dozens of buildings and lots had needed
to be developed or renovated; now, developers were moving north of 110th
Street because their work in the neighborhood was over—not one empty
lot was left. Has Ike seen who has been moving into the condos where Nee-
dle Park used to be? Has Ike seen what happened to that spooky old can-
cer center and nursing home on Central Park West? After the developers
briefly stopped construction following 9/11, gangbangers were hanging out
there again; now they're calling it "The Landmark." They built a high-rise
behind it where every apartment sells for seven figures, and the place looks
like a castle, "a fucking *castle*, man."

Ricardo says he had always looked forward to the monthly Clemente
board meetings—the heated debates, the free-flowing Ron Barceló. At one
time, this was an extremely political neighborhood. The Progressive Labor
Movement held meetings two doors down from the Clemente; members
of the Weather Underground holed up right on Central Park West; when
he first arrived in Manhattan Valley, Ricardo heard stories of beatnik parties, of private benefits for the Abraham Lincoln Brigade, of editors of *The
New Masses* being forced to leave their homes during the Red Scare.

But no one on the Clemente board wanted to discuss politics or the community anymore; the board members talked only about the value of their property. What's more, they were asking to be remunerated, and there was talk of hiring a private management company, of building an elevator, remodeling the lobby, hiring a white-glove doorman, all that kinda jive. Meetings had to conform to some bastardized version of Robert's Rules of Order, and Ricardo couldn't speak unless he was recognized by the new condo board prez, who didn't even live in the building, man.

He hasn't felt at home around here for a long time anyway, Ricardo says. Used to be that whenever a new business would start moving in on Broadway or Amsterdam, he would get excited, wondering what it would be, but these days, it's usually a drugstore or bank. He was always a great movie buff; he was at the Olympia the night the FBI shut down the Cuban Film Festival. Now, the Olympia's a bank; the only theater left is the Metro and that one's for rent; even his favorite video store on 105th shut down. Whenever he walks through the old 'hood with Buster, he sees dudes wheeling big black Dumpsters with PHASE ONE DEMOLITION printed on them. That name's a lie, man, Ricardo says, because once something's demolished, there's no phase two.

Ricardo and Marlena both knew it was time to cash in, he says. He knew the economy was cyclical; the pendulum always swung back. He remembered the late 1980s, when home prices plummeted nearly 50 percent. So they found a nice kid from Overman who sold their place for $600K straight up to a twenty-seven-year-old mortgage broker. He and Marlena now live in a house on the Jersey shore just like Marlena always wanted, and they barely come into the city at all anymore, only to see Marlena's parents on 109th, and when he's had enough of them, he goes out walking with Buster.

"You still talkin' to me now that it turns out I'm a capitalist sonofabitch too, man?" Ricardo asks, but Ike doesn't answer. Ever since he returned to New York two weeks ago, he's felt as if he has been playing one of his way-out solos while the band is trying to keep a straight 4/4 time. With the Funkshuns, Maestro let Ike get away with flourishes as long as everyone else kept the beat; he often said Ike's harsh, avant-garde improvisations

would make critics think the band's music was less derivative than it actually was. But for Ike, life has never seemed to work the same way that music does; all music used to help him do was to forget about his life for just
a little while. As he sits on the picnic bench beside Ricardo, Ike has the
sensation that time stopped moving when he was with his mother in
Chicago, but when she was gone, it started accelerating, and now he's rac-
ing to catch up.

Ricardo tells Ike he should think about selling too, maybe find himself
a pretty little house by the water before the next real estate crash. But when
Ike reminds him that, unlike Ricardo, he didn't have the foresight to buy
his place and Masler's kid is selling it, Ricardo puts an arm around his
friend, then asks if Ike needs money. Nah, but thanks, Ike says, he's hoping he can find some way to stay, but if he has to move, he can track down
some gigs or a construction job to pay for a new place; maybe he'll even
break down and call Maestro about rejoining the band. The men stand in
the dog run in the gathering dusk as Ricardo throws the tennis ball for Herbie. Ike asks if Ricardo really feels happier now.

"Richer than ever," Ricardo says, with a smile.

The sun is all the way down when Ike and Herbie walk out of the dog
run and head home via 105th Street, then north on Amsterdam Avenue,
then east once again. Herbie Mann smells the dank vestibules of churches,
doughnut grease, refried beans, samosas, carnations, dried eucalyptus. He
hears scissors snip-snap in barbershops, muffled conversations over cell
phone speakers, airplanes overhead, children playing. But when Herbie
crosses Columbus and sees a broad-shouldered figure walking purposefully
toward him and Ike, he starts growling, not even registering Ike's commands or the cries of the parrot in the beauty salon (*CoolitHerb-
CoolitHerb*).

As the figure continues to approach, Herbie's growl transforms itself
into a bark. Not the dog's traditionally impatient but cheerful "throw me
the damn ball already" bark. He sounds alarmed, uncharacteristically aggressive. With each bark, his paws ride off the ground and his jaws snap at
air. Ike again is telling Herbie to cool it when he espies Mark Masler.

"I'm gonna go take care of this right now, Josh," Mark is saying into his cell phone. Then he flips the phone shut and walks right up to Ike in front of the Roberto Clemente Building. What the hell is Ike tryin' to do to him, *man*? Mark wants to know; he pays little attention to Herbie, though Ike needs practically all his strength to prevent his animal from jumping up for a mouthful of Masler's overcoat. Ike has always held Herbie back during the animal's rare violent displays and wonders what the dog might do if he ever let go of the leash; he'd like to think Herbie wouldn't hurt anyone, but he can't be sure. Ike tells Mark to just hang on for a minute, then pulls the dog inside.

Moments later, Herbie's paws rest on the ledge of a window of apartment 2B. He is barking at the sidewalk below, but the barks are muted by the glass as Ike walks back downstairs where Masler is waiting. The dog can't quite make out the two men's gestures, can't comprehend the specific words that are all running together: **WhydoyoukeephasslingmebrotherNo-brotherwhydoyoukeephasslingmybuyer**. But he understands that Ike's voice is raised. He wants to protect Ike, protect his home, but at this distance, from inside his apartment, he can only bark.

Outside the building, Mark Masler heatedly recounts the conversation he just had with Josh Dybnick, how Josh entered the apartment with his customer and her father and saw the message Ike had painted on the ceiling: I'VE GOT A GODDAMN LEASE! That was a "punk move," Mark says, and he doesn't know what Ike was trying to prove by pulling it. Look, he says, if he himself had nothing but money, Ike could stay as long as he wanted. But this is New York, he says, this is America, this isn't the land of give-away-half-a-million-bones-just-to-be-a-nice-guy. His dad might have done that, but he had that luxury—his wives were gone, his daughters were established in their careers, and his son was just a fuck-up anyway.

Now, Mark tells Ike, they both know he's selling Ike's place and that can happen one of two ways: either Ike can be cool and cooperate or Ike can continue to interfere, and Mark will have to start contacting lawyers and repo men. Will Ike act like a mensch or will he keep asking for things that no reasonable human being would ever give him?

Ike takes a tight breath. Why is Masler treating him like some panhandler? he wants to know. He's not out on the street asking anybody for a handout; he's not looking for Mark to *give* him anything, only to honor the agreement that has already been made. For years, he offered to pay Mark's dad a higher rent, he says, but Jerry Masler always told him he was happy with their arrangement. "Save your money for the people who need it, Isaac," he'd told Ike. "Save it for your family; save it for when you have kids." Now Ike can feel the old frustration rising—the kind he'd felt when his father would go out and get drunk, spending the money he earned at the Regal Theater gambling at the Vincennes Chess and Checkers Club; the kind he'd felt when he would blow his clarinet until dawn to drown out the sound of his mother and sister arguing downstairs; the kind he'd felt after he left Chicago when his letters home were returned unanswered but his checks were cashed anyway.

Mark says he doesn't see any reason for Ike to get upset—the man had just about the sweetest real estate deal in the city; no one could have expected it to last forever. If Ike were in his position, he'd be doing exactly the same thing.

Ike considers Mark's statement. He doubts that, he says, but whether or not it's true, how often does someone like him ever find himself in Mark's position? When was the last time Mark heard of a brother from the South Side of Chicago with a messed-up dad and an overworked mom inheriting property he never had to work for? Maybe if Mark knew the feeling of having someone taking away the one home he thought was his, he might feel a little "upset" too.

Mark looks at Ike and sighs. Hey, he knows a lot more about having to leave a home than Ike would realize, he says. And sure, he guesses that if he were Ike, he'd probably think he was getting screwed. Still, that doesn't change the situation, and he's not going to change his mind about selling the apartment. Mark says he can remember his pop teaching him all about the history of this neighborhood, a history in which someone was always taking property from someone else. Jerry Masler called that history tragic, but you know what Mark calls it? Progress. That's what happens in every city; it changes person by person, apartment by apartment, building by building, block by block. By his father's logic, neither he nor Ike should have the apartment; they should give it back to the Lenape Indians. But this neighborhood is moving forward, both of them know that, and all they can do is to help it along by getting out of its way.

Look, Mark says, if Ike will let him and Josh do what they have to do, he'll give Ike a reasonable amount of time to move; plus, he'll even pay Ike's moving expenses and ask Josh to help him find a place he can afford, and he'll put this promise in writing. Maybe his father would do more, but he's not his father and he never will be.

Ike eyes Mark Masler closely. Yes, Jerry Masler would do more, he thinks, but Mark won't. This is the best the man can do.

"Fine," Ike says. "Just do what you gotta do."

Herbie is lying on his pillow, chewing on a tennis ball. When Ike enters, the dog wags his tail but without much vigor, doesn't even bother getting up, just keeps chewing his ball and spitting it out, completely indifferent to the slices of beef liver Ike sets out for him; he doesn't get up until he hears Ike taking boxes out of his closet. Now, his tail stands straight up; ears alert, he trots into the living room. The sound of boxes is one of his least favorite, almost as bad as suitcase zippers, almost as bad as cage doors slamming shut, almost as bad as *Seeyoulater*, the words Ike speaks whenever he is about to leave Herbie alone for more than an hour or two.

"We'll be all right, man; don't worry," Ike tells Herb. "Wherever I go, you know you're coming with me. You've got my word on that."

Ike fills one box with books and sheet music, another with clothes. He doesn't know whether he's planning to leave or just give everything away. All he knows is that, soon enough, he'll have to go—his time here has passed, that much is clear. He begins making up a third box, but before he is through, the doorbell rings. Herbie barks and runs to the door. Then Ike walks to the intercom and asks who's there. Herbie hears the voice from downstairs and the words a woman speaks all run together: *ItsRebecca-Youdontreallyknowme.*

THE BUYER'S REMORSE

Rebecca Sugarman walks nervously into the lobby of the Roberto Clemente Building while dialing Darrell one more time. She has just left her father on Broadway at Smoke, choosing not to stay and listen to him play his "licorice stick" for the umpteenth time in the jazz club's open jam because she wants to tell Ike Morphy personally that she can't in good conscience bid on his apartment. She already loves the building and can easily see herself and Darrell happy here, hates the idea of vetoing the apartment her husband has chosen. But as her father said upon seeing the message Ike painted on his ceiling, Manhattan does not exactly have a shortage of attractive apartments.

Halfway up the stairs, as Rebecca approaches 2B, Darrell still isn't answering his phone, so she hangs up. Lately, she doesn't like bothering him when he is trying to work on his dissertation; even when they go out, he seems only half present, the rest of him composing sentences, scanning his brain for appropriate citations, interrupting Rebecca to loudly insult himself while quoting from books he's taught but never read ("Slow, Trojan Aeneas? Are you *slooooow*?").

This morning, Rebecca was watching Darrell sleep, but after she began caressing his cheek, he sprang up, looked at the clock, and said *aww crap*, he was already behind schedule. So instead of starting in on the passionate morning she had been anticipating, Rebecca grabbed a red pencil and a stack of theater, film, and book reviews Chloe Linton had asked her to edit for *The American Standard*'s upcoming issue, and lay naked in bed working her way through the copy. Chloe had told Rebecca she hadn't intended for her to have so much responsibility so early, but Liz Fogelson hadn't given any notice, just decided on Rebecca's first day never to come in again. Chloe said that Rebecca would serve as acting literary editor, she would receive a $5,000 raise, and, if all went well, she would take over permanently.

While Darrell showered and dressed, Rebecca lay on her stomach, editing capsule book reviews. She was astonished by their brevity, by their lack of depth. They were also riddled with typos ("Zimmerman places an arm around her waste"), facile literary references ("Like Vonnegut, Hemingway, and Kerouac before her, Trinkelman's surname boasts three syllables"), and mixed metaphors ("In more sure-footed hands, this novel might have made for a splendiferously fragrant stew, shining a beacon onto the immigrant condition, but it fails to even pay lip service to the elephant in the room"). Also, some of the types of books that the *Standard* was reviewing seemed uncharacteristic. Instead of, say, a 2,500-word consideration of Liam Roth's six-volume defense of Zionism, *Without Forgiveness*, there were 125-word blurbs about romance novels, mysteries featuring feline detectives, inspirational and self-help texts, and pseudopolitical quickie books, such as cable news personality Remak Roland's *Five Liberals You'll Meet in Hell*.

But today, when Rebecca tried discussing the *Standard*'s anemic Arts & Letters section with Darrell before he left for the library, he seemed interested only in the topic of her raise; five thousand didn't sound like enough "scratch." He advised her to march into Chloe Linton's office, "swing [her] dick around," and demand "ten large." When Rebecca said that as a new employee she certainly couldn't ask for more money, Darrell accused her of lacking self-esteem. People were never paid their worth unless they knew their worth, he observed, citing the example of his pop, a genius who probably could have succeeded in any field but wasted his life trying to be some *Fachidiot*, teaching Wordsworth in Podunk towns *am Arsch der Welt* to a bunch of pud-knockers, making less than entry-level lawyers young enough to be his grandkids.

In the afternoon, while walking to the Clemente with her father, Rebecca tried to discuss the *Standard*'s weak editorial content, but Phil Sugarman just said that if her job turned out to be rotten, she could quit; he'd send her whatever cash she and Darrell needed. And once Phil and Rebecca arrived at apartment 2B and saw Ike's message on the ceiling, Phil, who owned every Funkshuns album on which Ike Morphy had played, wanted only to discuss Ike. Did Rebecca think they were really in his apartment? he wanted to know. Did she think they could wait around for him to come back to autograph an album and talk music? Could they maybe leave a note asking him why he had quit the Funkshuns, if he'd spent all this time wood-sheddin' just like Sonny Rollins?

"Absolutely not, Dad," Rebecca said, and yanked her father out of the apartment.

Rebecca Sugarman is now standing in the second-floor hallway of the Roberto Clemente Building as Ike Morphy opens his door. He looks weary, preoccupied, as if Rebecca has wakened him from some deep sleep or interrupted some profound thought. He hasn't taken off his coat or his boots since he returned from the dog run. At first he appears unsure whether to ask Rebecca into his apartment—Herbie snarls when he gets a whiff of Rebecca's coat but he is soon wagging; so Ike, trusting his dog's judgment as always, steps back from the door. Ike asks if Rebecca forgot something here, but she says no. As Rebecca enters his hallway, again seeming as if she belongs here, Ike remembers more clearly who she is and why she has probably come. He asks snidely if she has brought a tape measure to double-check his square footage; maybe she wants to test the water pressure or make sure all the sockets are working. Rebecca shakes her head. And when Ike finally asks why she's here, she stammers, then says she doesn't know. She has spent enough time at clubs and studios with her dad waiting to talk shop or collect autographs to feel comfortable around musicians and to be familiar with their moods and their quirks; still, now she wonders if Ike will think she's too self-important or self-satisfied if she barges into his place, then announces that she and Darrell won't be bidding on his apartment. She is being foolish and patronizing, she thinks. She is turning to leave when Herbie trots away to the bedroom, then reappears, dragging an empty cardboard box to block her exit; it's too big for the dog, though, and he trips over the flaps.

Eyeing the boxes in the hallway and the living room, Rebecca asks if Ike is moving. Ike says Rebecca should tell him whether he is or not, but she says the decision has little to do with her; she hasn't spoken to Darrell but has already decided against bidding on this place, she wouldn't feel right since Ike is still living here. Ike asks why she cares—apparently, someone will buy the apartment, why not her? No, Rebecca says, she couldn't.

Ike pauses for a moment. Ahh, what the hell, he says, he can't act the part of the asshole all night long—why doesn't she come in and they can talk? Rebecca says she doesn't want to bother Ike if he's busy. No, come on, he says—he loves his dog, but this place can get pretty boring and lonely since it's just the two of them here; sometimes it's nice to chat with someone who can talk back instead of just barking.

Rebecca laughs, and when Ike gestures to his worn tan sofa, she walks over to it and takes a seat. Herbie Mann leaps up on the couch beside Rebecca, and she scratches the dog's belly while Ike heads for the kitchen.

"I'm sorry," Rebecca tells Ike.

"Sorry for what?" Ike wants to know.

Rebecca pauses, then says, actually, she isn't sure. Her default response is usually to apologize, she says; she can almost always find something to apologize for.

Ike returns to the living room with two glasses and a carton of orange juice; he pours a glassful and hands it to Rebecca. He doesn't mind the company and Herbie always likes having people around, but he is still having a hard time figuring out why Rebecca has come. No woman has sat alone with him here since he walked out on the band and, soon after, broke up with Muriel, a woman who always seemed angriest in the moments when he felt most content. When would he cut a solo record?

Muriel kept asking him. When would he hustle some gigs, why was she the only one drinking now, would he ever play again or would he just leave the clarinet in the closet forever and work mindless jobs until he died?—she hadn't gotten into this relationship to date some tight-assed construction worker. The last time Ike saw her, she was sitting with a couple of neighborhood kids in the back of a gypsy cab stalled in front of Quierido's Barber Shop on Columbus Avenue. She rolled down her window. Dark shadows were under her eyes and she was wearing too much eyeliner. How was she doing? asked Ike. How did she look? Muriel asked. And when Ike didn't respond, she said, "That's how I'm doing—as well as I look."

Now, Ike sits on his couch, Herbie Mann between him and Rebecca. Ike has never spent much of his time apologizing, he tells her—when you don't talk much, you find you don't have to apologize too much for things you say. He's felt sorry for lots of things he's done, though. What does she usually apologize for, he asks—for things she said or things she did, or maybe for things that weren't even her fault to begin with?

All of the above, says Rebecca with a smile. Yup, that just about sums up her approach. She sips her juice as Herbie Mann rests his head in her lap. She is beginning to feel oddly comfortable here, can sense the years Ike and Herbie have spent in this apartment, and feels touched by the love she sees between the man and his dog. Now that she and Darrell are planning to become parents, she is heartened whenever she observes nurturing qualities in men and tries to imagine that home ownership and fatherhood will reveal those characteristics that she has always worked hard to bring out in Darrell. Does Ike know where he'll go if he leaves? Rebecca asks. Hell, he isn't sure, Ike says. When he was driving back from Chicago to New York, he had been planning to devote himself to his music without thinking about anything else, but ever since he's been back, he hasn't had a chance to get his mind clear enough.

Well, maybe someone could give him that chance, some time to think, says Rebecca, maybe her father could help. She tells Ike how much Phil Sugarman loves his style of playing, how much of a jazz fan he is, how he once described the Funkshuns as "Ornette Coleman meets Kool & the Gang," how he plays clarinet too and admires any musician who didn't sell out the way he thinks he did. Phil still owns a studio apartment in New York and a vacation house in Maine; he's a little bit of a dork about music sometimes, but he's a good guy and would gladly help a fellow musician if Ike needs a place to stay for a little while.

Ike says he's not crazy about that Kool & the Gang reference, but comparisons to Ornette are always welcome, and he's glad to hear that somebody out there still remembers him. Just as he feels his mood brightening, though, he catches himself and regards Rebecca with new suspicion. She's up to something, he thinks—why would anyone offer a place to stay to someone they don't even know?

How long does Rebecca mean by "a little while"? Ike asks.

Rebecca says she doesn't know; she hasn't talked with her father yet.

Well, how much would her pop charge him?

Probably nothing, Rebecca says, maybe a pittance; she doesn't know.

What's a pittance? Ike asks. Is that what she thinks he's been paying here? A pittance?

Rebecca says she really has no idea, only knows her father might help.

Just for a "fellow musician," asks Ike.

Yes, says Rebecca, always slow to recognize sarcasm, but hearing it now.

No, Ike thinks, irritated with himself for having been naïve and gullible—Rebecca is too forthright, too guilelessly honest to be credible. People don't just show up at strangers' apartments unless they want something. Ike says he doesn't believe anything comes for free anymore. What does her father really want? he asks. To manage his career? Get a cut of the action? Dangle a carrot in front of him to make sure he leaves his little girl's condo quietly? Take him on as some kind of equal opportunity charity tax write-off?

Does Ike always assume the worst in people? Rebecca asks. She gets up and starts walking for the door.

"I do now," says Ike.

Rebecca shakes her head as Ike watches her go.

Herbie trots after Rebecca, tries to follow her out, but Ike grabs the dog by the collar and holds him. The animal runs back to the window; he looks out and shivers slightly as he sees that rain is beginning to fall. Rebecca walks down the front steps, then proceeds west, taking an umbrella out of her shoulder bag. Herbie barks at her but she doesn't turn around or look up, just continues walking fast. Herbie keeps barking and runs to the door, begging Ike to take him out, so Ike puts on his leash, assuming that Herbie will just hop into a tree pit to do his business, then, because of the rain, turn around and go home where it's warm and dry. But Herbie leads Ike quickly west, his tail wagging until the moment he sees Rebecca step into a cab, at which point the tail suddenly droops and Herbie whines. Ike stands in the cold rain and watches Rebecca's taxi driving west toward Amsterdam. He can almost hear the faint hint of a sad, sweet melody.

THE BUYER'S HUSBAND'S LOVER

{ Or at Least He Can Dream . . .}

Jane Earhart lets Darrell Schiff kiss her good-bye in front of the Columbia University gates, but she keeps her teeth clamped together when he tries to slip in his tongue. Then, with a cryptic smile, she speeds east through the icy rain. Looking back every so often to make sure Darrell isn't following her, she walks through Morningside Park, down wet stairways, along a slippery curved path, around a muddy baseball diamond, up the steps, east on 110th Street, then on into Central Park. As the rain continues to fall upon her, she wends her way through the park, so familiar to her that she could easily find her way home blindfolded. She walks past the soggy lawn beside the Harlem Meer; through the Conservatory Garden; past the Untermyer Fountain, around which three stone maidens frolic; past the statue of J. Marion Sims; out at Girls' Gate; then south on Fifth Avenue until she reaches her building at East Eighty-fifth Street. She smiles at her doorman and vainly tries to strike up a conversation with him, even though after all these years he still barely speaks to her. Then, she takes the elevator up to 11. She enters her unspeakably messy apartment, steps over the papers and half-open books scattered about the floor, attempts to dry her hair with an already damp and fairly rank towel, glugs from a bottle of mouthwash, swirls the fluid around in her mouth, returns to her worktable, pushes the power button on her laptop, draws the blinds on her view of the rain falling onto the park and Fifth Avenue, then goes back to her bathroom to spit.

Jane takes a seat in front of her computer. On the screen is a sepia photo of Virginia Woolf, along with dozens of little blue folders, most labeled with unwieldy and all-too-literal titles. She opens the folder marked "More Damn Manuscripts That I Haven't Figured Out How to Finish" and scrolls until she finds a document entitled "The Time I Kissed This Married Guy but Didn't Let Him Slip Me the Tongue." She clicks twice on the document and it zaps open. Midway through the tenth page, she finds the passage she has been seeking; it begins, "Kissing him was like . . ." followed by a blank. She ponders the blank space for a moment, then types in the next phrase: "kissing one's reflection and finding one's lips have touched the cold, rough surface of a cracked mirror." She reads the sentence she has written, shudders, yells "Shit," and deletes every word after "reflection." Then she slams her fists on the table and cuts the whole damn sentence.

When Jane was growing up in this unnecessarily large four-bedroom apartment, books were always her favorite escape—the ones her late parents and grandparents used to read; the ones her mother had written; the ones her housekeeper, Raimunda Bonilla, read to her; and the one she herself was writing. She read books in all genres—biographies of entomologists and aviators, antique encyclopedias, annotated maps, first-person narratives of explorers and animal behaviorists, science fiction by Jules Verne, J. G. Ballard, Lewis Ridle, and H. G. Wells. But whenever she wrote, either in school or at home, she would write only one extended story: *Wizard Girl, the Blue Kingdom, and Her World Made of Glass.*

Wizard Girl's name is Iphigene; she is the daughter of an evil wizard named Sims who, upon discovering that his daughter's powers exceed his own, locks her in a glass cube, which he suspends high above his blue kingdom. He warns her that if she ever escapes, she will fall to the earth and die. Though Iphigene tries to escape anyway, all her attempts are thwarted. She conjures up a great storm, but the cube repels the lightning;

she guides her cube into space, tries to crash-land it into the moon, but the cube always tumbles back down toward the blue kingdom, above which it bobs and dances.

Lonely and despondent, Iphigene lives inside her cube until her thirteenth birthday, upon which she wakes, then stands. And when her head hits the cube's ceiling, she realizes she has grown too tall. She considers telling her father, but fears he would just cast a spell to shrink her. So she curls herself into a ball, then devises her own spell to make herself even larger, to make her hands ten times as wide, her arms ten times as long. And once she feels herself growing, she thrusts out her arms and legs and bursts through the cube, spinning toward the earth, a blizzard of shattered glass falling after her. And as she falls, she makes a pact with herself: she will not hit the ground until she has told one story for each shard of glass hurtling toward her.

In each shard, Iphigene envisions an entirely new adventure. In her mind, she journeys through the Land of Cherry Mountains, through the Land of Swimming Turtles and the Land of Eternally Optimistic Song Lyrics. She tumbles through the Land of Diminutive Mariners and Falling Azaleas, does battle with magical bears, sheep, and mechanical horses. Traveling above the Mirrored Stream, over fields, cliffs, and gullies, she befriends alligators; cavorts with Romeo and Juliet, Mother Goose, and Ludwig van Beethoven; does the Charleston with three naked nymphs. As she travels over land after land, over the Land of Lilacs, the Land of Green Meadows, and the Land That Encompasses All Other Lands, telling herself story after story, she does not know that the shimmering blue surface below her is water, and that when she falls into it, she will not die as her father warned, only float effortlessly back to shore.

When she began writing these adventures, Jane Earhart was Gigi Malinowski, the small, exceptionally mousy, blond-haired daughter of the late Twill Malinowski, heir to a funeral parlor fortune and author of two works of nonfiction (the highly praised generational memoir *By the Time We Got to Woodstock* and an indifferently received follow-up, *By the Time We Got to Westchester*). While Gigi was still in middle school, Twill and her husband, Alan, perished in a traffic accident on the Triborough Bridge, after which the girl took to creative writing with unprecedented fervor. Living with her grandparents, who were too old and ill to supervise her, she spent days away from school, conspiring with Raimunda to have her act the part of Gigi's grandmother at parent-teacher conferences, forging signatures on sick-day notes, then wandering the paths of Central Park, telling stories to herself about Iphigene, and then returning home to write them down. After her grandparents died when she was in high school, Gigi inherited the remainder of her family's money and, following her graduation from Trinity, she dismissed Raimunda, moved to California, dyed her hair orange, and changed her name to Jane Earhart—a name she created by combining the names of a literary and a real-life heroine. She entered the University of California at Santa Cruz, where she planned to pursue a degree in writing.

Upon her arrival at UCSC, however, Jane discovered that something significant about her, aside from her name, had changed: over the years, she had become pretty, and her distant, quiet otherworldliness was now a seductive inscrutability. At least that was what she deduced from her fellow students' behavior—they stopped their Ultimate games to chat with her on the beach, approached her after class to ask about homework. But the moment Jane knew she was supposed to express love or passion for one of her peers, she just felt indifferent or overburdened or angry. She still wrote stories, but now they were always literal, banal, and exceedingly cynical: "So I Arrived in Santa Cruz (Yeah, I Know, So Effing What?)"; "So I Met This Mega-Loser in the Repulsively Dank Laundry Room (Big Deal)"; "So I Lost My Virginity to Some Sweaty, Thick Rugby Guy Named Russ (Yuck)."

Four years ago, after leaving UCSC three credits shy of a bachelor's degree, Jane returned to her grandparents' old apartment here on the Upper East Side, hoping that coming back to New York would shock her system and awaken her creativity—but to no avail. The first story she wrote here was entitled "So I'm Staring out My Window Looking at This Big Damn City (Again and Again and Again)."

Jane is currently a continuing ed student in Faith Trinkelman's creative writing workshop, held in Dodge Hall on the Columbia campus. Trinkelman, who authored the critically acclaimed novel *Zimmerman's Daughter*, leads "writers' boot camps" and has published numerous writing memoirs, including *Faith-Based Writing*, *Take It on Faith*, and *Write On, Sistah!* Her workshop meets four times a week for eight hours a day, beginning at 7:30 a.m., when she locks the door—latecomers are not allowed to enter and bathroom visits are forbidden except during the noon break. Students critique one another's stories, perform composition exercises, and take notes on Trinkelman's Rules, such as "Never write in the first person because 82 percent of all best sellers are written in the third."

Unlike the rest of her classmates, Jane Earhart already has a literary agent and a publisher, Purple Prose. But the work Purple Prose will soon be publishing is not *Unimaginative Encounters with People I Probably Don't Know as Well as I Should to Write About Them*, the collection of short stories and sketches Jane has been working on throughout the workshop, but *Wizard Girl, the Blue Kingdom, and Her World Made of Glass*, which her late mother's agent Naomi Boldirev's son and partner Carter found while rummaging through files in Jane's apartment for posthumous works written by Twill. Jane had not even realized that Carter Boldirev would approach editors with the fantasies she wrote during middle school and high school, and she was stunned when Purple Prose offered to publish them. She agreed on the condition that the book be published anonymously, for she preferred not to be reminded of either the tragic circumstances that inspired *Wizard Girl* or the painful fact that she was obviously so much more talented and creative as a child; these days, her stories still stall when any imagination is required. How she was ever able to envision such worlds as the Land of the Shallow Water Alligators or the Land of Rolling Frankfurters is beyond her.

Boldirev has told Jane he will make every reasonable effort to keep her name secret, and has already sold rights in twelve foreign countries; he is enthusiastic about the prospects for a *Wizard Girl* film, a Saturday-morning cartoon show, and the licensing of *Wizard Girl* plush toys and video games. But he has expressed little interest in Jane's newest short stories; they don't capture the imagination the way her children's stories do, and don't resonate with life experience the way adult writing needs to.

Both Faith Trinkelman and Jane's fellow students offer similar criti-cisms of Jane's most recent stories; her characters lie flat on the page, their behavior and dialogue are mind-numbingly ordinary. Her only funny line is delivered in a library, where Jane's first-person narrator asks a suitor if he is a stalker and he says he doesn't have the time. Trinkelman keeps telling Jane she should have waited to try writing; she should have gathered more experiences first—88 percent of all first novels are based on one's own life, and as of now, Jane doesn't seem to have had much of one.

Taking these and other criticisms to heart, Jane has spent months on a scavenger hunt for experience. She now eavesdrops on conversations, chats up the owners of newspaper stands in subway stations, talks to strangers on the No. 6 train, takes notes of their physical tics, their clothes. And this evening, when Darrell Schiff moved in for the goodnight kiss, she consented. How else could she attempt to finish the story at which she is intently staring this very moment, the story entitled "The Time I Kissed This Married Guy but Didn't Let Him Slip Me the Tongue"?

THE BUYER'S HUSBAND

Darrell Schiff walks across campus through the rain toward Broadway with a new spring in his step, an unfamiliar lightness in his stride. He enters the Morton Williams University Supermarket and heads straight for the flower section to buy a bouquet of red roses for Rebecca. He knows she's allergic to one flower, but thinks it's either carnations or tulips. As he stands in the checkout line with his bouquet, he can still feel Jane's kiss upon his lips. He feels rejuvenated, doused with elixirs of love and youth. For a moment, he wonders why the checkout girl is laughing at him, then realizes he has been chanting Tupac lyrics ever since he walked into the store—"I'm a sucka for love." But he is not embarrassed. In fact, he wants to kiss the checkout girl, wants to smooch with every woman waiting behind him in line, wants to make out with every fricking woman on Broadway. Darrell has not felt this giddy in ages, maybe ever.

On his dates before meeting Rebecca, Darrell often felt like a talk show host with an uncooperative guest, having to keep the conversation moving. Rebecca, by contrast, has always asked him about his research, but he usually just repeats the same phrases ad infinitum, hoping she won't realize she is more interested in his work than he is ("Spent the day in the piles again, didn't write a frickin' thing"; "Gertrude McFuzz is pissed 'cause I haven't returned her paper"; "That peckerwood Ostrow's still flippin' me the bird"). When Rebecca returns home, she talks effusively to Darrell about her new colleagues at *The American Standard*; she talks about literature, about babies, and about ovulation, something that has seemed distressingly regular of late. On the bedside table stands a V&T Pizzeria calendar with the days of the month circled — in red when Rebecca will be menstruating, green when she'll probably be ovulating, yellow when she has a deadline at the *Standard* and will be home late. Meaning that, when Darrell avoids sex on green days, it seems as if he's doing it on purpose. Which he is. Not that he doesn't want kids, it's just that he'd prefer them when he's secure in his career, maybe in, oh, about ten years.

With Rebecca's wealthy-ass family and her real-ass job, Darrell sees himself transitioning all too easily into the role of stay-at-home dad, one of those ultraserious, soft-spoken Stepford husbands who talk only of playgroups and diapers and percentiles of weight and height and the Bradley Method; one of those Croc-wearing husbands with more hair on his face than on his head, who says things like "We're pregnant" or "We started *trying* six months ago" or "Hey, sorry, man, gotta go; my wife's ovulatin'" — guys with kids always seem inexplicably fruity to him. And Darrell just loathes the idea of making small talk with other people's kids, discussing *Dora the Explorer* and *Bob the Builder*, singing "The Wheels on the Bus (Go Round and Round)," like he really gives a shit, like he's some diddler or some other species of loser.

He sees the arrival of children as the end to his privacy; sees himself hosting interminable visits from both his and Rebecca's parents, calling Phil Sugarman "Dad," even though Phil obviously hates his pale slacker ass; sees himself spending holiday dinners once again noting how his parents fail to measure up to the Sugarmans, how they resemble at best the Simpsons or the Munsters by comparison. He sees himself living in a condo he could never have afforded on his own, then moving to fricking White Plains, driving in car pools, pointlessly fantasizing about *schtupping* the MILFs he meets on the playground, getting punched out by

belligerent jock dads at soccer practice, trying feebly to protect his intellec-
tually gifted but athletically retarded offspring from bullies named Cody,
Tyler, and Dakota when he'd really rather be drinking beers at the Dive
Bar, making lewd and facile references to Anthony Trollope ("Of Trollope
and Trollops: The Determinism of Surnames"), perhaps performing any of
a wide array of sex acts with Jane Earhart, or even just having one more
conversation with her.

Tonight, they spent three hours together at the Mill Korean Restaurant.
He adored watching Jane slurp her noodles. They kept ordering more rice
teas, more lime rickeys, more dishes of kimchi because she couldn't stop
asking questions about him. She wanted to know about his family, about
how he met Rebecca, about how he felt being out with another woman.
Even though she smirked at almost everything he said, she always asked for
more detail, as if what he was saying was so captivating that she just had to
write it down.

And then there was the kiss, that "what the hell I've got nothing to lose
I'm a dead man anyway" kiss he and Jane shared in the rain outside the
university gates; despite the disappointing lack of tongue, that kiss produced a sensation approximating an electrical charge coursing through his
body, so much so that he stopped in a Kent Hall washroom before going to
the supermarket just to make sure he hadn't ejaculated like some kid during his first slow dance—well, like him during his first slow dance with Jessica Bosman back in Madison. His only regret regarding his evening with
Jane is that, in his zealous responses to her questions, he barely asked any
of his own, only asked if he might see her again at the library, and she allowed, "Hell, dude, anything's possible." But before he could shout after
her to ask for her phone number or e-mail address, she was already a half
block away. When he returned to the library, he was dismayed to learn on
findanyonesnumber.com that she was unlisted. Still, she had left her umbrella on the desk where she had been working, which seemed to suggest
she would be returning.

Darrell arrives home just after midnight with his bouquet of roses and
thrusts it toward Rebecca, who has been lying awake in bed. Her eyes have
been red ever since she left Ike Morphy's apartment. When she returned

home and found that Darrell still wasn't here, she actually burst into tears, unsure why a few harsh words from a stranger had affected her so deeply. She checked the *Times* movie listings, rode the subway down to Houston Street, and caught the last show of *Los Olvidados* at Film Forum; she cried all the way through the movie, cried about all those poor, motherless children on the streets of Mexico, happy she had some reason to cry other than the cynical remarks Ike had made about her and her father.

Rebecca sits up in bed, rubs her eyes, and sees Darrell standing over her with the bouquet. Why the flowers? she asks. Darrell shrugs. For coming home so late; he lost track of time. They're pretty, she says. She takes the flowers and wipes away a tear. Darrell asks what the matter is. Nothing, says Rebecca, she has just always been allergic to roses. Darrell makes as if to take back the flowers, but she shakes her head; they're pretty enough to compensate for the tears. Rebecca gets out of bed, still holding the bouquet, and Darrell watches her walk naked to the kitchen, her long red hair cascading down, almost to the small of her back. She takes a glass vase out of a cabinet, runs the faucet—droplets of water spray her breasts and stomach. Darrell whips off his clothes, deposits them in a heap on the floor, and climbs into bed.

Darrell isn't certain whether the sight of his nude wife or, more probably, the memory of Jane Earhart's recent affirmation of his worth is making him feel so horny. Once, almost everything gave him the horn, and part of him suspects that the reason he pursued a graduate degree was not because his parents had urged him to do so and certainly not because he was so bloody interested in English lit, but because studying it seemed like the most effective method for discouraging his frequent and often ill-timed erections. He used to love when sex was transgressive and still hasn't quite gotten used to the fact that having sex with the woman who shares his bed is actually something he's supposed to do, not something that would be considered felonious in red states. When he and Rebecca stay at her parents' Maine vacation home or his parents' Madison ranch house, he still finds it odd that they get to sleep together and that she rarely wears pajamas. He is still not accustomed to the fact that his wife enjoys sex, apparently even more than he does. He still feels embarrassed when Rebecca parades around in the nude, when she goes down on him, when he sees her dildo on the dresser, or when she grabs his testicles hard, just like the *nafkehs* in Piccadilly. And now that they're planning for children, sex has been transformed—into something profound, beautiful, sacred. God, it sounds deadly.

But not tonight. No, tonight Darrell could make love for a thousand hours, could write a thousand pages of his dissertation. No, tonight Darrell loves Rebecca Sugarman, could live with her in any apartment she chooses. Rebecca feels Darrell's arms around her, feels him slide down her body and work his way upward, his lips against her right instep, her knee, then between her legs. She wonders at his passion, recalls once when he gave a similarly energized performance after returning from a Victorian scholars' conference in Sheboygan. He is so avid, in fact, that she closes her eyes and feels for the moment that her encounter with Ike Morphy happened only in the distant past. Ike doesn't matter, his apartment doesn't matter, nothing matters except the bright speckles and swirls she sees with her eyes closed. And after Rebecca feels Darrell's lips upon her breast, then his legs between hers, she wonders while using a hand to guide his penis if she should mention that she is ovulating, that today's date has a green circle around it. But given Darrell's uncharacteristic behavior, she senses he must know.

The next morning, Rebecca sleeps an hour past her alarm, and when she wakes up, Darrell—who usually pulls all-nighters, then sleeps until noon—isn't lying beside her. She smells brewing coffee and melting butter. Rubbing her eyes, she walks naked to the kitchen, and watches her clean-shaven husband shaking a skillet over the burner; on the counter is a blue ceramic bowl with beaten egg in it, slices of challah stacked on a plate. A pot of coffee is percolating.

After Rebecca has finished showering, she emerges from the bathroom, towel around her waist. Darrell has set the table with the wedding china and cloth napkins he once suggested they sell on eBay. Rebecca sees a pitcher of fresh orange juice, a bottle of champagne in an ice bucket, coffee in china cups, three slices of French toast and dollops of fruit preserves on each plate, and no sign of Darrell's usual paper plates or mismatched coffee mugs.

Rebecca asks Darrell what the special occasion is. Buying their first place together, Darrell says, then asks if "Daddy-O" liked the apartment. A swirl of memories returns to Rebecca—the graffito on Ike Morphy's ceiling, Ike's anger, her cheeks streaked with tears as she watched *Los Olvidados*. But the last thing she wants to do is ruin this moment. The apartment is perfect, she says without missing a beat, and, she adds, its second bedroom is large enough to accommodate a nursery. Darrell pops the champagne bottle and pours mimosas.

THE BROKER

Josh Dybnick wakes to the low, insistent moan of his vibrating cell phone. He reaches around on the floor, grasping three clumps of cat hair and carpet lint before finally finding it. He flips open the phone, too tired even to bother checking the number on the display, too hungover to remember he'd been drinking the night before and he doesn't normally drink. Hullo, he says, and the man lying in bed next to him asks, Hey, guy, *canst thou keep it down?*

Josh wonders who this scrawny young man is, Josh's covers over his head, Josh's cats at his feet, a furry spindly leg dangling off the side of the bed, pale toes clutching at sheets that are halfway off the mattress. Oh Christ, now he remembers. Josh hadn't gotten drunk since sophomore year of college, and he hadn't even considered the idea that the punch at last night's agents-and-clients holiday party, held on the top floor of Brad Overman's Riverside Drive duplex, would be spiked. This was supposed to be a business party, not some grain alcohol and Kool-Aid bash designed to facilitate date rape, and he wasn't hanging out with econ majors anymore as he had during those first one and a half years of college at Oberlin when he had briefly dated Gretchen Gruetke shortly before discovering men and the Drama Department at roughly the same time.

In Ohio, Joshua often fantasized about Broadway opening-night parties like the ones he had seen in musicals and plays, such as *Light Up the Sky*—he imagined tuxedos, champagne, martinis, canapés, bon mots. Sir Ben Kingsley or one of Joshua's other heroes would be entertaining a bevy of eager starlets; there would be a grand piano upon a marble floor; a handsome pianist would wave him over and ask him to sing Stephen Sondheim. But when he arrived in the city, Joshua couldn't find anyone in theater who could afford lavish parties. The get-togethers he attended were usually held in some cramped Chelsea walk-up and featured cheddar cubes, Triscuits, Lancers wine, and Mountain Dew. No dining room table strewn with crudités; no dining room, actually. No piano either; everyone would sit on the floor in a circle, listen to musicals on a boom box, bitch about shows they hadn't gotten cast in, then grumble about their measly *Law & Order* residuals. And soon, Joshua wondered if his fantasy New York had ever existed at all.

Then, last night, punch cup in hand, Joshua entered Bradley Overman's living room. The black Hudson River and the distant, twinkling white lights of the George Washington Bridge were visible through the north-facing windows, and Joshua realized he had arrived inside a slightly distorted version of his dream. Tuxedoed waiters were circulating through the rooms with trays of martinis, champagne, and appetizers. There was, in fact, a grand piano here, one of its legs chewed almost all the way through. A pale woman with freckles and dyed orange hair, martini glass in hand, purple notebook under an arm, was leaning against said piano and laughing hysterically while a slim pianist in a tuxedo with a slightly frayed collar serenaded her with original show tunes he was inventing on the spot for the apparent purpose of mocking just about everyone in the room.

As Josh strolled through Brad Overman's apartment, sipping punch and occasionally pausing to survey his boss's antediluvian record collection and his framed pictures of dogs, he smiled and nodded at authors whose photos he recognized from book jackets, at an actress he had seen in the touring production of *Wicked* in Cleveland over Thanksgiving weekend, at TV actors, Broadway dancers. And yet, no one was talking about art or shows; everyone was discussing closing costs, mortgage rates, co-op boards, flip taxes, operating fund revenues. And as for Sir Ben Kingsley and his fawning starlets, well, there was Brad Overman himself surrounded by a posse of nubile, twentysomething real-estate agents and mortgage brokers. Yes, this was the Broadway party Josh had always imagined, but he had not gotten here through acting; this was the Manhattan of his dreams, but it had nothing to do with theater.

Save for Brad, who had been hosting these parties ever since he opened his agency, Josh knew no one here, other than the other salespeople from his office, with whom he rarely conversed. He hadn't invited any of his clients; though he appreciated Brad's desire to maintain his company's community-minded image, he thought having a client meet him here among all the other Overman sharpies might sully his image, might create an effect similar to seeing a great actor without makeup in shabby street clothes. Is that all he is? his clients would think upon seeing him. *Is that all there is to a fire?*

Somewhat tipsy and vaguely depressed for reasons he couldn't pinpoint, Josh returned to the living room and interrupted the pianist in the middle of an original song entitled "(I'll Bet He Gets) a Really Big Split." Joshua asked if he could sing "Finishing the Hat," the song about a man sacrificing love for art that he'd sung in school in *One-Man Sunday in the Park with George*. Pianist Miles Dimmelow played the piece from memory, then applauded, whispered something to his orange-haired friend, winked at Josh, and told him he didn't sing too badly for a real estate guy. Miles led Josh back to the punch bowl and told him that he'd moved to New York from Muncie, Indiana, after having graduated from Ball State, and was now trying to break into musicals or cabaret. He was appearing in *Boysworld* right now, but, *sigh*, hadn't found the right producer to back his original material.

At the punch bowl, Miles spoke to Josh in an affected, condescending manner, seeming to imply with disdainful admiration that, as a real estate broker, Josh had little appreciation or understanding of an artist's struggles.

Miles spoke of Josh's field with what Josh interpreted to be thinly disguised scorn, layering his speech with innuendos that often went over Josh's head. "Can you get in trouble if you commingle?" Miles asked him. "What if a buyer wants an owner to flip, but he's just not ready? . . . How does a buyer show his package to a co-op board? . . . How do you generally like to handle your openings?" As Josh smiled blankly at Miles, it was surprising and somewhat disturbing to him how effectively he could perform his own role, how easily he had adopted the characteristics Miles seemed to ascribe to him. He began to feel a greater affinity with the condo owners and co-op board members who surrounded him than with Miles, felt oddly flattered that the struggling performer could seemingly no longer recognize Josh as one of his own.

Now in bed in his Washington Heights apartment, as Josh hears Darrell Schiff's voice on the phone telling him that he and Rebecca have decided "not to fart around anymore" and are making a full-price bid on the apartment in the Roberto Clemente Building, he wonders how Miles wound up in his bed anyway, how Miles wound up taking a good two-thirds of it. If he hadn't spent the evening continually refilling his own punch cup, he might be wondering if Miles had slipped him a mickey.

Josh informs Darrell that he will contact the seller and present Darrell and Rebecca's offer. Miles stirs and groans. "Keep it down, guy," Miles says again, then steps out of bed in sagging black bikini briefs. Josh watches Miles strut around his apartment, the knock-kneed young man apparently thinking he is auditioning for the role of boy toy. Even though if Darrell's offer proves genuine it will mean twenty grand in Josh's pocket before taxes, more than he made his entire first year in New York, he is paying close attention to Miles opening his refrigerator, making a face at its paltry contents, dragging a chair across the floor, standing on the chair, opening cabinets. Something about Miles Dimmelow's behavior is distressingly familiar.

"Hey, guy," Miles asks Josh, "where's thy coffeepot?"

"My name's not guy," Josh tells Miles. He is about to call Mark Masler to relay Darrell and Rebecca's offer, but Miles has found the pot and is spooning coffee into it. And now, Josh feels an urge to apologize to every date with whom he ever overstayed his welcome, understands the looks of pity and suspicion he received whenever he met someone at a party and revealed he was an actor. He had felt so insulted when he called Dan Perna, a title company rep who once treated him to opening nights of *Gem of the Ocean* and *Jumpers*, to ask if Perna might have tickets to *The Robbers of Madderbloom* at the Helen Hayes Theater. "Stop being such an unctuous *schnorrer*, Dybnick," Perna said. "Find yourself a real job; buy your own tickets." Joshua spent days trying to assure himself he wasn't a *schnorrer*, but now he's certain that he was.

Josh tells Miles he has a lot of work to do this morning. Miles nods as he fills the coffeepot with tap water. Josh says maybe he'll call Miles later in the week and they can see a play—he hears the disingenuous tone in his voice and feels almost proud he has so quickly mastered this tone, the same tone he used to hear when he himself was being hurried out of one apartment or another.

Miles Dimmelow takes two English muffins out of the freezer and places them in the toaster oven. He turns on the toaster, but Josh shuts it off, then removes the muffins and returns them to the freezer. He's sorry, he says again, but Miles has to leave now; he has business. Business on a Sunday morning? Miles asks. *Art thou serious?* At this, Josh starts losing his patience. Yes, he says, actually he does have business on Sunday mornings; he's not an actor, he works seven days a week, works damn hard.

Miles regards Josh with what appears to be a certain fearful respect, like a tardy millworker in the presence of his short-tempered foreman. He walks past Josh, opens the door to a closet, pouts, and strikes a pose. "Where's thy towels?" he asks, then stops, gapes at Josh, and laughs in apparent horror. Can't he at least shower before he leaves, guy? Josh frowns and shakes his head, then watches the young man get dressed, making certain Miles doesn't take anything from the apartment. He used to do that after he spent the night at someone's place and suspected he wouldn't be asked back. He'd take a book or some trinket, and he once took a watch that was far more expensive than he'd ever have guessed—he returned it right after the police called.

Josh waits for Miles to leave in a huff, but once the man is dressed, he lingers. So, he asks with a wink, will Joshua call him? He knows some people Joshua might want to meet. Definitely, Josh tells him quickly, we'll do something—though he wonders why he would ever want to meet any of the people that Miles knows.

Once Miles has exited, Josh double-locks his door and loudly slides the security latch. He remembers that lonely sound—standing in a hallway, waiting for an elevator, hearing that click. But from this side of the door, the sound is incredibly reassuring, as if he is locking the door not only against Miles Dimmelow, but against his own failed recent past. Yes, he can feel the universe continuing to shift, his role in it too, moving from bit player toward star once again. He leaves a message for Mark Masler, then pulls up the blinds of his living room windows and sees Miles Dimmelow's scuffed black shoes walking away fast onto Fort Washington Avenue. Some day soon, Josh will have made enough money to move to one of the neighborhoods where he sells apartments; he will secure financing for a condo on a floor above ground level, and then he'll be able to look down on the world instead of up at it.

THE SELLER

P olice scanner on, radar detector engaged, Mark Masler drives down the Henry Hudson Parkway, speed-dialing Josh Dybnick's number. He is on his way back to his office after having delivered a motivational speech to the Young Leaders Committee of the B'nai Akiva Synagogue in Riverdale. Following his bar mitzvah—during which he botched his haftorah portion and his infuriated rabbi stuck out his tongue, then blew a raspberry at him—Mark vowed never to return to a synagogue, not even for the High Holidays. But since his father's death, Mark has attended B'nai Akiva just about every weekend; at the funeral, his first wife, by then Holly Kovacs-Pools, suggested that Mark try attending shul. More than fifteen years after their divorce, Holly is Mark's oldest, closest, and now basically only friend, never mind that Tony Pools, her current husband and father to her three children, has drastically limited her conversations with Mark: no longer than a half hour; no more than once per week.

Mark had met Holly, a graduate of Suffolk County Community College, at the Culinary Institute. Before they married, they talked of opening their own restaurant—Mark would handle main courses, Holly desserts.

But their one experience working together in the kitchen of Meloche was fraught with tension. Mark said he swore at her only because he was trying to cultivate an image as a "kitchen jock" and didn't want anyone to think he was playing favorites, but Holly quit anyway, fearing their marriage would not survive if they continued working together. Even so, the marriage lasted only half a year after Holly left Meloche and started a mail-order snickerdoodle cookie company.

Before Holly sold her first snickerdoodle, Mark had fallen hard for Tessa Minkoff, a Meloche hostess and an aspiring actress and hand model. While Holly was a homebody who fell asleep after half a glass of champagne and whose favorite evenings involved eating take-out Chinese on the couch and watching Mets games while wearing her red sweats, which she called her "TV-watchin' pants," Tessa was a Jägermeister-pounding club girl who wore short leather skirts with no underwear when she went out dancing at Shaker's. Mark's marriage to Tessa didn't last even as long as his marriage to Holly. Tessa left Mark for Hollywood, appeared in the soft-core, straight-to-video slasher flick *Dark Wet Tunnel*, then married a Sears appliance salesman, converted to fundamentalist Christianity, and hawked skin-care products on the Evangelical Shopping Network. After Tessa left, Mark called Holly every evening, leaving rambling messages in which he would plead for reconciliation. On the sixth consecutive night that Mark was leaving a message for Holly, a man identifying himself as "Counselor Anthony Joseph Pools" picked up the phone and told Mark that Holly didn't want to hear any more of his pathetic messages; if Mark ever tried to leave another, he'd pound in his skull.

That evening, after snorting six lines of coke, then performing more than a hundred lats and squat thrusts at the gym, Mark Masler drove to Holly's apartment, fully prepared to roll Anthony Pools. But when Holly answered the door wearing an engagement ring and a pink maternity blouse, Mark muttered an apology and some words of congratulation.

Lately, most of Mark's dates have been arranged by Holly, and nearly all have given the man a very sobering impression of how his first wife views him. The women are usually in middle management or sales; they work the floors of outer-borough furniture shops, the front desks of auto dealerships; all have been divorced at least once. Still, on the occasions when he calls them for follow-up dates, they never call back. His efforts to find respectable dates for himself have proved fruitless. Telling a young South Asian woman on a downtown C train that he was "in the mood to try some curry tonight" won him a mention as "Ass-Clown of the Week" on the website knowyourcreeps.com, a fact he became aware of when Tony Pools forwarded him the link. Mark's forays into Internet dating have yielded scant results; his singles.com post (*igotsomerealbigarms*) was accidentally listed in the "Men Seeking Men" ads; his match.com listing (*I'mtotallycleanandsobernow*) yielded only one hit, a forty-eight-year-old divorcée from Riverdale who needed an AA partner; and his Chosen People Singles listing (*Ready2Bchosen4sum69*) was taken down for violating lewd-content restrictions.

After Mark admitted to Holly that he was becoming desperate to find a new wife and start a family to share in his imminent business success, Holly suggested that he volunteer at the synagogue, where he could meet eligible divorced moms who attended sisterhood meetings or double-parked outside the playground with their SUV motors running while waiting for their children to finish Sunday school and "Fun-a-Gogue" recess sessions. Though Mark still hasn't shared more than a smile and a wave with any moms—save for Holly, who usually greets him with a cheek kiss after services while her husband glowers—he has become an active synagogue member. Today, following morning services, Mark lectured the recent college graduates on the Young Leaders Committee, advising them to keep their feet on the ground yet still reach for the stars. He then stayed for the post-talk bagel breakfast and chatted with division leaders Beth Siegel, Ruth Pools, Zachary Kaganoff, and Allie Scheinblum—who asked if Mark might write her a recommendation for business school at NYU. Mark agreed and offered to treat her to lunch after they met in his office.

Even though the Young Leaders Committee is composed primarily of single young women who dress for shul in skirts, heels, and pantyhose, Mark is proud of the fact that he has had only the most innocent thoughts about them, with the possible exception of Allie. At the brunch, he even made a point of speaking more to Zachary Kaganoff than to Allie, despite the fact that Zachary is a skinny, helium-voiced runt while Allie seems like a freak whose body he would at one time have loved to slather with Nutella. Mark provided honest and mature answers to everyone's questions; when Allie asked whether YLC should raise money by producing a series of "Jews Gone Wild" DVDs, Mark told Allie that maintaining one's dignity would always be more important than making a quick buck. On the front steps of the synagogue, before Allie sashayed off to a waiting white Ford Escape driven by her brother Caleb, a black-clad teenager who had just procured his driver's license and was blasting Damage Manual tunes on the car stereo, she tried to sneak a good-bye kiss from Mark. But he stepped aside, pressed his lips to Allie's forehead, and advised her to "go in peace." He enjoys his newfound role as upstanding citizen and member of the synagogue elite.

Indeed, Mark Masler has found his place standing firmly upon the middle ground. His father would have allowed Ike Morphy to stay in his apartment as long as he wanted, paying only as much as he wanted to pay. Mark's lawyer Alan Ziegler counseled putting Ike and his dog out on the street. But today, when Mark Masler gets Josh Dybnick on the line, he says he will accept Rebecca Sugarman and Darrell Schiff's offer provided Josh makes a good-faith effort to help Ike find a decent place to live. He will pay Ike's moving expenses, broker's fees, security deposit, and first month of rent, and give him ninety days to move after Rebecca and Darrell are approved for a mortgage. He can't honor his father's unrealistic, old-school, handshake commitment, but he will act like a mensch and make this small gesture to the man's memory.

Once he's back in his office, Mark heads directly to his steel file cabinets, opens the top drawer, and pulls out the Roberto Clemente Building folder. Immediately following the death of Mark's father, the "Contracts and Deeds" file was still full, but now the Clemente folder is the only one left. He writes a brief note to his secretary, Maria Aquino, asking her to tell Alan Ziegler to prepare the contract, then messenger it to Josh Dybnick.

Mark is ripping the "Contracts and Deeds" label off the file drawer when the phone rings. He picks up and hears the voice of Allie Scheinblum. Breathless, she tells Mark that she's calling on behalf of the entire

Young Leaders Committee. Though they've hosted great speakers in the past (among them, Dr. Ruth Westheimer and former Buffalo Bills coach Marv Levy), he has been their favorite. No one has ever been more generous with his time; no one else has stayed for bagels; no one else has condescended to talk to Zachary Kaganoff. Allie tells Mark she wants to thank him for agreeing to meet with her to discuss the possibility of writing her business school recommendation. But she adds that Mark doesn't have to buy her lunch; instead, she wants to invite him to Riverdale for a home-cooked meal, at least so she can show her mom and brother how civilized people behave.

Initially Mark thinks he should refuse Allie's dinner offer—she seems far too young for him to pursue romantically, yet far too attractive for him to consider befriending for any other reason. But at the phrase "home-cooked meal," he stops. He imagines Allie carrying a bowl full of steaming mashed potatoes; Allie's mother at the stove, stirring gravy; Allie's brother setting the table. He imagines clearing that table, then scooping Rocky Road ice cream out of a cardboard carton, dousing it with Hershey's syrup and raspberry jam, then all four of them sitting down in the living room to watch *The Wonderful World of Disney*. Sure, why not, he tells Allie, a home-cooked meal sounds delicious.

At the JCC gym, Mark Masler bench-presses as he listens to the U2 song "Yahweh" on his iPod. The music isn't quite the kind of ass-kicking anthem he once enjoyed, but he's a man in his forties now and can appreciate the song's intellectual appeal. "Take this shirt and make it clean," Bono sings, reminding Mark that he really should pick up his dry cleaning soon. Mark sits at the juice bar with a towel around his shoulders, cannonballs a protein shake, then heads for the locker room, where he strips naked and retires to the sauna. He closes his eyes and sits until the sweat drips down from his forehead like rain. Yes, Jerry Masler's last apartment will soon be gone, Mark thinks; the city old Jerry knew is disappearing and a new one is rising to replace it—Rolls Restaurant & Wash, here we come.

{ II }

AN
OFFER IS
ACCEPTED

I like the sight and the sound and even the stink of it.

COLE PORTER,
"I Happen to Like New York"

THE TENANT, THE BROKER, THE BUYER, & HER HUSBAND

O n the January day when he will begin to realize that he is inconveniently falling in love with Rebecca Sugarman, Ike Morphy is touring Upper Manhattan apartments with Josh Dybnick, who has borrowed Mark Masler's Hummer to show him around. Ike has packed up just about all of his belongings, save for his Müller B-flat clarinet and a few changes of clothes. He has sold his truck for $3,000 to a foreman from Phase One Demolition, and has begun performing breathing exercises and scales as he prepares to find out if he still has the ability, focus, and drive to play and compose music.

Ike has seen the futility of opposing Mark Masler's plan to sell apartment 2B. He can either fight and lose, or face the situation and move on. He doesn't have any friends left in his building anyway. Gone are the days when the Roberto Clemente Building was full of artists, musicians, schoolteachers, and activists. Gone are the nights when he'd walk home from Birdland or Augie's and smell paint and sawdust, once in a while weed; when he'd hear Ricardo and Marlena's stereo blaring out Hendrix or Sun Ra. Now, Ricardo, Marlena, and Buster are living in Jersey, the Clemente's silent hallways gleam, the condo board agenda posted on the first-floor corkboard offers news of competing bids for a video security system, and the basement garbage compactor room provides evidence of his new neighbors' lifestyles: Ikea and FreshDirect boxes, recycling bags filled with empty Côtes du Rhône bottles. So Ike has accepted Mark Masler's offer; he will move out of the Clemente within three months after Darrell and Rebecca are approved for a mortgage.

As he sits in the passenger seat of the Hummer with the windows open and the stereo blasting *A Little Night Music*, Ike asks if Josh might be able to help find him another apartment in his neighborhood; he figures he could cover the first few months' rent with his savings, spend his days getting his chops back. But Josh says that's unlikely, seeing as apartment vacancies in the city are now well below 1 percent. And anyway, just about all Manhattan Valley landlords now want to see two consecutive pay stubs and evidence of three times their annual rent in a savings account. Therefore, Josh says he will take Ike a good deal north of 106th Street, which he still insists on calling "Ellington Boulevard." They'll have to view buildings with less-particular landlords.

But the problem, Ike soon realizes, is not the buildings or even the streets themselves, which seem at first glance to be as segregated as the ones he'd left behind in Chicago twenty years ago; no, it is Herbie Mann, who sits with his head poking out a back window of the Hummer as Josh and Ike make their rounds. Were it not for the dog, Ike could live anywhere, he tells Josh. Man, you could even throw him in jail, he wouldn't really give a damn, good place to think about his music, no distractions. But he made a commitment to Herbie and knows what would happen if he ever left the dog. Forty thousand animals are put down each year in New York City shelters alone; if the right person were to walk into the shelter, the dog might survive, but the odds are even slimmer than they were on the day when Ike chose Herbie among the fifty-odd dogs in the room full of cages.

The men begin their real estate search with a series of tenements near 147th Street and Adam Clayton Powell. "These might be a little sketchier than you're used to," Josh says, but is quick to point out that "West Harlem" is "one of the city's hottest new neighborhoods"—dark green banners emblazoned with sketches of brownstones fly from every other lamppost: YOU ARE ENTERING A HISTORIC PRESERVATION DISTRICT. Josh and Ike walk past townhouses with blacked-out windows, underneath the pale green awning of the Henderson Funeral Parlor. A gutted brownstone with arched windows and turrets has a banner over its portico: MORE THAN YOU IMAGINED FOR LESS THAN YOU EXPECTED. Every other home is a beauty, but Josh takes Ike only to the buildings that stand in between. The neighborhood reminds Ike of Manhattan Valley when he first came to New York, but there's no decent park within easy walking distance, and he says he can't stomach the idea of Herbie living so far away from green space.

Ike rejects a studio on Edgecombe with a layer of algae in the bathtub, no toilet seat, and roach control coasters in every kitchen cabinet ("First thing I'd do, I'd take down these walls," Josh suggests). Although Ike supposes he could tolerate the vague scent of urine in the hallways, he says Herbie would go berserk when he got a whiff of it. Plus a studio is really out of the question; the animal acts depressed when he's confined. Small spaces, Ike theorizes, probably remind Herbie of the shelter.

Ike and Josh tour the basement portion of an illegal two-bedroom conversion on Frederick Douglass Boulevard. "Basements are underrated; you never get noise complaints from downstairs neighbors," says Josh, but Ike keeps saying how sad Herbie would feel without a view—Herbie likes to look out windows, greet people, let Ike know when someone's coming. Josh and Ike climb to the top floor of a six-story walk-up just south of Macombs Dam Bridge. "Imagine how strong your leg muscles will get after living here a year," Josh says, but Ike only ruminates aloud about the time Herbie injured his paw—how difficult it had been to get the animal up and down just one flight of stairs.

Ike could return to Chicago, he thinks as he and Josh visit yet another apartment, this one on Lenox above a restaurant advertising a half-price curried goat special that incited Herbie's growls from half a block away. But man, if he wants to give music another shot, he can't see living in any city other than this one. In Chicago, even some of the best musicians he knows still teach part-time at junior colleges, scrounge up gigs in pit bands for

touring musicals, sell homemade CDs in the Randolph Street subway station. And, if he goes back to Chicago, how could he ever reconcile himself to the memories he came here to escape? Even now, living eight
hundred miles away with both his parents gone, he remembers every day
the words his mother spoke moments before he decided he would have to
leave Chicago as soon as he made enough money: "People can be so disappointing." He still can recall how he felt whenever another one of his letters was returned to him without the check he enclosed, still remembers
the burning sensation in his eyes when he heard his brother's secretary say
she would give Ruel his message, when he heard his sister Naima or one
of her boyfriends on the phone: "Mom says she won't talk to you"; "Mrs.
Morphy says she won't come to the phone." There are so many streets he
still can't drive down in that city, knowing who used to live there but is
gone now.

And besides, he still loves this city, he can't help it, still feels he belongs
here even if now it seems as if he might not be able to afford to live where
he and Herbie would be happiest. He still loves the sense of possibility that
permeates every building and block. He loves the view of the Hudson from
Riverside Park, loves watching the ducks paddle in the Central Park pond,
loves the almost-too-pungent scent of gingkos on Manhattan Avenue in the
summer. He loves watching his dog's tail wag when he pulls Ike toward
Strangers' Gate. He loves the sounds of baseball games in Morningside,
mah-jongg tiles on 107th Street, playing cards outside the Frederick Douglass Apartments, the subway underfoot, the flutter and clang of the flags
atop the Blockhouse—every bit of it is music.

He loves the liberating feeling that this city doesn't seem to give a damn
about him and never did, that he could succeed or fail, turn tail and flee
or persevere, pick up his music right where he left off or leave his clarinet
in the closet forever—every one of those possibilities would be a classic
New York story, each as likely as the next because the city is the only one
he knows that can accommodate any story he might choose to pursue.

After taking Ike to see more than a dozen apartments, Josh is driving
south on Amsterdam Avenue when he asks if Ike would mind sitting in the
car while he runs a quick errand. He advises Ike not to get disheartened;

real estate searches gather their own momentum, and he doesn't know anyone who finds what he's looking for on the first day. Josh parks the Hummer in a metered space across from Western Union. Then, cell phone and car keys in hand, the broker jogs toward Darrell and Rebecca's six-story redbrick walk-up, shutting down his phone when he sees that, once again, Miles Dimmelow is calling him.

Josh has been inside for nearly five minutes, when Ike—who is using his fingers to run chromatic scales up and down the dashboard while he contemplates how he'll be able to make some money quickly enough to pay for a spacious, cheerful, dog-friendly apartment with a view and access to a park—sees Rebecca Sugarman walking home, cheeks pale. "Chill, Herb," Ike orders when the dog starts whining and wagging, but Rebecca has already spotted the vehicle and the passengers inside and has started moving quickly past it.

Ike hasn't seen Rebecca since the night two weeks ago when she walked out of his apartment, and seeing her now fills him with regret and purpose. He gets out of the SUV to intercept her. "Hey, how're you doing there?" he says, forcing a smile. But Rebecca doesn't look up. These past few days, she has been feeling nauseous, and seeing Ike again isn't helping. She exhales sharply, shakes her head, and continues to walk toward her building. "About that night," Ike begins, but she just looks past him. Every night, the words Ike spoke to Rebecca have haunted her, so much so that she even repeated them to Darrell, who proceeded to rant about the misplaced rage of the American underclass, and she wished she hadn't mentioned the incident at all.

Aww, come on, man, Ike says, trying to keep pace, she knows that he doesn't apologize to many people, and the truth is he doesn't really know how—maybe she can help him do it the right way; she's the expert apologizer. What's that supposed to mean? asks Rebecca. She stops in front of her building. Is he trying to apologize, or insult her again? Right, Ike says, now she can see he was telling the truth; he's not good at this. Look, he says, he just wants to say he was wrong to have taken his frustration out on her. She just happened to be sitting in his apartment at the very moment when he had begun to see some of his dreams evaporating. He has lived in

2B for twenty-some years, thought he might live there forever, and when he saw someone who would now be able to afford to live there instead of him, he started feeling jealous and acted like a jackass. He tries to hide it, but these past weeks have been tough. He doesn't know what to say other than that he hopes Rebecca might understand. There, he says, that's about as real an apology as he can give.

Ike begins to turn from Rebecca, but now she touches his shoulder and their eyes meet. Wait, he says, *she's* not about to apologize, is she? Rebecca cracks a smile, and Ike tells her not to worry about him; he's out looking for a new place now and he'll leave 2B in good condition for her and her husband, and he's the one who should be sorry—apology accepted? Rebecca nods, then asks where Ike will be moving. Ike says he still doesn't know. Prices are pretty messed up down here—he'll probably have to head farther north. Nice, Rebecca says, adding that when she needs time to think, sometimes she'll jog all the way to Inwood Hill at the edge of the city; it's the quietest, prettiest place she knows. Ike says maybe some quiet would be good for him and Herbie; anyway, no hard feelings. And he adds, as he shakes Rebecca's hand, if what she told him about her father's fondness for his music is true, maybe the three of them can join him for a beverage sometime—Rebecca, her husband, and her pop. Ike feels his speech coming more easily now, as if some gray presence that clouded his vision for years is slowly lifting.

But after Rebecca takes Ike's phone number so that she can call him to set a date, the front door to her building swings open, and out walks Josh with a manila envelope containing the signed contract for 2B; Darrell Finneran Schiff is walking behind him. The two men are discussing the meeting Darrell will soon be having at Gotham Mortgage to lock in a rate, but talk stops when Darrell sees Ike with Rebecca. His face flushes. Before Rebecca can explain, Darrell asks Ike why he's here, then asks Rebecca if "this guy" has been hassling her again. Of course not, Rebecca says, but Darrell talks over her, telling Ike that if he has anything to say to Rebecca, he can say it to him directly; he doesn't care what Ike says about him, but about his wife, that's another story.

Rebecca begins to pull Darrell back toward their apartment by the tail of his anorak, but he wriggles free, then gestures to Herbie, whose paws are scratching the rear street-side window of Mark Masler's Hummer. Darrell informs Ike that he has no sympathy for animals who can't be controlled; when Darrell's "people" are visiting apartment 2B to "make their appraisals" and their "damage assessments," Ike had better "secure [his] animal," or else he'll call animal control. He drapes a protective and proprietary arm over Rebecca's shoulders, leading her away from Ike, asking if she's okay, honey, while Rebecca, with a roll of her eyes and just the hint of a smile, mouths the word "sorry" to Ike, who can't help but smile back at her. Ike wonders if Rebecca might call him in the next day or two to apologize again, then ask him to have drinks with her and her dad. But, Ike wonders as he gets back into the car with Josh, what's the point of daydreaming about married women anyway?

Nevertheless, the very next morning, Ike is walking through the cold toward Inwood Hill Park with his dog at his side and his clarinet in his backpack, wondering if he might happen upon Rebecca jogging there.

THE BUYER'S HUSBAND &
THE MORTGAGE BROKER

On the sixteenth floor of a steel-and-glass high-rise on Sixth Avenue, Darrell Schiff, who is still proudly reliving the moment last week when he defended his wife's honor, is carrying a brown accordion folder and wearing a visitor badge with his name scrawled on it. Walking past a group of nattily dressed young men and women gathered around a television, he approaches the front desk and gives his name to the Gotham Mortgage Company receptionist; he has an 8:00 a.m. appointment with Megan Yu. He has spoken to her over the phone several times and, in her flirty cigarette voice, she has told him that getting a loan for a $650K condo will be easy. "Solid gold" was the phrase she used to describe Darrell's pre-qualifying application.

Darrell sits beside a potted plastic fern underneath a framed poster of the Statue of Liberty on the only unoccupied black leather armchair in the reception area. He glances up at the TV, which is broadcasting a commercial—"Isn't it time you moved up to Overman?" a broker asks the camera, while Darrell laughs to himself, thinking about how all these brokers look exactly the same to him. Now, the television station returns to its featured program. Onscreen, five middle-aged white men in funereal suits are sitting around a conference table; the bug in the screen's lower-right-hand corner reads "The Financial Network." Numbers and percentages scroll across the bottom of the screen. All this looks like gibberish to Darrell, but for once, as he surveys the mortgage brokers around him, probably all his age or younger, he feels more sorry than proud that he doesn't understand; for once, he feels uneasy in jeans, Kurt Cobain shirt, and mud-stained hiking boots. Up by Columbia, he takes pride in his slovenly appearance; here in Midtown, he feels like a poverty-stricken *clochard*. He hopes these brokers will peg him for some rich *culo* dressing down instead of just another schlumpy professor's kid who can't afford to dress up.

On the wall above the TV, mortgage brokers' licenses from every state in the union are mounted, displayed behind glare-proof glass in dull black frames. Darrell turns away from the TV, unwinds the brown string to his accordion folder, opens the folder, and peruses the compartments, each labeled with far greater attention to detail than he has ever given to his dissertation chapters. The "Banking" compartment contains six months' worth of collated and chronologically ordered bank statements. "Employment" holds Rebecca's first pay stub from *The American Standard* and a letter from Columbia stating the value of Darrell's teaching assistantship. In the folder are three years' worth of tax returns, canceled checks from Columbia's housing department, a Xerox copy of the contract with Mark Masler, credit card statements, résumés, letters of reference, evidence of Phil Sugarman's $125,000 deposit into Darrell and Rebecca's joint account, even a copy of the teaching award Darrell won his first year at Columbia, the only year he received uniformly positive student evaluations, plus a red pepper icon beside a smiley-faced review on rateyourteaching assistants.net, meaning that the reviewer thought he was a "hottie." The documents help to alleviate some of Darrell's mounting self-doubt, allow him for the moment to consider himself a man of independent means.

Megan Yu, wearing a slim gray pinstripe suit with gleaming black buttons, her long straight black hair streaked with hints of red, approaches Darrell, shakes his hand, then asks one of the men seated in front of the TV—a fleshy, moon-faced twentysomething—whether he's learned anything new. The man shakes his head; the announcement is still a half hour away, he says, and asks if Megan will be joining them. Nope, says Megan. Darrell asks why everyone here is watching TV, and as Megan quickly leads him across gray carpeting, through a maze of gray cubicles toward her gray office, she explains that the Labor Department will be issuing its monthly jobs report this morning. Everyone at Gotham is bracing for bad news, she says. The previous month, they dodged a bullet, but the experience of waiting for the news was unnerving anyway. When a spokesman for Bear Stearns predicted that 250,000 jobs would be added to the workforce, Megan had run to the bathroom to throw up.

Why? Darrell asks. A quarter of a million jobs sounds like a lot. They are now sitting in Megan's office; pictures of her family adorn her desk—her parents in cheap, outdated business attire, her brother in a Little League uniform, a white poodle sporting a red bow. On the wall behind her is a framed poster of a parasailing collie gliding into the sunset, above it, the word ACHIEVE. On the wall behind Darrell is a poster of a Labrador retriever at the wheel of an SUV, above it, the word IMAGINE. Yeah, Megan says, but in this business, good news is bad; with so many new jobs, the Federal Reserve would most probably raise interest rates, which could lead to a sharp decrease in new homebuyers. Luckily, up until now, all the projections have been overly optimistic; last month, when the government announced that only 22,000 new jobs had been created, the president of the Overman Group, who is the nicest man she has met in this industry, sent her a stack of Rick Wakeman CDs, a case of champagne, and a note saying that everyone else in his office was celebrating the news, so he figured he might as well celebrate too. If the news is bad today, Brad Overman has promised to take her out to Dryden's for steaks.

So, Darrell asks, they're rooting for bad news?

With a dark cackle, Megan says that Darrell has described her life in a nutshell. "Sick, isn't it?" she says, remarking that altruism is hard to maintain when one's own livelihood is at stake. She and her family had moved to Fort Lee, New Jersey, with nothing, not even the poodle they'd had to leave behind in Seoul. And now that her parents' deli is going bankrupt and her brother is applying to college, she's taking night classes at New

York Law School because she will eventually need an even higher-paying job. "I have no life, not even a boyfriend; welcome to the American Dream," she says. Darrell offers some words of comfort but Megan waves him off, presses a key on her computer, and asks to see his paperwork.

Megan speeds through Darrell's files, seemingly impressed by the care he has taken in organizing them. "Good, good," she keeps saying. She plugs Darrell's and Rebecca's social security numbers into checkanyones credit.com and seems pleased with what she sees onscreen. "Good, good," she says. "Flying colors."

Music plays softly through Megan's white iPod speakers, one of the CDs that Brad Overman sent to her—"In the Court of the Crimson King." She bops along and mouths the words, takes further notes, and punches numbers on her calculator. Darrell finds something surprisingly erotic about having his whole life spread out before Megan, about her being able to peer into every nook and cranny of his and Rebecca's bank accounts. Like telling Jane Earhart his entire life story. Like standing buck-naked in front of Larissa the Piccadilly hooker, who eyed his erection, smiled, and said, "Is that all for me then, *luhv*?" As Megan types, Darrell fantasizes about what she meant by saying she has neither a life nor a boyfriend; he wonders if she finds time for quickies, given her work and law school schedule, or whether she is still clinging to her virginity while living at home with the overprotective parents in her pictures. Darrell is still fantasizing when Megan removes the rest of the papers from his accordion folder, arranges them in neat stacks, glances at her lead sheets, then asks, "Is that all you have, Darrell?"

Darrell swallows hard. His first instinct is to treat Megan's question as sarcasm. Yeah, he says, he has certainly brought a lot of material. He apologizes for overwhelming the poor woman with so much intimidating raw data. Megan regards him with a bemused smile. "But how can you live in New York?" she asks.

And now, Darrell truly does feel naked, as if Larissa has inspected his groin in Piccadilly, tittered, and asked, "Is that all you've got down there, *luhv*?" Once again, he remembers the mud stains on his boots, the frayed cuffs of his jeans, the way the collars of his flannel shirts never sit flat. He asks Megan what she means. Well, she says, there's not enough income for a loan of this size. How is that possible? Darrell asks. He reminds Megan that he and his wife have a checking account to which his father-in-law has added "more than one hundred large," and that they both have jobs that pay over $50,000 a year. Megan shakes her head before Darrell has finished speaking, then says Rebecca's salary history shows her making no more than $35K in the past, and the fact that her new job pays better can't be taken into consideration. Plus, according to Darrell's documents, he's barely making $22K. Right, Darrell says, but he's also getting thousands of dollars' worth of free tuition and subsidized housing.

Megan tells Darrell his free tuition doesn't count, then asks if he has any other "income streams." No, he says, looking away from her and down to the carpet. Any pension or retirement account? Fuck no, says Darrell. Well, maybe she can find some sort of loan, she says, but since Darrell and Rebecca's situation is no longer "solid gold," the process might take just a few days longer than she expected, and she won't be able to offer many of the "yummiest loan products" they have discussed over the phone. She'll probably have to negotiate a no-income-verification loan, which will mean a higher rate; perhaps Darrell and Rebecca will have to pay a couple of points too and come up with 25 percent of the buying price upfront. And they'll need a guarantor too, Darrell's father-in-law perhaps.

Darrell's eyelids sag. He has never been a materialist. Far from it. He has purchased three pairs of pants—all jeans—in the past two years. If he needs shirts, he shops at the closeout racks at Century 21, buys plain white underwear in three-packs at Old Navy; he wears dead guys' suits from the Salvation Army if he needs to deliver a retarded paper at some lame conference. And now, even though he works and his wife works, and they have a butt-load of money from her old man, Megan Yu, who works a job he figures he could master in a week, is sitting behind her desk below motivational dog posters, probably making a bazillion times more than his annual stipend, telling him he needs some parental permission slip.

He feels like a child. He feels like he still lives at home. He feels like Sam Elliott in the film *Lifeguard*—thirty-one years old and still spending summers at the beach. He feels like Adam Rich on the show *Eight Is*

Enough, trying in vain to sneak a kiss from one of Grant Goodeve's foxy girlfriends. He feels like Dilton Doiley in the *Archie* comics, attempting to move in on some of Reggie's action. He feels like Floyd Ellis, the man with no place left to go. Darrell Shit, that's who he feels like—*Darrell Shit*. Every school he ever attended, the same joke on the first day of gym class. The teacher would call roll—*Quigley? Here. Reyes? Here. Schiff?* And then some classmate, some hick, some brother, some blow-dried jock would start guffawing. *Darrell Shit? Man, what a name, heh heh heh.* He feels like hitting something, feels like having sex with any woman other than his wife. He looks down at the visitor pass stuck to his shirt—"Hello, My Name Is Darrell Shit." He can now see why his parents never lived in big cities, why his mother never pressed her husband to move when NYU and the University of Chicago offered her plum positions. In the college towns where Darrell grew up, professors were right up there in prestige with doctors and lawyers; living in New York as an academic, on the other hand, is just one serious fricking chode-suck. *Contemplate this on the tree of woe.*

After Megan's secretary, Lynette—who probably pulled Cs in econ at Chodesuck Junior College yet undoubtedly earns more than Darrell and Rebecca combined—has made Xerox copies of all of Darrell and Rebecca's now painfully embarrassing financial documents and handed him a guarantor's form for Rebecca's father, Megan walks Darrell back through the reception area and assures him that there really isn't any question of whether he and Rebecca will get their loan, just what kind of loan they will get and at how high a rate. But though Darrell grunts and nods, he is thinking of his frayed cuffs, of the dead men's suits in his closet. Not until he and Megan pass through the Gotham Mortgage reception area do any sounds pierce his reverie.

Suddenly, Darrell feels as if he has been beamed into some nightmarish, Big Ten football party right at the moment when the placekicker has booted the winning extra point through the uprights. The brokers who have been watching TV all spring to their feet. They hug, they high-five, they pump their fists in the air and affect African-American accents. "Yeahhhh, dawg," they holler. "That's what I'm talkin' 'bout, boy, *that's what I'm talkin' 'bout.*"

"How many?" Megan asks the moon-faced young man. "How many jobs?"

"Forty-five thousand," the man says with a snort, and he and Megan high-five. Megan's eyes sparkle, her face lights up with a somewhat embarrassed grin, and she spontaneously embraces Darrell, telling him thank God, the experts' estimates were wrong once again; they have a reprieve for at least another month. Once Darrell has sent Megan his guarantor's form and she has faxed Darrell his good-faith estimate, they can work on locking in a rate. Darrell can smell Megan's perfume as he holds her close, and he notices for the first time that she is not wearing a brassiere.

And as Darrell feels Megan's breasts against his chest, the smoothness of her neck against his left nostril, he feels that this proximity is nearly enough to compensate for the humiliation he felt just moments ago. Nearly. If he can feel her lips against his, her breath against his neck, maybe even her voice in his ear telling him to come back at lunchtime for a "nooner," he'll leave Gotham Mortgage with his self-confidence intact, then go straight home without stopping at the library. With the back of a hand, he touches Megan's hair; Rebecca has never dared to dye hers. He smells her perfume; Rebecca is too pure to wear any. Never mind that Rebecca has had one more sexual partner than he's had—that discrepancy can be corrected before the end of the morning. He sniffs Megan's ear and she giggles.

"What are you?" she asks. "A dog?"

"No way," Darrell says. "I hate dogs."

"Then you wouldn't like me," Megan says. Her secretary approaches to say that Bradley Overman is on the line, at which point Megan gives Darrell a limp handshake good-bye, then disappears back into her gray world.

As Darrell heads for the elevator, he tries his best not to think about Jane Earhart. But after he reaches the first-floor lobby, he can't help craving some form of affirmation or reassurance. And by the time he emerges onto Sixth Avenue, he can barely wait to get home, shower, change, leave a quick message for Rebecca telling her about the fricking guarantor's form, then sprint through Columbia's gates to try to find Jane.

THE BUYER & HER BOSS

Rebecca Sugarman lets another one of her husband's calls go to voice mail as she sits at a back table in Café Desjardins with Chloe Linton during what she fears may be her last-ever meal as an employee of *The American Standard*. She is sipping hot green tea while Chloe is already halfway through her second vodka and tonic. The women's conversation has been reasonably pleasant. Chloe, a self-described "sports nut," has discussed her all-time favorite National Hockey League goaltenders and the apartment that neither she nor her "patently evil ex-husband" is willing to sell yet; Rebecca has spoken of the incredible stress her husband must be feeling as he tries to finish his dissertation, not knowing exactly when they will be able to move into their new apartment. But before meal's end, Rebecca is fairly certain that Chloe will fire her.

In the magazine world, Chloe Linton has become known as a "turnaround artist," someone who, through sheer will and force of personality, can turn around a publication's fortunes. Wherever she's worked—from *Sluggo*, the bald men's fashion magazine, to *Teenage Bride*—subscriptions and advertising revenues have skyrocketed inexplicably during her tenure, but plummeted after her departure. Explaining this phenomenon in interviews with industry reporters, Chloe often likens herself to a well-traveled, inspirational sports coach, such as Mike Keenan or Bill Parcells—someone who can turn a 2–14 record into 14–2 in one season, but won't remain long enough to wear out her welcome.

Ever since the initial flurry of resignations and firings that marked Chloe's arrival, Nick Renfield, the *Standard*'s gifted-but-lazy, wise-ass journalist whose media column allows him to expense his cable, TiVo, and Netflix subscriptions and to charge his amazon.com cat food purchases to the company, has been publishing the Evening Noose. The anonymous blog offers snarky criticism and gossip about the entertainment and publishing industries, and posts weekly odds on which *Standard* staffer will next get the axe. In Nick's most recent posting, he listed the employee identified as "Yalie Redhead" at 3 to 1.

Staff morale at the *Standard* has been tracing a steady downward trajectory. Several months before Rebecca started work, Chloe hired Molinaro Communications, a consulting firm, to "maximize worker output." "Rules for Cubicle Etiquette" are now posted above every worker's desk; personal calls can be made only during one's lunch hour; every employee's e-mail is subject to surveillance. Occasionally, when a staffer instant-messages a friend or spouse, a note from Chloe's personal secretary, Bella Ratny, will appear on his or her screen: "Gotcha!" Private writing suites now belong to the marketing department; their previous occupants have been relegated to cubicles and pods. Staff librarian Myrna Lanzmann has received a severance package; her library has been converted into a new subscription manager's office and its contents have been sold for less than a thousand bucks to the Strand Bookstore. The antique liquor trolley has been moved permanently into Chloe's office.

When Rebecca interviewed with Liz Fogelson for the assistant literary editor position, editors sauntered in anywhere from nine-thirty in the morning to eleven, and production staffers who had stayed past midnight on deadline days usually arrived at noon. Now, the workday starts promptly at 9:00 a.m. no matter how late anyone worked the night before, and lateness is noted in every employee's file. These files are locked up with subscription and ad data in a cabinet to which only Chloe Linton and Bella Ratny—whose odds of departure are listed on the Evening Noose at 75 to 1—have keys. A dress code has been instituted: no shorts unless air conditioners are broken; no tank tops under any circumstances; feet must be covered at all times, which means that art director László Ruffcorn (7 to 1) can no longer attend meetings in flip-flops, and film and theater critic Norman Burloff (even money) can't go to the refrigerator in bare feet to retrieve his ham sandwiches and Maalox. Distressingly for many of the *Standard*'s old-timers, Chloe's policies seem to be having a positive effect; last quarter, for the first time since 2001, ad sales and subscription numbers increased.

This morning's staff meeting was one of the most tension-filled of Chloe's tenure. In happier days, when the age of the average reader wasn't approaching the life expectancy of the average American citizen, when subscription numbers were so high that ad sales figures were all but irrelevant, meetings were all-day affairs and habitually devolved into shouting matches. On one occasion, when Norman Burloff wrote an essay mocking theater director Harvey Mankoff's use of a production of *The Nutcracker* to protest the Vietnam War, Liz Fogelson slapped him on the mouth. Now, editorial meetings begin precisely at 9:45, when Chloe enters the conference room and sets her timer, and end at 10:45, when the timer buzzes off.

The main subject of today's meeting was the already slim editorial budget, which Chloe said she would slash by another $150,000 in order to increase the subscription-promotion and marketing budgets. On a Dry Erase board, she printed one of her mottos, EIEIO (Everyone Is Expendable in Organizations), and Rebecca suspected that this motto referred specifically to her. Clearly, she was the wrong person for her job; every time she proposed an article idea, Chloe would say, "Let's move on," and whenever Chloe made an editorial suggestion, such as cutting down one of Norman Burloff's reviews by 1,500 words or reviewing only books whose publishers purchased ad space, Rebecca couldn't help but sigh or shake her head.

After the meeting, as she walked with Chloe up Broadway—past smokers congregating outside office buildings; past Forty-second Street, where the Reuters news crawl was announcing JOBS REPORT LACKLUSTER; past a billboard on the side of a Times Square development that read WELCOME TO THE CENTER OF THE UNIVERSE, 19,000 SQUARE FEET AVAILABLE; past Alexander's Wind Instrument Center, where a dozen ebony clarinets were displayed in a second-floor window—Rebecca kept thinking about how much she loved the fact that she was working for the *Standard*. Simply imagining her name on the masthead of a publication that had been a staple of Manhattan's intellectual and cultural life since Phil Sugarman's childhood made Rebecca want to remain at any salary even if the magazine's editorial content was obviously going downhill. But she wondered how she could ever justify her job to Chloe; the only reason she might *not* be expendable, she thought, was that she would work cheap. Her first editing assignment had turned into a fiasco; three of the writers to whom Rebecca tried to explain her edits hung up on her. Half still haven't returned her calls. She spends her days on edge, feels pukey whenever Chloe walks by her desk or calls her name; in bed, she wakes up from vivid nightmares in which she is back at school and there is a test for which she hasn't prepared, a research paper she has neglected to write, a dissertation chapter she is handing in too late. And now, as she sits across from Chloe in Café Desjardins, she can feel her stomach slowly constricting, can feel every drop of tea dribbling down her gullet.

Rebecca tries to calm herself by focusing on all the preparations she has made for this lunch. For the "Books" pages, she has scoured every publisher's catalog and placed all the selected titles on a spreadsheet beside the names of potential reviewers. For the "Endword" page, she has created an alphabetized list of twenty-five potential essay topics. And she has already decided to refuse her raise. So it is beyond surreal to hear Chloe, after she has placed her lunch order and sampled her third vodka and tonic, say with a touch of the Atlanta twang that emerges after she has been drinking, "The only good decision anyone's made around here lately was hiring you."

Since she became publisher of this magazine, says Chloe, the one criticism she has been hearing from focus group readers is that the editorial voice is too negative. She says that one of her first jobs out of j-school was on the *Atlanta Journal-Constitution*'s sports desk, and a lesson she learned there was that nearly twice as many newspapers sold on days following Braves or Hawks victories. What she already admires about Rebecca, she says, the reason she wants to keep her happy, is that she is the only staffer with a positive attitude; she greets people, says hello, remembers everybody's name, works hard, dresses well, listens at editorial meetings, and doesn't snigger at her sports references.

More changes will have to come to the *Standard* if the magazine is to have any hope of continuing to attract new advertisers and subscribers. The *Standard* will need a greater Web presence, not the text-heavy snooze-a-thon that has barely changed since 1999. Every article will need both a "service component" and a "call to action." The modern reader can no longer be treated as a passive being who will read solely for the sake of reading; a reader has to feel inspired to do something afterward—buy a handbag, take a yoga class, make a dinner reservation, contribute to a cause, bet on a game. Chloe doesn't want to read any more "think pieces"—thinking isn't action. She wants to gut the Politics section; with the *Standard*'s six-to-eight-week lead time, what's left to say that hasn't already been said on the twenty-four-hour news networks, which are already feebly trying to keep pace with the bloggers? She wants to see fewer negative arts reviews. Last issue, Norm Burloff wasted yet another 2,500 words on the three-hour epic *Attila: A Love Story*, saying little more than that the movie sucked and had hokey CGI effects. Why not write 2,500 words about a movie somebody would actually want to see? Why make it that much more difficult to sell advertising to 20th Century Fox or Disney?

These days, editorial has to be dictated by what subscribers and advertisers will pay for, Chloe says. If 75 percent of surveyed subscribers like the "Dibbles 'n' Dops" upfront news column, she'll keep running it. If only 25 percent do, *sayonara*. If the Comedy Network continues to buy the page opposite Nick Renfield's media column, the column will remain, at 700 words. But if no one wants to buy the page, then the odds of Nick's staying, she says with a smile, are about 900 to 1. What she's saying may sound cynical to Rebecca, Chloe acknowledges, but it's the reality they're facing in the current marketplace, even though she knows editors won't be happy. So, she asks, what would make Rebecca happy?

Rebecca, whose relief at knowing her position is secure somewhat mitigates her distaste for Chloe's philosophy, says that she's really still learning her job and is happy enough. But is she happy making $50K? Chloe asks, and before Rebecca can say yes, Chloe says she shouldn't be; what about $65K? But wouldn't that mean someone else would have to leave? Rebecca asks. Not to worry, Chloe tells her; she has been trying to make the office as inhospitable as possible so that more editors will quit, thus saving her from having to dole out more severance packages; but either way, staff will be cut. A great team, she says, is never composed of twenty-two all-stars anyway; a couple of all-stars form the core and one builds around them with role players. But that core—and Rebecca will represent a big chunk of it—has to be happy. Would a $15,000 raise make her happy? Of course, especially since she and Darrell are trying to have a child, says Rebecca, and then wonders if this is the sort of information one should impart to one's employer. But in response, Chloe only smiles wistfully. Once she'd wanted to be a mother herself, Chloe says, but her ex-husband, who has spent his whole life making people believe he is actually the person he pretends to be, fooled her too.

What happened? Rebecca asks.

Nothing good, says Chloe; at any rate, it is too late now, but she does hope Rebecca will bring her child into the office sometimes.

Once the two women return to the *Standard*, Rebecca can already sense a change in the office and her role in it. Out of the corner of her eye, she notices production staffers and her fellow editors glancing suspiciously as she passes their cubicles en route to Chloe's office. Bella Ratny usually greets Rebecca with a sweet, maternal grin, but now she winks. And when Rebecca sits down in the publisher's office, Nick Renfield peers in and mouths the words "What's goin' on, Red?"

Chloe sits on her desk and says that, before Rebecca returns to her cubicle, she wants to briefly discuss book review and essay assignments for upcoming issues. Rebecca unzips her shoulder bag, pulls out her spreadsheet of potential assignments, and hands it to Chloe, who studies it briefly, then takes out a red pen, crosses out some of the titles Rebecca has listed, and adds others. She crosses out Joseph Mbekwe's *A History of Genocide*, Pavel

Vilkov's *A Return to Treblinka*, Rena Javits's *The Supersonic Moel and Other Tales of Magical Judaism*, and Dr. Eleanor Bingley's *Why Dogs Are Better Than People*. She adds bad-boy Irish playwright Seamus O'Hollearn's *O Ye Wicked Saints of Dublin: My Life to the Age of Thirty* and rapper Edward Scissorhands's South Central LA debut novel, *Westward, Ho'!* She adds sportswriter Stan Ascherman's *The Hit: How Stan Bahnsen's Last Pitch to Walt Williams Changed the History of American Culture* and humorist Neal Kagan's *If Anne Frank Had a Blog, and 99 Other Reasons to Love the Information Age*. Chloe then scans Rebecca's document, apparently attempting to find something she seems unable to believe is not there. She walks to her bookshelf and pulls down a purple paperback—an advance copy of a forthcoming book.

"We have to do something on this," Chloe says. "It's going to be one of the big books this year."

Rebecca takes the book and glances at the title: *Wizard Girl, the Blue Kingdom, and Her World Made of Glass.*

THE BUYER'S HUSBAND
& HIS LOVER

{ *Yes, He's Still Hoping . . .* }

or

THE TRAGIC CASE OF THE
MAD GOOGLER

Darrell Schiff glances down at the loan guarantor's form that he has placed next to his home fax machine and attaches a yellow sticky note to it: *Here's the damn thing to fax to Daddy-O; these people suck donkey dick. I'm at the fricking library. Love and all that jive, Darrell.* He strips, showers, changes, then returns to his laptop and decides to spend some more time obsessively Googling people before he leaves for the library.

Using Google and a variety of other search engines and databases to gather critical information is perhaps Darrell's greatest skill and most time-consuming activity. With his fleet-fingered research prowess, he can, within moments, discover obscure tidbits of biographical information about Victorian scribes, identify key quotations from hip-hop songs and B movies, ferret out plagiarists in his introductory English lit course, and determine the home address, occupation, and marital status of former girlfriends. Today, with his humiliation at the hands of Megan Yu fresh in his mind, he spends hours trying to gauge just how far he has tumbled in the universe: he Googles classmates from Madison West High School and Penn to find out if anyone has a less impressive career (Lainie Margerum is a regional ad sales manager for *Rotational Molders Magazine*); he Googles members of his JCC T-ball team in Lincoln, Nebraska (Marty Bierman teaches Judaic studies at Holy Redeemer).

Darrell feels cheered when he learns that some people never moved on, that on Ogg Hall Dormitory's home page, Floyd "No Place to Go" Ellis is still listed as a janitor, that Darrell's eighth-grade rival Abner Kravec is still in-house accountant for Kravec Plumbing Supply in Dousman, Wisconsin. But whenever he finds someone who seems more successful than he is (just about anybody aside from Abner Kravec and Floyd Ellis), he feels a soul-crushing sorrow, attempts to guess the person's annual salary, then types his or her name into homepriceestimator.com to determine the approximate value of the person's real estate. He Googles himself to see if he can find more than the usual thirty-four hits, but finds only thirty-three—more than a hundred fewer than Rebecca. He does find the Wikipedia entry he wrote about himself, but can no longer find a listing for his poem "Come Forth from These Loins," which won a 1991 honorable mention in the Wisconsin State Youth Poetry competition. And when he returns to rateyourteachingassistants.net, the red pepper near his name signifying that he was a "hottie" has been replaced by a green frownie face; a new review authored by someone calling himself "C.S." has been posted: "Avoid this slacker like the plague."

Before venturing out in search of Jane Earhart, Darrell stares into space and morbidly contemplates for the third time in a week how much other people accomplished before they reached the age of thirty-one. F. Scott Fitzgerald wrote *The Great Gatsby*; Carson McCullers wrote *The Heart Is a Lonely Hunter*; D. H. Lawrence wrote *Sons and Lovers*; Shakespeare wrote *The Comedy of Errors* and *Taming of the Shrew*; Thomas Mann wrote *Buddenbrooks*; Charles Dickens wrote *Nicholas Nickleby*, *Oliver Twist*, and *The Pickwick Papers*; Bret Easton Ellis wrote *Less Than Zero*; Orson Welles made *Citizen Kane* and *The Magnificent Ambersons*; François Truffaut made *The 400 Blows*, *Shoot the Piano Player*, and *Jules and Jim*; Quentin Tarantino made *Reservoir Dogs*; John Singleton made *Boyz N the Hood*; Spike Jonze made *Being John Malkovich*; Walt Disney created

Mickey Mouse; Chuck Jones created all the Looney Tunes characters; John Keats was dead; Christopher Marlowe was dead; Buddy Holly was dead; Tupac was dead; Janis Joplin was dead; Jimi Hendrix was dead; Kurt Cobain was dead; Eazy-motherfuckin'-E was dead; the Beatles had already broken up; Andrew Cunanan had already killed three people.

Darrell looks up the webpages of students with whom he started grad school back in the Precambrian age; they now have visiting lecturer gigs at NYU, Hunter, and Barnard; they have delivered more papers at academic conferences, have published more articles in journals and edited volumes; just about all have red peppers and smiley faces next to their names. When he learns that *Nineteenth-Century Reports* recently published Barnard assistant prof Graham Buggett's facile, kindergarten-level, only slightly reworked master's thesis about the role of clothing as a "signifier of status" in *Pride and Prejudice* ("Well, no shit, Buggett," Darrell said when Graham presented an early draft in a seminar), Darrell shuts down his computer, leaves his apartment, goes straight to the flower section of Morton Williams, buys a yellow rose, then walks to the library, where he spots Jane Earhart, kisses her on the lips, and hands the flower to her.

"Marriage trouble?" Jane asks. She takes the flower and places it in her bottle of iced tea, then tells Darrell that she was just on her way out. Darrell says he's had a rough day and would like some air too so that he can "decompress"; he asks if Jane wants to walk to the Grant Memorial, remembering that he and Rebecca once had sex on a bench there. Jane shakes her head—no, she's not planning to take any "couple's walk"; she's off to research a story, one she had set in Coney Island but that had stalled when she realized she had never been there.

In her most recent writing workshop session, Faith Trinkelman had criticized Jane's story ("The Time I Kissed This Married Guy but Didn't Let Him Slip Me the Tongue") for the banality of its setting—didn't Jane ever write anything that took place outside of Manhattan? Jane never disputed the criticisms that Trinkelman and her students leveled against her. She knew that her settings were unimaginative, that her characters' motivations were unclear, that since she didn't want to dredge up her past, she remained stuck writing vague, unilluminating, glorified diary entries. Often she felt awestruck in the presence of her fellow writers—Jha Robey, whose novella, *Eden's Scapegoat*, retold the story of Adam and Eve from the perspective of the snake; Gregor Poliakoff, who used his experiences as a white-collar grunt to inform a parable about a servant in Russia before the invention of flush toilets ("Pity poor Gregor, burdened with the responsibility of opening the royal windows whenever the czar chose to fling out the contents of his chamber pot"); even Jane's adolescent self, who wrote of magic carousels, of crystalline rivers and enchanted meadows, and who would surely have laughed at adult Jane, bereft of fantasy, struggling to write a story entitled "So for the Hell of It I Ride the Train to Coney and Whatever."

But after Darrell and Jane exit the library together, leaving behind the yellow rose in its iced-tea vase, Jane's new story slowly takes shape. In it, an unhappily married man's entire history is recounted in the span of a single train ride. The story opens en route to the train as the man tells a woman, "Listen, here's what frickin' happened to me today"; it ends with the man at the Stillwell Avenue stop saying, "So, I guess we're gonna get off here."

The D train ride to Coney Island takes just over an hour, and in that time, Darrell Schiff finds himself running the gamut of emotions—glee at his own transgression, fear of being caught, relief when he realizes he won't be, wistful longing when he looks out the train window and spots a billboard that reads DIVORCE $299! NO COURT FEE! SPOUSE'S SIGNATURE NOT NEEDED! But the emotions Darrell experiences as he and Jane walk down the stairs toward the Riegelman Boardwalk are most distressing of all. For, though he had once again approached Jane in the library primarily to restore his sense of worth, to offset the self-loathing he felt, as he and Jane stroll along the boardwalk past shuttered fast-food stands and gated carnival rides, he has the giddy, uneasy sensation that he might truly be falling in love for the first time in his adult life. He feels certain Rebecca loves him, while Jane doesn't really give a damn; he knows Rebecca cares about his struggles, while Jane finds them to be, at best, amusing fodder for fiction. He knows Rebecca is the smartest, classiest, most generous woman he'll ever meet. No matter. He is still captivated by Jane's intensity, by her curiosity, even by the pain he sees looming behind her nasty laughs and knowing smiles. Most of all, he is captivated by the person he feels himself to be in Jane's presence—optimistic, not jaded; twenty-nine, not thirty-one; Darrell Schiff, not Darrell Shit.

Darrell remembers how he experienced Coney Island the one time he came here with Rebecca and her dad. He feigned illness at the pervasive odor of fried food, politically correct outrage at the "Shoot the Freak" competition; he made scathing remarks about the appropriateness of the fact that the freak show was located near the U.S. Army Recruiting Center. He grumbled to himself about the prospect of parenthood while watching rug rats riding Blaster Boats and Go-Karts. He observed that the Dante's Inferno ride didn't have the requisite number of rings, decried the American scourge of obesity when Rebecca offered to buy him a hot dog, seethed with resentment when Rebecca predictably smoked him in the batting cages and the strongman competition. With Jane, he is willing to do anything—walk barefoot in ice-cold water at the beach, play crappy arcade games, hop a fence to sneak into the amusement park rides that are closed for the season.

The only time when Darrell felt the same sort of tremors he feels as he follows Jane into a dark car of the Wonder Wheel was in high school, senior year. Jessica Bosman's father was a visiting anthro professor from Kenya, and during the year Dr. David Bosman taught at Wisconsin, Darrell and Jessica were inseparable—they skinny-dipped in Lake Mendota, took overnight camping trips to Door County, borrowed his folks' jalopy to see Steve Earle in Milwaukee at the Eagles Ballroom. He pleaded with Jessica to attend college in the States. And when she said she had already been accepted by the University of Nairobi, he offered to move to Kenya. Jessica finally told Darrell that he was "too needy" for her, that she had a boyfriend back home anyway, and that she had dated him only because she'd known their relationship wouldn't last.

Darrell didn't learn that Jessica was lying until more than ten years later, when he Googled her and learned that she had become a feminist scholar whose widely anthologized essay "The Suffocating Male Embrace" spoke of feeling trapped in her first relationship and inventing the story of a lover in Nairobi just so her American boyfriend wouldn't follow her. Nevertheless, after Jessica Bosman broke up with him, whenever Darrell would start a relationship, he would always focus on how it would end, and on whom he might date afterward. If he ever sensed that a woman might dump him, he would dump her first. His relationship with Rebecca lasted long enough for them to marry partly because, though he always felt comfortable around her, he rarely felt any great passion, and consequently didn't have to fear experiencing devastation if she ever broke up with him.

As Darrell and Jane sit in the Wonder Wheel, a frigid wind is whipping through Jane's orange hair; her eyes are closed and her arms are raised as if she is trying to will herself to imagine that they are twirling, not standing still. Darrell is wondering in the Wonder Wheel. He is wondering whether the reason he feels so much lighter in Jane's presence is that he now sees that the man for whom Rebecca cares is really something of a *trou du cul*, while Jane, for better or probably worse, sees him for who he truly is.

As dusk approaches, they sit on the beach and watch seagulls soar over the dark gray ocean. Darrell tells Jane he's sorry that, when they're together, he talks so much and rarely asks her anything. But even though Jane answers the questions Darrell poses, he learns little more than he knew at the beginning of the day. Jane tells Darrell of long periods of isolation, of writing stories to keep herself company. She tells of her parents dying unexpectedly, even of how she contemplated committing suicide by leaping from her window onto the blue canopy below. But when Darrell asks for more detail, she merely shrugs, laughs, or says, "That's all you'll get out of me, dude."

Once Jane and Darrell begin walking back to the train station, Darrell asks if Jane is busy on Friday. She says she has already made plans to see a friend's show but might have time for a drink or a walk afterward. Darrell then proposes that they walk for a while instead of taking the train right away; he doesn't want this time with her ever to end, he says, doesn't want to have to return to his real life, to the person he is when he's back in Manhattan, to the *Arschloch* he is when he's not with her.

"Not if you're going to fall in love with me," Jane says.

Darrell takes a breath, makes as if to speak, then stops.

"Hell no, I'm a married man," he finally says as he takes Jane's hand. "It's just a nice-ass night for a walk."

THE BROKER & THE ACTORS

Josh Dybnick leaves a message for Mark Masler, telling him that he and his lawyer can set a closing date for mid-April, since Darrell Schiff and Rebecca Sugarman's loan has been approved. Then he enters the auditorium of the Manhattan Theater Project to find his seat for the first act of the musical *Boysworld* starring Miles Dimmelow.

Since he temporarily retired from acting and began working sixty-hour weeks for the Overman Group, Josh has not seen much theater. When he had barely enough money for rent and Campbell's soup, when he would make monthly phone calls to Shaker Heights, asking for far less money than he actually required to pay off his debts ("Dad, really, four hundred dollars is all I need, and it's just a loan, not a gift"), he would see shows all the time; he'd sign up for comps, get in free on actors' nights with his picture and résumé, hoping his fellow thespians would see him too if he ever got cast. He enjoyed watching even the worst shows, and would spend his time in the audience playing director, imagining how he'd redesign the set, refocus the lights. But now that he can actually afford to see shows, he rarely ever finds the time. The only reason Josh can justify being here tonight in MTP's mainstage space for *Boysworld* instead of at the office or an open house is Miles Dimmelow. Josh accepted Miles's invitation not for Miles's featured role, two solos, and striptease, but for Miles's vague promise of real estate business.

Miles has been calling frequently, and Joshua has been surprised by his perseverance. Every time he tells Miles that he is busy or that his datebook looks full, Miles laughs as if he finds something hysterical about Joshua playing hard-to-get. In the past, whenever Joshua himself was turned down for anything, he never called again. If he failed to win a role, he pouted for days but never questioned the decision. And now, as the houselights dim and he sits beside a sprightly, familiar-looking young woman with freckles and short orange hair, he wonders whether he should have been as pushy as an actor as he has become as a real estate agent, whether he could have won more roles, scored more dates. He had no plans to see Miles ever again, but when Miles called, saying he could introduce Josh to Manhattan Theater Project founder Harvey Mankoff, who was thinking of either selling the building or finding a new manager for MTP, Joshua said, "Uh, let me check my calendar again," and once again, Miles laughed like a hyena.

The mainstage space here at MTP hasn't changed much in forty years; it is still raw—only 199 seats, and about a third have been reupholstered with duct tape. Electrical cords dangle—it's not up to fire code. Paint is flaking off the ceiling, the floor creaks, the lighting booth hasn't been soundproofed—Josh can hear the stage manager curse the light-board operator, can hear someone click off the preshow music on what sounds like a cassette player, can hear the Broadway traffic outside. And yet, how he loves this space—the smell of flat-black paint and recently cut wood, the murmurs of anticipation in the audience, the footsteps backstage, the dusty red curtain. Since his parents' divorce during his first month in college, he has never felt as safe or at home anywhere as he does in a theater.

Squinting in the dark, Josh finds Miles's bio in the *Playbill* and is taken aback by all the credits; the bio takes up more space than that of any of the other actors. In the few children's shows in which Joshua appeared in New York, he padded his own bio with college shows and "favorite roles"—parts he wanted to play but never had. All of Miles's credits seem legitimate — gigs in regional theater, off-Broadway, Shakespeare festivals, touring productions of musicals. And though everyone else in the program has also appeared on *Law & Order*, Miles is the only actor who has played characters with names (Dr. Gordon, Principal Thillens), as opposed to First Bystander.

But even more perplexing and disheartening is the musical itself; Joshua spends Act I of *Boysworld* trying not to feel envious that it has been running for six months while all of his original scripts and literary adaptations are still languishing in drawers. The musical is a lighthearted romp about a controversial plan to build a gay theme park in the Bible Belt (*FOOTLOOSE MEETS ANGELS IN AMERICA!* reads the show's poster); it has been successfully targeting European tourists, even after having received damaging publicity when Evening Noose blogger Nick Renfield revealed that the musical's authors were a straight married couple who had been unable to find backers for their original moneymaking musical concept, *Heathentown*, a Christian rock opera about missionaries. They rewrote the show for an all-male cast, added new lyrics and nudity, then reset the action in the fictional town of Decorum, Kentucky.

Miles plays Mayor Charmless, who initially opposes the Boysworld theme park. His song at the end of Act I ("The Webelos That We Blow") is capped off by a striptease, after which the mayor, overcome by lust for the well-hung mascots of Boysworld, grants a permit for the theme park. At first, Joshua endures this musical number by once again playing director, but he stops when he realizes that his first move would be to fire Miles, who frequently breaks character, mugs, and steals focus. Nevertheless, the audience seems to love the clown. When he mugs, they hoot and holler; they laugh at his bitchy punch lines and burst into wild applause at the Act I blackout. When the lights go up for intermission, the young woman sitting next to Josh is still wiping away tears of laughter. After she catches her breath, she introduces herself and asks if Joshua is also a friend of Miles's.

What makes her think that? Joshua asks Jane Earhart.

"Everybody knows Miles," says Jane, adding that Miles mercilessly mocks every show he's in, always ad-libs and makes up his own lyrics, but still gets cast because he has such a long mailing list and can fill a house on opening night. She asks if Joshua is enjoying the show. Joshua demurs, saying he doesn't know much about theater—he's a real estate man; that's where the real dramas are—then asks for Jane's opinion. Jane scribbles a brief note to herself (*real estate's where the real dramas are*), then tells Josh that Miles loathes *Boysworld*, but as for herself, she's amazed by any writer who can create an entire world. She has started writing a new story called "Nothing Better to Do Than Go to the Theater, I Guess," but, as usual, she says, pounding her palm against her forehead, she can't find an ending; her goddamn imagination keeps failing her.

Jane says she met Miles in her writing workshop. Faith Trinkelman had grown frustrated with her students' flat, ponderous reading styles—98 percent of the money in literature was made by the 1.2 percent of writers who understood the performative aspect of writing, which made their work easier to adapt into screenplays—and had invited actors to read aloud. After class, Miles told Jane he thought her story "So This Lech in the Asian Library Keeps Looking at Me (What the Hell Is His Deal?)" was funnier than anyone else's. Hers was the only story that presented characters realistically, not as they saw themselves or as an author viewed them. Later that evening at her apartment, after Miles read more of her stories and became even more enthusiastic about her work, he suggested they work together to adapt the stories into a musical or cabaret show. Once they came up with a unifying theme, she could work on the book and he would start writing songs.

Knowing that Miles apparently intends his over-the-top, vamping performance in *Boysworld* to be ironic still doesn't help Josh to enjoy Act II any more than he did Act I. The musical's inevitable surprise twist comes when the staid Bible Belt town becomes so enthusiastic about their new gay theme park that the park's organizers close up shop and move to a more conservative city: San Francisco. Corny, Josh thinks. And the curtain call—in which all members of the Decorum City Council enter naked with strategically placed rainbow flags, after which Miles whips off his flag, turns to moon the audience, and receives a standing ovation—is just dated and crass. Josh shudders while frustratedly imagining all the shows he could stage here if someone just gave him one chance.

In front of the theater after the show, Jane tells Miles she won't have time to discuss their musical tonight, then runs off in the direction of the Grant Memorial while Miles and Josh head for the Ding Dong Lounge. Josh doesn't care for the bar—the Pogues' music on the sound system is too aggressive for him. He doesn't particularly care for Miles's company either; the man behaves like a pinball, caroming from person to person, shaking hands with just about everyone he sees, making a spectacle of himself with the bar's hula hoop, winking at Josh the whole time as if this evening is part of some elaborate private joke. Still, as the one real estate broker in a seemingly bohemian and increasingly foreign world, Josh begins to feel unusually important. Over the course of the evening, Miles returns to their table to introduce Josh to bartenders, to actors, even to a commercial casting director who once said Joshua lacked the range to sing backup on a shampoo commercial but, tonight, takes Josh's card because he wants to sell his town house. They pepper Josh with questions: How long before the bubble bursts? Should their daughter rent a place? Or should she buy, then sell when she graduates Columbia? Did anyone ever tell him he looks just like that guy on the "Isn't it time you moved up to Overman" ads?

"This is Josh Dybnick," Miles keeps saying, "good guy for you to know," or "You wanna know anything about condos, here's your man." And when a rumpled Harvey Mankoff finally enters, then passes their table, Miles grabs Joshua's longtime theater idol by the sleeve of his dandruff-speckled, moth-eaten blue blazer and says, "Here's the big-time real estate *macher* I wanted you to meet," and hands him one of Josh's last business cards.

Swaying slightly, Mankoff studies the card, then pockets it, mumbling that if Josh works for the Overman Group, he must really be "a big *macher*." And even though Joshua was wait-listed when he once tried to register for a class at Mankoff's workshop, now the man takes a seat at Miles and Josh's table and offers to buy their next round.

Mankoff smells of cheap liquor and stale lemon-lime aftershave. He has owned MTP since 1965; he purchased the building, a former Studebaker dealership, using money he had earned for character work in motion pictures and a recurring role as Dr. Henry Wilbon on the daytime soap

What Goes Around. Early on, he ran MTP's mainstage, upstairs, and basement studios. He directed two shows at a time, produced a third, managed the box office, taught private and small-group acting classes and monologue workshops, and appeared in nearly forty motion pictures. Now, as he explains to Josh over a tumbler of scotch, littering his speech with Yiddish words that the young real estate broker is far too assimilated to understand, the theater business in New York has become little more than the real estate business, his job that of glorified landlord. In this city, space has become the "Holy *verstinkeneh* Grail," Mankoff says. To pay his alimonies, he still plays uncredited roles in *chazzerei* with which he is embarrassed to be associated, but he hasn't directed or produced in a decade; when MTP holds classes, he now gives only the initial lecture and drops in on the final day to evaluate scenes and sign copies of his books.

As Mankoff lambastes the state of contemporary theater, Josh plays dumb, not allowing starstruck Joshua to blow his cover. He lets Miles describe plots of plays Joshua has already directed, lets Miles recite résumés of actors he has idolized for years, lets Mankoff recount the history of this theater in which Joshua has long yearned to appear, suspecting that if Mankoff ever discovers he is an aspiring actor, the man will flee. Instead, Josh becomes Mankoff's confidant—Harvey calls Josh "son," speaks to him with an Eastern European disregard for personal space, his face less than six inches away from Josh's. The economics of theater don't seem sustainable anymore, Mankoff tells Josh, it's "a rich man's ball game"—even the least ambitious, nonunion show costs fifty grand up front. You can't afford to use simply the best actors if you want to "make back your nut," you have to cast the actors with the longest mailing lists. "It's meshuga," he says— you come to this city thinking you're gonna be an artist, but once you get good at it, you have to turn into a businessman.

Over the course of their conversation, Mankoff offers Josh a half-dozen jobs. He asks Josh to find a buyer for his building, to lead the executive board of MTP. Finally, he says he doesn't know what he wants anymore. He had thought he would always uphold one of the world's most sacred arts, but if all he's doing is filling out leases and depositing checks, *feh*, who needs it? He asks if Josh could just come in sometime to analyze the theater's accounts; he'd like an opinion from someone with a business mind, someone who knows nothing about theater. Miles has told him that Josh is a sharp cookie with some *seychel* and might be able to make his theater viable again. If so, Mankoff might give it one more shot; if not, maybe Josh can just sell the damn place and he'll buy a villa in Spain and drink sangria all day long.

Joshua mouths a silent prayer thanking God for introducing him to Miles Dimmelow and Bradley Overman, who have allowed him to leapfrog over all the actors who pay $600 for six weeks of classes, after which Harvey Mankoff tells them they still can't act and bullies them into registering for the next session. He wonders whether he should inspect Mankoff's accounts, pull out a prospectus and a proposed season of shows from one of the imaginary theater companies he has always wanted to found, then tell Harvey he has researched the industry and what he really needs to do is produce an entire season of one-man adaptations of literary classics. But after Josh shakes Harvey's hand, then claps him on the shoulder, he says he will have to consult his office calendar to see if and when he can meet with him. Miles grins, then winks at Joshua, but Mankoff seems impressed; he says he doesn't trust a man who's free to meet with him right away.

Near dawn, when Miles is snoring in his bed, Joshua opens a desk drawer and begins to page through one of the scripts he performed in college—his solo version of *Candide*. As he reads, he is pleasantly surprised—the translation still sings. And later in the morning, when Miles is gone and Josh is holding his phone with one hand while speaking with Mark Masler to ask if he and Alan Ziegler have chosen their closing date yet, with the other hand Joshua is typing, "Manhattan Theater Project: An Idea Whose Time Has Come."

THE SELLER &
THE YOUNG LEADER

Mark Masler is contemplating the cashier's check that he will deposit after the closing on April 16 into his ever-burgeoning Rolls Restaurant & Wash bank account when he arrives at the front door of the Scheinblum residence in Riverdale, bearing one letter of recommendation to NYU's Stern School of Business and two bottles of nonalcoholic champagne from the dwindling cache that he had pilfered from his kitchen at Meloche after the Health Department's final visit.

Upon meeting Allie Scheinblum in his office, where the young woman wore a short, canary yellow skirt that kept creeping up and a loose white silk top that kept creeping down, Mark told her he was "quite impressed" with her "maturity" and would gladly write her business school recommendation, choosing not to taint her image of him by admitting that he never actually graduated from a four-year college himself. He told her again that she did not have to treat him to any sort of meal—he simply enjoyed the energy he received from being around young people, and helping them was a perk of being "a man of influence." But Allie insisted, saying she would be deeply insulted if he didn't come to Riverdale for dinner.

Sitting at his desk and peering at Allie over his new half-glasses, Mark vacillated between thinking she was either the most innocent girl he had ever met or the filthiest freak upon whom he had ever laid eyes. He longed to corrupt the former Allie, succumb to the latter, but, happily, he rarely allowed his gaze to drift below her collarbone. Throughout their meeting, he addressed her as "Ms. Scheinblum," provided advice while employing avuncular phrases such as "nowadays," "when I was your age," and "old *cockers* like me." He rubbed his knee and complained of his high school football injuries. They discussed her favorite book (*The Fountainhead*), her favorite living author (Tom Wolfe), her favorite album (*Funk That Hurts*), and her personal heroes, who included Margaret Thatcher, Condi Rice, and Monica Lewinsky—all three were women who knew what they wanted and, when they saw it, they "went for it," Allie said.

Frequently Allie would make sweeping statements, then punctuate them with the assertion "It's true" ("Everyone wants to live near rich people. It's true"; "Palestinians don't place the same value on life as we do. It's true"; "Nobody cares about anyone but themselves. It's true"). But even when he secretly agreed with Allie, Mark would only frown. And whenever Allie tried to discuss personal matters, Mark would steer the conversation back to the subject of her recommendation.

Mark only nodded sympathetically when Allie looked into his eyes and observed that she adored men with beards like his because they reminded her of the times when her father still lived with her family and she would feel his beard against her cheek whenever he kissed her goodnight. When Allie said she couldn't wait to leave her mother's "rancid house"—Caleb, her "creepy Goth brother," would murder somebody someday and it sure as hell wouldn't be her—he told her to cherish the moments she spent with her brother, for they would pass all too soon. He did not know how to interpret Allie's questions—"Why didn't your marriages work out?" "Are you physically involved with anybody?"—and responded by saying that love became more complicated as one grew older. And when he asked Allie what was the best thing she had done since graduating from college and she answered "Inviting you to the Young Leaders Brunch," he agreed that volunteer work was rewarding.

The Scheinblum residence is located in a neighborhood of cul-de-sacs, of tricycles and plastic toys strewn over snowy front lawns; a neighborhood of canopies, two-car garages, and mix-and-match houses made of equal parts brick, wood, stone, and aluminum siding. As Mark stands at the front door of the house, the neighborhood brings back memories of his early childhood in Sunnyside before his mother died and he moved with his pop and stepmom to Manhattan, a place that he never really warmed to—in the city, Mark had access to more money, but he didn't have an alley, a shed, or a lawn mower. In this section of Riverdale, Mark finds himself remembering Sunnyside's parks and playgrounds, the smell of leftovers warming in his mom's oven, his mother driving her Buick into car washes with uniformed attendants, idyllic locales where he longingly gazed at cars being scrubbed, buffed, *shpritzed*, and waxed.

Yet upon entering the Scheinblum house, where he hears the sizzle of oil in a hot skillet and smells garlic being sautéed, Mark feels his body slump. Immediately he understands why Allie has invited him here, and the reason has nothing to do with the whipped-cream-and-maraschino-cherry fantasies he'd tried to sublimate on the ride north by switching back and forth between the audiobook of Jack Welch's autobiography and the police calls on his scanner. In his yellow Hummer, he'd rehearsed respectful, mature statements to dissuade Allie if she was overcome by youthful lust and pounced on him. He wanted her to want him, but also wanted to demonstrate that he was man enough to tell her no. But though Allie greets Mark at the door with a smile and a kiss on the cheek before she takes his coat, she is dressed in ripped jeans, white athletic socks, and an inside-out gray sweatshirt; Allie's mother, Marilyn Scheinblum, is the one who appears ready for a date.

Mark meets Marilyn in the kitchen at the yellow Formica counter where she is pouring gin into a tumbler of Tang on the rocks. She wears a tight crimson dress, pantyhose, and no shoes, and when she shakes Mark's hand and flashes a pained smile, Mark sees bits of pale pink makeup flake off of her cheeks. Allie hands Mark a glass of club soda with a twist of lime—"clean and sober almost five months now," Mark boasts to Marilyn, who takes a slug from her Tang Blossom and eyes him dubiously, as if to say she's heard that story before and knows how it ends.

While Allie works in the kitchen making pasta sauce, Mark follows Marilyn into the living room. Marilyn's seventeen-year-old son Caleb—lanky and awkward, still not quite used to his height—is standing with his laptop balanced precariously on top of the TV; he is listening to music through headphones and typing. Can't he do that in his room without bothering company? Marilyn asks, at which point Caleb, who wears black Carhartt pants and a matching hooded sweatshirt, takes off his headphones and asks why his mother always feels a need to humiliate him. Marilyn says that as long as Caleb has no social life, dresses like a third-rate Ninja, and spends all day with his computer doing God knows what, he deserves to be humiliated. Mark tries to introduce himself to Caleb—ever since the shootings at Columbine, he has assumed that all disaffected, black-clad suburban teens might own large caches of weapons, and he would prefer to be the one trusted adult whose life they spare. But Caleb barely looks at Mark; he trudges upstairs with the laptop, and moments later Mark hears a door slam shut, furious typing, then a stereo being turned on.

Mark observes that Caleb seems like "a real good kid."

"You think so?" Marilyn asks. She finishes her drink and sucks on an ice cube.

As they stand in the living room, Mark tells Marilyn he has written a business school recommendation for Allie. Good, Marilyn says (looking Mark up and down with the air of one who spends every weekend being introduced to yet another of Allie's boyfriends and imagining they'll disappoint Allie in the sack), then at least one of them will finally have a decent job. Why, Mark asks Marilyn, what does she do for a living? "Next topic," says Marilyn. She chews on her ice as Mark sits beside her on a white leather sofa and relates the expurgated version of his autobiography that he offered in his speech to the Young Leaders Committee. As he speaks, he senses that he is boring Marilyn; she frequently interrupts to ask seemingly irrelevant questions (Where does he live? What address? What floor? How much did he pay? No kidding, that much?). But when Mark talks about how he kicked his drug and sex addictions, she tunes out, and Mark finds his gaze drifting from Marilyn to the view out the front windows—the frozen lawns illuminated by streetlights, the kids in coats, sweatpants, and boots playing football or riding bicycles with training wheels before their parents call them in for dinner.

Recently, to inspire himself in his quest to realize his business dreams, Mark rented the movie *Car Wash*. And the scene that grimly resonates for him now as he contemplates his distant youth is one in which a handsome gent visits the titular location, hits on a nerdy girl, and asks her for a date. Thrilled, the nerdy girl agrees, only to discover that the aforementioned gent is already dating her hot friend and has invited her just to keep his nerdy friend company. Watching the movie, Mark imagined himself the handsome gent, but he now realizes he's just the nerdy girl, sitting in the backseat with Marilyn Scheinblum. Who is he fooling? Allie flirted with him only for a business school recommendation and a date for her mom.

As far as love is concerned, this is just about all he has to look forward to, Mark thinks. Not long ago, had he met the Scheinblum ladies in a club, he might have invited them to a VIP room, then back to his apartment, hoping one of them would turn out to be a freak. Now, Mark can see his future; Marilyn Scheinblum, Viagra, and prostate care are stamped upon it. Marilyn is the appropriate age for him; though he is not particularly attracted to her, she is reasonably attractive. Yes, she seems weary, but life after forty is a wearying proposition to him too. Relationships of the sort he could have with Marilyn are something to which he will have to become accustomed—like using margarine instead of butter, like fixing himself a grilled-chicken salad instead of a cheeseburger, like drinking club soda instead of gin. At least there is a family for him here, ready made. How can he be forty-two years old and still have no family?

But the moment Mark is about to ask Marilyn how often she gets into the city, and whether she might join him for espresso at his favorite café (he doesn't have one, but figures that since he once had a favorite tit bar, he should now have a favorite café), Marilyn chomps her last ice cube, stands, then tells Mark she's already running late, and if Mark stays overnight with Allie, maybe she'll see him at breakfast. Where is she going? Mark asks. Don't ask, says Marilyn. She carries her tumbler to the kitchen, clunks it in the sink, puts on her heels, then heads for the front door, clutching a set of car keys. "Caleb, don't make me have to tell you again to take out the damn trash," she yells, whereupon a gust of profanity whooshes down from Caleb Scheinblum's room before the front door closes. Puzzled, Mark stands to gaze out the front window. He takes a pull of club soda and watches Marilyn at the wheel of a white Ford Escape without a license plate speeding out of the driveway. He doesn't notice that Allie has entered the living room until she has slipped an arm around his waist.

Mark asks if Allie's mother will be returning soon. *Huh-uh*, Allie says, shaking her head, she rarely comes home before morning—she'll probably spend the night with "another creepy, freeloader boyfriend" in some "down-ass apartment." Oh, she has a boyfriend, Mark says, beginning to understand. She always has a boyfriend, says Allie, and the boyfriend always has at least two girlfriends, sometimes a wife; even when she was married, she was always second choice, Allie says. "It's true."

And now, reality dawns on Mark Masler. Why, this is not a scheming young woman in need of a recommendation and a date for her mother after all; this is a lonely girl who needs a decent man for herself to compensate for all the thugs Marilyn Scheinblum drags home, who needs someone with big arms to sternly yet lovingly discipline her troubled-but-well-meaning brother, take him to Knicks games and the synagogue, help him with his homework, convince him to turn in his gun collection.

Mark touches Allie's neck. He hears her swallow; she's so close that he can even hear her blink. Instinct takes over. Mark barely notices that the curtains in the Scheinblum living room haven't been drawn, that Caleb is still upstairs typing. He doesn't know how Allie's sweatshirt comes off before his trousers do, can't figure out whether he already removed her brassiere or whether she wasn't wearing one, has no idea of the provenance of the ribbed condoms he wears. Only after Allie and Mark have slept on the carpet for an hour, her body neatly molded into his, does Mark take

note of a piercing sound—a series of incessant, high-pitched beeps that he
initially mistakes for the alarm on a clock radio. When he inhales, he feels
a harsh sensation in his nostrils, a slight tightening in his chest and throat.
His eyes are too dry; when he blinks, they burn. A thick fog hangs in the
air: smoke.

Mark grabs his pants, puts them on without bothering to find his underwear. He runs toward the kitchen, barefoot and shirtless. Fire extinguisher,
he thinks, where the hell is the fire extinguisher? But when he sees the tall,
hooded, shadowy figure of Caleb Scheinblum standing in the kitchen with
his back to him, Mark is seized by foreboding. He spent far too much of his
youth acting without considering consequences. He would drink without
remembering how he would feel in the morning, smash side-view mirrors
of sports cars without considering how much his hand would hurt, have sex
on carpets and floors without thinking about rug burns and splinters. Once
again, his lust has gotten the better of him, and now Caleb Scheinblum—
this sullen, nihilistic, fatherless youth with nothing to lose; this computer-
obsessed Goth, shunned by his peers, humiliated by his mother—has
witnessed the ultimate indignity: a forty-two-year-old man humping his sister. The lad has taken revenge; he has set the house ablaze.

"Just what the hell's going on here, son?" Mark Masler asks. Caleb
Scheinblum turns; he is at the sink, water rushing out of the faucet, smoke
billowing around him.

"If you're gonna make Bolognese sauce, don't leave it on the stove,
dumbshit," Caleb says.

Dumbshit. At the uttering of this word, Mark aches to grab the youth
by the hood of his black sweatshirt, drag him upstairs, dress him in clean,
colorful sports shirts, and make him listen to U2 or Springsteen. He longs
to teach the kid some respect. But because he knows that some youths benefit more from kindness than from harsh discipline and because he doesn't
want to die in a hail of gunfire, he forces a smile. That's right, he finally
says, though he doesn't appreciate Caleb's language, he has been, he admits, something of a dumbshit; he should have remembered that Allie had
been cooking pasta sauce. Mark offers his hand. "My name's Mr. Masler,"

he says. "I'm a friend of your sister's." "Whatever," says Caleb, who adds that he's going out, then advises Mark to turn off the smoke detector, put on a shirt, and zip up his fly.

Mark takes the batteries out of the Scheinblum smoke detector, cleans what he can of the saucepan, empties the pasta water into the sink. In the first-floor bathroom, he washes his chest, his armpits, and his crotch with a half-used bar of Ivory soap, then dries himself with a hand towel, wakes Allie, and suggests that they go out for dinner. But when they get to Vachon, having stopped twice to pull off the road and have sex in the back of his Hummer, the kitchen is already closed. So they head back to Mark's penthouse apartment at the Landmark, where they order out pizza from V&T and sit at his dining room table in matching monogrammed white bathrobes gazing east at the view—the dark expanse of the boulevard, the illuminated park entrance at Strangers' Gate, the icy cliffs and bare trees along Central Park West, the distant lights of the Triborough Bridge, the apartment buildings looming over the park's eastern border.

"You can practically see the whole city from here," Allie says, then turns back to Mark. "Yeah, I like this place, and I'm really gonna like spending time here," she says. "That may sound forward, but it's true." Mark runs a hand down Allie's back and over her buttocks. He rests his head against Allie's shoulder and inhales. She smells like burnt spaghetti sauce; she smells like home.

THE TENANT &
HIS INSTRUMENT

The B-flat clarinet that Ike Morphy had stored for more than six years
on a high shelf in his apartment, and that he now carries in his backpack in a beat-up, hard black plastic case while once again strolling north
on Riverside Drive, bears scuffs, scratches, and burn marks from its nearly
two-hundred-year existence. A long, beat-up boxwood cylinder tapered at
one end, fluted at the other, its body pocked with more than a dozen nicks
and dings, it was designed by early-nineteenth-century clarinet pioneer
Iwan Müller and manufactured by Jean-François Simiot of Lyon.

The Estonian-born Müller moved in 1811 to Paris, where he worked as
a musician and composer, playing a thirteen-key, purportedly omnitonic
clarinet of his own design. Proud of his invention, Müller, in an incident
that has been well documented by music historians, presented the clarinet
before the Conservatoire de Paris, certain his model would become the
standard for all clarinets. Unfortunately for Müller, an egotist and a hothead, the conservatory rejected his clarinet outright. Suspecting that this
rejection was based on nationalistic prejudice rather than the quibbles
with tonality the conservatory cited, Müller ordered J.-F. Simiot to cease

production of his clarinet and, instead, set about designing a seventeen-key instrument that predated by more than two decades the Auguste Buffet–Hyacinthe Klosé design that would become the basis for the modern clarinet. But when the conservatory approved his second B-flat clarinet, Müller, rather than express his gratitude, savaged his judges with an expletive-riddled diatribe, then stopped production on the new instrument before half a dozen had been made. He spent the rest of his life performing recitals using the clarinet the conservatory originally rejected. When Müller died in 1837, his will specified that his instrument was to be auctioned off to the highest bidder, as long as that bidder had no association with the Conservatoire de Paris.

Of the five surviving seventeen-key B-flat Müller clarinets, Ike Morphy's is the only one owned by a musician. One is exhibited in the Musée des Arts et Métiers in Paris, another in the Musée des Instruments Musicales in Brussels, the others in Stockholm's Royal College of Music and Munich's Bavarian National Museum. The model that Ike is now carrying as he begins to approach Inwood Hill was purchased at the 1837 auction by Roland Derain, a member of the Orchestre National de Lyon, who found Müller's instrument superior to his own Buffet-Klosé, particularly for his solos in the works of Georg Philipp Telemann and Carl Phillip Emmanuel Bach. After Derain's death, the instrument passed on to his nephew Robert Severau, a prodigy who ultimately forfeited the clarinet to satisfy a gambling debt to a card player named Guillaume Milliot, who in turn gave the instrument to his mistress, the former prostitute Clothilde Chadeau. Upon Chadeau's arrest in 1871, two years after Guillaume Milliot died of syphilis, her daughters Natalie, Christine, and Marie-Ange offered the instrument to Zurich-born Bernard Chabat in lieu of the sexual favors he demanded. Chabat played the instrument for twenty-nine years with the Paris Opera, for whom he composed his sole work, "These Three Coquettes of Arras."

None of Chabat's seven children showed any musical facility, save for his eldest son, Nicholas, who planned to take up the instrument in earnest once he returned from the army but was killed in action at Verdun, at which point his widow sold the Müller for far less than it was worth to itinerant merchant Charles Dufour, who immediately sold it for a 400 percent profit to Monroe Brannick, owner of the Pittsburgh-based M. Brannick & Sons department stores. Brannick was not a musician but a collector of antiques and objets d'art, which he displayed in the north wing of his Squirrel Hill mansion. During the Brannick Fire of 1947, which was blamed on house servant Mamie Reynolds but was later rumored to have been set by the Brannicks' son Monroe Jr., whose schizophrenia prevented him from ever rising beyond the Pennsylvania state legislature, the clarinet disappeared.

It turned up twenty-five years later in a pawnshop on Van Buren Street in Chicago, where Benjamin Sorey, a onetime thief and reformed arsonist who was now a preacher at the Pacific Garden Mission, had unloaded it with various other items pinched from the Brannick mansion. The priceless instrument was purchased for a mere $50 by Chicago Symphony Orchestra second-chair clarinetist Herman Vontagh, who worked part-time in his Hyde Park home teaching private lessons. After retiring from the CSO, Vontagh, a painfully shy man who lived alone and had no living heirs, gave the clarinet to his favorite student, Ike Morphy, whom he had first seen performing on a plastic clarinet with the Merit Youth Orchestra, for which Vontagh served as a board member. Look, Vontagh said, pointing to the "I.M." that Iwan Müller had etched into the instrument's barrel, the clarinet even had Ike's initials on it; he was destined to own it.

Ike played the clarinet throughout high school at Whitney Young, but not until his junior year would he discover the instrument's true versatility. He was struggling with Mozart's clarinet concerto in the upstairs bedroom that he had shared with his brother before Ruel started law school at Chicago-Kent, got married, and moved out of the house. At the time, Ike was a talented and dutiful player, skilled and dexterous but lacking spontaneity. He practiced the same measures over and over, yet could never play the tones as he heard them in his head. Briefly, he stopped, exhausted and frustrated with himself. But as he started playing again, he heard a clatter, followed by a thump, then two screams. His heart beating fast and his body suddenly cold with foreboding, he rushed downstairs, clarinet still in one hand, and when he entered the kitchen, he saw his father lying faceup on the floor, the contents of the refrigerator's vegetable drawer scattered around his limp body.

Ike watched his sister, Naima, who, like him, was still living at home then, futilely performing CPR. He watched his mother, Ella Mae, back stooped, arms dangling at her sides, standing frozen beside the telephone until Ike grabbed the phone himself and called 911. When the ambulance arrived, Ike was still holding his clarinet, and the refrigerator door was still open.

For the two weeks following his father's death, Ike didn't play the clarinet at all. The initial days passed in a blur—he always felt on the verge of collapsing, but managed to stay awake; his body was always too hot or too cold; the days were filled with telephone calls, visits from relatives, trays of rich food that he always felt too ill to eat. But after Ike's father's funeral, life at the Morphy house briefly returned almost to the way Ike had perceived it as a boy—before Ruel had started Chicago-Kent, before Naima had dropped out of Loop College and begun working as a secretary for their mother in the Horticulture Department of the Garfield Park Conservatory, before Ike had joined the Merit Orchestra and rarely returned home before eight, when all the Morphys were still living at home and Ike would practice in his bedroom and listen to the sounds of Ruel's study partners carousing in the living room, Naima typing on her Smith Corona, his father in the basement playing records or hammering wood, his mother listening to her kitchen radio, which was always tuned to classical music on WFMT. This was before Ike realized that all of these disparate sounds were not evidence of a happy, lively home but of a family in which people rarely spoke to one another at all.

During these days after the funeral, when Ike's mother, brother, and sister slept at the family house on South Colfax Avenue, Ike rarely saw Ruel's wife or Naima's boyfriends. The remaining Morphys ate all their meals together, saw movies at the Hyde Park, walked all the way to Rainbow Beach and back. His mother sat at his bedside and wished him pleasant dreams; his brother and sister chatted quietly, then embraced. From his bedroom, Ike would hear muffled voices and occasional, unfamiliar bursts of laughter. Then, the relatives and well-wishers finally stopped ringing the doorbell, and one night Ike's mother started crying at the dinner table; she just couldn't believe the whole family would never sit around this table again, she said. When Ella Mae stopped to catch her breath, the next to speak was Naima, who had always taken her father's side when her mother became emotional. Why was her mother crying? Naima wanted to know; this had never really been a whole family anyway. And moments later, when Ruel walked out with Naima, he said that his sister was right; there had never been any love in this house, and there never would be; the past days were nothing more than a fantasy. Naima walked into the winter night, and Ruel said, hey, wait up, and put his arm around her. When Ike and his mother were alone, she dried her eyes. "People," Ella Mae Morphy told Ike before she walked outside into the snow without her shoes to trim the bushes in her garden, "can be so disappointing." Later that night, after Ike stopped crying, he took his clarinet out of his case and practiced his Mozart. He nailed every note; then, he started to improvise.

Midway through his sophomore year at UIC, while Ike was still living in the house on South Colfax, Herman Vontagh told him that he would soon be moving into a nursing home and he had little left to teach Ike anyway; soon, Ike would be moving on too. New York was the right place for Ike, said Vontagh, who had studied at Juilliard before joining the Chicago Symphony; it was a city where people discovered who they were, even though, for some, it wasn't always the person they thought they were or the person they wanted to be.

After Herman Vontagh died, Ike left a note for his mother and sister, telling them he could no longer breathe in their house—he could no longer stand listening to Naima arguing with their mother about food, about boyfriends, about money. He was leaving for New York and would call when he was settled. He walked all the way north to the Randolph Street bus terminal, carrying a suitcase in one hand, his clarinet in a backpack. He caught the Greyhound, rode it eighteen hours to Port Authority. He slept in the north end of Central Park, the emptiest spot he could find, one where he assumed that cops wouldn't bother him. He played his clarinet in the subways for three straight days until, in a Columbus Avenue coffee shop, he met a young professor named Ricardo Melendez who asked if

Ike was looking for work and a place to live. Ricardo told him about this neighborhood called Manhattan Valley. The community was starting to take control of it again; oh, it might not have looked like much now, man, but someday, every building around here was going to be worth a million bucks. Ricardo handed Ike a slip of paper with Jerry Masler's phone number on it.

When Ike began to help renovating what would become the Roberto Clemente Building, he often tried to call his mother either at home or at work, but his sister Naima always answered. "She won't talk to you until you come home," she would say. And no matter how many times Ike asked her to put their mother on the line, Naima would say, "Not unless you're coming back." But Ike said he wouldn't come back—Herman Vontagh was right; he already knew his home was in New York. Still, whenever Ike received a check, a small one from Jerry, or later, a larger one from Lyman Wishner, who managed the Funkshuns until Maestro fired him, Ike would send half the money home to his mother with a letter telling her how he was faring. The letters always came back, but the checks were always cashed.

Eventually, Ike gave up and stopped calling home—thinking that his mother didn't want him back made breaking from her seem easier. Nevertheless, he started drinking, and the more he drank, the more creative and free his clarinet playing became. Ike knew little about popular music and assumed that, when Maestro John Wilkins Jr. saw him playing on a Monday night at Augie's and asked if Ike wanted to join a band he was forming, the Funkshuns would never be anything more than a side project, a bunch of dudes gigging in basements and lofts. The music wasn't deep enough to be anything more, Ike assumed, unaware of the power of Maestro's shrewd eye for business, talent for mimicry, and knack for a catchy pop hook and a titillating lyric. Though the Funkshuns' songs rarely exceeded five minutes, Ike invented short passages within them that were as complicated as miniature symphonies. On a break during a video shoot in a Chelsea loft after the band released its self-titled debut album, which reached number 37 on the *Billboard* R & B chart, Ike met a model named Muriel who was nearly as tall as he was, and nearly as estranged from her family as he had become from his. They found in each other an easy and willing audience for what frustrated them. For Muriel it was her father, a philandering scholar with an eye for women who resembled her all too closely; for Ike it was his mother, who had apparently taken her elder children's side against him. In Ike's apartment on West 106th Street, or on the Funkshuns' tour bus, Ike and Muriel would huddle together, relate stories of their past, drink bourbon, read novels to each other, work crosswords, play chess until one or the other passed out. During the years they were together, Muriel often felt too high or too low, too joyful or too angry, but Ike helped make her feel even, she said.

One night, nearly ten years after Ike had left Chicago, he and the Funkshuns were warming up backstage at the Arie Crown, preparing to play the first of three sold-out shows. The band would soon be returning to New York, and in a preshow meeting, Maestro mentioned that they would be recording a beer commercial when they got there. Ike, rolling his bloodshot eyes behind the sunglasses he wore to conceal them, said hell, man, shilling for beer companies wasn't why he played clarinet. If any other band member had made that statement, Maestro would have fired him on the spot. But Maestro treated Ike with more respect than he did the other Funkshuns; he only grinned before asking Ike, well, then why did he play, brother? Ike didn't respond, but he thought about Maestro's question all night. *Why?*

The following morning, before any of the other band members rolled out of bed, Ike asked their tour bus driver to take him past his old house for the first time since he'd left his hometown. South Colfax looked the same as he remembered it, but he could barely recognize his home—the sidewalk and steps were cracked; the glass in the front door was broken; the canopy looked as if it had been stripped bare. Only the garden, immaculate as always with every color of the rainbow represented five times over, was familiar. His mother, her hair now the color of cigarette ash, was on her hands and knees in the front yard, pulling weeds. Ike stepped off the bus, but when he tried to speak, the words caught in his throat. Ella Mae

Morphy, still on the ground, spoke to him before she even looked up. Why hadn't he ever called or written? she asked. Naima had told her Ike would never call or write, but she always hoped that someday he would.

At the kitchen table, the mother and her son talked through the past decade—the house in Oak Park that Naima, now a social worker for South Side Elder Care, and her boyfriend Sal had bought, most probably with the checks Ike had sent; the documents that Ike's brother, Ruel, who now worked as an estate planner, had urged Ella Mae to sign. Ike told his mother he would move back to Chicago, try to make up for all the shit that had apparently gone down in his absence, but Ella Mae told him to go back home. "There's nothing for you here," she said, but at least they could talk on the phone now. She missed their talks; at one time, they had been such good friends.

The next night, during the Funkshuns' second concert, Ike froze the moment he tried to play his first solo. And each subsequent time he tried to play his Müller, the notes were either wrong or absent altogether. He kept wondering why was he playing, what the hell was he doing here, just how much of his life had he already wasted, playing through an anger and pain that he may not have even needed to feel. He wished he knew how to play something hopeful or carefree, like his clarinet idols Sidney Bechet and Benny Goodman, or even the flutist Herbie Mann, but he didn't know how. Finally he whispered to Maestro; he was feeling lousy, he said. Then he walked offstage and caught a train back east.

Ike thought only a few days would pass before he picked up his instrument again and either rejoined the band or started a solo career. But once he placed the clarinet in the hall closet, he found it easier not to play at all. The clarinet stayed in the closet when he was sober and it stayed when he was drunk; it stayed when he was high and it stayed when he forced himself to go straight. It was there on the day when Ike realized that royalty checks weren't coming anymore and he rode the subway down to Jerry Masler's office to ask if he still needed men to work for him. Ike didn't take out the clarinet when he asked Muriel to leave because they weren't doing each other any good anymore, or when she came back, or when she left for the last time. On their final night together, Ike told her that he was talking to his mother again, and he was just starting to feel better about himself. "That's fine for you," Muriel said. Still, the clarinet stayed in the closet. During the late summer afternoon when Ike walked through East Harlem in the direction of the loudest, steadiest A-flat he had ever heard, the instrument remained in the closet; and, when Ike brought home the creature that made that sound to keep him company—a black mutt that answered to the name of Lucky—the clarinet was still on a high shelf, its case covered by a thin layer of dust.

When Ella Mae Morphy learned she was ill, Naima was living a half hour away from South Colfax in her Oak Park home with Sal; Ruel and his second wife lived thirty miles north, in Evanston. But the first call Ella made was to Ike. That same incongruously beautiful, early spring day, he drove his pickup all the way from New York to Chicago in twelve hours. For the months of his mother's life that remained, he lived in the same house where he'd played as a boy. Two weeks before she died, Ella Mae Morphy asked Ike to play his clarinet for her, but it was still in New York. Ike promised her he would play again the moment he got home, but then he arrived at the Roberto Clemente Building and home wasn't something that belonged to him anymore.

On this still winter night, Ike is walking up a path on Inwood Hill with Herbie through the last remaining natural forest in Manhattan. His time is short. He needs a new place, money to pay for it. Josh Dybnick has told him to call when he knows how much he is prepared to spend. And though Ike knows he could find some construction job, music is all he's ever been truly good at, his only talent that can pay for the sort of place he and Herbie need.

Man and dog follow the path they have been taking practically every day for the past month; they hike up dirt trails, climb over rocks, wind upward following pink chalk arrows on the ground, ascending more than two hundred feet until they reach the park's highest elevation and a clearing called Butterfly Meadow. Through a fence, Ike can see over the northern border of Manhattan, across the Harlem River to the dark curtain of evergreens beyond. Herbie settles upon the wet grass beside the trunk of a black ash tree, front legs tucked under his chin. Ike sets down his clarinet case and flips it open. Inside, five wooden segments lie encased in red velvet; there are packets of reeds, an old matchbook from Alexander's Steak House, a tin of wax, a little bottle of tea tree oil. Ike takes a reed, places it in his mouth, and screws his instrument together, polishes it with a rag until the keys glint again in the light of the haloed moon. As he wets the reed, he runs scales, and where the keys still stick, he takes a match, lights it, and melts the wax between the keys and pads until the smoothness returns.

Ike places the reed on his mouthpiece, tightens the ligature, forms the embouchure, puts the tip of the instrument in his mouth. He takes a deep breath, closes his eyes until he can once again hear the scales as they have been played on this instrument for nearly two centuries. He plays softly at first, then louder as the music begins to transport him as it used to. He plays for his mother, wishing she could hear him now, wherever she is, if she is still anywhere. He plays for Herbie too. He keeps playing even as a cold, wet wind begins to blow, even as his cheeks grow sore, even as his embouchure slips, even as his breaths become so heavy that he feels each one in the corners of his eyes. He keeps playing even as he hits wrong notes. After all, he thinks, no one can hear but the river, the black ash and the tulip trees, and Herbie Mann, who starts barking when he smells a familiar scent just before the sun begins to rise.

THE TENANT & THE DOG &
THE BUYER & HER BOSS
& HER BOSS'S OB-GYN

One day before she will happen to meet Ike Morphy and his dog on Inwood Hill, Rebecca Sugarman is waiting for a table at the sleek oaken bar of Maniago's Bistro with Chloe Linton, who has been looking her up and down this afternoon with an unusually attentive air. Now that Rebecca has been officially installed as *The American Standard*'s literary editor, these lunches with Chloe have become a daily event. They are lavish, lengthy affairs involving appetizers, main courses, desserts, coffee, even vodka tonics. The idea of dining so frequently with her boss flatters Rebecca, but she still almost always returns nauseous to the *Standard* office, for she spends most of her lunch hours advocating for her colleagues, trying to persuade Chloe not to fire Norman Burloff, because, yes, the man's film reviews are almost always published months after the movies have left the theaters, but he is still one of the *Standard*'s most eloquent writers, and who cares how he dresses? Rebecca has managed to win a temporary stay of execution for art director László Ruffcorn, insisting that more technique is involved in designing a magazine page than "converting text into Quark, choosing a font color, and Photoshopping the hell out of a picture." And although Rebecca could not mount a winning defense for Nick Renfield, whose snarky media column was the least popular item in every focus group survey, and who has already found a job at *Groom*, a start-up men's marriage-and-horse-enthusiast magazine, Chloe has agreed to let Rebecca keep Nick under contract as a freelancer should any story require his investigative skills.

This afternoon, as she sits on a stool at the Maniago's bar beside Chloe, Rebecca is about to order a vodka tonic to settle her nerves. But before she can utter a word, Chloe breaks in. "She'll take a Sprite," Chloe tells the bartender. Rebecca, somewhat embarrassed that she has spent every day this week thoughtlessly ordering drinks without asking Chloe's permission, apologizes for draining the *Standard*'s finances. Chloe says that as far as she is concerned, the two of them can spend as much of the magazine's entertainment budget as they want, but Rebecca should not drink, given her condition. Just how far along is she? Chloe asks. Rebecca gazes at Chloe, mystified. When was her last period? asks Chloe, whose questions are always so direct that Rebecca never seems to have the option of deflecting them. Maybe two months ago, Rebecca says, but she's been late before. How many times before? Chloe asks—Rebecca doesn't strike her as the sort of person who is ever late for anything. Does Rebecca really not know she's pregnant?

Chloe Linton's ob-gyn, Lisa Belfour, featured in *New York* magazine's "Gotham's Top Docs" cover story, has a sontag of white down the middle of her jet-black mane. She greets Rebecca in her office with a cool, firm handshake and tells her that she is seeing her only as a favor to Chloe— she sees very few new patients, most of them celebrities (she rattles off some names and gestures toward the headshots on her walls). And if her new patients aren't famous, she adds, they are usually television producers to whom she owes favors for putting her on talk shows to discuss birthing methods.

While Rebecca strips, Dr. Belfour chitchats with Chloe, detailing the argument she and her husband, Alan, have been having about whether to sell their weekend house in Pound Ridge (she thinks they should) or to wait until the kids graduate high school (her husband's opinion). Frankly,

Belfour observes, given that her husband opposed the idea of the Pound Ridge house to begin with ("Slip on this gown, Miss Sugarman," she tells Rebecca), she doesn't see why she should consider his opinion ("Can you get up in the chair?"), and even if his opinion might be worth considering (Dr. Belfour snaps on a pair of plastic gloves), his logic is flawed because the weekend house is only an investment ("Lift the gown, would you?"), and therefore the market should dictate the time to sell (she kneads Rebecca's stomach as if manipulating particularly stiff dough).

The way she sees it, Belfour says, New Yorkers are living inside a real estate bubble, and she doesn't want to be stuck with a useless secondary property when the bubble gets pricked (she reaches for a white, pump-top dispenser and squirts three dollops of lubricant onto a glove). Belfour says she was smart enough to sell off her tech stocks right when dot-coms were cresting (she inspects Rebecca's labia, inserts her fingers). "Relax," she says, adding that she has an inkling that what happened in Silicon Valley will happen right here. "So you're pregnant," she tells Rebecca, then withdraws her fingers, removes the gloves, flings them into the trash, and furiously washes her hands. "Should we keep the bugger or not?"

Spontaneously, Rebecca feels a moment of euphoria and exhilaration, but this moment is so brief that she cannot entirely separate it from the anxiety that follows. Until now, she has easily been able to picture herself with Darrell and a baby in the apartment on West 106th, but here in Lisa Belfour's examining room, she just can't call up that image anymore. Perhaps Rebecca's expectations are too grand, but the most anticipated events of her life somehow always turn out to be anticlimactic. Her bat mitzvah was held on the same day as that of Mallora Reichlin, whose postsynagogue bash at the Copley Plaza was far better attended than Rebecca's comparatively sober affair at the jazz club Wally's Café. Rebecca missed orientation day at Yale because her father's rental van broke down on I-84 and they spent the night in a Days Inn outside Hartford, Connecticut. She feared that losing her virginity to her first college boyfriend, Ross Terpel—an event for which she had two diaphragm fittings at her mother's office—would be painful, but just as she was beginning to enjoy the experience, Ross rolled off her and asked if she had enjoyed the sex as much as he had.

She remembers Darrell's marriage proposal: at the costume jewelry counter of a San Francisco Woolworth's during the Modern Language Association convention, he purchased a seventy-five-cent ring and asked, "Should we do this frickin' wedding thing?" She can only imagine the experience of giving birth: she'll probably be doped up with Stadol, and Darrell will enter with the child, then ask, "So, should we do this frickin' circumcision thing?" She has always assumed that fatherhood will bring out the respectable qualities that only she seems to see lurking beneath Darrell's ever-more-prickly surface, but she has hardly seen Darrell at all lately, and now she can't help but wonder.

As Rebecca lies in a paper gown on cold vinyl in this strange doctor's office, the only reason she is not bursting into tears is that Darrell is not here. At least she has time to plan how to relay the news. She feels confident that, in the right mood, he will be ecstatic. Maybe he will even take her in his arms and cry; she has never seen him cry. She has heard him speak frequently of crying—"Man, when they called Florida for Bush, I was bawling, man"; "No shit, when I saw *Fly Away Home*, I wailed through the whole frickin' thing".—but never actually cry. She hopes he is having a good day, hopes his dissertation chair has told him something encouraging, hopes someone on rateyourteachingassistants.net has awarded him a smiley face and a "hottie" red pepper, because she knows how susceptible he is to even the slightest perceived affront. She doesn't know how she might react if she tells Darrell her news and he makes some caustic, vulgar remark.

After her appointment, Rebecca wishes she could spend some time alone to understand why the best news of her life comes accompanied only by a daze in her head, a wobble in her knees, and a sloshing in her stomach, but first she shares an uptown cab with Chloe, who spends the ride telling Rebecca how lucky she is to be expecting a child, yet once again demurring when Rebecca asks why she never had one herself. In the taxi, Chloe pesters Rebecca, asking, when will she tell Darrell her news, why hasn't she called home yet, is she sure Darrell will be happy about this? Chloe is so persistent that Rebecca, quite possibly the worst liar in the world, finally pretends to punch in a number on her cell phone, then leaves a bogus message: "Just got back from the doctor. Great news. We'll talk as soon as I'm home. Bye, honey. Love you." Leaving that message makes Rebecca even more anxious, not so much because it is a lie, but because she wants it to be true; it is the message she would like to leave but can't. Not until she returns home and gauges Darrell's mood.

The taxi drops Rebecca off in front of her apartment building. Chloe advises Rebecca to pay closer attention to her health now that she is pregnant; she removes the orange scarf she is wearing—it smells vaguely of her perfume—places it over Rebecca's head, and tells her to keep warm. It looks like rain, Chloe says.

Darrell is not home yet, and to Rebecca, their empty apartment feels heavy and dark as she enters, the air thick, as if she has to push through it. She places Chloe's scarf in the bedroom closet, takes off her clothes, and flops on top of her blankets. And when Darrell does come home, long past midnight, yet again, singing "(I'm a) Love Man" to himself as he sets down his book bag, she pretends to sleep, even though she can't sleep at all, tosses and turns and stares at the ceiling, then listens to Darrell snore on the futon. After Rebecca has dressed for her morning jog, Darrell is still sleeping; he doesn't stir when she opens the front door.

Just before dawn at the northern tip of Manhattan—when the uptown bars have closed and the soccer fans have gone home, but the newspaper and bread trucks have not yet started their delivery runs; when the late-night gypsy-cab drivers have turned their cars over to their morning partners, who are hosing them down before taking them back onto the street; when pigeons sleep in pairs on window ledges and atop air conditioners; when LaGuardia's last flights have landed but its first flights have not yet taken off—the sounds of New York seem to travel unusually long distances. As she jogs north through something colder than rain but wetter than snow, Rebecca can hear empty buses rolling down Amsterdam, wind rustling through the bare branches of sugar maples in Fort Tryon Park, the Hudson River rippling below, the day's first garbage truck beep-beep-beeping as it backs onto Broadway. And as she hears a B-flat clarinet playing atop Inwood Hill, the sound so smooth, effortless, and free that at first she mistakes it for a night bird, Rebecca feels as if she is in a different city altogether.

Higher up, the icy, leaf-strewn paths of Inwood Hill Park become steep and rugged; tree roots snake across the ground; bottle caps and shards of broken beer bottles claw out of black mud. Rebecca runs faster, as if, this early in the morning, gravity too is still asleep; it pulls her up instead of pushing her down. Through the criss-crossed maple branches above her, she can see patches of the dark blue dawn sky, and even though her breathing is becoming heavier, the breaths feel no more a part of her than the other sounds of the waking morning: a car speeding south toward the George Washington Bridge, a twittering sparrow, a cackling black squirrel, the whoosh of LaGuardia's first takeoff, the call of the clarinet.

As Rebecca runs, her mind not yet clear—it never truly is; it always whirls with memories of what she has done wrong and what she could do better—she wonders whether she may be to blame for all her own unmet expectations. Maybe, she thinks as she skips over roots, then passes under the low-hanging branch of a beech tree that scratches her below the eye, she spends too much time swinging back and forth between hope and fear. She should have more faith in Darrell. Deep down, he is truly a kind man, a gentle lover, capable of great passion; he just needs her patience, love, and confidence. Love requires hard work sometimes—she needn't protect Darrell all the time as she did early in their relationship when she told him she had had only a measly five sexual partners so that he wouldn't feel inadequate. She will return home immediately, she decides.

But just as she turns to head back down the hill, she hears a loud bark, and as she turns back toward the source of that bark, her right shoe slides on the ice and her ankle twists. Rebecca's pulse quickens and she throws her hands in the direction her ankle seems to be turning, ready to tuck and roll the moment hands touch earth. But the ice is too slippery, the mud beneath it too loose, and she is accelerating too quickly.

Her knees and elbows hit the ground at the same time and as she yells, she slides, her hands grasping at branches and roots until she slams into the trunk of a tulip tree; she has to close her eyes and wait for her heartbeat to slow before she can move again. She breathes deeply, brushes off her hands, tries to swat away the bigger clumps of mud from her clothes. The damp earth is now soaking through her pants; the sleeve of her sweatshirt is torn, and, through the hole, dark pearls of blood ooze out. She reaches for the tree trunk, waits for the panic to pass, considers briefly then rejects the possibility that the fall may have harmed her child. Still, this will certainly be a grand way to tell her news to Darrell, she thinks, her pants soaked, her sweatshirt ripped, her hands covered with muck like Caliban's. She lets go of the tree and takes a step, but a sudden pain knifes through her left ankle and she falls back down. And each time she tries to stand, the pain from her ankle pulses through her leg. The wind has picked up, the night bird has stopped singing, but the dog is still barking.

Herbie Mann reaches Rebecca only moments before Ike Morphy does; the dog approaches her by tracing a series of gradually tightening circles. He wags and barks as he completes one circle. He pants excitedly, then circles closer; he begins to make a third circle, but before he can finish, Ike steps between the woman and the dog. She was right, he tells her, this has to be the quietest place in all of New York, at least it was until this morning. Rebecca smiles, then wipes her hands on her sweatpants, but as she pulls herself up and tries to take a step, she loses her balance and, wincing, grabs for Ike's hand. "I gotcha," Ike says. Soon the two humans are proceeding downward gingerly, one walking, the other hopping, the dog trotting ahead, then circling behind, listening to the man and woman speak as they approach the bottom of the hill.

*WasthatyouIheardplaying**Idontknowhowditsound**Nice**Probablywasntme**Stilldontknowhowtoplayanythingnicethatsmyproblem.*

Rebecca, Ike, and Herbie move slowly over wet meadows, alongside the murky Harlem River, past a plaque affixed to a boulder—here, in 1626, Peter Minuit purchased Manhattan for sixty guilders' worth of trinkets. The woman has a hand on the man's shoulder; the man has an arm around the woman's waist as they reach Indian Road. Here, Rebecca leans against the hood of an old white Mercury Comet. She unlaces her shoe and takes off her sock, now gray and wet. She massages her ankle, already swollen, and presses her fingertips hard against the skin; she can see pale impressions between the patches of drying mud.

WherewereyougoingBackhomethentoworkWheresthatTheAmerican-StandardYeahIusedtoreaditbutithasntbeengoodinyears.

Rebecca sits in the back of a taxi with Ike and Herbie, who pokes his head out the window as the vehicle zooms south on Broadway. The city is waking up now, and the reality of Rebecca's situation is beginning to seem more concrete to her. Men are unlocking steel grates in front of stores and sliding them open, fluorescent lights are flickering on behind plate-glass windows in bodegas, barbershops, and storefront Realtors. Buses are moving more slowly now, stopping every other block to pick up umbrella-toting passengers.

WhatwereyoudoingupsoearlyCouldntsleepMeneitherNevercananymore.

As the taxi passes nail salons, Irish pubs, and liquor stores before turning west toward the Hudson Parkway, the woman rubs her ankle while the man moves his fingers up and down his dog's fur, the music in his head sounding clearer now. Damn, he wishes every note he's hearing didn't sound like a theme about unrequited love, but at least he can still play, he thinks—just a little more practice and maybe he'll call Maestro after all.

Ike glances over to Rebecca. Is she all right? he asks.

YesnofuckIdontknowChristImsorry, Herbie hears her say.

Ike asks Rebecca what's wrong.

Impregnant, Herbie hears.

Rebecca blurts out the words before she can contemplate why, when she has been debating how to tell Darrell, when she has been wondering whether to call her parents first, she feels most comfortable confessing to a man she barely knows.

"Isn't that good news?" Ike asks.

"Probably," says Rebecca. She blows her nose, then apologizes, "Yeah, probably it is; I'm sorry."

Thatsenoughsorries, Herbie hears Ike say.

The taxi eventually deposits its passengers at the corner of Amsterdam and 123rd; sleet has resolved itself into an insistent rain, which Herbie shakes off, spraying the cars parked outside Darrell and Rebecca's apartment building. As Rebecca limps, again clutching Ike's shoulder, she says she'll have to find some way to repay him—does he need to stay a few months longer in his apartment? No, Ike says, he'll figure something out; no use standing still anymore. Rebecca then proposes that they at least set a date so Ike can meet her father. Ike agrees as Rebecca buzzes her apartment—no response. Her keys are in her pocket, but she doesn't want to ask Ike to help her all the way up to her apartment; he's done enough already. She stands under her building's canopy and calls her husband on her cell phone to see if the buzzer isn't working. When she hears the voice-mail message, she tells Ike that Darrell is probably in the shower; Ike can leave if he wants and she'll wait in the stairwell for Darrell to help her upstairs.

Ike tells Rebecca he can wait with her—at least until Darrell comes down and tells him to get lost again.

DarrellsgotalotonhisplateHesreallyagoodguydeepdown, Herbie hears Rebecca tell Ike.

Couldafooledme, says Ike.

The three of them stand under the canopy—Ike, Herbie, and Rebecca. They watch the rain.

WouldyoumindwalkingupwithmeYoudonthavetocomein, Herbie hears Rebecca say.

They walk to the top floor with Rebecca pressing hard on Ike's shoulder while Herbie squeezes past and between them, dashes up then down flights of stairs, sniffs each door until he stops and sits expectantly in front of Darrell and Rebecca's apartment, tail wagging at a familiar scent. The door is double-locked; Darrell is already gone. And before Rebecca can invite Ike in, Herbie has already nosed his way inside and has started sniffing everything—the books and newspapers on the floor, the pigeon roosting on the planter outside the front-room window behind the unmade futon, the egg-stained plate atop the tiny kitchen table.

Rebecca apologizes for the mess, then apologizes for apologizing. Grabbing a tall black umbrella from the hallway closet and using it as a cane, she hobbles toward the bedroom dresser. While Ike stares at Rebecca's shelves ("Damn, you've got a lot of good books," he says), Rebecca searches for a bandage in the drawers, but when she says she can't find one, Ike says he'll run down to the pharmacy. Rebecca says she appreciates how kind Ike is being to her; Ike says that anyone who wouldn't offer to get a bandage for a hobbling, pregnant woman would be a jackass. "True enough," Rebecca says.

Herbie does not seem alarmed when Ike walks out. After all, Ike tells him *Berightback*, not *SeeyoulaterHerb*. Still, he cocks his head toward the door as he hears Ike walking down the stairs, then trots nervously about. Suddenly, he stops pacing and stands in front of Rebecca's bedroom closet. He growls. Rebecca asks Herbie what he wants. He pokes his nose against the closet door. Rebecca limps into the bedroom; Herbie wags, then growls again. Rebecca wonders if a ball is in the closet, remembers that her family's chocolate Lab, Mistress Quickly, used to whine at doors until someone found a ball for her. *Theresnoball*, Herbie hears Rebecca tell him, *justclothesandshoeboxes*. But Herbie growls again, so she slides open the closet door, and now the dog's paws are digging into boxes and he is sniffing Darrell's bunched Salvation Army jackets and Rebecca's dry-cleaned coats. Herbie puts his paws up on one box and then another until he espies the orange scarf that Chloe lent to Rebecca. And before Rebecca can tell Herbie no, he snags the scarf, trails it across the floor, snarling; he leaps over it, then whips it back and forth as if trying to snap its neck.

When Ike returns with a pair of bandages for Rebecca and two packets of cheese and crackers for Herbie, he asks his dog just what the hell he thinks he's doing. At the sound of his owner's voice, the animal immediately drops wet orange swatches of scarf onto the floor. He is slinking away to a corner and curling up amid Darrell's papers and books when he hears Rebecca tell Ike, *GodIwassoluckyyouwerethere*.

Yeahlucky, Ike says, at which Herbie pricks up his ears.

THE BUYER'S HUSBAND,
HIS DISSERTATION ADVISER,
& HIS LOVER

{ *This Time for Real* }

Now that he has divested himself of a deposit check worth well in excess of his entire annual Columbia stipend at Starbucks, which on Wednesday afternoons serves as attorney Gretchen Gruetke's uptown Manhattan office; now that he has delivered an earnest-money check to Megan Yu that is worth either twice his and Rebecca's monthly rent or a year's worth of pizza slices at Sal & Carmine's; now that the bank appraisers have come and gone; now that Bernard Ostrow has agreed to meet with him regarding his funding for the following academic year, Darrell Finneran Schiff is standing at the door to Ostrow's Philosophy Hall office shortly before another tea date with Jane Earhart. The idiosyncratic nature of Gretchen Gruetke's schedule—she's a licensed real estate attorney in New York, New Jersey, and Connecticut who works three days a week out of her Stamford home and comes into the city only once a week—had allowed Darrell to briefly procrastinate handing over the deposit check without drawing attention to his mounting ambivalence regarding just about every aspect of his future. But now, Darrell knows a time of reckoning is upon him, a time in which he will discover who he truly is and who he just might be becoming. Will he really continue to take the path of least resistance, become a married condo owner, struggle to complete his miserable dissertation? Or will he plunge into the abyss of the unknown—admit he has been treading water in grad school, then face the ultimate rejection by telling Jane he has fallen hopelessly in love with her? As he stands outside Bernie Ostrow's office, chewing Bazooka and wearing a battered vintage 8-Ball jacket, Darrell can hear Sean Connery's voice from *The Untouchables* urging him on: *What are you prepared to do?*

Darrell pushes open Ostrow's door.

Three long years after he passed his preliminary exams, Darrell actually felt frightened when Bernard Ostrow told him the department might not continue to fund him, since his T.A. evaluations were getting worse every year and he wasn't making adequate progress in his research. Consequently, Darrell spent the next twelve months working fourteen-hour days, preparing lectures, submitting inane articles and conference proposals, traveling to London to study the papers of George Eliot and to get serviced by Larissa, and to Sheboygan to deliver a conference paper and to perform a sex act on Millie Werling, only to return for his annual evaluation meeting during which Dr. Ostrow told him once again that his research was lacking, that he might have to apply for outside funding if he wanted to continue.

That time, when his funding was once again renewed, Darrell assumed this conversation with Ostrow to be little more than a yearly hazing ritual, and decided to blow off all his work. Even though Ostrow told Darrell he had only one more year to prove himself, the man's words no longer had any power over Darrell; when his adviser chided him, Darrell imagined himself as James Bond in *Dr. No* telling his would-be assailant he was out of bullets: *That's a Smith and Wesson, and you've had your six.*

For the subsequent academic year, Darrell based lectures only on cursory readings of CliffsNotes; he recycled research papers, presented them at conferences with only the font and title changed, spent hours on eBay and stealware.com bidding on action movie posters, or illegally downloading MP3s, or reading dozens upon dozens of blogs. He whiled away afternoons like a mad twenty-first-century Moses Herzog, typing letters to companies in hopes of getting free swag ("Dear Miller Brewing Company, the other evening while enjoying your Genuine Draft product, I was dismayed to find a sliver of glass in my bottle"). He popped virtual bubble wrap, racked up high scores playing games on damnimsobored.com. He assembled "fuck-off lists," enumerating archenemies, whom he'd tell to fuck off the moment after he nabbed his first job at Harvard. He composed politically incorrect Victorian rhymes, anonymously submitted them to journals, and tried to pass them off as the work of Robert Louis Stevenson ("When the evening sun goes down / We tell tales of recompense / The Christian gives away his pounds / The Jew doth hoard his pence").

When delirium truly set in, he invented obscene wordy-gurdies (Clue: Possible evidence of scrotum reduction surgery; Answer: Nutsack cutback; Clue: Possible sexual reconciliation offered by Popeye's seafaring nemesis; Answer: Seahag Teabag). Via spoonerisms and other forms of word play, he created porn titles out of pop songs, e.g., Paul Simon's "One Prick Tony," Dolly Parton's "Y'all's Come." Sometimes he banged on an out-of-tune guitar that he called "El Kabong," smoked joints, and invented fake early 1970s drug songs, such as "Sweet Mary Jane" ("Mary Jane's so sweet when I'm smokin' her / But The Man says that our love is wrong / So I've packed my bags for Amsterdam / That's where I can smoke her all day long / Sweeeeeet Mary Jane / Sheeeeeeee's the sweetest bud I know / She's part of what I do / She's everything I am / Sometimes you gotta take love by the gram"). And when Ostrow read him the exact same riot act, Darrell once again promised his work would improve but secretly decided that now he would work only at his own pace: slooooooooooooow.

Today, as Darrell enters Ostrow's office, he knows how their conversation should proceed. He should nod and smile while Ostrow rips him *ein neues Arschloch*—even though Darrell's mother has pointed out that Ostrow has barely published anything original since he achieved tenure in 1978 and now attends academic conferences only when they are held in exotic locations, where he lounges on the beach, enjoys massages with happy endings, rides the motor coach to tourist attractions with faculty spouses, and unsuccessfully hits on his female junior colleagues. When Ostrow finishes his monologue, Darrell is supposed to tell Ostrow please, losing his funding now would ruin his career—isn't there anything he can do? Ostrow will hem and haw, then say he'll do what he can, but this will probably be the last time he will ever go out of his way to help the son of an old grad school chum. A month or two later, Darrell will receive a form letter in his third-floor mailbox congratulating him on having his slave-wage stipend renewed.

But with the hour when Darrell is scheduled to meet Jane Earhart rapidly approaching, he wonders which is really more important—receiving another year of crap funding or meeting Jane on time. Ostrow is speaking pedantically of his concern for Darrell's scholarship, while Darrell begins to study more closely the trappings of the man's office, Ostrow's reward for years of hard labor: an unventilated room with a partially obstructed view of the Quad, a ceiling that hasn't been repainted since he was hired, a wall of creased paperbacks, a shabby corduroy sports coat, a battered squash racket, plus this opportunity to strike fear into the heart of some weedy grad student by threatening to take away his future opportunity to work in a dingier office, to wear a shabbier jacket, to play squash and live in subsidized housing in a city he couldn't otherwise afford or in a cluttered ranch house in some jerkwater college town—like Darrell's own parents, still riding around on the hamster wheel of academia: Margaret Finneran, still busily organizing marches on Washington and incurring the wrath of her English Department by issuing flaming memos regarding the suspicious disappearance of Post-its, Liquid Paper, and ballpoint pens; Peter Schiff, still intoning the same Wordsworth passages year after year to posses of hungover undergraduates in sweatpants and flip-flops. This is Darrell's own future playing out for him, he thinks, as he once again eyes Ostrow's squash racket; this is his future without Jane, a woman whom Bernie Ostrow never could have scored even in the 1960s and '70s, before the era of political correctness when harassment was part of the job description and leering academics like Ostrow actually got tail. Which future will he choose? *What is he prepared to do?*

Ostrow is reciting the usual bunk about the benchmarks Darrell should have reached eons earlier, but Darrell finally cuts him off. Listen up, he says, then, feeling energized and empowered by his own decisive tone, briefly segues into hip-hop lingo. He tells Ostrow he will do the man a favor and "break the situation down for [him]." As of this very moment, he is through with this whole clientelistic relationship, through working on the plantation for Mister Charlie. He tells Ostrow that he will "put [him] on the tip." Maybe he'll finish his dissertation, maybe he won't, but either way he'll do it on his own terms. He'll teach how he wants to teach regardless of what some spoiled nineteen-year-old *culo* writes on an evaluation; he'll publish articles if and when the mood strikes him. He'll prepare his lecture material if it interests him; if it doesn't, he'll blow it off because, frankly, he has a ton of more important shit to do. And if Ostrow doesn't like his new, honest approach, well, he can either renew his funding or kick his ass out, but Darrell won't be one of Ostrow's boys anymore and he won't trifle with this annual circle jerk.

Darrell bursts out of the office without even bothering to see Ostrow's reaction. Then he skips down three flights of stairs and out into the rainy February afternoon, gleefully imagining himself the hero of some 1970s cinematic paean to the American underclass, sticking it to the man just like Richard Pryor in *Blue Collar* or Ron O'Neal in *Superfly*. "You don't own me, pig," he bellows to whoever might be listening, even though he's never even participated in any graduate student strike for better contracts and working conditions. As he sees it, he might have the capacity to lead a rebellion, but he could never merely participate in one, holding some lame sign, chanting some dumb-ass slogan, beating a drum like a retard. Today, as he dashes across campus, flipping off Alma Mater as he does so, his only regret is that the door to Ostrow's office had been closed and his fellow grad students could not have heard him speaking truth to power.

Crossing Broadway, his heart pounding, Darrell feels certain he is in love. Nothing else can explain his newfound strength. In the past, he courted infidelity only when he felt depressed or angry or bored, only after he Googled Jessica Bosman and discovered her union ceremony photo album online. But at this moment, when he feels nothing less than exhilaration, when he doesn't care that his most recent, frownie-faced review on rateyourteachingassistants.net written by "C.S." calls him "the Renoir of bullshit artists," he is standing here on Broadway outside Caffe Swish, staring at Jane through a window, thinking only of her. This has to be love.

In the past three weeks, Darrell has seen Jane more than half a dozen times, and the most encouraging aspect of the hours they spend together is the fact that at the end of each date, Jane always leaves something behind—a book, an umbrella, a cell phone, a pack of cinnamon gum. Jane says her forgetfulness results from thinking too intently about the present moment to focus on anything else, but Darrell presumes that this is her way of ensuring they will see each other again. Either way, their time together has been blissful, frantic, intense, as with young lovers on their last night together, knowing one of them has only a few more hours left to live. They have consumed three meals together, eighteen cups of coffee, a dozen bubble teas, nine pitchers of ale, four steins of root beer. They have made love five times and Darrell hasn't even thought to ask if Jane has had more sexual partners than he's had. They have rented Rollerblades and traversed miles and miles of Central Park's paths, attended a screening of A Man Escaped at Anthology Film Archives, eaten steaming bowls of congee on the Bowery, and, most recently, ridden the Adirondack Trailways Bus to New Paltz, then made out in a cab bound for the aviation center in Gardiner. Once there, Darrell happily signed the most terrifying document he had ever read ("Are you willing to risk your life while participating in skydiving?"), then took Jane's hand and boarded the prop jet on the runway.

Thirteen thousand feet up in the air, before they took their first tandem dive, Darrell told Jane how daring she was, the most frickin' fearless chick he had ever met. But Jane just shook her head like a baseball pitcher rejecting a catcher's sign. He was wrong about her, she yelled over the din; the only reason she sought out danger was not because she had so few fears but because she had so many. Darrell had always been too chickenshit to ride roller coasters with Rebecca, who instead rode them with her dad or brother. But with Jane, he didn't feel afraid even while leaping out of a plane. Every moment he spends with her, he feels as if he is seated beside Tom Cruise playing the role of Vince in Collateral ("Most people—same job, same gig, doing the same thing ten years from now . . . Us, we don't know what we are doing ten minutes from now").

Seeing Jane through the Caffe Swish window, Darrell allows himself to wonder for the first time if she is in love with him. The fact that she is already here to meet him suggests this possibility. He watches her hands cup her glass, her lips encircle her straw as she sucks up the black tapioca marbles in her bubble tea. He watches her fingers grasp a small square of carrot cake and bring it to her mouth. Poetry and perversion immediately insinuate themselves into Darrell's mind, poetry of Shakespeare, perversion once attributed to England's Prince Charles. *O, that I were a glove upon that hand that I might touch that cheek. O, I wish I were a whole box of Tampax.* He stares at her neck, watches her hair brush against the strap of her knapsack when she turns toward the back of the café, then toward the door, then back again. He knows he is in love because he feels flattered that she appears to be looking for him. And he knows he is in love because he feels murderously jealous when he sees another guy approaching her.

A short, slender young man in a white ruffled shirt, black tuxedo pants, and an undone bow tie sits down beside Jane, puts an arm around her, then forks a chunk of her cake. Darrell knows he is in love because he has no clue who this clodpole is, and yet he feels his whole future being vaporized and replaced by the world he has just decided to escape, the future of play dates and pack 'n' plays, of sexy au pairs who'll call him a scumbag behind his back. *This is a dead man talkin' to me*, he says to himself. Darrell stands under the bus shelter, counting seconds, wondering when Jane will notice he is here, asking himself who is this guy next to her—this guy who makes Jane laugh harder than he ever has, so hard that she has to wipe her eyes with a napkin.

Looking up and down Broadway, Darrell can't help but think that every sign on every lamppost and in every window pertains directly to his predicament: ROOMS FOR RENT—soon he may need one; WE NOW SELL KNITTING NEEDLES AND YARN—all the better with which to impale or strangle himself; HALF OFF ROAST TURKEY—turkey, that's him. A sign in the window of Ivy League Stationers reads DO YOU NEED CHANGE?

Jane's tablemate finally kisses her on the cheek, grasps his umbrella, exits the café, then calls out to her, saying, "I'll see you at the fund-raiser, Earhart." The man steps outside, assesses Darrell with a knowing grin, and walks quickly into the wet day singing a show tune, whose lyrics, to Darrell, sound like "Just another cuckold in the rain." Darrell bumps the man's shoulder as he walks into the café and heads right for Jane's table; he doesn't say hello, just asks miserably, "Who was that guy?" Jane chuckles. "My husband," she says.

Darrell is now so upset and so in love and so happy to be with Jane and so sad she might not love him that he takes a beat before realizing she is joking, and even then, he can't find her remark funny. What time were they supposed to meet today? he asks. Jane says she doesn't know, maybe four? And what time is it now? he asks. Jane says she never wears a watch; she always loses them. It's practically four-fifteen, says Darrell. Oh, Jane says with a smile, she doesn't mind that he is late. Darrell points out that he isn't late; he's been waiting outside since four. Well, why didn't he come in? asks Jane. Because that guy was here, he says, that guy sipping her frickin' bubble tea, eating her frickin' cake. But she and Miles weren't having a private discussion, Jane says, he is just some guy with whom she has been writing, God help her, a *musical*. Darrell was welcome to join them; he could have pulled up another chair.

Shit, Darrell says, then apologizes, his voice wavering, his eyes watery. Can they start over, please? He can't think lately; something has been driving him nuts. Jane asks what has been driving him nuts, and even though Darrell knows this is the most embarrassing cliché he could ever utter, he says, "Baby, it's you."

Darrell Schiff does not know how to speak romantically, never mind the literature he is supposed to study and teach on a daily basis. Usually the only way he can express enthusiasm is by swearing. After he first reached climax with Rebecca by the Grant Memorial, he pounded his fists into the Arctic-themed mosaic bench and yelled, "Fuckin' A, man! Motherfuckin' A!" Driving back to New York from their first visit to the Sugarman vacation home in Croix-de-Mer, Maine, Rebecca told Darrell she loved him and he shouted out the window, "That fuckin' rocks, man! That shit just rocks!" And now, as he gazes across the table at Jane, he tells her he fricking loves her—can't she see that? Does she have any idea of how strongly he feels?

Look, Darrell tells Jane as he swallows hard, not pausing long enough for her to respond, part of him thinks that what he should do right now is walk out; she can lead her life; he'll lead his. But he can't do it. He is trying to imagine life without her and every time he succeeds, he feels as if he will burst. Looking at his life in the present, he is imagining himself as Gerald McGrew from *If I Ran the Zoo* ("But if I ran the zoo . . . I'd make a few changes"); looking at his future, he feels like a contestant on *Let's Make a Deal*, and Monty Hall is handing him a check for $10,000. And Darrell knows what Monty Hall's $10,000 check means: Monty Hall's $10,000 means security; Monty Hall's $10,000 means a nice bit of money, a lovely wife he'd have to be a crazy, selfish, self-destructive, mean-spirited asshole to lose, a kick-ass condo he'd never be able to afford on his own, maybe a cute little rug rat or two. All his life he has settled for that $10,000 check. He married the obvious woman, chose the obvious career. But he never had the *guts*—he almost says "nuts" but gets the *g* out just in time— to risk anything, to check behind Door 3. Maybe it's just a room full of Ball Park franks, but maybe it's what he's been seeking all his life.

Jane makes as if to speak, but Darrell keeps talking. He knows what she'll say, he says. He knows he's married, knows he has only just met Jane, knows he doesn't make much scratch, knows that ten dozen other pud-pullers, excuse his French, ten dozen other *suitors* are probably vying for her heart. But he's in love with her, and nothing else matters to him. Does Jane share any of these feelings? Any at all?

Jane's face remains immobile. She finishes her bubble tea before she speaks. Darrell barely even knows her, she says. He knows nothing of who she is.

Darrell says he doesn't give a shit. Too much emphasis is placed on people knowing one another. In some countries, husbands don't meet their wives until their wedding day, and some of those wives turn out to be cool. How well does he know her? Well enough to know he wants to spend the rest of his goddamn life with her.

It just can't happen, Jane tells Darrell.

Why not? he asks.

Because it won't, says Jane. She tells Darrell she has no interest in breaking up a marriage. Darrell counters by saying that whoever either of them has known before they met doesn't mean dick. Jane tells him that soon Darrell will tire of her just as he has apparently tired of his wife. Darrell says no, he can honestly say he has never had these feelings for anybody. Only when Jane stands, warns Darrell not to follow her, not to approach her in the library, not to speak to her ever again, then bolts out of the café and starts sprinting across Broadway, does Darrell begin to get the message. He considers whether he should quit right now—obey Jane's wishes; get out of her life; return to Rebecca, safety, predictability; finish his damn dissertation already; move into the Clemente condo; sire a pack of offspring. But once he has paid his bill, then zipped up his jacket, he notices that Jane has left her knapsack behind. He runs outside to return it, but she is already gone, so he heads directly for the grad student office in Philosophy Hall, makes sure it is empty, then locks the door.

Darrell has never rooted around in the drawers and diaries of his significant others. He has never been sufficiently in love to care about their secrets, and where Rebecca is concerned, his greatest fear has always been that she might not have any at all. Nevertheless, he unzips Jane's bag, reaches past the Chap Stick and the dented chewing gum packs to find a black leather wallet, which contains a driver's license with Jane's home address on East Eighty-fifth. Then, after he replaces the wallet, he takes out four identical, brand-new violet paperbound volumes of a forthcoming novel: *Wizard Girl, the Blue Kingdom, and Her World Made of Glass*.

Three paragraphs into the novel, Darrell is hooked; he realizes that this is just the sort of book he wants to be reading now, not another chode-sucking article—"Forms and Formations of Sexual Ambiguity in *Bleak House*"—in *Nineteenth-Century Reports*. Briefly, he can put out of his mind the fact that Jane has rejected him. He reads the book in one sitting; he loves books he can read in one sitting. He loves the straightforwardness of the writing—short chapters, limited vocabulary. He loves reading about cool shit like wizards and trapped maidens, dragons and unicorns; loves the idea of magical sheep in enchanted hills, of crimson mountains made of cherries, of carousel people who walk in circles all day long.

Once Darrell has finished the novel, having savored every page, he notices a folded sheet of stationery inserted after the last page. Darrell rereads the book's last sentence ("There was no glass left in the world made of glass. That was all right. The blue kingdom was no longer blue. That was all right too. And the wizard girl was no longer a wizard girl and she did not know if that was all right or not. But that's the way it would have to be"). He then unfolds the sheet of stationery, which bears the name and address of the Boldirev Agency; a brief note is addressed to "Gigi" from "Carter B." Darrell Schiff grins; Jane's wishes for anonymity will be no match for his mastery of Google, LexisNexis, and findanyonesaddress.com. In less than an hour, he learns nearly every secret to which Jane has clung for the past decade, the tragic childhood she is still trying to escape. He learns of Gigi Malinowski's mother's books, learns of the accident that claimed Gigi's parents' lives, learns of the boring short stories a young woman named Jane Earhart wrote for the literary journal of the University of California at Santa Cruz before she returned to New York.

When Darrell arrives back at his apartment on Amsterdam Avenue, Rebecca is asleep, but when he turns on the bedside lamp, sits beside her, and strokes her hair, she stirs. Darrell is so focused on what he has to say that he does not notice that Rebecca's ankle is bandaged or that shreds of orange scarf are scattered over the floor.

"Hey, honey," he says. Rebecca smiles and embraces Darrell, who asks if he has woken her. Rebecca says yes, but she needs to talk to him anyway. Darrell says he needs to talk to Rebecca too, and he should probably speak first.

And for one of the first times Rebecca can recall, Darrell speaks with the eloquence of which she always knew he was capable, and it takes a few moments for her to realize she is not dreaming. For Darrell does not swear, does not even use the word "fricking" or quote from *Conan the Barbarian*. As he speaks, Rebecca cannot remember any time when he has appeared so confident. He says he knows this is a bad time for this discussion, but there will never be a good one. The truth is that he has met someone. He didn't intend for it to happen, but sometimes, no matter what people intend, fortune intervenes. He cares deeply for Rebecca, and feels fairly certain that he will regret walking out on her now and that he will soon beg for her to take him back. And he knows she will be perfectly justified when she slams the door in his face. But he hopes she will accept what he is telling her and that they can still be friends. She needs a better husband than him anyway; he knows that he's been a drag, pretending to be rebellious when the truth is that he's been little more than a self-absorbed sloth. As far as the divorce is concerned, he'll take all the blame, and he won't lay claim to any of her belongings. The apartment will be hers alone—it is a good investment, and she can consider it his gift to her; he never would have thought it was his anyway and, as their broker has repeatedly said, Duke Ellington Boulevard looks like a great place to invest. He wishes he could explain his feelings better, wishes he could explain what it feels like for him to finally be in love, to know that, sadly, what he felt with Rebecca was not love at all, just safety and comfort. What makes him feel somewhat less guilty, he says, is that he is making this decision before Rebecca has become pregnant, long before they've moved into the new place and had a couple of kids. Imagine how difficult it would be to endure this madness if a kid were on the way.

Rebecca is too stunned to respond, but her eyes grow larger when Darrell produces *Wizard Girl, the Blue Kingdom, and Her World Made of Glass*, with whose author he says he has fallen in love.

"You really should read it," he tells her as he begins to pack his suitcases. "It can explain things a whole lot better than I can."

When Darrell appears at Jane Earhart's door, she smells of shampoo and cigarettes. Though she forces half a smile and a sullen thank-you when Darrell proffers her knapsack, she does not invite him in. But when Darrell says, "Can you hold on a second, Gigi?" she blanches. Then Jane Earhart née Gigi Malinowski mutters the word "Fuck."

THE ACTOR & THE BROKER

or

THE BROKER & THE ACTOR

{ *He's Having Trouble Deciding* }

Josh Dybnick will not receive his commission check for 64 West 106th Street, 2B, until closing day in mid-April, which is just about sixty days away, but he has already spent most of it anyway on lumber, paint, and equipment rentals, as well as a new suit from Barney's that he wears as he stands in the wings of the upstairs studio space of the Manhattan Theater Project. Although Joshua has appeared on a New York stage as recently as two and a half years ago (a Kidstuff Productions adaptation of *Snow White*, whose producer fired Joshua once he realized he could afford only six dwarves), he feels as if he hasn't appeared before any audience in decades.

Josh watches from the wings as the houselights fade out to a slow, steady count; the song "Something's Coming" fades in over a loudspeaker. The music swells; a screen is lowered. Two spotlights criss-cross each other and settle on the screen. Flashpots explode, a gong is struck; on the screen, a question is superimposed in white over a rear-projected image of a hang-gliding schnauzer: WHERE DOES A GREAT IDEA START?

A baby spot bursts on and follows Josh as he walks toward a centerstage podium. He has waited for this moment ever since he arrived in New York, waited to appear before an audience as the star of a show for which he has written the script; designed, built, and painted the set and the flats; focused the lights and programmed the special effects; chosen the sound track; even catered the reception. He can feel the audience's eyes upon him, can hear Mark Masler and Allie Scheinblum breathing there in the front row. This is why Joshua moved to this city; this is precisely what he came here to do.

The projected image behind Josh cross-fades to a new one—a wind-surfer upon an ocean—and a new phrase: WHAT MAKES A GREAT IDEA GREAT? More images follow—sweaty, mud-streaked men playing tug-of-war, a lone marathon runner crossing a finish line, a mountaineer scaling a snow-dusted peak. More words and phrases too: ASPIRE. ACHIEVE. IMAGINE WHAT CAN BE. A medley of inspirational tunes plays—"(To Dream) The Impossible Dream," "(You Are the) Wind Beneath My Wings," "(I Wanna) Soar," "(I Believe I Can) Fly"—one tune segueing effortlessly into the next. The music fades out, the screen fades to black, glitter tumbles from the ceiling, a wind machine blows soap bubbles across the stage. And then, another image is revealed: the dilapidated facade of the Manhattan Theater Project on Broadway. A phrase scrolls below it: EVERY GREAT IDEA STARTS WITH A DREAM. Flashpots. Smoke. Fade to black. Silence. Josh leans into a microphone. "We are standing on the threshold of a new city," he says.

Once contracts are signed, most of Josh's real estate colleagues consider their job essentially done. They move on to the next deal; they communicate with their clients and customers primarily through faxes, messenger services, text messages, and e-mail; they leave any unfinished business to the attorneys and lackeys, and send their junior colleagues to the final walk-through and the closing, having forgotten that these are the best places to get referrals. For his part, rather than merely overnight copies of the executed contracts and the canceled earnest-money and deposit checks for apartment 2B, Josh insisted on meeting personally with Mark Masler, hand-delivered all of his documents, then asked if Mark would be interested in learning about an investment opportunity. Ever since Harvey Mankoff named him executive director of development for MTP, he has asked all his clients the same question.

When Josh called Mankoff back after their first drunken conversation at the Ding Dong Lounge, Mankoff suggested they meet at his apartment, and on the day of the appointment, Josh left the Overman office earlier than usual to get to Harvey's place on time. He knew he could convince Mankoff that Miles was right: he, Josh, was just the man to reverse the fortune of Mankoff's theater building. He'd navigated the emotional world of residential real estate, mastered the corporate lingo of commercial sales; MTP would require both Josh's savvy and Joshua's artistic sensibility. But when Joshua arrived at Mankoff's bleak green door, then entered his dim, acrid apartment, his heart plummeted. The opening notes of "Conquering the City" that he'd been whistling to himself were suddenly drowned out, replaced by the voice of Peggy Lee—*Is that all there is to a fire?* Mankoff's ceiling was stained brown with water damage; his floor was warped; his windows appeared to be painted shut; his furniture seemed disposable yet permanent, as if the apartment's occupant had intended to stay for only a year, counting on his luck to change; but the luck never changed, and he had remained for forty. Was this what became of all actors, Joshua wondered—was this what the city did to them? *Was this all there was to a fire?*

Still, as Joshua sat with Harvey Mankoff on a lumpy, mustard-colored couch with tired springs in an apartment that he would have had trouble selling for more than half a mil, he could not conceal his awe of the man whom he had road-tripped in college to see performing *One-Man Misanthrope*. Joshua regaled the venerable actor with his purportedly new theater acumen, hoping Harvey would act as impressed as his clients usually did when he demonstrated just how extensively he had researched their properties. But Joshua's apparently stagestruck enthusiasm only made Mankoff suspicious. To him, business savvy was incompatible with a familiarity with theater in general and his own career in particular.

When Joshua told Mankoff he was sorry he was too young to have seen him perform King Lear, Mankoff, an odd glint in his eye, asked, "How do you know from Lear?" Joshua, assuming that Mankoff was enjoying receiving accolades as much as he always had, remarked that he wished he had seen Mankoff's legendary performance as Torvald in *A Doll's House*, tearing off his clothes and writhing naked on the floor during the play's final moments. "What are you giving me with Ibsen?" Mankoff asked. And when Joshua continued trying to discuss Harvey's craft, the man only wanted to discuss money. Mankoff's cameo appearance as Godot at the end of Beckett's play, in which he told Vladimir and Estragon, "So go already," then strung the two tramps up by the neck? "Barely cleared fifty bucks from that meshugas," Mankoff said. His sole cinematic directorial effort, the still-unreleased *We Are All Moby Dick*, shot underwater from the whale's-eye view? "That sure cost the studio a few shekels." Mankoff's controversial decision to demonstrate the universality of evil by refusing to perform Adolf Hitler with a German accent in the TV miniseries *The Year Was 1939*? "*Feh*, I'm still waitin' for my check."

And when Joshua effused about Mankoff's modernization of *The Nutcracker* in which Herr Drosselmaier appeared as Mankoff's archrival, acting guru Lee Strasberg, a glow-in-the-dark skeleton took the place of the fairies, and Green Berets served as tin soldiers, Mankoff grumbled that this was the only *Nutcracker* production in ballet history to lose money. Well, surely the money had never mattered all that much to Harvey, Joshua said. "No, that's the whole ball game," said Mankoff, who then asked whether Joshua was, in fact, a real estate man or instead a dog. Joshua smiled and squinted. Why a dog? he asked. "Because you keep sniffing my balls and licking my ass," Mankoff said.

For the rest of the meeting, Mankoff eyed Joshua warily. Whenever Joshua asked a question about Mankoff's hopes for his theater, Mankoff would say Josh was there to give answers, not ask questions. But when Joshua would make a concrete suggestion, such as updating the theater's technical equipment, Mankoff would either mock him ("What, you're a monkey now? You like shiny objects?"), fix him with a dark stare and say, "Is that what they teach in school?" or ask, "What the hell kind of real estate man are you anyway?"

Joshua made more detailed preparations for the second meeting—budgets, schedules, a virtual tour of the theater, a PowerPoint presentation—but Mankoff, apparently senile, drunk, or some combination of the two, seemed distracted all the while. First he misplaced his glasses, then he walked out while Joshua was trying to show him a mock-up for a prospectus and a proposed season of shows for MTP. Mankoff returned more than half an hour later with a soggy box of take-out Chinese, whose contents he studied with a nauseated facial expression while muttering "I-yi-yi-yi-yi" over and over as Joshua, who had been spending his time thumbing through Mankoff's depressingly yellowed *Playbills*, tried to schedule meeting number 3.

That night, following the second meeting, while Miles snored and wheezed on the pillow next to his, Joshua lay awake, replaying these encounters with Harvey Mankoff, the man who he had dreamed would someday play Polonius to his Hamlet; yet he felt no closer to appearing on Mankoff's stage than on any other. He felt the same sinking sensation that he had as a child in a taffy shop without any money, the same emptiness as when one of his dad's clients gave him a tour of the Cleveland Federal Savings vault and let Joshua hold a million dollars. "You'll probably never get that close to a million again," Paul Dybnick had told his son.

As dawn broke, Joshua thought about the kind of person Harvey Mankoff would want him to be, the kind of person Miles had told Harvey that Josh was, a person who, frankly, much more closely resembled Harvey Mankoff than Joshua Dybnick. He thought about the times when he had been Joshua and the times when he had played Josh. He thought about the roles for which he was always deemed too young, too clean-cut, too unassuming, too short, too nice. "What the hell kind of real estate man are you?" Mankoff had asked, and Josh realized that Harvey had no idea how actual real estate men behaved, only knew the parts he'd played in movies or onstage, where salesmen were either shuffling sad sacks taking the gas pipe or foul-mouthed cutpurses hustling swampland in Florida. Joshua had never met any brokers like the ones in movies, but those roles were easy to play.

The next day, when Josh called Mankoff, he barked into the speakerphone and said he would be late to their six o'clock appointment, and, frankly, since he'd be having meetings downtown, traveling all the way to Harvey's Upper West Side apartment was too much of a pain in his ass — why didn't Harve grab a cab down to the Meatpacking District so they could have dinner at Sawchuck's Chop House? Mankoff, noticeably more docile, agreed.

Josh arrived at Sawchuck's twenty minutes late, and though he had never been to the loud, glittering restaurant before, he acted like a regular. He wore his most expensive suit, but rolled up the sleeves and loosened his tie, as if to suggest that this was the cheapest one in his wardrobe. He ordered a gimlet straight up, tipped the bartender a five-spot, slapped Mankoff too hard on the shoulder, said, "How's it goin', Harve?" then asked who had given him this shitty table. Throughout the meal, Josh lectured and patronized Harvey, on two occasions calling him "son." While Harvey was relating a story of a sword fight involving Laurence Olivier, Josh said, no offense, but he didn't think they were having a business dinner so Harvey could tell war stories, and who the hell was this Olivier ponce anyway? Joshua felt a twinge of horror at the ease with which he was bullying the venerable old man, but one day later, he was MTP's executive director of development with full access to Harvey's Rolodex, keys to all of MTP's theater and classroom spaces, and Harvey's approval to host the first of several elaborate PowerPoint presentations to attract investors.

Working with Miles to hastily plan a viable season of one-man adaptations of classics for the MTP prospectus that he would distribute at the initial presentation required another sort of reverse psychology. Since he wasn't supposed to know anything about theater, he needed Miles, whom he named executive director of audience development, as his front. At first, he thought that Miles, hard at work with Jane on their musical, *Ellington Boulevard*, which Jane had suggested they structure around the theme of real estate ("That's where the real drama is," she'd said), would embrace all his ideas. But Miles's image of Josh seemed no more realistic than the one Josh was presenting to Mankoff, and Miles, even though he'd been born in Muncie, Indiana, seemed to enjoy treating Josh like a rube. To Miles, Josh was apparently little more than a wheeler-dealer sugar daddy—prudish, uncultured, hopelessly mainstream, and Midwestern.

Any evidence that might have contradicted Miles's assumptions never seemed to have any impact. Miles explained Joshua's cheerless Washington Heights apartment by theorizing aloud that this was only one of several properties that Josh owned; someday Josh would trust him enough to take him to his house in the Hamptons. Whenever Josh denied the existence of this Long Island home, it acquired additional rooms and floors, an ocean view, access to a private beach. Whenever Miles noted that Joshua's walls were decorated with framed posters of plays, that his bookcases were stacked three deep with scripts, Miles would say that they must have belonged to some former boyfriend, or that the books and posters were actually his.

Miles immediately mocked any show Joshua proposed to include in an MTP season but rushed to embrace any play Joshua questioned. So that, finally, when Joshua wanted Miles to approve of his translations of classic French literature, all he needed to say was "The one thing I really don't want to see is something old, boring, or French," after which Miles would tell Josh he wouldn't recognize good theater if it bit him on the ass. Joshua thought he might have trouble dissuading Miles from insisting on a prime-time slot for his musical, so he told Miles the show should open the season. *God*, Miles said, real estate brokers were so ignorant. You never slotted a world premiere to open a season, you workshopped it, then tried it out in a late-night slot—they needed to open with *One-Man Candide*. All the while, Joshua flattered Miles, called him "sexy pinup boy," told him he looked like Daniel Day-Lewis. Miles grinned proudly at every improbable compliment his boyfriend proffered. Not even in *Cyrano* had Joshua ever given such a convincing performance.

Sometimes, when his brain was all atwirl with dreams of quitting his Overman job and reading glowing profiles of himself in *American Theater*, *Backstage*, and *The American Standard* (to which he had received a new, free subscription), Joshua would ask himself whether to feel guilty for conning Harvey and Miles. But all success required some willing suspension of disbelief. A bare stage and some lights and you were standing on the battlefield at Agincourt. A hobbling gait and a pillow under your cape and you were Richard III. Tear down that wall, caulk those holes, varnish those floors, hide those glue traps, slap on a new coat of paint, reglaze that bathtub, and a 500-square-foot one-bedroom was worth a million clams. A blow-dryer, a good suit, and a business card and you were executive director of development for MTP.

For the PowerPoint presentation at MTP, in less than two weeks, Josh had photocopied and bound his prospectus, proposing five seasons' worth of one-man shows and Miles Dimmelow–scored musicals, paid for by ticket sales, foundation grants, and the money gained from selling the rest of the MTP lot for a condo complex with commercial space available for lease. He scripted his sales pitch down to every last gesture and sip of water. He designed and timed his slides; chose, then recorded, his music and sound effects. He told Harvey Mankoff to stay as far away from the theater as possible because no one needed to be reminded of the man's checkered career. He planned the route of the postshow tour of the theater space, which he would treat as an open house; first thing he'd do, he'd say, he'd take down these walls. Before and after work, he manned the phones, called his clients, leaned on Miles to call everyone on his mailing list. He wanted a full house.

Now, he has one.

As Josh Dybnick stands onstage, behind him is the screen upon which is projected one final phrase, THE NEW MANHATTAN THEATER PROJECT: AN IDEA WHOSE TIME HAS COME. Four flashpots explode, Carl Orff's *Carmina Burana* echoes through the theater, and the image cross-fades to a sketch of MTP, and on its marquee: *ONE-MAN CANDIDE:* THIRD SMASH MONTH! *ELLINGTON BOULEVARD:* A NEW MUSICAL! COMING SOON!! The houselights go up and, as Josh takes a bow, a scale model of MTP quickly descends from the ceiling and lands onstage with a dramatic and resounding bonk. The clapping grows louder.

Josh basks in the applause. He has often said that he loves an actor's work more than the acclaim, but this has always been the moment he likes best. Finally, he steps offstage and into the lobby, where Mark Masler, standing hand in hand with his new fiancée, Allie Scheinblum, is first to greet him. Maybe the three of them should sit down sometime and look over one of these prospectuses together, Mark says. Josh Dybnick shakes Mark's hand, nods, and smiles.

"Let's do it," he says. Then he walks past Mark to greet the rest of the crowd.

THE SELLER & HIS BROKER
& HIS NEW FIANCÉE

Moments after Mark Masler proposed to Allie Scheinblum—down on one knee aboard an ice-cold ferryboat bound for Ellis Island, where his mother had arrived with her parents eighty years earlier, and where he'd recently donated $1,000 to have their names etched into the memorial wall—Allie told Mark that she would prefer to elope. Mark said he chose the Ellis Island ferry for his proposal because, to him, it symbolized his family's journey from persecution in Europe to the promise of wealth and freedom in America. Nevertheless, Allie told Mark she still didn't believe in wasting money on fancy ceremonies, nor did she need her family's approval. Her brother was a Trenchcoat Mafia wannabe who didn't have the nuts to shoot up a school and so spent all his time at the computer "with his pants around his ankles"; her mom was a lush and a thief who would probably steal the floral centerpieces; and, as far as her estranged father was concerned, if anyone could even track down the geezer, he probably wouldn't be sober enough to remember the event anyway.

Still, on the morning when Josh Dybnick arrives at Mark Masler's office, ostensibly to once again update Mark on the smooth progress of the Clemente deal now that Darrell Schiff's name has been removed from all relevant documents, but moreover to discuss the prospectus and business plan for the Manhattan Theater Project, Mark and Allie already have a wedding date. Mark has paid the deposit for a ballroom in the Puck Building downtown, even though neither he nor Allie has any idea of who will actually come. Mark's first wedding was beautiful, his favorite aunt, Sandy, told him; the second was trashy but fun. But who would attend three weddings for anybody? How many gravy boats could a person be expected to buy?

Mark thought that his sisters, who hadn't attended either of his earlier weddings, would come once they learned he had undergone anger-management counseling and was reembracing the ideas of family and Judaism. But Miriam didn't return either of Mark's messages, and Bess only listened briefly to Mark rhapsodize about his fiancée before interrupting to ask how old was this Allie and how long had Mark known her, and when Mark told her, she laughed for nearly a full minute. Holly Kovacs-Pools, on the other hand, already knew how old Allie was, had served as Allie's den mother in Brownies, and knew Allie's mother through Hadassah and the B'nai Akiva sisterhood. But when Holly realized that Mark was engaged not to Marilyn Scheinblum but to her daughter, Holly exploded—how could Mark ever marry a "mixed-up, innocent little girl" who was as young as she had been when the two of them had married?

"What could the two of you possibly have in common?" Holly demanded, then said that her husband, Tony, had been right all along: Mark was just an "inveterate pig." Mark reminded Holly of the agreement they had made long ago, that in their conversations she was not allowed to use words he didn't know. But Holly didn't hear him, for Anthony Pools picked up the phone to tell Mark never to call them again, to stay away from their synagogue, and to stay away in particular from Ruth, Tony's daughter from his first marriage. Mark started to tell Tony Pools that staying away from Ruth wouldn't be hard considering that Allie could pass for a supermodel while Ruth Pools had hardly any tits at all and, frankly, looked like a guy, but Tony hung up before Mark could finish the thought.

That evening, in the Eighty-third Street mikvah, where Mark and Allie had bribed the night guard to let them in to bathe after hours, Mark considered how his first wife had scolded him because Allie was no older than she had been when they'd married. This was true; Holly Kovacs had been twenty-two. Tessa Minkoff had also been twenty-two on the day Mark married her. But while Holly seemed to regard this fact as proof that Mark had not matured in two decades, Mark found inspiration in the number 22, as if God was giving him one final chance to fix his life. Listen, Hashem was saying, you can start over again.

Allie captivated Mark. Every night he spent beside her, Mark would fantasize about standing under a chuppa with her, cutting the ribbon for the first Rolls Restaurant & Wash with her, attending fund-raisers and listening to Benjamin Netanyahu with her, being lifted up and down in a chair next to her while men in tuxedos clapped and shouted *Hai! Hai! Hai!* like sushi chefs. He imagined their pictures in the Sunday Styles section of the *Times*, where the entry would conclude with "The groom's two prior marriages ended in divorce." Less confident men might have felt ashamed of those two divorces, but to Mark they meant that he was in constant demand and that he was a perfectionist.

What difference did it make that he had known Allie for only a matter of weeks, that Allie was born just four years after he'd attended Camp Sholem in the Adirondacks, where counselor Melanie Rittenbauer took his virginity and gave him the clap while all the other campers were singing "David Melech Yisrael"? Age was meaningless; in many ways, Allie was more mature than he had ever been, and though, for the first few weeks, he struggled to keep up with her in bed, keeping up with her outside of it proved even more challenging. Without a doubt, she was the sharpest woman he had ever met; after her parents' divorce, she balanced her family's checkbooks and prepared their taxes, used her bat mitzvah money to buy stock in Exxon, IBM, and Dow Chemical, sold her shares four years later to pay for her education at SUNY, where she majored in business, ran the Libertarian Club, and hosted an anonymous website on which she offered stock tips and invested her own money whenever she got more than a thousand hits.

Allie made Mark honest, made him justify his beliefs. While they were bathing in the mikvah, she suggested that Mark reconsider his whole Rolls concept. The car wash/restaurant idea wasn't a bad one, but a better bet would be a car wash/tit bar called "Convertibles," which would advertise with the slogan "The Place Where Everyone Pulls Down Their Tops." Mark admitted that "Convertibles" might be potentially more lucrative, but said he found "gentlemen's clubs" too exploitive, even though he had only recently torn up his VIP card to Moneymakers Adult Cabaret, and only in part because it had expired six months earlier. Allie scoffed at Mark's high-mindedness. Hell, she said, strippers made good money, no one was exploiting them, and, *hello*, if some pathetic Viagra addict wanted to pay her fifty doubloons to whip off her top and flash her boobies, she wouldn't say no to that money.

Holly Kovacs-Pools had asked what Mark and Allie could have in common. Actually, they had just about everything in common. Allie liked getting rim jobs; Mark liked giving them. She liked going commando, and so did he. He liked taking pictures of her; she liked posting them on her MySpace page. He was into foot worship; she thought that was kind of nasty, but if he was into it, hey, knock yourself out. Yet, despite all these points of harmony, sometimes Mark enjoyed even more the few times when they disagreed, for they allowed him to mentor Allie, to school her in the new moderation he was trying to embody.

Wedding preparations represented one such area of disagreement. After Mark's proposal, which was consummated first in the ladies' room of the Ellis Island ferry, then against a wall in the receiving room where all of Allie's great-grandparents had been processed, Mark said he wanted Allie's family's permission to marry her, and insisted they drive to Riverdale that very night to get it.

At the Scheinblum dinner table, Marilyn, who became increasingly crass after each slug of gin, made lewd remarks while consuming the meal Mark had whipped up (turkey tetrazzini casserole, mashed potatoes with gravy, a red velvet cake with frosting that tasted just like the Spry shortening his mother had used). Marilyn said she was glad her daughter had found a man who could support her, but the size of his bank account was less important than the size of his package. Before she left with two empty shopping bags in hand, she agreed to Allie and Mark's union, observing that once Allie left home, thankfully, neither of them would have to hear the other party screwing all night, though she allowed that if Caleb got a little action for himself, he wouldn't have to spend so much time hacking or watching porn or whatever it was he did with his computer, at which point Caleb—a vegetarian who had refused to eat Mark's food—scarfed up every last morsel of turkey on his plate, then stormed up to his room, slammed the door, and started typing.

"Lemme talk to him," Mark said, remarking that sometimes boys needed to talk to a man.

In Caleb's bedroom, Mark pulled up a chair next to the teen's desk, and Caleb quickly shut down his computer before Mark could see what he had been typing. Mark told Caleb that he understood his rage. Caleb might not believe this, he said, but once he had been seventeen too. He remembered asking his pop to buy him Roman knuckles for his birthday, his pop saying no, and having to fight with a roll of quarters taped to each hand. He remembered his first year at Wadleigh when his grades bounced him from the football team for Homecoming and he got so pissed that he biked to the George Washington Bridge and chucked rocks down at passing cars to see if he could break windshields and make the cars crash. But even when he hot-wired his coach's Camaro, drove it to the parking lot of the old Acme Zipper Company, then placed a brick on the accelerator, leapt out of the car, and watched it slam into a line of Dumpsters, the person he was really hurting most was himself.

Caleb asked if Mark had really done everything that he had claimed, and when Mark said yes, Caleb said that Mark was "pretty fucking wacked." Mark said he wanted Caleb to understand that the two of them would be seeing a lot of each other at family functions, and if Caleb ever wanted to ask about women or drugs or booze or college, he'd be there for him. Caleb said he didn't have any questions about college, which, by the way, he wouldn't be attending since he had already read more books than some of the professors there. Furthermore, he didn't have any questions about drugs or alcohol because he'd been straight-edge for his entire life, and why was it that only former addicts felt a need to lecture others about drugs? And finally, no, chief, he and Mark wouldn't be seeing more of each other; as soon as he graduated high school and earned enough money to buy a car, he'd be driving out of this shit town with his girlfriend. Mark told Caleb that he still wanted his blessing, at which point Caleb told him to just fuck off already, which, Mark supposed, would have to suffice.

In the days following Mark and Allie's engagement, Mark continued to enjoy all of their disagreements, which persisted even as they sat in the front row of the Manhattan Theater Project during Josh Dybnick's presentation. Whenever an image flashed on the screen—a hang glider or a mountain climber, for example—Allie would make an obscene gesture or pretend to put a finger down her throat. When Josh told his audience that they should "dare to dream," that they should "reach the top of the mountain, then try to climb even higher," she remarked that this sales pitch was far worse than the ones she usually heard at United Jewish Appeal fundraising dinners.

But Mark loved listening to motivational speeches; he loved listening to leaders, loved the idea of daring to dream. He had heard and repeated upon countless occasions these same bromides that Josh intoned, and yet they still moved him. He felt shivers when he heard "I Believe I Can Fly," the same shivers he felt whenever he heard the theme to *Rocky II*, whenever he watched the entire rematch between the Italian Stallion and Apollo Creed and worried that he'd remembered the movie wrong and maybe this was the one in which Rocky lost. This wouldn't be such a bad investment, Mark told Allie in the MTP lobby—support the arts, get their names on a plaque, solidify their reputations as pillars of the community. But Allie just snorted.

Mark is alone in his office at 7:30 a.m. when Josh enters. Mark is somewhat saddened that Allie isn't here yet; her absence seems to indicate that she has no interest in discussing Josh's theater plan. Allie, who has taken over the recently dismissed Maria Aquino's desk and has postponed her business school plans in favor of a job as chief financial officer of Rolls Restaurant & Wash, is usually correct about matters relating to business. But Mark comes from a more sentimental generation, one more appreciative of high culture, and he figures he'll have to convince Allie that invest-ing in theater isn't a waste of money.

But then, just after Josh and Mark have begun their meeting, Allie bursts through the doorway and apologizes for arriving late to discuss Josh's "awesome prospectus," a creased copy of which is under her arm. At first Mark wonders if she is being sarcastic, but her blue eyes seem too sincere, her speech too effervescent. When Mark tells Josh he really isn't consider-ing an investment over $25,000, Allie glares at him. Well then, why are they wasting Josh's time? she asks. And when Mark finally sits back and lis-tens to Allie and Josh discuss increasingly large dollar amounts, he realizes with pride that she has given serious consideration to his statements and now understands the benefits of supporting the arts.

Later that morning, after Josh has left, Mark and Allie are spooning naked on the floor of the office. The blinds are drawn, the lights are dimmed to a barely perceptible gray, U2's "Crumbs from Your Table" is cranked up loud. Mark briefly nibbles on Allie's ear, then asks why she'd changed her opinion about MTP so quickly. Because Mark is incapable of bluffing, Allie says. If she had told him her idea in advance, he might have given both of them away—Mark doesn't really want to invest in some the-ater, does he? Why not? Mark asks, the building has a lot of history, a great location, just as Josh said. Sure, Allie says, but not for a theater; in fact, it's the perfect place for Rolls Restaurant & Wash.

And at this moment, Mark Masler feels a chill—the same chill he feels when he hears Rudy Giuliani speak about reaching your true potential, the same chill he feels when he hears the opening riff for "Where the Streets Have No Name." God, he thinks as he runs his hands through Allie's hair, as he drags his tongue from her neck to her *pupik* and back, *God*, he thinks as he feels around in a desk drawer for his box of Trojans, he loves this girl. Still, he couldn't do that to Josh, he tells her, steal the kid's dream.

Sure he could, says Allie.

But Mark just shakes his head. When Allie's older, she'll understand, he says.

THE BUYER & THE CRITIC

Rebecca Sugarman, now two months pregnant, exits the C train at Eighty-sixth Street and Central Park West with a purple paperbound book she has not finished reading tucked into a front pocket of her black leather shoulder bag; in another pocket, she carries a sublease form that she purchased this morning at Staples. As she emerges into the unseasonably warm March afternoon, she leaves a message for Ike Morphy, asking him if he has time to meet her and her father this evening at the Ding Dong Lounge. Then she walks toward an apartment building she has never visited to ring the doorbell of a woman she has met only once before.

Now that she has been back in New York for nearly three weeks after having spent far too much time at her parents' house in Cambridge, Rebecca has gotten used to doing just about everything alone. She eats her breakfast at Crepes on Columbus and prepares for the morning *American Standard* editorial meeting alone. She rides the No. 1 train to work and back alone. She soaks her ankle, wraps it, then tries to jog alone. She sees movies at the Lincoln Plaza Cinemas alone, browses the shelves at Morningside Bookshop alone, edits copy and dines at Toast, L'Exquisitus, or

the Abbey Pub, drops off her clothes at the dry cleaners, lies in bed reading one book per night, always alone. It is the state that she once hated
above all others—being alone—and yet she hasn't cried once since Darrell
left her, hasn't even fought back tears. If anything, she has felt a profoundly
surprising sense of relief; at least now she no longer has to concern herself
with whether Darrell will be a good or bad father, whether he'll finish his
dissertation, whether she'll have to work even harder to turn him into
someone he's obviously not.

   While she was back in Cambridge, Rebecca only felt sorrowful when
she realized that she hadn't become the emotional wreck for whom her
family had obviously prepared. Her mother canceled all her appointments
and forwarded pages to the other physicians in her practice, even though
Rebecca told her not to. Her father took her to the Brattle Theater for a
double bill of *Small Change* and *The Man Who Loved Women*, and kept
apologizing for having chosen movies that dealt with children and infidelity. But Rebecca enjoyed the films and wondered if she should have stifled her giggles during the funny parts. Rebecca's brother Brian drove in
from Maryland on his birthday, having canceled his appointment at the
fertility clinic so that he could comfort his sister, but when Brian spoke of
Darrell's "unconscionable behavior," Rebecca found herself defending her
soon-to-be-ex-husband if only to shut Brian up. She denied that she was
"a victim of Stockholm syndrome" and told her brother that, even though
she was touched by his offer to adopt her baby since he and his wife, Alli-
son, had been trying to conceive for two years, she could raise the child
alone.

   While at her parents' dinner table, Rebecca occasionally pretended
that Darrell's departure was affecting her more deeply than it was, for fear
of depriving her family of the opportunity to demonstrate righteous outrage
on her behalf. While the others were discussing the imminent divorce, she
would contemplate which articles in *The American Standard*'s Arts & Letters section she might assign either to herself or to Nick Renfield. Her father would notice that her attention had drifted, then ask if she was
thinking of What's-his-name. And she would have to say yes: Yes, it hasn't
quite hit me yet. Yes, I do need some time to let it all sink in. Yes, I really

do need to sit down. Or lie down. Or stand up. Or go outside. Or stay in. Or whatever. When, in fact, the topic of Darrell Finneran Schiff's departure had already begun to bore her. She had arranged to take even more time off from work—Chloe, who said she knew all about miserable, mendacious husbands, had told her to take as much time as she needed—but Rebecca returned early to the private office to which she had graduated now that art director László Ruffcorn had been replaced by his assistant Patricia Ko, whose previous professional design experience was limited to East Side Methodist monthly events calendars and who was happy to work in any cubicle no matter how small.

At *The American Standard*, defiance toward Chloe Linton's reign had now transformed into vague depression and specific dread. Most of the old guard had already accepted severance packages; most of the new guard had found other jobs. Nick Renfield and Norm Burloff were working freelance—$1 a word, no benefits. Those who remained spent their workdays polishing résumés, waiting for the moment when Chloe would ask them to a quick breakfast from which they would return to find a burly Romanian security guard at their desk ready to escort them out.

But Rebecca began to notice that her attitude was changing at the *Standard* too. She still never spoke rudely on the phone, but she spent no more time in conversation than was required. When Carter Boldirev would call to ask whether his client's book would be reviewed in the next issue, Rebecca would let his calls go straight to voice mail. Darrell would leave conciliatory messages saying he just wanted to make sure she was doing okay, honey, but Rebecca always star-sixed those messages the moment she heard his voice.

At the same time, Rebecca's energy seemed boundless, as if she were finally free of some great burden. Her ability to edit and rewrite copy to Chloe Linton's specifications was becoming so razor-sharp that, over pasta at Favell's, Chloe said she would fire webpage editor Bret Dalrymple if Rebecca could take over her duties, and Rebecca didn't even bother speaking up for her colleague. She no longer took issue with Chloe's contention that she could do the work of four mid-level editors and that, once Patricia Ko had designed a template for the magazine, the entire design team could be "replaced by button pushers." And when Chloe again reminded Rebecca that Purple Prose's marketing department would "shit a brick" if the *Standard* didn't assign a reviewer to *Wizard Girl, the Blue Kingdom, and Her World Made of Glass* since they had purchased a four-page advertising spread for the book, Rebecca did not say she found the text's first pages to be simpleminded, did not even say she was averse to covering a novel written by a woman with whom Darrell said he had fallen in love. Instead, she tucked the book into her bag, walked to the Thirty-fourth Street subway station, and boarded the C train bound for Elizabeth Fogelson's apartment.

Though some small part of Rebecca secretly relished the idea of Liz Fogelson's savaging the anonymous author's work, the former literary editor of *The American Standard* was not the most far-fetched choice to review *Wizard Girl*. In her heyday, Fogelson—while she was butchering just about every twentieth-century novelist—always expressed a great fondness for children's literature. One of her most notorious essays, published in a 1968 issue of *The American Standard*, was "The Greatest Children's Authors of Our Time," in which J. D. Salinger, John Updike, and Philip Roth were among the authors discussed. Though Fogelson raised hackles by asserting that those men were best suited for writing fairy tales, hidden within her jeremiad was a genuine plea to end distinctions between so-called adult and children's literature, and to return to the finely crafted romances and adventures that she had enjoyed so much as a child and that she tried to emulate while writing her own now-long-out-of-print children's books, which included *The Amorous Aardvark, The Bilious Baboon, The Caterpillar Caravansary, The Draconian Duck,* and *The Secret Sicilian Salami Society*.

Rebecca checks the building directory, smiles, and walks past the uniformed doorman, who smiles back and does not question her—she knows she has a trustworthy face. She heads for the elevators and rides up to 14. The door to her right is dark green and the paint is peeling; a NO MENUS! sign is pinned to it and two pieces of black tape are criss-crossed over the eyehole. The door on the left is bright red; there is a straw welcome mat with gray kitty-cats in front of it, and a God Bless Our Happy Home sticker above the buzzer. Rebecca makes a move for the green door, then realizes 14A is the red.

As she approaches the door (FOGELSON appears in shimmering rainbow letters above the apartment number), Rebecca hears voices and laughter—a party, perhaps, a puppet show, or daytime TV. She rings the doorbell and hears howling beagles, footsteps on a hard floor, then "Shoo, now! Shoo shoo shoo!" When she first met Liz Fogelson, the woman appeared wan, bleary, polite to Rebecca as a matter of course, yet ready to lash out if Rebecca challenged her on any point. But the woman who answers Fogelson's door resembles less the terrifying figure who interviewed Rebecca than Fogelson's improbably glamorous 1971 author photo—skin pearl white, chin jutting outward, eyes black and penetrating, the hint of a knowing smile upon her face. Most disarming is Fogelson's uproarious and infectious laugh, not bitter at all, but playful, as if Rebecca has come to the door dressed as a clown, bearing a bouquet of balloons.

Rebecca had presumed that Fogelson would not remember her. But after the woman has used a stockinged foot to clear away from the entrance her quartet of beagles (named Eenie, Meenie, Miney, and Moe), she proffers a warm handshake and invites "Rebecca, my talented child" into her apartment.

Apartment 14A is on the top floor of one of the most desirable blocks on the Upper West Side; however, since some apartments in this neighborhood are still rent-controlled and Rebecca knows that *The American Standard* never paid well, she would not be shocked to see old, dingy furniture; warped, unvarnished floors; or a lopsided radiator. But the giant plasma screen TV surprises her. So do the piles of board games and puzzle boxes on the floor. Also, the white shag rug and the hot-pink vinyl couch with canary yellow piping and the half-finished tomato jigsaw puzzle on the dining room table and the open cabinets full of sugared cereals and Cheez Whiz. And yet, what surprises Rebecca even more is what is not here: books. Rebecca does not see one book anywhere.

Rebecca knows it is wrong to judge a person by her belongings or to pity a woman who apparently has gone mad. But as she watches Elizabeth Fogelson's dogs leap over LEGO sets and joysticks, she feels exceedingly uncomfortable. When Fogelson asks if Rebecca wants some grape or straw-berry soda, Rebecca quietly says no, thank you, water will be fine. When Fogelson asks if she'd like some cereal, Rebecca thanks her again but says that she just ate. As they sit at a cluttered kitchen table where Fogelson pours herself a bowl of Cocoa Puffs and a glass of strawberry milk, a thought occurs to Rebecca. She asks hopefully whether Fogelson's grand-children are napping, at which Liz Fogelson claps her hands, then laughs more loudly than ever. No, she says, she never married and she is the only child in this apartment. She eyes Rebecca with a glimmer of glee. Well, she asks, how's life at the old rag-a-zine? Has Linton fired everyone and "turned it around" yet?

Rebecca nods grimly. She now understands that what she's suspected all along was true, that Chloe fired Liz or forced her out. She looks around this madhouse and everywhere sees signs of depression. What would it be like, she wonders, to have your livelihood taken away from you after more than forty years? Suddenly, it all begins to make sense, this grown woman unable to cope with adult problems, turning herself into a child. I'm so sorry, Rebecca says. Sorry for what? asks Fogelson. For everything that happened to her, says Rebecca. Nothing happened to her, Fogelson says, she just left the *Standard* when the time was right. Rebecca nods un-certainly; when was that? she asks. When you came along, dear child, Liz Fogelson says.

As Liz Fogelson slurps her cereal, Rebecca says she doesn't understand. She thinks back to her interview in Fogelson's *American Standard* office, where the two of them did not find any points of agreement. When Fogel-son asked her to name the twenty-five worst books she'd read in the past year, Rebecca said she read only books she thought she would like, and one of the reasons she dropped out of Columbia was that, there, she fell in love with just about every book she read and didn't have the stomach to criticize them. Liz Fogelson laughed so hard at this response that Rebecca worried the woman might be having a coronary. How could she possibly have influenced Liz's decision to leave? Rebecca asks.

Fogelson lifts her cereal bowl with both hands, brings it to her lips and tilts it, gulping the remaining milk, which has become tan and gritty with

Cocoa Puffs residue. She tells Rebecca that the interview forced her to re-assess her entire view of literature. For years, she had built her career on demonstrating how authors didn't measure up to their forebears, imagin-ing some idyllic, literary Eden that contemporary writers had betrayed. The truth was, by the time Rebecca had come to interview with her, she'd realized she was just sick of books altogether.

"Sick of books?" Rebecca asks. But surely Liz loves books; only some-one with so much appreciation for literature could write about it so pas-sionately.

Liz Fogelson weighs Rebecca's argument, shrugs, glances down at her *TV Guide*, and dog-ears a page. Nope, she says, actually she's just sick of them. For a while, she had thought she just didn't like contemporary writers—the sense that their sentences had been flogged to death in some workshop, the experimental punctuation and typography, the use of non-linear narrative to disguise the lack of any through-line. But then, after meeting Rebecca, she reread some of her favorite authors. She did see why she had once admired their talent, but she couldn't say she wanted to piss away more time rereading their work. Books—she just had to admit that she couldn't stand the damn things anymore.

She has never even liked holding a book, Fogelson says now—hardbacks are just too heavy, they make unsightly creases on her belly if she tries to read them while lying down, and she hates the tiny print of paperbacks, hates how the pages always come apart when she bends the spines. She hates reading book-jacket blurbs; they're all full of lies. She says that she doesn't like authors much either, doesn't understand the effort they put into an essentially useless product, doesn't see why an author can't write just one book, be done with it, then do something productive with his or her life. She has never enjoyed the company of writers, and, by the way, she has never had a satisfying sexual experience with one either—the short story writers tire too easily; the novelists have no sense of pacing; the poets know only how to pleasure themselves; the mystery writers have poor bod-ily hygiene, and the sci-fi writers are even worse in that department; the ac-ademics are too damn grateful and accommodating; the historians just lie there the whole time and expect someone else to do all the work; the journalists have no sense of humor; the essayists are all panting, slobbering horndogs; and as for Norman Mailer, well, that man's just gross. She can't understand why publishers continue to print so many books—aren't there already enough to go around? Really, she asks Rebecca, does she truly enjoy reading?

Of course, Rebecca says; she still can't imagine an experience more wonderful than curling up in bed beneath warm covers, in the glow of a good reading lamp, seeing life through another human's eyes, imagining entirely different worlds into which she can escape. Liz Fogelson pauses for a moment, regarding Rebecca as if she is some delicate, endangered animal, then shakes her head with wonder. Well, she says, Rebecca has just explained why she is better suited to her job. As for herself, she has now become intrigued by so many things she once pooh-poohed. TV, for example. Once she loathed it, but now she loves flipping through every one of the zillion channels in her digital cable package. She spends nights on her laptop, watching videos on YouTube, betting on poker, writing to the men she meets in chat rooms with whom she has such interesting conversations. She even thinks she may have fallen in love with one.

Rebecca says that she is glad to hear Liz is enjoying her retirement, but she sees that she has come here for no good reason. What reason? Liz Fogelson asks. An impish smile forms on her face. Why, she asks, what sort of mischief has Rebecca been planning in that evil mind of hers? No mischief, Rebecca says, she had only wondered if Liz might still be interested in writing book reviews, but clearly, she isn't. Liz Fogelson says oh, now she is intrigued. What book could be so important that Rebecca has bothered to seek her out? It must be something so wretched that only she can torpedo it out of existence. Not necessarily, Rebecca says, she always hires fair critics. Nonsense, what a horrible liar Rebecca is, says Fogelson, she has never been a fair critic. No, no, she says with a grin, Rebecca must have brought something truly dreadful. She reaches her hands out in front of her, opening and closing them rapidly. "Let me see, let me see, please please please," she says.

Rebecca reaches into her shoulder bag and takes out the purple paperback book, which Fogelson snatches out of her hands. She flips to page

67, paragraph 3. It is one sentence long: "Iphigene vowed she would disappear the moment anyone learned her name." Who wrote the book, Fogelson asks, an adult or an infant? Rebecca shrugs and says she doesn't know—no author is listed. Liz Fogelson remarks that this is the oldest trick in the book: disguising the identity of an author in order to give heft to substandard work. Does Rebecca really want her to review this book? She will do it, but only on one condition: she wants to know why Rebecca has asked her. Rebecca stammers, then says that Liz is the sharpest critic she knows. Yes, yes, Liz says with a wave of the hand, but why this book in particular? Rebecca says that she recalls Fogelson's fondness for children's books. Sure, sure, Fogelson says, but that isn't the reason either. And in this moment, Rebecca feels suddenly trapped, feels that she has already turned into a petty, dishonest, and cruel person. But though she considers retracting the offer, petting Liz Fogelson's dogs good-bye, then taking the book with her and apologizing, she does not move, nor does she say she's sorry. The final time Liz asks why she wants her to review *Wizard Girl, the Blue Kingdom, and Her World Made of Glass*, Rebecca barely recognizes her own voice. "Because my husband left me for the author," she says. Liz Fogelson laughs riotously. Oh, she is evil, she tells Rebecca, a girl after her own heart, evil to the core.

THE TENANT & THE
ORIGINAL FUNKSHUNS &
THEIR NEW MANAGER & THE
BUYER & THE BUYER'S FATHER

On the way home from the 106th Street dog run, Ike Morphy stops at a pay phone and retrieves his message from Rebecca Sugarman telling him that she and her father will be at the Ding Dong tonight. It would be a relief for Ike to meet and talk with some people, Rebecca especially, but right now he has other, more pressing concerns. Ike takes a breath and dials Maestro's number. He has been putting off calling Maestro, having told himself that only after he regained more of his stamina and fluidity would he ask about rejoining the band. He told himself that Herbie might react poorly if he started playing music again and going out on the road. But the fact is that Ike's playing has already become nearly as strong as it used to be; as for life on the road, Herbie could come with him and would probably love it. And as far as Ike's original material is concerned, he will never find enough session gigs or club dates in time to earn the money he needs for the kind of apartment he wants.

As he stands at 106th and Columbus, phone in hand, Ike expects that one of Maestro's minions will answer his call; Maestro always liked having people work for him. Even when they first became friends—when Ike was working odd jobs for Jerry Masler and hustling $30 and free drinks on off-nights at Augie's; when Maestro was named John Wilkins Jr. and was spending his last summer off from Princeton working in the file room of his dad's medical practice, hanging out at jazz clubs, and organizing his band—he always liked being in charge.

At the first Funkshuns meeting, Maestro insisted that the other band members take nicknames, all from famous sidekicks: Ricki Hodge would be Sancho; Ron Pickett, Tonto; Eddie Watts, Watson. Toward the end of the meeting, Tonto Pickett pointed out that Ike still didn't have a nickname. Ike didn't need one, Maestro responded; Ike would always be Ike.

Throughout the years Ike spent with the band, from the adolescent pleading of the debut single "Can't We Funk Jus' a Lil' Bit?" to the confident swagger of "Won't Funk U 'Less U Beg," Maestro's comment about Ike being Ike held true. If band members showed up late, Maestro docked their pay; not Ike's. Every Funkshuns show was identical, every note and move scripted, save for Ike's. If Ike didn't want to wear the same black suits as everyone else, he didn't have to. He could wear sunglasses for a whole show, turn his back to the audience, walk offstage during songs he didn't like, go off on some ten-minute riff right in the middle of a tune, blow off photo shoots and interviews, play his clarinet upside-down, breathe or hum into the bell instead of the mouthpiece, show up at rehearsal fucked up, and if any roadie cracked wise about Ike or looked too long at his girlfriend Muriel's ass, Maestro fired him. "Ike's rules," Maestro would always say. "If you don't like 'em, there's the door."

Even though nearly seven years have passed since Ike walked off the stage at the Arie Crown, Ike's rules still seem to be in effect; Maestro answers his call. Ike doesn't even have to identify himself; Maestro recognizes the voice immediately—"My man," he says. Ike has never completely trusted Maestro, or, rather, has always trusted Maestro—who based his approach to the music business on Sun-tzu's *The Art of War* ("Make no move unless you see a clear advantage")—to do only what would benefit Maestro. So when Maestro says he isn't busy today and would love to see him, Ike is leery but says he'll get on a train and come right over—he'd like to talk.

"I like to talk too," Maestro says.

Ike exits the subway at 135th Street and walks along St. Nicholas Park, then turns west when he reaches 139th. Crimson banners flutter from lampposts: YOU ARE NOW ENTERING THE ST. NICHOLAS HISTORIC DISTRICT. The street's late-nineteenth-century townhouses, most already renovated, a few still in the process, remind Ike of his favorite exhibit that he saw as a child at Chicago's Museum of Science and Industry: the idyllic Home of Tomorrow with its giant see-through dishwasher and washing machine. Here on Strivers' Row, Ike can see not only the present, but also the past and future. Through those windows that aren't masked by taut sheets of opaque plastic, he sees unfinished wooden beams, stacks and bundles of two-by-fours, scaffolding, the skeletons of what homes once were and what they are becoming.

Ike is still amazed by the fact that a city can change so quickly, not just year to year but week to week, from something so familiar into a place he can barely recognize. Time passes faster here, almost as if it moves in dog years—seven times faster than anywhere else he's ever been. Chicago always felt slow, solid, flat, deceptively permanent. On the South Side, nothing ever seemed to change—same stores, same churches, same sand on Rainbow Beach, same wild lake, same neighbors until someone was evicted or somebody died. In Chicago, he was always the same person, always the same age. One reason he warmed so quickly to New York was that whereas Chicago seemed to be all steady 4/4 time, in New York, the meter was constantly shifting.

Ike rings the doorbell of Maestro's once-shabby building that is now the prettiest townhouse on 139th. No name beside the bell anymore, but now there is only one button. No butler answers, no personal assistant—no, it is Maestro John Wilkins Jr. himself, swigging from a bottle of orange Vitamin Water. He wears clogs and a belted black satin robe over a black tank top and shorts. No doubt he has a dozen outfits just like this one; the man could never be bothered to shop for clothes, he'd see someone else wearing something he liked, then order a dozen. Same with food: he looked at other people's plates and ordered that same meal for breakfast, lunch, and dinner until he got sick of it. "Just like Elvis," he said. Early on, before the band started selling out concert halls, he would bedeck himself with jewelry; now, he wears only one piece—a gold wedding band. Maestro kisses the air by each of Ike's cheeks, bows, then opens the door the rest of the way so Ike can take in the view.

The interior of Maestro's building blends opulence with austerity, no more belongings than necessary but each one worth a small fortune. The floors are marble, but only a few pieces of furniture are in any given room; only a handful of artworks are on the pristine white walls, but every one of them is a Warhol, a Rosenquist, a Barbeito, a Paschke, or a Flavin. Someone must have told Maestro that these were good artists, Ike thinks as his old bandmate leads him up to his outdoor roof deck, where he tells Ike he has moved his exercise equipment now that the weather is starting to get a bit warmer. Ike remarks that Maestro appears to have done well for himself. Maestro shrugs. Maybe so, he says; at any rate, he won't unload the building for at least another year.

Maestro offers Ike a seat on the wooden bench that wraps the roof deck's perimeter, then proffers a glass of club soda. He lets Ike do most of the talking while he takes off his robe, folds it, places it on the bench, puts on a pair of gym shoes, mounts his stationary bike, turns on the Lifecycle's TV, and pedals. The TV is tuned to the Financial Network—as Ike speaks, he can see numbers reflected in Maestro's glasses.

While discussing how he spent these past years, Ike waits for Maestro's mood to shift, for some caustic word to issue forth from the man's lips as it always did during band meetings, for him to make some cutting reference to Ike's ignominious departure and presumptuous return. But as the conversation proceeds—Maestro's attention divided equally between Ike and the stock market—the man offers no hint that he ever felt slighted. He offers condolences for the passing of Ike's mother, then asks if Ike ever hears from Muriel. Ike is listening for jealousy or admonition—Maestro often seemed resentful when Ike's stoned or sullen demeanor attracted more women than Maestro's calculated gentlemanliness, and Ike always sensed that Maestro, who only ever seemed to pursue women whom others found attractive, thought he and Muriel would make a better match—but Ike can't find it. He tells Maestro that after he quit the band, he quit just about everything else too—drinking, smoking, playing music, Muriel too. No love had ever really existed between them anyway—all they had in common were bad memories, crossword puzzles, books, negative energy, and need. Yeah, Maestro says, sometimes you have to let people go.

Finally Ike stands, places his forearms on the cement ledge, and gazes out at the city. Yes, spring is approaching already, and buds are forming on the trees in St. Nicholas Park. Trucks emblazoned with PHASE ONE DEMOLITION are stalled on 139th. Turning to the south, Ike sees cranes, girders, half-finished high-rises. He clears his throat and turns to Maestro. He says that lately he's been wondering if he made a mistake by leaving the band. Then he stops and swallows. No, Maestro tells Ike as he pedals, he doesn't think so; Ike did what he thought was right at the time, and no one can ever fault a man for doing what he thought was right. Ike was always Ike, played to his own rhythm, never gave a damn about what others thought.

Ike shakes his head. He doesn't know about all that anymore, he says. Sometimes he wonders whether the reason he acted as if he cared so damn little about everything was that he really cared too damn much—about the music, about his family. He figured the only way he could cope was to keep to himself. But that was a selfish way to live and he can't live that way forever; he realizes that he has to start playing again. Still, he's trying to play for different reasons now, not to blow away the anger and the memories, just for the joy of doing it. He thinks he could contribute to the band again, take up where he left off.

The timer on the bike dings and Maestro stops pedaling. He picks up a towel and wipes his chest and forehead, then walks to the roof door and exits, leaving Ike alone outside in the fading afternoon. The sun has disappeared behind a cloud, and a new, sharp chill is in the air. Ike looks at the stationary bicycle, at Maestro's empty hot tub. The emptiness reminds him of Herbie at home alone on his pillow, time passing seven times faster than it does for Ike; he considers if the animal even understands the passage of time, or if each time he leaves his dog alone is an eternity, a minute no different from a day or a year. At the same time, he wonders if a stranger could take his place in his apartment, feed Herb, walk him every day and night, and the dog would feel just as happy.

Maestro pushes open the roof door and, smelling of baby powder, reenters the outdoor area. You know, he says as he takes a seat on the bench beside Ike, he's been waiting almost seven years for this conversation. When Ike walked offstage, he admits he felt jealous of him, even admired him, because he had no idea how Ike could leave right when everything was clicking. For years he was pissed off at Ike, leaving as if their time together didn't make a damn bit of difference, abandoning Muriel like that, pretending he didn't matter to people. Ike may have been perfectly content working his construction gigs, caring for his dog, and taking trips to Chicago to see his mom, but he missed Ike, Maestro says. Ike was the only member of the band he could ever talk to about music; in fact, he says he wasn't surprised to hear Ike's voice on the phone today because he has imagined so many conversations and arguments with him. But the truth is that grudges are never good for business. Ike is still one of the best players he knows, and he has no good reason to stand in Ike's way. If Ike really wants to rejoin, though, he won't create any more special rules for him; there will be suspensions for missing rehearsals, docks in pay, zero tolerance for drugs or liquor. Ike says he never wanted to be special, and he's clean now. Well, then, welcome back, brother, Maestro says.

Maestro shakes Ike's hand, then adds that they should put their agreement down on paper now, sign their names to it before they have time to reconsider; remember, this is a business, he says with a smile. Maestro puts an arm around Ike; all they need to do, Maestro says, is find a contract, sign it, and Ike can be on his way until rehearsals start up again—his manager can draw up the contract. Ike asks if Maestro's manager can do paperwork on such short notice. She'd better, Maestro says; she's his wife.

Ike says he had noticed Maestro's ring. Yeah, Maestro says, he's settled down, has his priorities in order now—money's still number one, but at least some things are vying for number two. He never would have imagined himself married, but he's been thinking about having some kids, and lately, everything he writes turns out to be a love song. Love does mad things, he says.

Maestro beckons Ike to follow him through the roof door, down two curved flights of metal steps, back to the third floor, where light prisms through stained glass, casting blotches of red, yellow, and blue upon the white marble floor. Ike and Maestro approach a glass-enclosed office and recording studio with a steel door. Ike says he'll start playing nonstop now; on days when the band isn't rehearsing, he will keep heading out to Inwood, start playing at sunrise. Only when Maestro puts his hand on the office doorknob does Ike take note of the woman seated in the office with her back to him. She is shuffling the stacks of paper in front of her on a desk beside a mixing board and a silver laptop. Maestro asks Ike what the matter is. Ike keeps staring through the glass.

The hair is straighter than Ike remembers it. A different color too—hints of blond where all used to be black. But he recognizes the sweep of her neck as it descends into the iridescent royal blue of her blouse, knows too well the bend of that arm. He doesn't recognize her outfit, why should he, so many years have passed. He remembers seeing her, that last time, gazing out the back window of the gypsy cab stalled on Columbus before he walked away from her—*How do I look? That's how I'm doing—as well as I look.* Maestro should have told him, Ike says.

What for? asks Maestro. For courtesy?

Something like that, Ike says.

Like the courtesy he had shown her? asks Maestro.

Ike makes as if to speak, but Maestro interrupts. No, he says, he won't have this conversation, not this way. Look, he says, he didn't have to talk after he heard Ike's voice on the phone, didn't have to invite him into his home, offer him something to drink. When Ike asked to come back, he could have told him go to hell, could have said the same thing Lennon said to McCartney—*It's not like the old days, mate; you can't just stop by*. This is the deal, he says—rejoin the band? Yeah, sure, but only with Maestro's rules now. Ike plays the way Maestro tells him to play. Ike's schedule is Maestro's schedule, Ike's rhythm is Maestro's rhythm, and Ike's woman is Maestro's woman. If Ike doesn't act like a team player, he's gone. If Ike misses rehearsal, he's gone. If he does anything to piss Muriel off, he's gone too. She appeared at Maestro's door when she had no one else. He saw the track marks, saw her hands shaking; she could barely hold her cigarette. He could have taken advantage of her but didn't. Got her cleaned up, gave her a job working for him. He had no plans to love her, only wanted to help; love happened later. So, Maestro asks Ike, does he still want to come back?

Ike's voice is low, almost a whisper. Why would Maestro even want him back? he asks.

Because he won't have Ike Morphy haunting him his whole life, Maestro says. Lately, every time he plays one of his new songs for Muriel, she tells him she likes it fine, but something's missing. He never asks her what that something is, but they both know. He doesn't want Muriel to spend every day wondering whether Ike might come back someday. Now she'll see Ike whenever she wants, but this time he'll just be some other dude in the band, no one she ever should have given a damn about. Maestro might even give Ike a nickname after all.

"Now, what do you say about that, brother?" Maestro asks. "In or out?"

Ike gazes at Muriel through the glass. He shifts his gaze to the steel door, then to Muriel again. He takes a breath. He makes as if to shake Maestro's hand but can't bring himself to do it. "Sorry, man, but I think I'll have to pass," he says, then heads downstairs without saying good-bye, walking fast out the door toward home even though he knows that he can't really call it home anymore.

Maestro John Wilkins Jr. waits for Ike to close the front door behind him, then enters the office. Muriel turns to him and asks if Ike is still upstairs, but Maestro says no, the man has already gone. Muriel asks what Ike said about rejoining the band, but Maestro shakes his head. They're better off, he says. Ike hasn't changed at all, still only knows one way to play: his. They can stop talking about Ike now, he says, he's not coming back. Then Maestro tells Muriel he wants to play something for her, a new song. He turns a dial on the mixing board, hits a key on the laptop, and a ballad begins to play. And even though the love song that Maestro is playing for his wife does not contain any of the surprising notes that Ike Morphy used to bring to his band's music, even though every rhyme from "above" and "love" to "my girl" and "my world" is one Muriel has heard dozens of times before and that she and Ike would have mocked together, the woman's face brightens slightly as she listens. And when the song is over and

Maestro asks if Muriel thinks anything is missing, she says she can't think of anything.

So, how does she feel? Maestro asks, placing a hand on her shoulder.

How does she feel? says Muriel. She feels like she looks, that's how she feels.

Does that mean she feels happy? Maestro asks.

Not yet, not really, says Muriel, but at least now she is starting to feel even.

WHEN IKE MORPHY reaches the Ding Dong Lounge, Rebecca and Phil Sugarman are already seated at a window table beneath faded Bob Dylan and Patti Smith concert posters. They seem pleased to see Ike—Rebecca, wearing her sunglasses on her head, kisses him on the cheek; Phil leaps up, shakes his hand, pulls him into a hug, calls him "brother," says, "Let me buy this cat a ginger ale," then lopes to the bar—but Ike does not feel as if he belongs here any more than he belonged in Maestro's building. Hell, when he first arrived in New York, he thought he could achieve whatever he wanted. The city wasn't a place as much as an idea, he thinks—escape, freedom, such potential. Now, it seems as if all he's been trying to do is hold on to the place when it's the idea that's gone.

Phil returns to the table, and Ike tries not to appear too preoccupied when Phil pesters him with questions: What sort of embouchure training exercises does he use? Was he trying to mock Eric Dolphy in this or that song? Has Ike ever had his clarinet appraised? Is it a real B-flat Müller? Wow, it must be worth a fortune. Ike's responses consist of barely more than a handful of syllables. He drinks his ginger ale, impatiently drums his hands against a thigh, looks out the window past the locust trees and across Columbus Avenue—an Under New Ownership sign is in the window of the Esmeralda Grocery and the new owner is telling the *compañeros* to move their milk crates and their boom box away from his door. No, this sure isn't Ike's city anymore; his place, wherever that will be, is somewhere else. Finally, Phil asks if Ike wants another ginger ale and Ike says no, he probably should get moving soon. Ike asks when Rebecca's husband will be coming, figuring that, when Darrell arrives, he will make his excuses, then return home to call Josh Dybnick to tell him he's ready to start looking for a much smaller apartment in a much lower price range. Rebecca looks directly at Ike.

"You mean my ex-husband?" she asks.

Ike returns Rebecca's gaze. Seconds pass before he realizes Rebecca is serious.

Maybe he will take another ginger ale, Ike tells Phil Sugarman. But before Rebecca can tell Ike what has happened, Phil is back with more drinks, asking Ike more questions until Rebecca tells her dad to stop trying to talk shop and "give the man some peace." Ike sits back and listens to Phil and his daughter banter—Phil effusing about being in the presence of a musician he has always admired, Rebecca telling him fine, Dad, but can't he lower his voice anyway because everyone's looking at him. The Sugarmans' exchanges are so different from the ones Ike remembers from his own repressed family, where his dad regarded any expression of emotion as low-class and manipulative. Here, even as Ike discusses his own troubles—the changing neighborhood, Mark Masler's betrayal of his father's intentions, his meeting with Maestro, his glimpse of Muriel, his dim prospects for a desirable living situation—Phil Sugarman is all warm, nervous energy, monopolizing the discussion, gleefully gainsaying every one of Ike's statements of self-doubt.

Over his daughter's futile objections, Phil, a man who created his multimillion-dollar jingle business from scratch and has seen few problems he couldn't fix with money and hard work, blithely tries to solve every issue with which Ike has been struggling using only a single sentence. Ike shouldn't have bothered seeing Maestro Wilkins, he asserts; the Funkshuns are a hack band and their puerile music needs Ike more than he needs it. Well, that's easy for Phil to say, Ike says. Not really, says Phil, challenges are only as easy or difficult as one makes them; the hard part is deciding what you want. All Ike needs to do, he says, is decide what he wants.

What do I want? Ike asks.

Yeah, says Phil, what does Ike want?

Rebecca tells Ike he doesn't have to answer; as usual, her father is demonstrating his inability to hold his liquor. But Ike says sure, why not, he'll play Phil's game. What does he want, brother? Okay, he'll tell Phil exactly what he wants because he's been thinking about that very topic ever since he walked in here; he's been thinking about it ever since he drove back to New York from his mother's funeral, ever since he and Herbie arrived at what he thought was his home and saw three strangers in his apartment. What does he want? How about freedom and a decent place to live? What does he want? Man, that's easy. He wants a place where his dog can roam and play, where he doesn't have to keep the poor animal on leash whenever some jackass cop with time on his hands and an attitude wants to hassle him. He wants to play the music he's begun to hear again and not worry about why the hell he's doing it or whether anyone will buy or listen to it. What does he want? He wants his parents to be alive again, if only for a moment, yeah, he wants his mother to listen to him play one more time, wants her to be able to walk through her garden again, wants to have lived in a house where people loved and didn't hurt one another. What does he want? Same thing everyone wants. He wants to fall in love; to feel alive; to live a good, long, healthy life; to run, to sleep, then wake up without a care other than to love the woman he is with, the dog that needs him, and the clarinet he can now hear playing even in his solitude.

And barring that, Ike Morphy says as he finishes his ginger ale, he'll settle for a cheap crib, a daytime gig where he won't have to think too much so he can keep focused on his tunes, and maybe a date or two. There, that's all he wants, he says. He's looking at Rebecca, but Phil speaks first. "Hey, you got it, man, he says. He drains his beer. "Yeah, you got it, bro. Why don't we give it a whirl?"

Phil reaches into his blue-jeans pocket, takes out his key chain, removes one key from it, and places that key on the table. He and his wife own a house in Maine, the last house on Croix-de-Mer Road just across the bay from Canada, he says. Now that their kids are grown, they rarely use it anymore. When Ike needs to leave the city and wants some time alone, he can go there, take time to write and play; Phil will even advance him some cash, and in six months or a year they can meet again and see if Ike has written anything worth recording. If he has, he'll try to help Ike get a deal; if not, no hard feelings, and Ike won't owe him anything. How would that be?

Now, why the hell would Phil want to do some crazy shit like that? asks Ike.

Because he has faith in Ike, Phil says.

Why would he? asks Ike.

Because Ike knows what he wants, says Phil. He presses the key into Ike's hand.

NEAR DAWN, Ike Morphy and Rebecca Sugarman are sitting on the front steps of the Roberto Clemente Building, watching the garbage haulers taking away the week's trash—old records tied together with twine; a computer drive and a pair of monitors; framed posters from art exhibits; good chairs and dressers; hardback books with ripped covers; full plastic bags, which are hurled onto the back of the truck before it creeps forward another ten yards to the next building, the next pile of garbage. Ike is tossing a crushed plastic Diet Pepsi bottle for Herbie, who scampers down the sidewalk after it, retrieves it, scampers after it again until Ike says, "Rest."

Rebecca unzips her black shoulder bag and produces a legal-sized document. She says she wants Ike to read it, and if he agrees with its contents, to sign; it is a sublease for 64 West 106th Street, 2B. The monthly rent is listed at $350. Hey, man, Ike says with a laugh as he scans the document, the place has to be worth more than $350 a month by now. Yes, says Rebecca, but if Ike is to share the apartment with her, she won't expect him to pay any more. Unless, of course, he'd rather go by himself to Maine.

In the morning, inside apartment 2B, Rebecca stands atop a chair with a bucket of black paint and a brush. She signs her name on the ceiling just below where Ike had written I'VE GOT A GODDAMN LEASE! As he watches Rebecca, Ike feels an unfamiliar burning sensation in his eyes, one he hasn't felt since he was a young man on South Colfax Avenue. But Rebecca does not notice, for she is crying for the first time since Darrell Schiff walked out her door.

{ III }

A DEAL
IS CLOSED

*I'm a M-A-N-N man, you blink your eyes
and I'll be gone.*

LOU REED,
"NYC Man"

LOVERS IN THE BUBBLE

A Mostly Romantic Manhattan Valley
Interlude Before Closing Day, for
Humans, Pigeons, and Dog

The Pigeons of 2B, Part 1
(*34 Days Before Closing*)

One day before Ike Morphy will first tell Rebecca Sugarman he loves her, a pair of gray-black pigeons with purple throats, dull red feet, orange eyes, white beaks, and splashes of cream on their ruffled wings settle once again on the Amana air conditioner outside a second-floor bedroom window of the Roberto Clemente Building in a nest they have fashioned out of twigs, mud, cardboard, orange fabric, and strips of discarded pages of the *New York Post* and *The American Standard*. This air conditioner has served as the pigeons' home for nearly half a year, for as long as the birds, lifelong Manhattanites, have lived anywhere in the city. Perhaps in a smaller town they might live eight years or more, but here in New York, the four years they have already survived is a significant accomplishment.

Throughout these four years, save for two protracted stints near the Blockhouse in Central Park, the pigeons have resided within the borders of Manhattan Valley. Though they have rarely moved far, they have moved often. They have felt the bristles of supers' broomsticks against their bellies, the cold spray from janitors' garden hoses upon their wings, the sting of hooligans' snowballs against their bodies and beaks. They have been splashed with water, bleach, ammonia. Some people have taped steel wool to the tops of their ACs or glued nail boards to their window ledges. The pigeons' nests have been hurled into the trash, their eggs swept onto the street, after which the birds have spent mournful days patrolling the sidewalk barely able to muster the energy to find another place to live. Still, they have managed to produce more than two dozen offspring, seven of whom have survived, finding mates and staying ahead of the exterminators, never remaining too long in any one place before taking flight for another free window ledge, rooftop, or construction site. It is the only way a bird can manage to survive in this town—keep moving, keep building new nests.

This nest is sturdier and more elaborate than most, since 2B had been an exceptionally quiet apartment—no conversations or music, blinds always drawn—and the pigeons had remained undisturbed. Lately, though, the birds have started hearing new sounds from inside the apartment— conversations, cries, a clarinet. Though the noises have made them restless, the pigeons have remained. They have made love, gathered food from Dumpsters and grocery store trash heaps; they have found new twigs and strips of newspapers and magazines to reupholster their nest, where now a new creature rests inside her egg, waiting to be hatched, to be fed, to fly from her parents' nest, then return to the air conditioner outside of Ike Morphy and Rebecca Sugarman's apartment.

Rebecca & Ike
(33 *Days Before Closing*)

Rebecca Sugarman, lying naked in bed well past 10:00 a.m. in the apartment that will soon be transferred from Mark Masler to her, has already let her cell phone ring on three separate occasions without bothering to pick up. When the phone rings a fourth time, Rebecca supposes she could answer, but in doing so she would upset the covers, which have preserved the perfect temperature and protected her from the cool, wet March air seeping in. She would have to throw on a shirt that's so far away at the foot of the bed, perhaps even find her underwear.

In the past, Rebecca never ignored phone calls, never stayed home from work, rarely allowed herself to take a real vacation. At best, she traveled with Darrell during summer and winter breaks to her folks' places or to visit his parents in Madison. But wherever they went, Darrell would just complain that the trip was interfering with his work. He would insist on finding his own way to LaGuardia, then show up late, harried, always almost missing their flight; he would cut trips short by a day or two, spend afternoons taking "power naps" that would last upward of two hours, but whenever Rebecca would wake him to suggest some sort of activity, Darrell would shake his head, bite his lip, then say damn it, Becca, she knew he had to work.

Invariably, on so-called vacations, Rebecca would spend evenings alone struggling to write her own dissertation, reading paperbacks, dining at the Sugarman home with her mother, father, brother, sister-in-law, and an empty chair. She would take Sunday drives with Darrell's father in the Finneran Schiffs' "Crunk Car," their dank semiautomatic 1970 Volvo, and struggle to make conversation while visiting the Milwaukee County Art Museum or Mader's Restaurant, after which she would return to find Darrell asleep once again, either in bed, on the couch in the glow of the TV, or with his head on his hands in front of the computer screen, on which Rebecca would see the Microsoft Word helper tapping his foot or twiddling his thumbs—that, or a series of cartoon characters and a blinking message such as GAME OVER! or CONGRATULATIONS, DARRELL FINNERAN SCHIFF, YOU HAVE SUCCESSFULLY DOWNLOADED TUPAC'S *RESURRECTION*!

Rebecca lies in bed and shifts from her left side to her right—every moment she believes she has found the perfect position, she finds a better one. Until now, she has been unschooled in the art of laziness, even as a child felt guilty about enjoying the privilege of free time and instead packed days with piano lessons, dance camp, jogging, softball. But what has Rebecca done this past week aside from not returning phone calls, aside from not editing one word of *The American Standard*? Happily, deliciously, wonderfully, just about nothing. She and Ike have listened to his favorite Eight Bold Souls and Moving Pictures albums on the stereo, watched her favorite old Jacques Demy movies on the TV that the movers carted over from the apartment that she once shared with Darrell and is now subletting to Barnard assistant professor Graham Buggett. Rebecca and Ike have slept late; read nearly a dozen books between them; walked Herbie through Riverside, Central, and Morningside parks; played hours of catch and tug-of-war with the dog. They have worked the difficult crossword puzzles Darrell was too competitive to enjoy; they have played the chess games Darrell hated to lose; they have discussed the abandoned draft of Rebecca's dissertation that Darrell always said was "too earnest and 'up with people'" for him to finish reading; they have attempted the sexual positions that Darrell always dismissed as "too porn star-ish" for him to assay without snickering. Rebecca has committed adultery with Ike more than two dozen times, and she has delighted in every instance of commandment breaking. And today, most important of all, Ike has told her he loves her and she has said that she loves him.

Rebecca's college boyfriends all said "I love you," but to her, it always sounded as if they were attempting to utter a password. Darrell frequently said he loved Rebecca, but could never do so without interposing some vulgar modifier—*I frickin' love you; I love you, goddamn it*. "Can't you just say it for real?" she once asked. But today, just before he left for the park with his clarinet and his dog, Ike kissed her on the cheek, said, "I love you, Rebecca," then headed out into the dawn. The words seemed so simple and matter-of-fact when Ike uttered them that Rebecca never doubted he was telling the truth. Rebecca was barely able to say "I love you" in return before Ike shut the door, and she was once again happily dreaming.

The phone rings again, but Rebecca still does not answer. She pulls the covers tighter and closes her eyes. Just over a week into her relationship with Ike Morphy, she is still somewhat surprised to find herself in this bed. She had figured that Ike would opt for her parents' place in Maine, as Phil Sugarman suggested, or that the two of them would agree to live together as roommates—a shared bathroom, divided chores, separate refrigerator shelves just as in college, where her apartment-mates routinely snarfed down the good food that had the name "Rebecca" taped to it. She wasn't certain that Ike had any opinion of her whatsoever until he placed an arm around her on the steps of the Roberto Clemente Building, wasn't even sure he knew her name until he uttered it after they kissed.

She feared Ike would find her boring, told him that's what she always suspected Darrell thought she was. Ike said she had to be kidding. She was beautiful, open-minded, knew so much about books and art—what was boring about that? Walking around in a dark mood, brooding, and drinking didn't make a person interesting; he knew that better than anyone.

At noon, when her cell phone rings yet again, Rebecca wakes from another beautiful dream—she was lying in a green field by the ocean; lilacs were all around her. Now she stretches her arms, scrunches her toes, wraps the blanket around her, lets it drop, wraps it even tighter, drops it again, feels the warmth then the chill then the warmth again. She stands, reaches toward the ceiling, looks down upon the boulevard; sunlight shines through the blinds, casting slat shadows on her body as she watches deliverymen lug bags of Italian bread into the Parkside Mini Supermarket. She gazes up and down the street. Mah-jongg players are out; the *compañeros* are blasting Mongo Santamaria. She takes a towel from the closet, walks to the shower, stands under the water for what seems like only a few minutes, but when she steps out and walks back to the bedroom, Ike and Herbie have returned from the park, and as the dog licks water off of her toes, Ike is handing a ringing cell phone to her.

Rebecca takes the phone, places it to her ear, and hears Chloe Linton's voice.

"Rebecca," Chloe says, "we need to talk about Liz Fogelson's *Wizard Girl* review."

Darrell & Jane
(*28 Days Before Closing*)

Darrell Schiff returns from dropping off a copy of his latest dissertation chapter in Bernard Ostrow's mailbox, the second chapter he has completed in the past two and a half weeks, his best and quickest writing in years. He then opens the door to Jane Earhart's apartment and espies Jane, her face, eyes, and fingers red as she runs toward him, holds him tightly, then pushes him away. She darts back to her laptop to type, then stops, runs back the other way, throws open a window, yells "Yougoddamn-motherfuckercocksuckersonsofbitches" out toward Central Park, slams down the window, then returns to her seat. Darrell asks if everything is all right. Jane nods but keeps typing. Darrell shrugs, then shimmies his laptop case off his shoulder, unzips it, pulls out his computer, sets it down beside hers, turns on the machine, and starts typing too, trying to keep up with Jane's pace.

Two laptops are positioned side by side on the long mahogany work-table in Jane's living room; the occupants of two black, cushioned swivel chairs sit half a foot away from each other; two pairs of headphones are tuned to two songs playing for two sets of ears, four hands typing, two piles of paper beside them. Since Darrell has left his wife for Jane, sex has been remarkably efficient, but to his surprise these moments have been most blissful: the pure, passionate, unadulterated writing.

Writing has always been what Darrell needed to do only to get his doc-torate and a reasonable job. He has lived in eternal terror of the conversa-tion he overheard one night while dining on the upper level of the Pinnacle Pizzeria on Broadway with some fellow graduate students and dissertation chair Bernard Ostrow, back when any of them still spoke to him. At a nearby table overlooking half a mushroom pizza and a pair of old calzones, two high school toughs in lettermen's jackets were eating pepper-oni slices. The heavier kid boasted that a university had offered him a football scholarship. Which team? the other asked. "Ever heard of the Gauchos?" he answered. His friend shook his head. "Yeah, me neither," said the heavy kid. "Turns out they're some shit school out west." After that moment, Darrell tried to motivate himself by imagining that a subpar per-formance in grad school could result in his teaching at a university that a random high school hooligan would label "some shit school out west." Still, he would always tell himself he could write the next day, the next week or month, but not just now because there were games to play, songs to download, power naps to take, reality shows to watch. He never considered the possibility that work could be fun.

But observing Jane work, he had an epiphany. He watched her type, ball up papers and whip them into the trash can, leap off her chair and pump her fist with satisfaction. Watching Jane wasn't like watching a scholar, wasn't like watching his mom, her lips pursed as she dutifully used a red pen to mark the hell out of student papers while sitting in her unreasonably well-organized home study. Watching Jane wasn't like watching his dad in his musty little university office, rubbing his smooth scalp and shouting in anguish at a typically blank computer screen, "Aww, bloody hell! Bloody hell!" Watching Jane was like watching a rock star; she typed like Keith Fricking Moon; she tore up pages as if crashing cymbals together, bobbed her head, danced; and when she wrote yet another sentence she hated, she swore, using curse words that even Darrell was too timid to use around her.

This was what Darrell's life had been lacking—passion. As far as he was concerned, Rebecca inspired none; she was too nice for him, too even-keeled, too perfect, too Waspy somehow. Was it Darrell's fault that he told Rebecca he fricking loved her when he didn't know what love was and imagined that being in love and pretending to be in love were basically the same thing? He started asking himself how his life could change if he channeled the passion he once felt for illegally downloading music and playing Screaming Monkey Solitaire into work.

Within days, he transformed himself into an ass-kicking T.A., the kind who would receive hottie peppers and smiley faces and would have lines of students outside his office door just to shoot the shit, then drink beers with him afterward. He saw himself becoming the ass-kicking scholar that Rebecca always said he could be. He would reread his work and get pissed that Bernard Ostrow had been so lenient, giving him the benefit of the doubt, even though his riffs on sexual metaphor were hopelessly shallow. When, in fact, he had not realized that, in his vulgar rants, he had accidentally made a truly revolutionary discovery, one that could conceivably change literary studies altogether, one that he could not have learned without having met and fallen in love with Jane. Why, he had not invented the sexual references in the works he mocked, had not invented Thackeray's lewd names or Meredith's perverse metaphors, but he had never stopped to see their greater purpose, the entire subtext historians had ignored, an untold love story encoded within the metaphors. What all great authors knew, but most literary critics and professors—his parents in particular—did not, was that writing was not an intellectual act but a sexual one, just as it seemed to be for Jane Earhart, just as it was becoming for him: intro, rising action, climax, denouement; foreplay, thrusting, orgasm, cigarette. Every sentence he wrote was an act of love, just as it had been for the Victorians. Now, he only hopes he has enough time to commit all these observations to paper before Bernard Ostrow makes his final recommendation to the graduate committee about funding renewal.

At dawn, the two typists stop typing, save their documents, download their most recent versions to their SuperDrives, whip off their headphones, put their laptops on standby, brush their teeth, take off their clothes, shower, and jump into bed. And when both typists are too tired to sleep, one puts his arm around the other and asks why she seemed so upset when he came home.

"I fired my agent," the second typist says.

Jane Earhart is aware that after Darrell revealed his knowledge of her history and the two started living together, he has been viewing their relationship as a long-term proposition, even though she has warned him not to. She doesn't really believe in discussing the future, she's told him; it always turns out worse than anyone could ever imagine.

And yet, though she erupted with fury after Darrell arrived at her door and greeted her for the first time as "Gigi," though she flung three books and half a manuscript against the wall, broke one glass, two pencils, and a pair of ice trays whose cubes smacked Darrell in the chin and in the right nipple, though she told him that if he ever revealed what he knew, she'd fucking flay him, after she calmed down, she too began experiencing a new spurt of productivity. The fact that her secrets have been shared with another human being whom she is beginning to trust has granted her some small sense of peace.

Plus, Jane understands that her fiction has suffered as a result of her isolation. She does not really believe workshop leader Faith Trinkelman's recent assertion that her writing is so lacking in soul that she will only ever find work writing press releases or catalog copy for ball bearing companies. But if she wants to succeed as a writer, she cannot remain at such a great distance from her fellow human beings.

Jane cannot honestly say she loves Darrell; still, the proximity has fascinated her. She has never observed someone up close uninterrupted for such a long period of time, and now she has begun to write with so much depth and specificity that Miles Dimmelow has told her that her most recent story, "I Can't Sleep Because This Guy in My Bed Keeps Swearing (What's the Deal with That?)," is her most hysterical ever and will help flesh out another character in their musical. And even though Faith Trinkelman declared Jane's story implausible, because the unappealing titular character would never have left his wife for the story's inscrutable narrator, and said narrator would certainly never pursue a relationship with some foul-mouthed slacker who concocts obscene wordy-gurdies and uses the words "fricking" and "chode" in everyday conversation, Jane sent the story to Carter Boldirev, who, upon receiving it, invited Jane to lunch.

Jane tried to downplay her expectations for the meeting. At best, Boldirev would say the story still needed work before he could send it to a literary magazine. At worst, though, he would have to admit that Jane's work was improving. But moments after Jane sat down to lunch with her bow-tied agent at Chez Villemure, she realized the man hadn't even bothered reading her story.

Before the waiter took their orders, Carter Boldirev was already talking about *Wizard Girl*. When Jane asked if he had read her new work, Carter said he thought he had already explained his agency's opinion of short fiction—nobody read it and nobody bought it—then steered the conversation back to *Wizard Girl*, telling Jane that reviews would be forthcoming in *The American Standard* and other publications, and the PR department at Purple Prose wanted to know if they could reveal at least some vague biographical information about her. And then, suddenly, there Jane was, explaining everything again—how she didn't want to revisit the period of her life when she wrote about Iphigene, how she didn't want to be known as the precocious girl who became another washed-up adult, didn't want to respond to a whole lot of BS about how she survived the loss of her parents. Carter offered the opinion that journalists seldom wrote about new authors without compelling backstories. Jane's history of loss and redemption could aid book sales.

Jane couldn't stand this conversation any longer. She said no, her answer was final, and if Carter said the words "Wizard Girl" ever again, she'd find a new agent to represent her. Carter advised Jane to think very carefully before she said anything else because he had invested in *Wizard Girl* and would protect his investment in this "property." But Jane said she didn't have to think any further; her story wasn't a property and Carter was fired.

Jane walked home through Central Park, she tells Darrell as she lies in his arms; she zoomed past the carousel, past the statues of William Shakespeare and Balto, past Mother Goose, the boat pond, and Alice in Wonderland. At first she had trouble sublimating her fury. But once she reached the Glade, she began transforming the lunch from a vexing incident into one rife with dramatic possibility. And in the evening, while Darrell was writing another ten pages of his dissertation, Jane was banging out a story entitled "So I Had Lunch with This Preposterously Bow-tied Pain in My Ass," with most identifying details changed.

Dawn casts the typists' apartment in a soft lavender glow; the pair have slept barely more than an hour and a half, significantly less than even the shortest "power nap" one typist would routinely take during afternoons while his wife was at work. They have talked, they have made love twice with the lights on and their eyes open so that Jane could study Darrell's facial expressions. Jane has memorized Darrell's heartbeat, the rhythm of his breaths, and she has listened as he has shared with her his favorite and most secret dreams—lately, they almost always involve some professor or public intellectual in a position subservient to his own: Bernard Ostrow is a barista at Starbucks and fixes Darrell a mocha frappuccino; Christopher Hitchens is a waiter at Olive Garden and asks whether Darrell wants alfredo or marinara sauce on his pasta; Stanley Fish directs him to the men's jeans section at the Gap; Noam Chomsky wants to know whether he'd like sprinkles on his Blizzard at Dairy Queen; Camille Paglia asks if he'd like fries with that; Harold Bloom sells him a Lotto ticket; Fredric Jameson washes his windows; Gary Wills tops off his wiper fluid; and Henry Louis Gates Jr. pumps his gas. But mostly, the typists have lain awake thinking of the next sentences they will write. And when they arise, they do not shower, choose fresh outfits, or even make new coffee; they just warm up yesterday's dregs, sit in their wrinkled clothes, punch their laptop power buttons, put on their headphones, and once again begin to type.

Caleb & the Birdwoman
(*23 Days Before Closing*)

Alone as usual in the dark Riverdale house whose only illumination emanates from a laptop screen, Caleb Scheinblum sits on the carpeted floor of his upstairs bedroom, typing. He has the iTunes volume turned up all the way. He is listening to the Damage Manual, a song called "Sunset Gun," for the twelfth time tonight.

Are u there? he types.

Moments later, the response comes: *Why, yes.*

Caleb wears a black hooded sweatshirt and a pair of army fatigues; his toenails and fingernails are painted black. He glances over to his bedside alarm clock; it is nearly three o'clock in the morning. He is typing to the pulsating music and muttering along. "It's all fake as they come," he says. "Burn my eyes like a sunset gun."

What were u doing?

Wondering if you were awake too.

Caleb's sister has already moved in with her fiancé and is planning a wedding that the young man would not be attending even if he were invited; tonight, Caleb's mother is off again somewhere that he'd prefer not to know, and thankfully, he is now able to spend even more time alone up here with the door closed, the lights off, his music as loud as he wants it. He keeps his black hood up as his long, pale fingers type fast.

Will I ever get to meet you?

You might be disappointed, my dear.

In the chat room, her name is Birdwoman, but that doesn't tell Caleb much. He identifies himself using his real initials, but only because he lacks the patience, the creativity, and the need for deception that nicknames require. Still, he has refrained from using his full name because he fears that when she learns more about him, as she ultimately will if this relationship is ever to move beyond their computer screens, she will lose interest, as has happened with most girls once he meets them. He is too young, they tell him, he is too tall, too scary, or just too freakishly intense; the reason is always different, but the meaning is always the same: no. Caleb desperately fears the day when these conversations too will end; when he's in school, they are the only reason he looks forward to going home.

Did you get that book I sent you?

Yesterday.

What do you think?

Maybe the best I've ever read.

Caleb and the Birdwoman chat about the books she sends to him through the mail; they chat about the music he sends to her; they chat about going away together. Well, mostly Caleb chats about this last topic while the Birdwoman, he fears, humors him. Sometimes, he suspects she might only be idly fantasizing; she might have a husband who works all day and leaves her with a houseful of kids; she might have a boyfriend or two; she might be conducting three other conversations online; she might be some twelve-year-old home-schooled genius living on an Iowa farm; she might be a guy. Who knows? Someday he'll have to find out.

What did u think of that song I e-mailed to you?

Loud.

U hated it.

No, I've always liked things that are loud.

But then again, when it comes right down to it, Caleb is probably the true fantasist in this communication, he thinks as he types. He's the one talking about getting out of town, hitting the open road, asking a woman or a girl or a guy or whoever to move to Canada with him. He hasn't mentioned the facts that he's only seventeen, still living at home with his mom, doesn't have the credits to graduate, just got his driver's license, doesn't have a car, hasn't even scraped together the money to buy one—what's the point of having a job, really, when his mom just bogarts his cash when he's sleeping?

What are you doing now?

I'm closing my eyes. You're closing your eyes. I'm kissing your neck. You're kissing my neck. I'm touching your hair. I'm holding you close.

Someday, though, he'll have to do something or else he'll burst. He can't expend all this passion in a relationship if this is all it will ever be; he can't take much more of sitting in the dark typing as his frustration and rage build.

Are u there?

In the distance, Caleb can hear a car approaching his house. He turns down the volume of his music.

Are u still there?

Caleb can hear tires on the driveway, a motor being turned off, a door opening, then slamming shut.

Hey, are u still there?

He can hear footsteps on asphalt, then on the front steps, the screen door being opened, can hear his mother fumbling with her purse. "Caleb," she calls. He can hear her swearing before she calls up to him again. "Hey, Caleb!" Again, she has forgotten her keys or lost them or left them in somebody's apartment—some boyfriend, some stranger, some fucker, some jerk, somebody Caleb will most probably never meet. He heads downstairs to open the front door. He has to get out of here, he thinks, he has to figure out a way.

Caleb is turning the knob of the front door when a message appears upstairs on his screen:

I'm here.

Mark & Allie
(*18 Days Before Closing*)

As he is hoisted up in a chair, dropped down, then hoisted up again, Mark Masler, even with "Hava Nagilah" being played by a nine-piece band, even with photographers and sushi chefs clapping along, feels that his wedding has been a perfect demonstration of his still-young life philosophy of moderation and compromise. He wanted a lavish, black-tie reception in the Puck Building; he wanted sushi chefs who could speak both Japanese and Hebrew as they sliced lox (*"Yitgadal! Yitcadash! Hai!"*); he wanted a band that played Jewish wedding standards, such as "Raisins and Almonds," "Sunrise, Sunset," and "Boobalitchky," along with his favorite old power ballads, "Winds of Change," "Rough Boy," and "Here I Go Again on My Own." He wanted **Mark Masler** and **Allie Scheinblum** listed in boldface in gossip sections, wanted pictures on *The American Standard*'s brand-new "Parties" page, wanted hot chicks in white tuxedo shirts and tight black pants carving roast beef and scooping mashed potatoes. He wanted the hunkiest trainers from the JCC gym lifting him up and down in his chair, wanted to dance around his wife on his knees like a Cossack, to remove her garter belt with his teeth and shoot it across the dance floor. He wanted midnight to strike, at which point he and Allie would strip off their formal attire, then return to the dance floor in muscle shirts, shorts, and sandals, wave good-bye to their guests, and follow a porter who would tote their luggage to a limo that would drive them through the city toward JFK airport while they made love in the back.

Allie, on the other hand, nixed the idea of a big reception. Which was how, while lying in the new, king-sized, vibrating water bed in the master bedroom of their apartment, they forged this solution: a ceremony at B'nai Akiva Synagogue followed by a formal reception at the Puck Building—no guests, but every moment captured by a photographer from the *Times*'s Sunday Styles section, where, six days before the ceremony, Mark was elated to read, "The groom's first two marriages ended in divorce."

The "no guests" policy at the Puck Building proved to be an inspiration. No guests meant no waiting in line at the buffet. No guests meant no drunken pervs cutting in to dance with the bride. No guests meant no one bitching about the fact that Mark and Allie forbade alcohol at the bar and supplied only Martinelli's Sparkling Cider and six-packs of O'Doul's and Buckler. No guests meant $200 saved for each guest who would otherwise have arrived. No guests meant no reception line where Mark would have rolled any male guest who attempted to tongue-kiss the bride just as he had always tried to do. And perhaps most important, no guests meant not worrying about Caleb Scheinblum appearing in a hooded sweatshirt and army fatigues, with criss-crossed ammunition belts and an AK-47, laying waste to the wedding party.

During the reception, Mark never feels lonely, only privileged, like a sultan who has rented out Madison Square Garden for a private U2 show. He and Allie request the songs to which they dance, return for seconds and thirds at the buffet table and never have to wait, and when it's time to change their clothes for their limo ride, they strip in the center of the dance floor and dance naked for the better part of a half hour. Arms around each other, they sway to power ballads, his *schwantz* resting ever-so-comfortably above her pubis. As the couple slow-dances naked, Mark closes his eyes. He hears the flutter of Allie's eyelashes as she closes hers. And as they kiss, Mark now knows the past is gone, and so is the man he used to be—the bully, the underachiever, the angry coke-addicted sex fiend with the mullet. With Allie, he has been reborn. Praise Hashem, who gave him a second chance, he thinks, and also this third one.

Wearing only their bathrobes and sandals, the newly married couple step into the back of their white limo and hold each other close in the glow of the vehicle's overhead purple fairy lights. While the limo rolls along Central Park West, Mark and Allie Masler are too occupied with each other to notice that all the lights in their apartment are blazing.

The Pigeons of 2B, Part 2
(*1 Week Before Closing*)

Two pigeons stand on the air conditioner outside the bedroom window of apartment 2B. The birds have been taking turns. She sits on the egg and he forages for food; then he sits on the egg and she gathers twigs to fortify the nest. She struts along the pavement; he waits impatiently for her to return, hops nervously off the egg then back onto it. And every time she does return—never a sure thing in this city—he jumps up, beak juddering, wings fluttering, and then they preen, circle each other, and coo.

The egg is warm; small cracks are visible on its surface. She leaps off the egg and now the two birds stand on the AC, one on either side of the nest. Through the window of the apartment, two sets of human eyes are watching too. The birds and humans watch the tiny beak slicing through the eggshell—once, twice, three times. Sections of the shell flake off and are caught in the wind. They swirl up in the air and then down the airshaft into pools of old rainwater. The birds' feet march right then left, right then left; their heads move back and forth. They've witnessed the same scene more than twenty times, have vague memories of each hatching imprinted on their brains, and yet they still watch, rapt. Their bodies now shudder in the wind. The couple behind the glass hold hands. The wind blows. Rain falls. The beak slices. The shell cracks. And then there is a slam against the window and the air conditioner vibrates. Through the window, the birds can see a set of paws and the face of a black dog. And as the baby bird finally breaks through the egg and looks upward, at first all she can see of the great, new world is a blur of gray sky overhead. Her parents are flying to a ledge opposite their nest where, even though they no longer see Herbie Mann, they can still hear the animal bark.

CLOSING DAY

The Mortgage Broker

Closing day for 64 West 106th Street, 2B, has arrived, the beautiful, clear morning of April 16, and Megan Yu is bursting past the unoccupied reception desk of the Gotham Mortgage Company, past the unilluminated television, past empty wastepaper baskets, past closed office doors with bagged newspapers in front of them, past the desk of her all-too-efficient, busybody secretary Lynette, who is, thankfully, vacationing in Aruba and therefore will not be in the office if Megan's parents call this afternoon and ask where she is. As for any other calls she might miss, Megan doesn't mind if they all go to voice mail. Megan used to turn on her computer first thing in the morning; she would commit her lead and rate sheets to memory, study Bloomberg.com, then return every one of her phone messages. But lately, the news has been so good that she can afford to relax; she can get a mortgage for just about anyone now. So today, when Megan turns on her computer, she checks only her personal e-mail just to make sure her lover hasn't canceled their meeting. Then she cranks up "I've Seen All Good

People" by Yes and signs onto the Zagat site to determine where she will tell her parents she lunched today.

Megan darts out of her office, zigzagging between cubicles, moving too quickly to even try to say hello to her colleagues, many of whom are just arriving, not understanding the difference between clocking in at 7:59 and at 8:01, though they should have gotten a clue when bonuses were announced. She is not like the others, she thinks, she never churns and burns her way through clients the way they do, never bait-and-switches them, knows that treating them fairly is the best tactic for assuring repeat business. As her boyfriend has told her, the loyalty one earns through playing by the rules more than compensates for any short-term gains one might make by hustling. Sometimes, honesty is the cleverest sales tactic of all.

Megan heads for the company kitchen, keys poised in one hand. She approaches a locked cabinet, stands on a step stool, unlocks the door, and opens it, revealing rows of champagne bottles. She snatches a bottle of pink bubbly, hops off the stool, carries the bottle to the sink. She inserts the drain-stopper, turns on the hot water. When steam billows forth, she places the bottle in the water and waits for the label to float off. And when it does, because she has always been a perfectionist, she scrubs the bottle with a Brillo pad until she cannot see any trace of the label. She dries the bottle with a towel, steps on the stool again, takes down a sheet of labels, and pulls off a silver one that reads "Gotham Mortgage: A Truly Vintage Company." She presses it onto the bottle, finds a red ribbon and bow in a drawer, then writes a congratulatory note to Rebecca Sugarman, knowing full well that little touches like these are what have allowed her to rise so quickly in the company. A sheet of gold wrapping paper in one hand and a bottle of "Gotham Champagne" in the other, Megan returns to her office to call her boyfriend to tell him to be sure to arrive at the Warwick Hotel before one.

The Tenant & The Buyer

On closing day, Ike Morphy returns from a long early-morning walk through Central Park with Herbie. He kisses Rebecca just before she heads out for work. Damn, she looks good, he tells her, then asks her to wait so he can walk her to the subway. Ike takes off the dog's leash and hangs it on a hook by the door. Even though on-leash time officially starts at 9:00 a.m. in city parks, Ike always keeps Herbie's leash on now. Such a shame he has to do this, but his life has improved so radically that he sees no reason to attract the attention of the law.

In the mornings, he wakes up with Rebecca beside him and Herbie underneath the bed, sighing, uncertain whether to feel irritated that his status in the pack has been downgraded, or to feel content that his pack has grown. The two humans lie in bed. They talk and make love, then walk to the air conditioner to watch the baby pigeon in her nest, mouth opening, then snapping as the mama bird upchucks into it. During the days, Ike practices alone on Inwood Hill; he can visualize notes even before he plays them. Sometimes, they appear to him in color—dark greens and blues. He has begun composing again, a tribute to his adopted city and his surprisingly happy new life in it. The piece, Rhapsody in A-Flat, will begin with a chromatic progression based on the steps at Strangers' Gate that he and Herbie climbed upon their return to Manhattan on the night they first saw Rebecca. The steps always remained the same, but Ike now senses he wasn't the same person the next time he climbed them. Rhapsody in A-Flat will be an uncharacteristically hopeful work, Ike has told Rebecca, filled with the sounds of their street—speeding taxis and car horns and cooing pigeons and barking dogs and kisses on his front stoop. Rebecca returns home between seven and eight; they eat, make love again, take Herbie on his last walk of the day, then lie in bed and talk about how their lives will change when Rebecca's child arrives. Ike's looking forward to it, doesn't give a damn that the kid's not his, no more than he cares that he's not Herbie Mann's dad; everyone needs someone to take care of them.

On today's walk to the subway station, Rebecca tells Ike she won't return to her office after the closing; she'll meet Chloe for lunch, then come home. The weather is supposed to stay warm today, so maybe the two of them can go out for a picnic. Ike kisses Rebecca good-bye, wishes her good luck, watches her descend the steps of the 103rd Street subway station, and begins walking quickly north with his clarinet in his backpack.

The Sellers

On closing day, as he places a call to Josh Dybnick in advance of their meeting at Gotham Mortgage, Mark Masler flicks off the last shards of glass clinging to the sleeves of the charcoal gray suit he last wore to his father's funeral. Since Mark and Allie have been back from their Hawaiian honeymoon, nearly every one of their days has been spent, in part, dealing with some aspect of the robbery that Mark has decided not to report either to the police or to his insurance company in order to protect the individual who he still assumes committed the crime. Mark and Allie have itemized all their missing jewelry, furniture, and appliances; supervised the installation of new locks and an alarm system; purchased new silverware, a toaster, a microwave, a DVD player, and a set of dumbbells.

After the return limo ride from JFK, Mark lifted Allie and kicked open the door to their apartment, planning to once again carry his new wife over a threshold, then into bed. But every light was on, clothes were scattered over the carpet, the stereo was blasting, the master bed was unmade and madly vibrating. Mark knew he had been robbed, knew exactly who had robbed him, and as soon as he and Allie cleaned up, then made love on the sheets heaped on the floor, Mark was in his yellow Hummer, driving to Riverdale to confront Caleb Scheinblum.

Allie had said she was certain the culprit was her mother, who had once hocked Allie's computer and printer to pay her Discover Card debt. Allie told Mark she had had enough of her mother's shenanigans, but when she reached for the phone, Mark asked her to put it down. "No cops with family," he said.

Mark arrived alone at the Scheinblum house during the late afternoon, when he figured Marilyn would be out. He was dressed in a tight suit and stiff shoes, ready for a serious discussion with Caleb about family and responsibility. No one answered when he rang the buzzer, but the door to the house was open.

Caleb was in the kitchen, fiddling with the microwave. The kid was wearing his black sweatshirt again, hood up, saggy black jeans, black high-tops. Mark mustered a polite hello, and when Caleb grunted in response,

Mark reminded Caleb that he had said hello. Caleb gazed into the microwave as if studying a particularly intriguing science experiment. Mark feared that Caleb might be microwaving a living creature, some family pet; kids these days did that sort of thing, no conscience whatsoever, not like the harmless animal pranks of his youth—slipping LSD into dog food or duct-taping the legs of a cat. Hey, he asked, what was Caleb microwaving? Lasagna, Caleb said. He removed it from the microwave, sat down on a stool at the kitchen counter, and began consuming it with a fork.

Listen, Mark said while Caleb ate, he had heard that Caleb's father had never been much of a dad. He understood that. His own father was a good parent to just about everybody except his son, and as a result, Mark had never accepted male leadership. But even when he was punching out the side-view mirrors of Coach Hatfield's Camaro, he was really crying out for love. Mark said he knew why Caleb took his belongings; this was a cry for attention, a test to see if Mark would still love him and give him the attention he craved.

Caleb Scheinblum looked up and cocked his head; his lasagna-laden fork seemed to float midway between plate and mouth. Mark told Caleb he wouldn't call the police or ask Caleb to return his stolen items, because family members couldn't steal from each other. Caleb finished his lasagna, rinsed his fork and plate, and placed them in the dishwasher. He flipped his hair out of his eyes and leaned against the stove. You know something, man? Caleb said to Mark. Sometimes, if you called a person a name too many times, that person actually became what you called them, even if they hadn't been that thing in the first place.

Mark Masler beamed. Yes, he said, this was exactly his point. That's why he would never call Caleb a thief. Instead, he had come here with respect, generosity, and understanding, knowing that if he treated Caleb as a mensch, then that's what he could become. He offered his hand, but Caleb just walked past Mark down the hallway toward the front door, opened it, and walked outside. Mark remained at the counter, thinking Caleb might be searching for a present—perhaps his father's old pipe or a book of photographs. He didn't get up until he heard the sound of tires squealing: then he looked out the front window to see his Hummer being steered out of the driveway. And by the time he had the wherewithal to give chase, Caleb had turned a corner and sped out of sight.

When Marilyn Scheinblum drove Mark to the train, Mark was too angry at Caleb and himself to notice the remaining items of silverware still on the backseat of Marilyn's car. He had wasted time with Caleb, he now realized. He had tried to be a mensch like his old man, and what had he received for his troubles? A ransacked apartment and a stolen car. He wouldn't report the kid, but from this moment forward, he would trust no one save the members of his family, and that meant only him and Allie. Period. With anyone else, he would do whatever he could get away with: shove people who got in his way; hock goobers into the Jacuzzi at the gym to make sure that no one would get in with him; take both armrests on airplanes; sit in exit rows to make sure that, in an emergency, he could get out first; sit up front in the boxes at the Met, and if anyone said he was blocking their view, he would roll them during an aria. Everyone was just out for himself anyway, like Allie always said. It was true.

And now, when he gets Josh Dybnick on the line, Mark says he won't be donating to his theater, not unless he can put in his own business on the ground floor. And when Josh tells Mark that his plan is unworkable, Mark says well, maybe he'll call up Josh's boss now and tell him exactly what Josh has been doing without his company's knowledge. And before Josh can respond, Mark hangs up and calls Brad Overman to inform him about his moonlighting associate broker. Then, Mark and Allie hail a taxi for the Eighty-third Street mikvah, where they barge into the ritual baths and barricade the door until the time comes for them to head down to Gotham Mortgage to collect their check.

The Soon-to-Be-Former Associate Broker

On closing day, which happens to be Joshua Dybnick's twenty-ninth birthday, Josh is on his way out of the Overman Group office when he stops to grab a doughnut from the table in the commissary. He is debating whether to select a butternut-cake or a chocolate-glazed when a hand reaches past him and slams the box shut. Josh looks up to see Bradley Overman, who tells him that those doughnuts are for vice presidents only; there aren't enough to feed Josh too. Assuming that Brad is joking, Josh reopens the box. He reaches for a doughnut, but Brad grabs his hand and says hey, what is this, kindergarten? If Josh wants doughnuts, why doesn't he generate more sales and attain the position of VP; then he can eat all the damn doughnuts he wants.

It's time for a serious talk, Brad tells Josh; they have to meet privately — now. Josh says he has a closing at Gotham, but Brad tells him this conversation can't wait because he's leaving the office soon and won't be returning today. "Let's go," he says. "Chop chop."

Bradley's tone is unfamiliar to Josh. Brad usually greets him with "Hey, Josh-O" and a back slap, then lends him CDs of bad music. Today, Brad's attitude seems all too similar to the one Josh still cops every day with Harvey Mankoff. Josh isn't positive why Brad might be barking at him. He has racked up more points lately than any other associate broker in this uptown office, and he has been putting in sixty-hour weeks aside from the fundraising and script development work he is doing for MTP. He can't imagine that his job could be in jeopardy. But lately, he hasn't spoken much to Bradley, who has been spending most of his lunch hours out of the office and having calls forwarded to the Warwick Hotel. As Brad leads the way out the front door, Josh tries to dismiss his boss's gruffness, but assumes Brad might be angry about what Mark Masler has told him — the man won't even look at him.

As the two men step out onto Broadway, Josh clutches his right knee to keep it from shaking. He sees Bradley's black Ford Explorer parked across 109th Street between a pair of other SUVs, recognizes Bradley's LUCKYDOG license plate, but when they reach the car, Bradley doesn't open the door, just leans against it, looks north and south on Broadway, then asks Josh to tell him exactly what he sees. Josh asks if this is a test. Bradley says Josh can call it what he wants, but he wants him to answer the question — what exactly does he see on this street? Come on, he says, he's waiting. Warily, Josh plays along.

Okay, says Josh, looking down, he sees the ground.

Good, Bradley says. What else?

The sky, says Josh.

What else? asks Bradley.

What is this about? Josh asks.

No, says Bradley, interrupting, tell him what else he sees.

Buildings, Josh says.

Wrong, says Bradley, who then makes a *ning-ning-ning* "wrong answer" sound. Those aren't buildings; they're commissions. He tells Josh they are standing in one of the most expensive zip codes in the country, where an average apartment costs $1.3 million. Each apartment in the city possesses, on average, five visible windows; thus, each window they can see potentially represents nearly $200,000 to the company after commissions. Does Josh understand what he is saying?

Sure, Josh says, everything is worth something—it is what his father always says while making summations to juries. Every limb, every lost day of work, everything has a price.

That's right, Overman says. But, he adds, some people can stand here, look at the buildings, and not see any commissions at all. You know what they see? Josh shrugs. *Theaters*, Bradley says. He says he has just received a phone call regarding a certain broker representing a property without his company's knowledge, and this broker isn't even trying to sell the thing for what it's worth; apparently, he wants to develop "a repertory theater company."

Oh shit, here it comes, Josh thinks. As he imagines the phone conversation that he now knows Bradley must already have had with Mark Masler, he looks across Broadway and can almost feel his new life receding from him. He can imagine everything he has gained from working at Overman being subtracted—he imagines his suits fraying like Miles Dimmelow's, his cuff links tarnishing. His throat suddenly parched, his voice sandy and dull, Josh asks Bradley to let him explain. No, Bradley says, then tells Josh to look at him and tell him something. Josh nods. What? he asks.

Bradley asks Josh to tell him if what he is doing is something he would expect an associate broker to do—pass up his commission just to fulfill some mad theater dream? Josh shakes his head. And why isn't it something an associate broker would do? Bradley asks. Josh begins to speak, but Bradley interrupts. No, he says again, he'll tell Josh exactly why. Because, he says, pointing a finger at Josh, not one of the firm's salespeople would have the *balls*; not one of them would have the creativity, the vision, the ambition. That's right, Bradley says, grinning now. All of them are too worried about their jobs, about their commissions, about making as much as they can now so someday they can sit around and do less.

So, Bradley asks again, is Josh's MTP plan something an associate broker would devise? Hell no, he answers. He reaches into the front pocket of his slacks, pulls out a key chain, and pushes a button on his remote. The trunk of his Ford flies open to reveal a small box wrapped with navy blue paper and tied with sky blue ribbon. And when Josh opens the box and finds the business cards on which are printed "Josh Dybnick, Vice President and Associate Broker, The Overman Group," Bradley roars with laughter and pulls Josh into a hug. "Happy fucking birthday, you slick, double-crossing, thespian son-of-a-bitch!" he cries, then says he wants to ask Josh only one more thing. Why hasn't Josh ever approached him about investing? How come Josh has never shown him one of his prospectuses? Anyone with Josh's talents is worth an investment, he says, and he might like to come aboard; he has always loved theater people—as Josh may have noticed, he's not a bad actor himself.

When Josh and Bradley return to the office, a giant shout of "SURPRISE!" is heard and lights burst on to reveal the office walls strewn with pink, blue, and yellow streamers. Red and white balloons bounce against the ceiling, a white banner with red letters reads HAPPY 29TH, JOSH! A new song by the Funkshuns suddenly blares. "(Girl, You Know That You're the) Best Funk of My Life." Josh's colleagues start dancing. There are party hats and noisemakers, flutes of champagne, grapes, hors d'oeuvres. The scene looks just like an opening-night celebration from *Light Up the Sky*.

Joshua watches the revelry as if he is already drunk; everyone is moving too slowly, speaking too fast. He doesn't register faces, just buffed shoes and tailored suits. Bradley Overman called him "slick." He still doesn't feel completely slick, but, who knows, maybe he already is. Sometimes onstage while playing D'Artagnan or Candide, he would feel as though he were moving with grace, speaking with beautiful diction, and afterward he would watch the videotape of the performance, and he would look clumsy, sound too self-consciously theatrical. He was never sure whether his true performance was the one he had felt inside or the one he later watched on video. All this while, he has only been acting the role of slick salesman, and yet he wonders if, at some point, he has become what he only pretended to be. And as a white twelve-tier cake shaped like a high-rise with more than a hundred windows is wheeled in on a handtruck, Joshua wonders why he doesn't feel happier. Still, once he catches a cab to Gotham Mortgage, a familiar Leonard Bernstein tune is beginning to play in his head: "Conquering the City." Yes, Josh thinks, yes, he just might.

The Buyer's Ex-husband & His Lover

On closing day, Darrell Schiff sits at the worktable in Jane Earhart's apartment, consults his datebook, and takes note of the scheduled meeting at Gotham Mortgage. In previous years, he has always bought a datebook in late December, filled it dutifully, but lost it by April and, invariably, upon finding it several months later, has been too discouraged by the months he missed to start filling in those that remain. But as Jadakiss once observed, that time is *over*. To spend as much time as possible with Jane, Darrell now breaks down every day by the hour, and he finds he has more time to write, more time to research, more time for his students. His classes go overtime, he stays in the T.A. office an hour later than anyone else, attends departmental functions and rarely finds them boring. He sits in the front row of lectures and actually cares about hearing answers to the questions he asks. He dresses for class in suits and sport coats, shaves every other day, interviews job candidates with the rest of the grad student committee even if a free meal isn't part of the bargain. And ever since he moved into Jane's apartment, he has not downloaded a single song, has not invented one obscene wordy-gurdy, has not even Googled anybody—save for once-hapless Abner Kravec, who has, believe it or not, won the fricking Wisconsin State Lottery, twenty-seven million bucks, God bless his balls, and Floyd "No Place to Go" Ellis, who received an Alert Citizen award for saving twelve kids from a fire.

Darrell sits on the edge of Jane's bed, watches her sleep, her body stiff, her eyes shut tight, her breaths short and fast. When she awakes, she looks into Darrell's eyes and sees them fill with tears. When she asks what the matter is, he says he never knew joy until he met her, was always most comfortable expressing dissatisfaction. Before he met her, he never would have settled for anything less than a job at a top-flight research university, despite the fact that he never gave two flips about research or universities. But even though he has begun to feel passionate about his work, if Jane wants to stay in the city, he'll find a job here even if he has to give up academia to do it. And if she wants to leave, well, he'll all-too-happily do that which he once feared; yes, for the sake of love, Darrell Finneran Schiff will teach at some shit school out west.

After Jane sits down at her laptop and begins to type, after Darrell knots his tie and grabs his new dead man's overcoat out of the closet, he pages through his datebook again. The words "Gotham Mortgage" float up to him like a letter from an old lover, a distant memory of a life he led before he scammed on Jane and changed his destiny. He truly hopes the closing at Gotham goes well. He wishes Rebecca great happiness, not like the times when he broke up with women or women broke up with him and he told them he wished them happiness when in truth he wished them years of abstinence, years of hell, or years of being boiled in Bezelnut oil. But Rebecca of all people deserves to be happy. Perhaps seeing her today embarking upon her new life would give him the satisfaction of learning that both of them have moved on.

For nearly an hour, Darrell lurks on the corner of Fifty-fifth Street and Sixth Avenue, leaning between the V and the E in Robert Indiana's *LOVE* sculpture, staring across the street at the steel-and-glass office building that houses Gotham Mortgage. As he stands and watches the life he might have led, the advertisement in the nearby Commerce Bank window resonates: CASH IS GOOD: CHANGE IS BETTER. Darrell watches the working people of midtown Manhattan and feels happier than ever that he is not among their number. He sees men and women in crisply tailored suits and $500 shoes, laptop bags over their shoulders, cell phones or iPods in their hands. Darrell's suits are all secondhand, the elastic on his briefs has gone crackly and limp, the soles of his shoes are worn through, but he possesses a gift he is certain these people do not have. If a man speaks in the tongues of mortals and angels, but has not love, then really what is he? he wonders. A fricking noisy-ass gong, that's what. If any of these people could find a love comparable to his, they would happily ditch their suits, their cell phones, their jobs, and leave this city behind.

Finally he sees Rebecca walking out of Gotham Mortgage and tears gather in the corners of his eyes. She looks awful. No makeup, he can tell that from here. But more important, Darrell notices that Rebecca has something she never had before—a beer gut. She practically looks pregnant. She must have started binge-eating the moment after he left her, he surmises. When he was with Rebecca, she was a strict vegan; now, she looks as if she spends her nights drinking Heineken, eating Cheetos and Funyuns. Darrell wishes he had never come here; this sight is just too grim.

Darrell walks slowly north, thinking of what his life would be like if he hadn't left Rebecca, imagining which boring and demeaning tasks he would be performing if he had closed on a condo today, if he hadn't escaped just in the nick of time. He spends the afternoon walking along Broadway, wandering in and out of bath, home fixture, and stroller stores, glad there is nothing here he needs to buy. He pays no attention when, early in the evening on 100th Street, a patrol car speeds past him with its sirens off and its flashers going. He takes no note of that police car until he sees it again, stalled outside 64 West 106th Street. But Darrell does not stop when he sees an officer getting out of the squad and hears the sound of howling from the building's second floor. He figures that Rebecca may finally have to evict that vagrant and his dog squatting in the apartment. He considers ringing the doorbell of 2B, offering to lend support to Rebecca, but instead he continues heading east toward the park, whose paths will lead him back home to Jane Earhart.

Just About Everyone at the Closing
(Save for the Dog)

On closing day, Megan Yu arranges and rearranges a dozen chairs around a long, varnished table in the Executive Conference Room of Gotham Mortgage, and opens the blinds onto a northern view encompass-

ing Central Park and the high-rises on either side of it—always a good idea
to offer a view of buildings with apartments that cost considerably more
than the one the client is buying, always smart to feed the client's aspirations. The mortgage broker shoves a beribboned champagne bottle into a
pewter ice bucket, then eyes her watch, hoping the closing will take no
more than an hour so that she won't be late to meet her lover.

On closing day, Alan Ziegler, the attorney for the seller, sits in the backseat of a taxicab creeping along Fifty-fifth Street, and once he has berated
the driver for not taking Fifty-third and has complained loudly to himself
about Gretchen Gruetke, the buyer's incompetent attorney, to whom he
has referred in negotiations as a "mommy lawyer" because she has three
children, he phones his secretary, whom he calls "Little Dummy," to ask
her to check his calendar to see if he has any other appointments scheduled for the afternoon or if he can spend the rest of the day at the club before meeting his wife, Lisa, to once again discuss selling their weekend
home in Pound Ridge. Then he clicks over to his other line, where today's
client, Mark Masler, asks if he will have time to "talk some car wash business" after the closing.

On closing day, Gretchen Gruetke, the attorney for the buyer, rides the
Metro-North into Grand Central from Connecticut, where she lives with
her four-year-old triplets and their round-the-clock nanny, Raimunda
Bonilla, who costs $200 a day plus expenses. The nanny was hired when
Gretchen's husband, to whom she had been introduced by his former college roommate, Josh Dybnick, who was incidentally the only man she ever
loved and who she now suspects has no soul whatsoever, departed for the
Marshall Islands, thus forcing Gretchen—who had hoped to take time off
from her job when her children were born—to work 364 days a year, handling real estate sales in three different states, all to endure the indignity of
being referred to as a "mommy lawyer" by the seller's attorney.

On closing day, the seller's estranged brother-in-law, Caleb Scheinblum, wears an ill-fitting sport coat as he drives a yellow Hummer up Central Park West. A cooler and a duffel bag that he surreptitiously filched
from his mother's house are in the back of the vehicle, and "Sunset Gun"
is turned up loud on the stereo. Caleb is wondering whether he should

park his car and meet the woman with whom he has communicated only via e-mail or keep driving rather than risk having her tell him he is too young for her. He turns west on Eighty-sixth Street, then drives fast around and around the block. He decides to stop, decides to keep driving, decides to stop again; no, he must keep driving. The music is too loud and he can no longer stand listening to it. He pops out the CD, flips on the police scanner instead, and drives around the block again, listening to police calls.

On closing day, the seller, Mark Masler, his hair still wet from the mikvah, tells his attorney, Alan Ziegler, over the phone that he needs to meet with him after the closing to discuss a possible "prime location" for Rolls Restaurant & Wash if they can find a way to circumvent the broker. Then he and his wife, Allie Masler, step out of their taxi and head for the elevators, one of which they initially intend to ride directly to Gotham's offices. But when the elevator starts moving, both instinctively smack the stop button and proceed to copulate until the alarm sounds only moments after their simultaneous orgasms, meaning that, once again, they have timed everything perfectly—making love in the time allotted, selling at what appears to be the peak of the market.

On closing day, the real estate broker, Josh Dybnick, walks into the Gotham Mortgage building with a stack of business cards in a jacket pocket. He is talking on his phone to his boyfriend, Miles Dimmelow, about a potential new "angel investor" for MTP, to which Miles remarks *woo-woo-woo-woooooooooo*, then tells Josh he will call Jane to tell her the good news. Josh informs Miles that he'll call back after the closing, then looks up to see the buyer, Rebecca Sugarman, waiting by the elevators, one of which appears to be stuck.

On closing day, Megan Yu pops a bottle of newly labeled champagne to celebrate not only the sale she has facilitated, but also the $3,250 commission she will receive, and the passionate afternoon at the Warwick she will soon enjoy. On closing day, buyer's attorney Gretchen Gruetke collects a $3,000 flat fee, which she will sign over to her nanny immediately upon her return to Connecticut, and seller's attorney Alan Ziegler collects $5,500 based on his hourly rate, which will just cover this month's dues at his club. On closing day, Mark and Allie Masler receive a check for $487,500 to cover the remainder of the apartment's purchase price, after which Mark will try to track down the owner of the property he is eyeing for his restaurant/car wash and make a solid, all-cash offer. On closing day, Josh Dybnick receives assurance that, within three days, his company will get a check from Alan Ziegler's escrow account for $31,500, of which 70 percent will be his to spend on a down payment for a new apartment so that he can finally leave Washington Heights, while the other 30 percent will go to his boss, Bradley Overman, who, unbeknownst to his ex-wife, Chloe Linton, with whom he still shares an apartment, will soon be in the Warwick Hotel awaiting his girlfriend Megan Yu's arrival. On closing day, buyer Rebecca Sugarman writes checks to Gretchen Gruetke and Mark and Allie Masler, then heads out to dine with Chloe before returning home to her boyfriend, Ike Morphy, and his dog, Herbie Mann.

On closing day, the aforementioned dog waits at home. Alone.

The Aforementioned Dog

On closing day, Herbie Mann is lying under Ike and Rebecca's bed when he hears the front door to the Roberto Clemente Building open, at which point he scampers out from his makeshift den, then dashes to the window and looks out onto the boulevard. When Ike and Rebecca have left for the day and the dog is alone, he usually shuts down, tries to block out feelings of boredom and abandonment by sleeping. Sometimes he dreams of squirrels; sometimes he has nightmares about that fateful day when he was taken away from the only home he knew—grabbed hard by his collar, muzzled, shoved into the back of a taxi, and driven to the shelter where he was surrendered. Sometimes he dreams of Ike's boots; sometimes he moans a low A-flat in his sleep as he dreams of the tiny, dirty cage where he learned to shut himself down like this, to curl up, to block out the sounds of the other dogs, to channel rage and despair into indifference.

He can lie in one position for hours, but when he hears keys jangle or a downstairs door open, he springs up, shakes off the sleep, and sniffs the air, hoping to smell Rebecca's shampoo or Ike's jacket. And then the tail comes to life, the heartbeat quickens; he feels pressure on his bladder, emptiness in his stomach, thirst. He trots to the bowl to lap up the water he hasn't tasted all day, hunts for the treats he refuses to eat when he is alone, gobbles them, then searches for a tennis ball, which he drops, then catches, drops, then catches as he listens for footsteps. When he is certain that Ike or Rebecca is approaching, he gallops impatiently from the window to the door to the window and back. But when the scent is unfamiliar or the footsteps are too heavy or too light, he lets loose with a warning howl, then barks as loud as he can until the danger passes, the hallway is silent, and he can return to his den, close his eyes, shut down once again.

The building's front door closes; the inner door opens. Herbie cocks his ears and sniffs. He hears two sets of steps, smells two scents, hears two voices; he recognizes both. He hears the voices in a duet, the words as always rushing by in a single stream: *HereweareChloehomesweethome***Sothisiswhatyougetforsixhundredfiftygrandthesedays**. The dog's heart pounds hard against his rib cage; saliva fills his mouth. As he runs back and forth, listening and sniffing, he feels two conflicting emotions. Smelling each scent, he is filled with love and with fear. Hearing each footstep, he wants to dash forward and he wants to slide under the bed. Listening to each voice, his tail wags, then droops. He runs, he stops; he struts, he cowers; he leaps, he shivers; he growls, he stops in mid-breath. He hears a key in the front-door lock of apartment 2B, and he sniffs, he stops, he listens, he waits.

The New Owner & Her Boss & the Dog

On closing day, Rebecca Sugarman and Chloe Linton climb the steps to the second floor of the Roberto Clemente Building, where Rebecca hears Ike's dog making strange, uncharacteristic noises: Herbie seems to be growling, whimpering, pacing the floor. Rebecca has become well aware of Herbie's usual routine, but none of this is familiar. At this point, she should be hearing Herbie's traditional welcoming bark. Then, she should hear the animal bark two more times, trot to the door, shake off the day's sleep. As she and Chloe approach the door, Rebecca should hear Herbie finally drink his water, crunch the fish-skin treat Ike left for him, then pant while eagerly waiting to greet her.

Rebecca puts the key in the lock and pushes open the door, and the animal turns from her glance, then dashes away. Rebecca considers whether she should ask Chloe to remain outside until she can determine whether Herbie is sick. But Chloe has already entered, and though Herbie is now running away faster, his growling is becoming louder.

Immediately following today's closing, Rebecca walked out of the Gotham Mortgage building, bade Josh Dybnick farewell, took several of his business cards, then met and embraced Chloe on Sixth Avenue. Before she could take note of the familiar figure lurking on the other side of the street, leaning against Robert Indiana's *LOVE* sculpture, she was in a taxi-cab bound for Esposito's Ale House, seated beside Chloe, with whom she still lunches every day.

After Rebecca moved in with Ike Morphy and Herbie Mann, she received a half-dozen messages from Chloe regarding the *Wizard Girl* review, and she worried that she might have irreparably harmed her relationship with her boss by assigning the book to Liz Fogelson. She was certain Liz would pan the book; making this assignment had been Rebecca's lone act of subversion since beginning work for *The American Standard.*

But when Rebecca finally spoke to Chloe on the phone, Chloe told her that the decision to assign *Wizard Girl* to Fogelson was "an act of beauty." Arriving at her office at the *Standard* to find Liz Fogelson's 5,000-word encomium, which hailed the unnamed author as the second coming of J. R. R. Tolkien, Carson McCullers, and Sir Thomas Malory, Rebecca assumed that Liz was joking. But that evening, when Rebecca entered Liz Fogelson's apartment and joined the critic, who was at her dining room table splitting a Big Mac and a large fries with her beagles and listening to loud, industrial music, Liz gushed forth with gratitude, thanking Rebecca for giving her a book that had made her enjoy reading again. She had even sent her copy of the book to her new boyfriend, who was loving it too. She couldn't remember any time when she had read a book and hadn't skipped the boring parts, which was what she had always done with Henry James, even when she had claimed he was her favorite author. Clearly, whoever wrote *Wizard Girl* had had a rich and difficult life, and this had informed her deceptively childish novel. Liz said she was sorry she couldn't trash the book as Rebecca had wanted, but she guessed that at heart she was a fair critic after all.

When Rebecca left the apartment, her recently renewed self-confidence had already taken a dive. She had never completely trusted her own literary taste, had spent much of grad school wondering how her fellow students could identify so many flaws in works she considered perfect, and this one time when she had felt sure of herself, felt certain that the portions of the book she'd read were heavy-handed and infantile, a woman who hated everything had utterly contradicted her. Now, Rebecca no longer knew what was good or bad, whether she was right or wrong, and furthermore she decided that she shouldn't give a damn. She had a new place to live, a new man, a child on the way, a dog devoted to her, and what she did between ten and six was inconsequential. Chloe had an editorial vision; Rebecca's job was to implement it and ignore her own opinions. From now on, she would assign the stories Chloe wanted to read; insert phone numbers, website addresses, and "service components" into columns; field calls from the marketing department, then insert references to advertisers' products into articles without raising any questions. Not quite how she had imagined the life of a New York editor, but maybe her vision had always been a fantasy.

Today at Esposito's, after Chloe and Rebecca sat down to another lunch, during which Rebecca assumed she would once again do little more than follow her boss's directives, Chloe, who was wearing the new orange scarf that Rebecca had bought to replace the one Herbie Mann had destroyed, announced that she had a surprise; this meal would celebrate more than Rebecca's first real estate purchase and more than her relationship with the "no doubt enchanting clarinetist" whom Chloe had not yet met. This week, Chloe said, she had received official audit numbers for the *Standard*'s circulation; they had risen for two quarters in a row for the first time since spring 2001. Plus, ad sales were inching up again. Barring "an act of God or a terrorist attack," the next issue would continue the trend.

Chloe asked if Rebecca understood the meaning of this good news. Rebecca said that, if Chloe wanted, the *Standard* could now hire back some of its recently departed editors. Chloe said that this was possible, then asked Rebecca what else the good news might signify. Rebecca asked if bonuses might be due to the advertising team. They might, Chloe said; in fact, everyone remaining at the *Standard* might get a raise, but she wouldn't be in charge of that decision and neither would Rebecca. She took a pull from her highball. Rebecca had not yet guessed the best news of all, she said. Come next year, the two of them wouldn't work at the *Standard* anymore.

One rule of being a turnaround artist, said Chloe, was to "never stay too long at the dance." Sooner or later, a downturn was inevitable, and she had already enlisted a headhunter for both of them. Next year, she would be turning around a new magazine, and Rebecca could join as second-in-command. They could have lunch together, take the subway to and from work together; Rebecca's child could toddle back and forth between their two offices.

None of the magazines Chloe mentioned—*Sloppy Seconds*, a cooking magazine for divorcées; *Tube*, a digital television lifestyle magazine; *Home Boy*, an urban real estate quarterly—had the same appeal for Rebecca as *The American Standard*. Rebecca had little interest in working for magazines focusing on such topics as prostate care, pleasure boating, or wine connoisseurship. But as all the publications Chloe named began to fuse into one, Rebecca told herself she shouldn't care. Her life with Ike should matter, the life of her child, her relationship with Chloe too. Her own editorial contributions would always be negligible; apparently, she still wouldn't be able to tell a good book from a bad one.

After lunch, Chloe suggested they go somewhere else for dessert or a nonalcoholic cocktail, but Rebecca asked if Chloe would mind if she went straight home to celebrate with Ike. Chloe consented but said that if Rebecca was taking the rest of the day off, she wanted to see this apartment, see what $650K bought in Manhattan these days.

Now, as she enters her new apartment with Chloe, and Herbie runs away, Rebecca notices with growing trepidation that the dog's tail is not wagging, that it is tucked between his legs. When Rebecca moves closer, Herbie scurries into a corner of the living room, seemingly unable to lift the tail more than an inch, twitch it twice, then tuck it back between his legs before running to the bed, then sliding underneath it.

Rebecca tells Chloe she doesn't know what's wrong with Herbie. Normally, he is so affable, always willing to play. She wonders aloud whether he has hurt his paw or if he is sick. "Herbie," she says, holding out her hand, "it's okay. Come out, boy." Chloe laughs and tells Rebecca not to worry; she has never had successful relationships with animals, has no patience for them; she believes they have feelings, sure, but neither souls nor memories, and she is certain that, once she leaves, the animal will act normally once again. In fact, she adds, her ex-husband's old dog looked just like this one. Rebecca asks her what was the name of that dog.

"Lucky," says Chloe.

"Lucky," Rebecca says.

LuckyLucky, Herbie hears.

A low growl is heard, followed by a clumsy pattering of paws as a flood of memories washes over Herbie Mann: the life he had before Ike named him Herbie, the life before he was muzzled and shoved into the back of the taxi, before the ride in darkness to a cold, dark room full of cages, where he howled every time someone entered, fearing they were there to destroy him.

As Chloe stands in the bedroom, gazing at the pigeon dung on Ike and Rebecca's windows, the dog dashes out from underneath the bed. He has now recognized the woman's voice, recognized her perfume, even the hands that grabbed his collar and led him to the shelter.

Herbie is at the foot of the bed, ears at attention, tail twitching. He breathes heavily, growls, snaps at the air. His lips are curled, teeth bared. To Rebecca, the animal is virtually unrecognizable. She has only seen him walk on leash and play in the dog run; she has never seen his full strength, never witnessed his true speed. Until now, she has never looked carefully at Herbie Mann's teeth; they are gleaming white and dagger sharp, worked down to fine points by a diet of raw meat and bones. The animal is staring at Chloe. Saliva from the corners of his mouth drips to the floor in long, thin strands that gather in pools. He breathes faster, fearful memories transforming themselves into aggression. And when Chloe's eyes meet his, the dog leaps up, mouth wide, paws extended, his growl as loud as a bark, only so much deeper, echoing in his chest as he pounces, and his paws collide with the woman's shoulders.

Rebecca screams. Chloe, hands raised, yells "Stop it, Lucky!" She tries to duck out of the way of the leaping dog, but her heel slips in a pool of Herbie's spit; her knee buckles, she falls backward, her head smacks the air conditioner, then the window ledge. As Chloe's head slams against the floor, the pair of alarmed pigeons in the nest outside flutter their wings, then fly for safety.

Herbie stands over Chloe's body, moans softly, then howls with fear and regret. Blood oozes from the back of Chloe's head and onto the hardwood floor. Chloe does not wake to hear Rebecca yell "Get away, just get away" to the dog, does not wake to see Rebecca run to the hall closet for a towel to wrap around Chloe's head. She does not wake to see Rebecca, cell phone in hand, call 911; or to see Herbie, shaken by Rebecca's screams and the sight of the blood, retreat to a corner of the living room and curl up, tail between his legs, his body shivering. Chloe does not wake to hear police cars and ambulances approaching; to see paramedics carrying a stretcher up to apartment 2B; to see Herbie corner the police officer, Wayne Cahill, snap at him, and lunge until the officer leaves, then returns with a muzzle. Chloe does not feel herself being lifted onto the stretcher, taken downstairs and into the back of the ambulance. She remains unconscious as that ambulance speeds away with Rebecca pressing a bloody white towel against her head, while Officer Cahill roughly yanks Herbie out of the apartment, and the dog howls and howls and howls.

{ IV }

CLOSING
COSTS ARE
ASSESSED

*Leaving New York, never easy
(it's pulling me apart)* . . .

R.E.M.,
"Leaving New York"

A MANN ESCAPES

On the night when Ike Morphy will discover that he will have to leave his city and his lover, Rebecca Sugarman enters the apartment she has owned for less than a day and sees him hanging up the phone in the kitchen. Ike has just finished talking yet again with animal control; he still has his backpack over one shoulder just as he did this morning when he went off to practice in Inwood. Since returning home to find the apartment door open and blood on the bedroom floor, then speaking with the four *compañeros* across the way, who mentioned the ambulance, the stretcher, and someone leading the black dog away, Ike has walked up and down just about every block in Manhattan Valley asking people whether they had seen Rebecca or Herb. But he barely recognized anyone now, and, more important, hardly any of his new neighbors seemed to recognize him. Most eyed him warily as he approached, realizing too late that he was not some homeless man selling newspapers or begging for change. They remained unmoved by Ike's questions, shook their heads, murmured a barely audible "Sorry," and Ike was left to ask yet another passerby had he seen a red-haired woman, about six feet tall, or a black Lab mix about yea big with a white tuft on his tail and snowy sprinkles on his muzzle and his front paws.

Ike pressed the buzzers of his neighbors' apartments; nobody came to the door. The police never called back. Ike called hospitals: no record of Rebecca. His emotions have zigzagged from fear to confusion to sadness to fear once again, a little pinprick of fear that bleeds into his entire body, then transforms to hope the moment Rebecca enters the apartment. He moves forward to embrace her, but her hands remain stiff at her sides and she feels cold: Ike sees that Herbie is not beside her.

"Where's that dog?" he asks. "Is the boy okay?"

Rebecca shakes her head; she has sat for nearly six hours at Chloe Linton's bedside, held Chloe's hand, waiting vainly for her to regain consciousness until a nurse told her that Chloe needed rest and would probably awaken by morning. Rebecca wants to rest now too, wants to sleep even though she knows she will probably not be able to, wants to lie alone in bed even though the apartment has only one bed. She wants Ike to sleep on the couch, on the floor, anywhere—is that really such a terrible thing? she wonders. Until now, the fact that she has known Ike for such a short time has been exhilarating, a blessed change from her predictable tendencies; now, she feels troubled that this man is here with her, this man who will probably care more about the fate of his animal than that of the woman his dog attacked without apparent provocation. She does not even want to tell Ike what happened, fears what he might do or say when he learns, has grown to care deeply for him but has seen his bitter anger once before in this apartment, such a seemingly arbitrary anger that somehow reminds her of the way in which Herbie Mann leapt at Chloe, sent the woman crashing to the floor, then turned on the police officer who had no obvious choice other than to take the animal away. Part of her now wishes she had listened to Darrell, who had never trusted Ike or his dog. She walks past Ike, her eyes not meeting his as she nearly collapses onto the couch. "The police," she says.

Ike stands in the dark kitchen gazing through the partition that gives out onto the living room as Rebecca tells the story. His body is pitched ever so slightly toward Rebecca as if he hasn't stopped moving yet, as if he has just stepped off a ship and is still not used to the feel of the earth beneath him. He is beginning to feel the same cold dread and powerlessness he felt one time as a young man in his parents' kitchen—his father motionless on the floor, his mother moaning, vegetables scattered all about. When Rebecca finishes telling him all she knows of what has happened and Ike asks questions, he can barely hear his own voice over the heartbeat thrumming in his chest and his ears; the apartment already seems so damn empty without Herbie in it, emptier still as he sees the cold, distant way that Rebecca is looking past him, almost as if now that Herbie's gone, some part of him is already gone too. Somehow, he feels, he has let everybody down.

Moments pass in silence. Then Ike walks to the hall closet and takes down his mother's old gardening kit. From it, he removes his pair of shears, grips them tightly in one hand, feels their weight. He pauses and looks toward Rebecca, waits for her to ask what he is planning to do, but she doesn't say anything. He moves closer but sees her body become tense again, her face turn paler. Ike stops. Still carrying his backpack with his clarinet inside, he turns and heads for the door. "I love you, Rebecca, but I gotta find Herb. I made a promise to him," he says, but Rebecca still doesn't respond, just shrugs; she feels numb, unsure at this moment whether she cares for Chloe or Ike or no one at all. She does not ask where Ike is going or when he'll be back. She does not look up when he walks out with his garden shears and backpack. She hears the outside door of the Roberto Clemente Building open and close, then Ike's footsteps on the sidewalk below. She sighs, closes her eyes tight, hugs her knees to her chest. Her eyes, her throat, her hands, her belly—everything feels cold, dry, alone. She owns this apartment now, but it sure doesn't feel like home.

Ike does not try to conceal the implement in his right hand as he proceeds through a now strange and unfamiliar city down Columbus Avenue, upon which an oily spring rain is beginning to fall. He feels a sensation well beyond exhaustion, as though his body has seeped out of him and no frame is left for his skin. Still, his body feels like that of a younger man, one with a guiding mission. He walks through the rain, stepping from light into darkness, then into light again, passing a beauty salon, a ninety-nine-cent store, Los Compadres restaurant. Then he reaches the Frederick Douglass

Apartments, beside which he walks in darkness again. On a sign in front of the housing projects, there is a quote from Frederick Douglass: "If there is no struggle, there is no progress." At the corner of 100th Street, Ike turns west again. Across the street, more than an entire city block has been leveled. What used to be there? Ike can no longer remember. He walks past an asphalt playground where a lone girl spins Xs and Os on a vertical tic-tac-toe game that is taller than she is. A posse of teenage boys is laughing and smoking cigarettes behind the project fence. In the distance, Ike can see cranes hovering above new Broadway condo buildings already taller than the spires of Trinity Evangelical Lutheran Church.

Tonight, the police station is the only bright building on the block. It has the eerie white glow of an all-night diner on a dead-end street, and in its incandescence, the accelerating rain looks like falling snow. Ike has seen the cold, fluorescent-lit interior of the station only once, came inside to return a checkbook he'd found on the Great Hill, then watched the officers, most all of them white, wearing navy blue uniforms as they walked back and forth in front of a framed, wrinkled American flag and beneath tarnished gold letters that spelled out "Courtesy, Professionalism, Respect." They cracked jokes as Ike sat and waited to file a report, eyed Ike as if he were some shady character, as if any black dude who entered the station had to be guilty of something; they asked if Ike had stolen the checkbook and was now looking to claim a reward. Ike knows that some folks in the city idolize the cops, but all he's seen them do lately in this neighborhood is arrive long after they're needed, hassle the people who've lived here for years; they drive fast, leap from their cars, guns and nightsticks drawn, tackle some poor crackhead or shoplifter, knees in the perp's back, cuff him and shove him against a wall, holler with unconvincingly affected ghetto slang—*Yeah, motherfucker, how you like me now?*

The sidewalk in front of the police station is empty and, across the street, a yellow Hummer is driving slowly past the dim Bloomingdale Branch Library. The teens from the projects are peering at the police station's driveway, where a white Crown Vic police sedan is parked. Ike stops walking about fifty yards from the station; he already understands what has captured the kids' attention. Even at this distance, Ike can hear Herbie Mann whimpering from the backseat of the police car. He recognizes that sound, the soft, back-of-the-throat stutter that comes accompanied by a wet nose and glassy eyes, that deep *humm-hmm-hmm-hwaaaaaaaah* that Ike first heard on the day he adopted Herbie, the A-flat Herbie emits whenever he is ill and smells food he cannot eat, when he sees other dogs playing on the Great Hill and he can't join, when he sees Ike and Rebecca leave the apartment, knows he's not coming with them, and starts to sing this mournful solo.

Herbie paces the back of the vehicle, performing tight little laps. The dog tries to look out, tries to poke his nose through the thick, sharp wire separating him from the back window. He claws at the wire, shoves his nose into the windows, against the bulletproof-glass partition. His ears ring from his own barks. But soon he lies resignedly on the backseat once again, curls his head into his body, so small now, his tail brushing his nose, his voice barely strong enough even to whine anymore. He is shutting down, imagining a park full of squirrels to chase, a cool blue lake without another dog in sight; a place where he can swim all day. The animal closes his eyes.

Ike stands, holding a bar of the project gates. He imagines a future unfurling before him to the distant, lugubrious sound of a muted clarinet. If he does not move forward, he will stand here and watch an officer leave the station, get back into his squad, probably drive the vehicle to animal control, where Herbie will be shoved into a dirty cage, no one to hear whether or not he even bothers trying to make another sound. Ike truly has no idea of what will happen to him or to the dog; maybe he'll get off with merely a fine, maybe the animal will be destroyed. Forty thousand are put down in Manhattan every year; he knows that number by heart.

Perhaps he should just go home, Ike thinks, sleep beside Rebecca, apologize to her, take the blame for all that has happened. He could say to himself that his responsibility to Rebecca and her child is more important than the fate of one unlucky mutt, say that the animal has lived a good life, has known greater friendship than most of his brethren, has most probably outlived just about every creature who was in the shelter the day Ike brought him home.

Garden shears in hand, Ike moves into a white halo of streetlight, then into another blotch of shadow. His heart still thrums, but he feels the icy calm that comes with certainty of purpose. He steps forward and light glances off of the shears, now wet with rain; the gleam bounces into the eyes of the project teens who wonder aloud who that tall brother is with that big-ass scissors in his hands. They whisper, they laugh, and they shout as they follow from behind the fence.

The backseat of the squad is dark. Ike hopes Herbie will stay down, hopes the animal won't recognize his scent. He moves slowly now, in the shadows, steps oh-so-quietly. *Don't stand up, Herb, stay down, down, stay down*, he says to himself, hoping the animal will understand. *Stay down, man*, he whispers, *down*. But the animal senses Ike approaching, and now he stands again and paces the backseat of the squad. *Quiet, Herb*, Ike whispers as the dog tries to bark; no dog is as loud as this one even with a muzzle on. *Down*, Ike says as Herbie whines. *Goddamn it, Herb*. The dog is so loud now that the kids from the projects laugh harder ("What's that crazy motherfucker gonna do with that scissors?").

Ike raises the garden shears high above one shoulder, grips them hard using both hands, then brings the blades down into the center of a rear, passenger-side window. A whoop goes up from the kids, a whoop and a "Damn, motherfucker!" The car alarm pierces the night, but Ike doesn't stop, brings the shears down, as if he's driving a pitchfork into the center of the earth, down, down, and down again until the window crumples like tinfoil that Ike swats away, barely feeling the glass that cuts his palms as Herbie leaps through.

Cops in uniform and plainclothesmen in baseball jackets, polo shirts, and clean white tennis shoes burst through the front door of the station, guns drawn. They see the shattered window of the white Crown Vic, hear the alarm, see the project kids approach the car, then take stock of the cops and run across 100th Street toward Trinity Evangelical. The cops start chasing the teens, oblivious for the moment to both the man and the dog. "Yeah, motherfucker, hold it right there, boy," one cop is shouting as Ike and Herbie creep slowly west, turn north at Amsterdam, then start running fast. The sound of the alarm is becoming ever more distant to them as they run through the city; it is fading like the last note of a symphony.

CHASE!!!!!

Ike Morphy and Herbie Mann are running. They have not stopped since 106th Street, and there they'd paused only briefly. No, they couldn't go home, Ike thought. Herbie would no longer be safe there. "Follow, Herb," Ike finally called out to the dog, and they turned around and started heading west. "*FollowHerb*," the parrot at Ana Beauty Salon repeated as the man and the dog crossed Columbus Avenue, passing the site of the old Felipe Grocery, where the *compañeros* were packing up their radio, lawn chairs, and milk crates to get out of the rain. *Heyblackdogblackdog*, Herbie heard one *compañero* shout with a laugh as he and Ike ran by.

No leash restrains Herbie, and his legs feel more elastic without it; his paws barely touch the ground. He and Ike zip past the Jewish Home and Hospital, where elderly patients, some with oxygen tanks, some with nurses by their sides, gaze out at the blur of man and dog running by. Across the street at Mama's Pizzeria, young toughs are gathered outside under the canopy eating pizza slices while seated on mini-motorcycles; Ike and Herbie run past the Empire Corner Chinese Restaurant, where a man in matching tweed hat and jacket barks into a megaphone, asking passersby if they have been saved by Jesus. Herbie lunges for the man, but Ike grabs the animal's collar and pulls him away. Ike and Herbie run toward Broadway past shuttered copy shops, past newly rehabbed condos with Security Watch cameras mounted above their doors. They dash across Broadway through tiny Straus Park, past its memorial fountain with a plaque honoring Isidor and Ida Straus, who died on the *Titanic*: IN THEIR DEATH, THEY WERE NOT DIVIDED.

In the darkness of Riverside Park, Ike and Herbie walk fast upon wet leaves, the black Hudson River to the west, the lights of New Jersey beyond. Ike washes the blood and remaining slivers of glass from his hands in a drinking fountain, wipes them on his jeans. Herbie laps from the fountain. Ike checks to see if, by some coincidence, Ricardo and Buster might be in the dog run, but no, they are long gone from this city. On this wet night, the whole park seems empty. Ike hears a crash of thunder and sees a patrol car rolling along the path; he pulls Herbie by the collar back east, up the stairs, out of the park, back toward Broadway.

Ike and Herbie are heading uptown. The rain is beginning to fall so forcefully now that everybody on Broadway is looking either straight ahead or down to the ground; nobody's watching. Restaurant deliverymen wear hooded, rain-slicked, green or black ponchos as they bike through the storm; umbrella-toting pedestrians maintain their distance from curbs where buses and taxis kick up dirty water that is pooling in potholes. Ike and Herbie walk briskly, though not fast enough to call attention to themselves; they are merely a man and his dog out for a quick stroll in the downpour, Ike keeping pace to the forceful beat of his heart.

Farther up Broadway, professors, students, and the students' parents are closing down Korean, Mexican, and French restaurants. The Olympia Theater at 107th has been razed; up goes a condo complex and a Bank of America; a Commerce Bank has moved in across the way. Gristede's has been shut down to make way for another condo. Yet another condo rises in the distance above a gleaming new supermarket. Ike and Herbie pass through the blue-and-white glow of a new bank sign: CHASE.

Ike and Herbie walk past the Overman Group's uptown office, where a few night-owl brokers are hunched over computer screens, typing with one hand as they speak on cell phones, glugging coffee out of giant mugs, grabbing pages of listings from printer trays. Looking ahead across 110th, Ike can see that the entire building complex he remembers has disappeared—the bagel shop and revolutionary bookstore are gone now; more condos and groceries are already here.

Acting students in sweaters and scarves are waiting for taxis in front of the Manhattan Theater Project. Two posters are taped to the ticket booth. One reads BOYSWORLD! LAST WEEKS! MUST CLOSE SOON! Another declares WATCH FOR OUR UPCOMING SEASON! Man and dog walk past gleaming new supermarkets, past Starbucks and the Broadway Presbyterian Church, where a homeless woman sits on the steps beside the church's sign: NEEDS: DONATIONS, CLOTHING, MUSICAL INSTRUMENTS. Ike and Herbie amble past university dorms, the public library, the gates of Columbia. But when Ike hears police sirens coming from the north, he charges across Broadway and he and Herbie run down 116th Street, underneath scaffolding, past Dumpsters overloaded with cardboard boxes, across Claremont, back to the park.

Ike and Herbie are running along Riverside Drive through the rain. Herbie gallops through the shadows cast by Riverside Memorial Chapel. The pair run past the Grant Memorial; then, at the sight of dark green security booths, they cut back over a faded hopscotch court, across Riverside Drive. Ike and Herbie run over dead grass alongside lengths of rusted black fence, past idling gypsy cabs, hookers and their johns in back. The Hudson River, the highway, the lights of the George Washington Bridge are all visible through the branches of oak trees as man and dog run over the highway, whizzing past billboards: NEW YORK LOTTERY: THE JACKPOT IS NOW and FOR SALE: COOPERATIVE APARTMENTS. As they run, Ike cannot shake the sensation that they are being followed. At every siren, his heartbeat quickens; at the sight of any Crown Vic, sweat forms on his wet neck and forehead; when he glimpses a yellow Hummer driving too slowly, the sounds of police calls blaring from its scanner, he runs faster.

As he and Herbie run farther north, past the entrance to Riverbank State Park, Ike checks his pocket for his keys—the one to Phil Sugarman's house in Maine is on his chain. That key represents the only solution Ike has been able to devise, the only way to reach safety and retain some connection to Rebecca. Ricardo and Marlena have moved away. Ike cannot go home. Chicago is too far, and everyone he cared for there is gone. He has no easy way to get out of town, no truck anymore. Hitchhiking's risky, and Herbie can't ride with him on the bus or the train. They have to keep running, past yellow caution signs, locust trees, barberry bushes. They run past a cut-out sculpture dedicated to Ralph Ellison; there is a sign upon it: I AM AN INVISIBLE MAN.

Ike's knees are killing him as he runs past the Milstein Hospital Building—he's thirty-nine years old, and he's really feeling every one of those years tonight. But Herbie's eyes are bright, his tail alive as he scampers up 165th Street, then north again at Fort Washington Avenue. They pass playgrounds, basketball courts, a restaurant called Shangri-La; parks, pigeons, bus stops, churches, a synagogue, swing sets, a hip-hopper rapping on a street corner, Mother Cabrini High School, dedicated to the patroness of immigrants.

For a few moments at the top of the steps of Fort Tryon Park, Ike and Herbie catch their breath, but then they descend fast—lone men in jogging suits are waiting for other single men to arrive; they whistle as Ike and Herbie run past them, then out of the park at Aster Street. The two pass a car wash, a paint shop, Laundromats, the True Love Wedding Center; in a window, a mannequin groom holds hands with his bride. On a lamppost, Ike sees a photocopied sign for a pet care center: LUCKY DOG. Ducks are quacking in Inwood Hill Park, and Ike and Herbie are running toward them when the rain stops at last.

Near the top of Inwood Hill, at Butterfly Meadow, where Ike and Herbie stop running, the ground is soaked. Herbie collapses, then falls fast asleep under a black ash tree; Ike leans against the tree, wipes his eyes, and shivers as he gazes past the edge of Manhattan across the Harlem River. If Rebecca wants to look for him, she will come here. Waiting on the slim chance she might arrive, all too certain she won't, Ike passes the hours by writing music in his head; he hears new sounds that he might incorporate into his Rhapsody in A-Flat—handslaps against the keys and the body of the instrument, signifying the escape he and Herbie have made tonight; fingers flicking metal to represent Herbie's claws on a cage; a long, piercing police siren. Every note he hears is melancholy; more so when he realizes that Rebecca won't be coming. People can be so disappointing, he thinks—yeah, himself most of all.

As Herbie continues to rest, Ike massages the dog's legs with the tea tree oil he keeps in his clarinet case, and he tries to develop a plan. One night, they can sleep; the next, they can walk. Daytimes, they will lay low—beneath trees in parks, under viaducts. Slowly, they will make their way north. Maine is much too far, of course, but at least it is a goal. The trick is to divide the journey up, view it in small steps, like math exercises using fractions—half and half and half again. Never try to memorize a piece of music all at once, Herman Vontagh taught him, memorize it measure by measure, note by note. They may walk only ten miles on any one night, but that ten and ten and ten will add up. Ike can see Manhattan ending as he stands underneath the ash tree and gazes downward; the Harlem River is narrow, and though it flows fast, he could swim across. He closes his eyes and pictures both of them floating the whole way—from the river to the ocean. Herbie always loved swimming in Lake Michigan.

Ike uses his garden shears to carve the words "Ike and Herbie Love Rebecca" in the trunk of a tree. Then, when Herbie wakes up, the pair make their way back down the hill and across the park's muddy fields. No dogs or people in sight. No cars driving by. A nearly empty bodega stands at Indian Road and 218th. Ike puts Herbie in a down-stay underneath a park bench, tells him to rest until he returns. The animal shimmies down to the pavement, chin against a paw, and sighs.

In the bodega, Ike orders corn muffins, water, two cheese sandwiches, a tall coffee, four hard-boiled eggs. The dreadlocked young woman at the register pays more attention to the purple book she is reading than to her customer. The news is on television, but she's not watching; neither is the short-order cook. Ike tries to call Rebecca from the pay phone but hangs up when his call goes straight to voice mail; he feels certain she has turned off her phone and doesn't want to hear from him.

Ike glances out the window to see that he can detect the glint of a streetlight in the eyes of his dog. Whenever he hears a car, he looks again, makes sure the vehicle passes and Herbie has remained still. Ike looks and Herbie

stays; a yellow Hummer passes and Herbie stays; a hooded dogwalker am-
bles by with four beasts on leashes, and Herbie stays nonetheless. The
young woman at the register hands Ike his coffee, his food, and his drinks,
keeps the change, wishes him good night, returns to her book, and Herbie
stays. Ike sips his coffee, turns to the door, takes a breath, and steps outside.
Venus is out; stars are becoming visible through the patches between the
clouds. They can walk ten more miles tonight, Ike thinks. They will start by
walking into the Bronx, underneath the elevated train tracks; when dawn
approaches, they'll find someplace to hide.

"Come on, Herb," Ike says as he crosses the street toward the dog. But
Herbie doesn't move. "Come on, man," Ike repeats, but the animal slides
farther under the bench, curling himself into a ball, as if trying to become
as tiny as possible. "Herb," Ike says. He reaches into a bag, breaks off a
chunk of corn muffin, holds it under Herbie's nose; the animal won't take
it. Ike peels a hard-boiled egg; Herbie turns away from the odor and
whines. Ike grabs the dog's collar and tugs, dragging Herbie out from underneath the bench. But after Herbie reluctantly emerges, Ike turns to see
a white Crown Vic with a broken rear window double-parked at the corner
of 218th and Indian; Officer Wayne Cahill is getting out of the vehicle,
one hand moving toward his holster.

Herbie growls as Ike Morphy takes a deep breath, sets down his coffee
and bag of food, and clutches his knees. Ike looks left to the Baker Field
football stadium, back to the river and the park, then down to his dog. Give
up or keep running? he asks himself. *Give Herbie up or just goddamn run?*
"Follow!" he suddenly shouts, and now they are running again, past the
padlocked football stadium, across Park Terrace West. They can hear a
door slam, the Crown Vic back up fast on the narrow street, shifting into
drive as Ike runs up 218th so fast that his knees practically slam into his
fists. The squad car's highway lights are hot and bright on their bodies, the
rumble of the Crown Vic's accelerator palpable in their chests and legs.

They will not stop running anymore, Ike tells himself as they dash
across an empty doughnut shop parking lot, never stop running. The squad
is gaining, but they keep running; the traffic light on Broadway is red, but
they keep running. The yellow Hummer appears, speeds north on Broad-

way; the driver of the Hummer lays on his horn, but Herbie and Ike keep running across the avenue straight for the traffic island. The officer sounds his siren; the Hummer's driver blares his horn; the Hummer's brakes screech. The Crown Vic clips the back of the Hummer and spins into Broadway's southbound lanes, at which point the Hummer suddenly stops, and its passenger door flies open. The radio in the car is still tuned to police calls. The eyes of the Hummer's driver lock onto Ike's, then Herbie's, then Ike's again.

"Are you that dude with the dog?" the driver asks, and when Ike nods, the driver asks him to get in.

Ike makes as if to start running again, but Herbie has already jumped, first onto the passenger seat, then into the back. He finds an empty space between a cooler full of sandwiches and bottled drinks and an open duffel bag with stacks of clothes, CDs, and a battered purple paperback inside. Ike gets in and shuts the door, and the driver speeds forward. Ike asks where he is headed. Canada, Caleb Scheinblum says. Then, he lays on the gas.

WELL PAST MIDNIGHT, Caleb Scheinblum is driving through Massachusetts on I-95. The roads are still slick; taillights and headlights cast red and white streaks upon the asphalt. Trucks spray droplets of mist on the windshield. Herbie sleeps in the back of the Hummer, sighing as he dreams of swimming. The two men have spent the drive talking and confessing, each finding comfort in revealing his hopes and fears to a stranger, one he will most probably never see after this drive. Ike has told Caleb about a small A-frame house on the South Side of Chicago with the neighborhood's most beautiful garden, about a life full of moments when everything he took for granted suddenly became precarious. He has spoken of leaving Chicago and never wanting to return, of blessedly arriving in New York but now having to leave again. He has told Caleb stories he has never told Rebecca, mostly because they concern her—the sense that he has known and will know her always, the frustration he feels wondering if he has made another mistake by leaving her tonight.

Caleb drives onward, both hands on the wheel, radar detector and police scanner still on, careful not to draw attention to his stolen car or the quarry he is carrying. Unlike Ike, he's glad to be going. New York was beat, he says, and he knew the time was right to go—who cares what city you're in if you can't be with the person you love there? Caleb says that he knows this woman is the right one for him—every night they discuss music, movies, TV shows. She has recommended books to him, one of which has become his favorite. But when she agreed to meet him, he lost his nerve. He drove around and around her apartment building wearing the only sport coat he owned, but never stopped driving; he was certain she would leave when she saw how young he was. Tonight, he has written her an e-mail telling her he is leaving home for Canada, and when he finds a place to stay, he will send his address. He has written that he doesn't care what her real name is, doesn't care whether she is rich or poor, a young babe or some old bat—they know each other's souls; that's enough.

Caleb asks if Ike thinks he's crazy to be leaving without knowing exactly where he's headed, but Ike says no. He remembers what his mother told him when she was still healthy and he said he could move back to Chicago. "No, brother," he tells Caleb, "there's nothing for you back there."

Morning breaks, and Caleb and Ike ride in silence. Ike is wearing one of Caleb's black hooded sweatshirts while his jacket dries. The car is warm, and Ike no longer starts at the sight of police cars. He gazes out the window at the green blur of fir trees, iridescent in the glow of last night's rain. When Ike falls asleep, he dreams longingly of stillness, of standing in place; of a sky with motionless clouds, an ocean without waves; of men and women frozen in blocks of ice, mountains and valleys as still as if captured in a photograph; of a day when he no longer feels any need to run. But when Ike finally opens his eyes onto the overcast day, Caleb is still driving.

The roads have become narrower, two lanes instead of four. The Hummer winds through small villages, not quite ghost towns, not quite living ones either. The marquee of an abandoned movie theater they pass advertises *Collateral Damage*, a film that opened and closed more than half a decade earlier. Paint has peeled off the wooden slats of churches; tall, yellow grass is growing over abandoned train tracks; FOR SALE signs lurk in the windows of shuttered diners, grocery stores, houses. Everywhere are Realtors' signs: OCEANSIDE PROPERTIES. MAINE REALTORS. PRECIPICE HOMES.

Caleb stops the car at the side of the road just outside Croix-de-Mer, the last town before Canada. From a pay phone, Ike calls Rebecca, and when once again she doesn't answer, he makes another call and leaves a message for Phil Sugarman, telling him where he is going; he says he can't see any other choice. If Rebecca makes her way to Inwood Hill Park, he says, she will find a message for her on a tree near the top of the hill.

When Ike returns to Caleb's car, Herbie is standing on the backseat, pacing, ears up, tail stiff. The dog makes low, muttering noises and high-pitched whines—he smells water and he aches to swim. You know, dude, Caleb tells Ike, if you want, I can take Herbie. He says he's good with animals and he didn't believe the story he heard on the police scanner; he doubts the dog acted randomly—people are irrational sometimes, never animals. He knows what it's like to be misjudged, knows he and Herbie could get along. Ike can sense that Caleb is a decent kid, and that leaving home will make him a better one. Yeah, he could say good-bye to Herbie and Caleb here, wish them good luck, return to Rebecca if she'd even have him anymore. But the dog was abandoned by his owners once, and that's enough for any lifetime. And besides, Ike can only imagine how he would feel standing at the side of the road, watching Herbie ride toward Canada while he had to find his way home alone, never knowing for sure if Herbie was still alive.

The two men part at the intersection of the highway and Croix-de-Mer Road. Caleb shakes Ike's hand, then thumps Herbie's flanks. "Be good, dudes," Caleb tells Ike and Herbie. "Thanks, brother," says Ike. Backpack over both shoulders, he walks with Herbie into fog and darkness; they hear two toots of the Hummer's horn as Caleb speeds to the Canadian border.

The sky seems lower here at the very edge of the country, and, walking into the mist of Croix-de-Mer, Ike has the sensation of moving through clouds. He can hear the low moan of the foghorn, the flutter of clothes on laundry lines, the hiss of the ocean, the cackles and howls of coyotes. At the end of the road, a damp, rocky driveway leads to the front door of the

Sugarmans' 150-year-old Cape Cod. Ike walks into the house and the dog runs to the bay. But when Ike calls Rebecca again, she still doesn't answer. He leaves a message telling her where he is, that he called her father to tell him where he was going, that he has left a message for her on Inwood Hill, that he hopes she will come here to join him or at least call, but he doesn't expect that she will. It will be just him and the dog now, he says, the same way it was in the city before he met her. After he hangs up, he takes his clarinet out of its case. As he sounds a low A-flat, in the vague haze of moonlight, he can see Herbie swimming.

ELLINGTON BOULEVARD: THE MUSICAL!

Music & Lyrics by Miles Dimmelow
Book by Jane Earhart

A Medley from Act I, Draft 1

The music starts out upbeat, vintage Broadway. Snare drums and brass, their sounds redolent of subway cars and traffic. We see hot-dog vendors, tourists with shopping bags, Madison Avenue bustle. All the melodies are in major keys.

Lights up full.

Behind a scrim, pedestrians walk the boulevards of old New York—men in business suits carry bag lunches and briefcases; women in smart skirts clutch shoulder bags as they jostle past one another. Car horns honk; policemen blow whistles; lady cab drivers lean out their windows—"Watch where yer goin', pal." A drumroll, the music reaches crescendo, and everyone onstage belts out "This Is New York (Outta My Way)." Suddenly, cymbals crash, the scrim rises, the score shifts—electronic drums, a rock 'n' roll beat; the melody turns minor. Businessmen pull cell phones out of briefcases; businesswomen insert iPod earbuds; taxi drivers curse one another in a babel of tongues.

Alone in his office, The Broker looks down onto the city and continues the song, but the lyrics turn cynical; the upbeat Broadway patter song metamorphoses into a lament of urban loneliness—"Cloud on My Title" ("I'm so *single / I can't commingle / I have no covenant or trust / Is there no one I can lien on if this boom goes bust?"*). Into The Broker's office step a Man and Woman seeking an apartment (*"A cozy place for you and me / A cozy place for two . . . or maybe three"*). The Broker leads them through his office, where he and the other brokers sing the show-stopper *"Bing Bang Boom,"* about the explosion of Manhattan real estate prices (*"First, they went SPLAT, then they went BING, then they went BOOM / The market looked FLAT, then it went SCHWING, now watch it go ZOOOOOM / If you have an interest in low interest / No need to forage for a mortgage / First you go BING, then you go BANG, then everybody goes BOOM-BOOM-BOOM-BA-BOOM-BOOP- BOOP-BOOP-DEE-DOOP-BOOM-BOOM-BOOM-BA-BOOM-BOOOOOOM!*). Then a group tap-dance, after which all fall to a knee and throw their hands out Al Jolson–style.

Scene shift: West 106th Street, Duke Ellington Boulevard. A scrim is lowered. Again the images behind it are suggestive of another era's New York: men and women steppin' in colorful suits and evening gowns; a blare of low-down-dirty trumpet; a raunchy jazz number called *"The Showdown"* (*"Everybody's goin' to the showdown; we're all gonna git down at the show / I ain't talkin' 'bout no hoedown; no, we ain't gonna get down with no ho's / So c'mon there's no use in feelin' lowdown / 'Cause everybody's on the down-low"*). But then the scrim rises and the revelers are pushed offstage by The Chorus of Gentrifiers, who sing *"It Don't Mean a Thing If It Don't Go Ka-Ching."*

The Broker enters an apartment building on Ellington Boulevard with The Man and The Woman and sings *"I Think You're Gonna Like This Place."* The Man and The Woman agree (*"I Think We're Gonna Like This Place"*), after which The Tenant enters with his Dog and they boot Man, Woman, and Broker out of their apartment. The Man tells The Broker that he and his wife will buy the place anyway. *"Make me an offer, maaaaaan,"* The Broker sings, then walks off to a swanky party, where he meets the incomparably handsome Miles, who sings a highly suggestive torch song (*"[Will I See You at] My Opening"*). Wild, passionate sex and gratuitous nude scenes ensue.

The next morning, The Broker wakes up next to Miles and confesses that he has nearly everything he needs in his life (*"Except Love"*). Miles says that he too has nearly everything ("Except Fame"). After the two men sing a duet ("Except You"), The Broker tells Miles he can help him realize his dream ("[I've Got] A Perfect Space for You"). They walk toward an empty theater. A scrim is dropped; a scene plays out from Broadway's heyday—men and women in their finery line up for a sold-out musical; they whistle the show's hit song ("That's Show Biz"). But when the scrim is lifted, the marquee reads "For Rent," and panhandlers mill about outside. The Broker introduces Miles to a Dissipated Theater Owner, who decries the state of Broadway in the vaude-villesque number "Feh!" ("Nothing's good / Nothing's bad / It's just FEH!").

The Broker tells The Dissipated Theater Owner that Miles's new show can reinvigorate his theater. But when Miles and The Broker are alone, Miles admits he's never written a show. The Broker tells him that writing a show should be easy; in fact, even his newest clients could be perfect subjects for a musical: "That's a Great Story Right There" ("There's a girl and her beau / They're ready to buy / But this man and his pooch / Say they won't move till they die / And the buyer will have to be bewaaaaaare / Now that's a great story right theeeeeeere!"). Miles and The Broker dance a jig, then repeat the chorus: "Yessirreeeeee, that's a great story riiiiiight theeeeeeere!"

Miles begins writing his show. He follows The Broker as he tries to sell the Ellington Boulevard apartment ("[Why Don'tcha] Tear Down These Walls"), observes negotiations with mortgage brokers ("Selling loans is oh-so-glamorous; amortizing always makes me amorous"), witnesses The Woman falling in love with The Tenant ("I love you floor to ceiling, not just head to toe") and out of love with The Man ("It's the same sad story all throughout the land / When my supply increases, down goes my demand"). The Man returns to take another look at the apartment, at which point The Dog leaps upon him, singing "Woof! Bite! Ouch!" ("First I go WOOF! Then I go BITE! Then you go OUCH!"). Tenant and Dog run offstage; searchlights sweep the auditorium; police sirens sound.

Blackout.

JANE EARHART IS sprawled barefoot on a black leather couch in Josh Dybnick's apartment, swigging from a bottle of wine, when Miles

Dimmelow finishes playing the climactic stanzas to Act I of their musical *Ellington Boulevard*, then flips the off switch on his electronic keyboard. It's not a bad first act for a musical, Miles tells her as she applauds and hands him the bottle, kind of like *Rent* but in a more expensive zip code and with a more affluent potential audience base and funnier songs, particularly "Cuckold in the Rain" and "Please Release Me (from Your Clause)." He sits beside Jane on the couch that he purchased for the apartment with the credit card Josh lent him, and finishes off the wine. Still, Miles says, the musical needs an ending.

While Josh Dybnick has been working longer hours for Overman to demonstrate his worthiness and his loyalty to his boss—who has committed to fully funding the first year of the Manhattan Theater Project, which will be renamed the Overman Theater—Miles and Jane have spent every other evening writing this musical, slated to premiere as a late-night workshop. They have cobbled the book together from Jane's urban character sketches and slice-of-life vignettes that her workshop leader continues to eviscerate, tales Josh has told Miles about his clients, and blog entries from the Evening Noose regarding the fallout from one of Josh's most recent sales. Miles has already written more than three dozen songs.

The only problem is that Miles and Jane's leading characters have not yet reached resolution. Devising a scenario about what may or may not have happened after Ike Morphy and his dog escaped from a police station would involve speculation—Jane's weak spot. Her newest stories seem less imaginative than ever, for her life with Darrell has become exceedingly domestic, her contacts with the outside world limited mainly to walks with Darrell, writing sessions with Miles, and hours of abuse at the hands of fellow workshop students. While recently browsing at the Morningside Bookshop, she and Darrell noticed a certain purple book on the Staff Recommendations table beside a blown-up Xerox copy of Liz Fogelson's review ("All Hail the New Wizard of Fantasy"), and ever since, she has wanted to stay inside a great deal more than usual.

Miles has been unable to suggest dramatic uses for Jane's most recent vignettes ("So Anyway, the Boyfriend and I Humped All Night Because Everything on TV Was Such Crap"; "I Have the Impression That the

Boyfriend May Finally Be Kicking Some Serious Ass on His Dissertation"). Not one can be adapted to pertain to the fate of the man who escaped New York with his dog, and according to the latest entry on the Evening Noose, the search for Ike and Herbie has gone cold. Chloe Linton, who has offered a reward for the animal's capture, is recovering from her injuries and hasn't returned to work yet. The dog owner's landlord and roommate, Rebecca Sugarman, has told the police that she has neither seen nor heard from Ike since the escape.

Miles tells Jane that once they can agree upon a plausible, heartbreaking, or rip-roaring conclusion, they can begin the workshopping process. But Jane resists every ending Miles suggests; they all ring false—the happy ones are too happy, the tragic too demoralizing, the others just too absurd to be credible. She keeps saying she is just no longer capable of imagining the way things might or should be; she can only tell how they really are.

When Jane finally returns home, no further along than when she had arrived at Miles and Josh's apartment, she is surprised to find that Darrell is sitting on her couch, not at the worktable; his computer is off, his bare feet are up on the magazine table. He wears a light-blue Gromit T-shirt and smiley-face boxer shorts. He holds a remote control in one hand and is flipping channels while listening to "Air Algiers" by Country Joe McDonald. Normally, whenever Jane enters, Darrell is typing like a fiend, whipping through one journal article after another, or furiously grading blue books. But tonight, the worktable has been wiped clean; Darrell's laptop is packed away; his library books, all overdue and long-since-recalled, are in neat piles. Yo, why isn't he working on his dissertation? Jane asks.

A smile erupts onto Darrell Finneran Schiff's face. He has finished that fat bastard, he declares, then whips out a velo-bound manuscript from underneath the couch and slides it across the floor toward her. "Read it and sleep," he says, then rises to his feet, wraps his arms around Jane, lifts her off the ground and spins her around and around; her red sneakers twirl above the dissertation. Oh, but this would be such a beautiful ending, Jane thinks as she spins in the glow of the television—too bad that it's for the wrong story. She feels certain that anything she writes will have to end badly.

REQUIEM FOR A
REAL ESTATE BUBBLE

or

SSSSSSSSSSSSSSSSSSSSSSSSSSSSS!!!!!!!!

or

GLUB GLUB GLUB GLUB GLUB!

or

UH-OH!

Bradley & Megan

In a king-sized bed on the top level of a duplex apartment on Riverside Drive, in the glow of bubbling lava lamps and blacklit Emerson, Lake & Palmer and King Crimson posters, in the flicker of a flat-screen television broadcasting images of polar bears, Megan Yu rolls over onto a remote control device and inadvertently changes the channel from the Mammal Channel to the Financial Network, which at this very moment is broadcasting the worst news ever to arrive during her career as a mortgage broker. Megan leaps up, grabs her glasses, and gapes at the screen and the words and numbers scrolling by. She listens with mounting horror as somber, black-suited men discuss the news. Feeling faint, she runs to throw up in the bathroom, where Bradley Overman has been showering for the last half hour.

During the past months, the flower bouquets that Bradley Overman once sent to Megan to celebrate poor economic news from the Labor Department were supplanted by prog-rock CDs, the CDs by cases of champagne, the champagne by steak dinners, which were then replaced by afternoon trysts at the Warwick Hotel. Bradley and Megan's relationship is nearly half a year old, but since Megan is always expected back at her parents' house in Fort Lee by nine, she never spends more than a few hours at any one time with Bradley. To him, Megan always seems to be hurrying in or running out, fussing with her jewelry, nervously checking her cell phone, gathering up her books for night classes at New York Law School, calling her folks to tell them she is still at the office but will soon be on her way.

Which is how Bradley has lately preferred to conduct both his business and his love affairs—quickly, intensely, with a set closing time usually no more than ninety days in the future. For him, sales and love have always been acts of seduction; once deals are closed, little is left to say or do—a handshake, a kiss on the cheek, a signature on a piece of paper, and it's on to the next transaction. Whenever a client accepts an offer or a woman accepts a proposal, he knows on some level that the relationship will soon be over.

But this month, Megan's family is visiting relatives in Seoul—a trip Megan has paid for. And the previous Friday in the Warwick bathroom, after she revealed that her parents would be leaving town for the first time in her adult life, Megan suggested she and Bradley spend an entire week together to see if they were as compatible as she suspected they might be. Internally, Bradley bristled at this suggestion, assuming that so much time spent together would surely hasten their relationship's demise. With the other women he has dated after his most recent divorce, he has never issued invitations to his apartment, usually offering the excuse that he does not want to provoke his ex-wife, never mind that he and Chloe use separate entrances and always blast their preferred forms of audio entertainment— "For Headphones Only" satellite radio shows for him; college sports for

her—to drown out any voices, footsteps, or creaking bedsprings eman-
ating from the other's floor. But the news has been well documented that
Chloe, despite her nearly full recovery, is still residing in the Jerry Masler
Memorial Wing of St. Luke's Hospital. And when faced with the options of
an unnecessarily pricey week at the Warwick or another hotel, a week in
Fort Lee, a week alone, or a week *chez* Overman, Bradley relented.

Still, when Megan arrived at his apartment today with two suitcases and
a cosmetics bag, Bradley, accustomed to the bachelor environment in
which he has lived for more than the past half-decade, was uncertain as to
how he should proceed; he didn't know whether to begin removing his
clothes, or Megan's, or to remain clothed and order in breakfast. There was
no need to rush, but he never conducted any relationship without rushing;
to him, rushing was a relationship's very essence. Relationships were based
on conversations that couldn't be finished, apartments that motivated sellers needed to unload now, mortgage rates that might never be this low
again.

Megan, however, began this day by luxuriating in the time. Upon entering Bradley's bedroom, she placed her cosmetics bag on his nightstand,
hung up a skirt and blouse in the closet, popped her favorite Procul Harum
CD into his disc player, then opened her suitcase, pulled out a book with
a purple cover, and told Bradley she would read in the bathtub before joining him in bed. When Megan showed him the book, Bradley was astonished to realize that he had recently started reading it too.

While Megan bathed and read her novel, Bradley undressed, got into
bed, pulled the covers up to his waist, picked up the remote control, and
waited for Megan to return for the inevitable intercourse that, as always,
would be gratifying yet somewhat dispiriting, reminding him yet again that
Megan Yu was half his age. He searched for a TV program worth watching, finally settling on the Mammal Channel, which was broadcasting
a show about service animals. Huskies panted their way through the tun-
dra; a yellow Lab led a blind woman across a city street; a Springer spaniel
leapt toward the sun and came down with a Frisbee. He missed his old dog,
he mused as he watched; he never should have married a woman who
liked sports more than animals. But then again, he thought, Chloe should

never have married a man who said up front that he preferred puppies to children.

When Megan emerged from Bradley's tub, book in hand, she was wearing a white, hooded terry-cloth robe. She untied the robe, placed her book on the nightstand, and slipped into bed beside Bradley, who turned from the TV, touched Megan's ankle, then her knee. But when he reached her thigh, Megan grasped his hand and pushed it away. Couldn't he wait? she asked. How long? asked Bradley. At least until the program was over, Megan said. And when Bradley asked why, Megan said she loved watching dogs. In fact, when it came right down to it, she usually liked dogs more than people, which was why she already knew that she would never have children. She leapt off the bed, wrapped herself in a blanket, and moved to the floor in front of the TV, where Bradley let her watch the rest of the program undisturbed.

Bradley Overman watched Megan Yu watching dogs on TV, watched this woman who said she preferred dogs to humans, who apparently cared about her clients almost as much as she did about making her commission, who enjoyed the same books and CDs that he did. Twenty-five years separated them, but right now, he could not think of any passion they did not share. Bradley and Megan spent the following hours watching nature programs and discussing animals. Bradley spoke of the dog he once had, the one who had been taken away because, he admitted, he'd acted stupidly and selfishly. He had arrived at the shelter to retrieve the animal, but found that Lucky was already gone. He wondered how Megan would react to the story, worried that she might despise him after he finished telling it. But Megan pulled Bradley close and kissed him more passionately than ever before. And while they made love, this time with unprecedented abandon, they discussed their favorite breeds, ultimately deciding that mutts were best of all.

Now, as Bradley Overman showers, he allows himself to fantasize about the upcoming week he will spend with Megan. They will have sex, order Chinese, listen to satellite radio, and watch *Ring of Bright Water*, *White Fang*, *Never Cry Wolf*, and every other animal movie he owns. But when he hears Megan cough, he pulls open the shower curtain and sees her on her knees, hunched over the toilet, wiping her mouth with a tissue. He shuts off the water, grabs a towel, steps out of the tub. He asks if Megan is sick, but she shakes her head. She reaches out a hand and leads Bradley back to the bedroom where the news is still crawling across the TV screen: 255,000 jobs have been added to the workforce, and now the Fed chairman is making a speech, signaling an inevitable rise in interest rates. Bradley pulls Megan close, but she feels limp as she continues staring at the TV.

Bradley shuts off the set, and after he and Megan return to bed, he holds her in his arms and tells her that she shouldn't worry. He'll make sure that everything will be all right. He strokes her hair, then reaches for the phone and dials Chloe at the hospital; he leaves a message telling his ex-wife that the time has come for them to sell their apartment and move on with their lives, adding that he'll make sure this happens if she agrees to do one thing in return. Then, he calls Josh Dybnick and asks if he has time for a quick meeting. He kisses Megan softly on the forehead, tells her he needs to go to the office, then asks what she wants to do when he returns. Bradley assumes she'll want to spend more time in bed or go out for food. Instead, Megan asks if they can go to the East Side shelter on 110th Street to look at dogs. This is the most romantic suggestion Bradley could ever have imagined, he tells her.

While Bradley gets dressed, Megan grabs the remote control and turns the TV back on. The same information is still crawling across the bottom of the screen. But even if the worst is happening, even if the bubble is really bursting, maybe this won't turn out so badly after all, she thinks— she still has a job, a man who loves dogs is in love with her, and Megan has a whole week with him ahead of her. She pushes a button on the remote, hoping the dog program is still on. And as Bradley leaves for the office, Megan blows him a kiss. She meets a lot of men in this industry, but he is truly special, she says.

Josh, Joshua & Miles

Josh Dybnick has been obsessing all day about the new employment numbers and the Fed chairman's speech. He was feeling seasick long before he received Bradley Overman's call from home asking if they could meet. Earlier today, several of Overman's sales agents and associate brokers had been watching the Financial Network and parsing the statements of National Association of Realtors spokespeople; then they stopped by Josh's desk to commiserate. Josh put his feet up on his desk and chomped the end of a pen. They would weather this storm, he said. No one ever made money betting against New York real estate; even if prices started going down, there would be a soft landing.

But as Josh now enters Bradley Overman's office, he has a nagging sensation that his boss will tell him the jig is finally up. Even before today's news, he has noticed his colleagues' rising inventory; he hears the other brokers talking at the water cooler about apartments moving off the market too slowly. Unlike those brokers, Josh still gets his full asking price most of the time, but rarely more, and whereas half a year ago he needed only two or three open houses to get that price, now he usually needs at least six. Bidding wars for apartments are becoming rare; buyers are acting more rationally and have more inventory to choose from. Josh's once-solid network seems flimsy too; Megan Yu rarely returns his calls on time anymore. And the frantic newspaper and magazine headlines predicting a housing crash haven't been helping either. This morning's news has made those headlines seem prophetic.

As he approaches Bradley's office, Josh is certain of the reason his boss has returned from his day off and called him in for this meeting. He knows that if the real estate climate worsens, an Overman Theater will seem foolhardy and Bradley will want to pull his investment. When the market appeared to be unstoppable, MTP was an easy sell. Today, Josh will have to either admit that the theater could become a boondoggle or somehow convince Bradley that it won't.

Joshua enters the office and takes a seat, observing that Bradley looks uncharacteristically disheveled. The man's shirt is out of his pants and buttoned wrong. Joshua's initial inclination is to tell Brad that current price fluctuations and job numbers are only a blip, that the market is merely becoming normal again; real estate prices will continue to rise, as will the market for live theater, particularly one-man adaptations of classic literature. But then, he stops in mid-sentence. What is he saying, he wonders, and above all *why*? He can't help but think that every word he is about to say sounds false; worse, out of character. And at this moment here in Bradley's office, he finds himself finally unable to speak like Josh in order to do Joshua's bidding, as if he has mastered his one role so completely, he can no longer play the other. Joshua has never cared much about Josh's job per se, only wants Josh to do anything in his power to get him back onstage. But if Joshua's optimism about the prospects of the theater proves ill-founded, Josh knows his ass will be on the line—and really for what? He can imagine what might happen.

Bradley might fire Josh, then hire some other actor to serve as pitchman; on a screen eighty feet high, Miles Dimmelow will ask, "Isn't it time you moved up to Overman?" Harvey Mankoff will sell his theater and its air rights, but another broker will collect the commission. When the crash comes, no respectable broker will want to hold Josh's license, to assign a desk and a phone to a dilettante who fumbled the only decently paying gig he ever had. He'll celebrate his thirtieth birthday alone, bartending at the Ding Dong, circling open casting calls in *Backstage*, waiting for another check from his pop; searching Chelsea bars for dates to buy him drinks, dinners, and theater tickets; taking the bus back to Washington Heights just like any other fool who moves to New York and thinks he'll make it big. Does he still want to act and direct? Sure, but not if he'll have to give up this career to do it, not if he'll have to return to a life of rejection after so much success, not if he'll have to keep living 140 blocks north of Times Square, not if he'll have to wait at least another two years before he can show a steady income and put a down payment on a condo, not if he'll have to face rejection from co-op boards as a result of his uncertain career, not if he'll have to give up platinum credit cards and cable and unlimited wireless minutes and his health club membership, not if he'll have to go to Kinko's or Starbucks for high-speed Internet access, not if he'll have to pay for his own health insurance or go without it as he did for so many years— God, he can't go back to being some peon in the world he came from when, in this world, he's already becoming a star.

Josh tells Bradley that he assumes he wants to discuss his investment in the theater in light of today's news. And when Bradley says he has no concerns about Joshua's theater plan, Josh says he is happy to have Bradley's faith, but nevertheless, he has arrived at a difficult decision; he now has deep misgivings about moving forward. The time isn't right for an expensive, risky scheme. The MTP building is one of the last desirable uptown properties he knows of that isn't already under development. He pursued the theater project only because it made sense financially, but it doesn't anymore. With Bradley's approval, he will table the plan, after which he will set up a meeting with himself, Bradley, Harvey Mankoff, and Mark and Allie Masler—he says he wants to make a sale that will benefit everyone involved, especially the company.

Bradley Overman contains a smile as if somehow he has known all along that this was how events would unfold. He tells Josh he is so moved by this transformation, so touched by Josh's willingness to forego a cherished project for the sake of a more secure future, that not only will he award Josh another bonus, but soon he may scale back his own involvement in the Overman Group's day-to-day operations, and he thinks he may finally have found someone to manage his uptown offices. Only when Josh is halfway out the door does Bradley remember why he called the meeting. He asks if Josh will personally handle the sale of his and Chloe's duplex; he knows of no other broker who could get a better price. And as Bradley is calling Megan Yu to say that he will be home soon and she should get dressed so that they can start looking for dogs, Josh calls Harvey Mankoff, who says he is so glad that he enlisted the services of a *macher* who knew nothing about art.

Walking down Broadway in the direction of the Ding Dong Lounge through a light rain that falls from the foreboding late-spring sky, Josh plots how to tell Miles that he is ditching their plans for MTP. He will tell Miles that his first priority will be to move out of his ugly, cramped, viewless apartment—Miles is always complaining about it anyway, saying the only advantage to looking out the window and up to the street is that you can scope out people's shoes and no one will accuse you of being a fetishist. Plus he will offer to produce the musical *Ellington Boulevard* in a small downtown venue. When it comes right down to it, Miles is obviously a pragmatist and a social climber; once he realizes he will continue to date an associate broker and vice president, but now in a roomier apartment at a swankier address, he will be content, just as Joshua would be were he still in Miles's position. Two and a half years ago, if a good-looking broker had taken him in and offered to bankroll one of his shows, not only would he have agreed, he would have killed for the opportunity.

But when Josh arrives at the Ding Dong, waves at a harried Darrell Schiff, who is gazing into the bar, and then, over a round of gimlets, informs Miles of his decision, Miles, his bow tie undone, his face and fingers red, stares at Josh with beady black eyes. "You piece of slimy shit," he says. Josh tells Miles he understands and has even expected Miles's initial resistance, but once they have spoken outside, where no one can overhear them, Miles will see that he has made the right decision for both of them.

While rain pit-a-pats upon the canopy of Jimmy's Pizza & Coffee on the corner of Columbus and 106th, Josh tells Miles that he has always had the wrong impression of him. He grasps Miles's hands; Miles pulls them away and snorts, but Josh grabs them again and says he wants to let Miles in on a secret that just might shock him: he's not really the man Miles thinks he is. Sure, he confesses, he can play the role of a businessman well enough, but once, he too dreamed of acting and directing on Broadway. He remembers waking up at five for auditions, being a schnorrer, just like Miles. He wouldn't trade those days for anything, because they taught him to appreciate having a job, a home, and a relationship. The two of them will be able to afford a decent apartment now—one with video security, central air, a washer-dryer.

But Miles shakes his head. *Art thou serious?* he asks. What does Joshua expect him to be? A kept man?

Whatever Miles wants, Josh says. He'll be pulling seventy-hour weeks, open houses on weekends; Miles can devote his full attention to *Ellington Boulevard.*

What about the one-man Shakespeare and Voltaire shows? Miles asks.

Candide can wait, says Josh; right now, the housing market is just too uncertain, and to tell the truth, the Manhattan Theater Project has always been something of an eyesore on Broadway anyway.

And so this is what Joshua will be permanently? Miles asks. A salesman?

Vice president, says Josh, maybe uptown manager too. Bradley Overman appears to be grooming him to rise in the company and at long last he is becoming what he was only pretending to be. Didn't Miles ever wish he could be the prince instead of just playing him? Didn't he wish he could be the lover instead of walking offstage and going back to being himself?

No, Miles says, actually not. But then again, he says, he never gets cast as leading men anyway; he always plays scheming villains, second bananas, salesmen, slimy little shits.

But Miles assumed he was a salesman all along, says Josh. What's wrong with the job now?

Miles stares in disbelief. Joshua has to be joking, he says. He actually thinks Miles bought his act?

Why, Josh asks, who did Miles think he was?

An actor, says Miles. Who else has shelves filled with play scripts? Who else uploads Stephen Sondheim ringtones onto his cell phone? Who else asks a pianist to accompany him on "Finishing the Hat"? Who else wakes up humming "Conquering the City" from *Wonderful Town*? Who else quotes Peggy Lee lyrics? Who else lives with two cats named after British playwrights in a ground-floor shithole in Washington Heights?

Then why did Miles pretend he was some honcho with a house in the Hamptons? Josh asks.

Miles says that he assumed they had been teasing all along, the same way Joshua was teasing when he called him "sexy" or "pinup boy" or "Daniel Day-Lewis." He knows he isn't a pinup boy; he looks nothing like Daniel Day-Lewis. Does Joshua have that little respect for him? Does he really think he is that suave, and Miles is that vain and dumb? Does Joshua really think he's that good of an actor? How can someone be so good at his job and so clueless about everything else? Hasn't Joshua noticed the way Miles winks at him all the time? Ever since the night he met Joshua, he thought the two of them were playing a game; as real estate honcho and his kept boy toy, they would con both Harvey Mankoff and Brad Overman, and soon they would have their own theater with which to play. But now, it seems as if Brad Overman has conned Joshua—tricked him into doing exactly what he always wanted Joshua to do. No, Josh says, this is entirely his own decision; Bradley had nothing to do with it. That's what a good con artist makes you think, Miles says. But either way, he adds, if they're supposed to play their roles for real now, he wants no part of it. Frankly, he's had just about enough of Joshua's act and he hopes that if the real estate bubble is really going kersplat, Joshua will lose his job and find himself on the streets; that would be a great ending for his musical and not a bad topic for a one-man show, guy. He walks briskly east through the rain, heading for Jane's apartment to suggest this new ending, and darting out of the way of an unmarked police car speeding north against the light on Manhattan Avenue.

Josh returns to the Ding Dong and joins the after-work crowd that is beginning to fill the bar. He finishes his gimlet, then finishes Miles's too and orders a third. He will miss Miles, he thinks. Well no, he corrects himself, he probably won't miss Miles much. He feels more self-confident than ever and doesn't need some actor to make him feel complete. Still, he will miss all the introductions Miles has provided for him, the opening-night-party invitations, the bartenders who gave free shots to Miles's friends. But all is really for the best; he has never tried to find a significant other while pulling in the kind of money he'll be making now. With a new partner earning a comparable salary and without Miles and his expensive tastes, Josh can only imagine the apartment he will be able to afford.

Jane

Jane Earhart begins another dreaded workshop day with breakfast at the Deluxe Diner, Darrell's treat. Afterward, at the university gates, they embrace and kiss. Darrell swats Jane's mitt with a vigorous high-five, salutes her with a surfer's "hang loose" gesture (middle fingers down, thumb and pinky splayed), then advises her to kick some ass in her writing workshop. Jane wishes Darrell luck for his meeting with Bernard Ostrow. Then Darrell walks straight ahead while Jane turns left, wishing only briefly that Darrell could come along to defend her from the drubbing she will surely receive when Faith Trinkelman discusses her latest story, "So the Boyfriend or Whatever the Hell He Is Is Still Waiting to Hear About His Funding but I'm Not Real Worried (Does That Make Me a Jerk?)."

In the classroom on the fourth floor of Dodge Hall, Jane takes her usual seat overlooking the Columbia quad. She folds her hands tightly over her story and waits for Trinkelman and the other students to arrive. She knows all too well how the workshop should proceed. Her classmates, preparing for the kill, will avoid eye contact with her, whisper among themselves as if in the presence of the bereaved. She will read her story aloud, endure the criticism, lamentably agree with just about all of it, and after class, she will slam-dunk her manuscript into the trash, swear to herself, and return home, where she will swear out loud, kick chairs, break a glass or plate, then start writing again.

But today, when class begins, Faith Trinkelman doesn't regard Jane with her typically scornful or, worse, pitying eyes. The other students don't avoid Jane's gaze either. On their copies of Jane's story, passages are underlined, notes scribbled in the margins, smiley faces, asterisks, and exclamation points drawn next to sentences that seem to warrant particular attention. And when Faith stands in front of the blackboard and says she would like to begin by discussing Jane's story, everyone spontaneously applauds.

Assuming the applause to be sarcastic, Jane smirks and, in her self-effacing monotone, reads the story's opening sentence: "The Boyfriend's wearin' a light blue Gromit T-shirt; he's sittin' on the couch, listenin' to dumb drug tunes and flippin' channels when She comes home." But the clapping continues. Barb Biggins, seated to Jane's right, caresses her shoulder; Byron Weems, at her left, offers a soul handshake; across the table, Gregor Poliakoff pantomimes a champagne glass. "*Nazdarovye!*" he shouts with a grin as he pretends to toast her. Faith Trinkelman says that today, class will be conducted in a different manner than usual; they will dispense with reading and critiquing and, instead, spend the whole session discussing Jane's "exquisite style." As Trinkelman speaks, she turns every previously identified liability in Jane's writing into an asset. What once was "boring" or "uninviting" is now "stripped-down" and "spare." Vulgar phrases, such as "chode-sucking" and "fat bastard," are now evidence of "realistic, urban argot." Stories with "no beginnings or endings" are now "refreshingly and realistically indeterminate."

The others in the room offer similarly effusive responses. Oswalt Kolle, a bedraggled John Fante and Gregory Corso fan, who has been refining a memoir of his childhood in an Evangelical Christian cult entitled *I Am the Resurrection and the Blight*, and who once declared women incapable of writing literary fiction and accused Jane in particular of writing "breezy prose" best-suited to a "hometown rag," such as the *Bangor Daily News*, for which he wrote obituaries for half a year, now says Jane's style is an "ironic, existential antidote" that "splits the difference between Hemingway and Sartre." Meanwhile, Barb Biggins, whose novel-in-progress *The Rain Comes Hardest in April* charts the unlikely love affair between a defrocked nun and a prostitute who decide to start a book group in Somalia, asserts that Jane's "plainspoken prose" offers a "critique of contemporary gender roles in the tradition of *Jeanne Dielman*." Jane Earhart does not have the slightest clue why everyone's opinion of her seems to have changed overnight, and she becomes even more puzzled when, during the noon break, a beaming Faith Trinkelman asks if she can buy her coffee after class to hail her arrival as "a writer of merit."

Following the workshop, the two women consume cappuccinos and black-and-white cookies at a back table of Nussbaum & Wu on Broadway, beneath a mirror that takes up half the wall. Faith begins by discussing stories of her own that are jammed into a burlap shoulder bag filled with manila folders, some wrinkled where her cats urinated, some stained by coffee mugs; she asks whether Jane might read her latest stories because only she has the sophistication necessary to appreciate them. As Jane munches her cookie, gazes distractedly into the mirror above the table at her own ragamuffin reflection, and listens to Faith, she begins mentally penning a story entitled "My Neurotic, Formerly Abusive Writing Teacher with a Gazillion Jangly Bracelets on Her Wrists Offers Her First Compliment, Then Treats Me to Coffee and Asks for Professional Advice (WTF??!!)." When Faith finally takes a breath, Jane asks what has changed her impression of her writing; she was convinced that Faith thought she was her worst student. Faith apologizes but says that's how she treats her best students—

motivates them with negative feedback. For the first half of the course, they hate her, but eventually 87 percent of them write publishable work; to wit, Jane's story "So the Boyfriend or Whatever the Hell He Is Is Still Waiting to Hear About His Funding. . . ."

During the second round of cappuccinos, Faith asks if an agent is representing Jane's work. When Jane says that, until recently, Carter Boldirev represented her, Faith says that her own career has "reached a crisis point." She is very dissatisfied with her own agent, who recently told her that no market exists for *A Faith Worse Than Death*, a semiautobiographical police procedural ("The names are all real," says Faith, "but some facts have been changed"). Faith says her financial situation has become "extremely dicey," and what with this morning's economic news, she fears that what she had considered her last resort, i.e., selling her co-op, will prove difficult, and she'll soon need to supplement the "subsistence wages" she receives for her workshops. She has long admired the Boldirev Agency's exclusive client list. Might she contact Boldirev using Jane as a reference?

Jane has no plans to talk to Carter Boldirev again but nevertheless agrees that if she does happen to run into that unscrupulous, gravel-voiced dandy on the subway, she will mention Faith. At which, Faith exhales with profound satisfaction. She then leans across the table and traps Jane in a tight embrace. The embrace is so tight, in fact, that her bracelets dig into Jane's shoulder blades; the embrace is so effusive that Jane feels hot, heavy breaths upon her neck, so expansive and demonstrative that, when Jane manages to wriggle free, Faith Trinkelman's manila folders tumble to the floor of Nussbaum & Wu. Her papers scatter across the café, they flutter in the direction of the pastry counter, they somersault toward the other customers in the café, they sail past paninis, bagel schmears, and hamantaschen.

Jane takes to her knees and begins to help Faith gather the papers— crumpled student essays, rejection letters from literary periodicals, scrawled lecture notes, photocopied lesson plans, underlined and dog-eared copies of magazines. Trinkelman, laughing and apologizing for her jitteriness, picks up the papers and the periodicals. She grabs *The New Yorker* and *Harper's*; she stuffs the *New York Review of Books* back into her shoulder bag; then she reaches for the brand-new issue of *The American Standard*, but notices that Jane already has a tight grip on it. Jane is staring at a headline: WIZARD GIRL REVEALED.

Faith blushes. Then, after a long silence, she stammers and says *ohhhhhhhh*, she hasn't had a chance to read that issue yet, but she intends to, and, "Oh my Lord, Jane, is that a picture of you? How terribly odd. What's that doing in here?" But Jane is not listening to Faith; she is holding *The American Standard* in her fists, staring at the article and the pictures of her East Side apartment building, of her mother's books, of herself as a child, of her parents before the taxi accident, before she was left alone. The words and phrases in the article pulse out at her—"Triborough Bridge," "UC Santa Cruz," "Nick Renfield," "Twill Malinowski," "And then she returned to the same apartment in Manhattan. . . ." Only the magazine remains in focus, while everything else—her own reflection above the table, Faith Trinkelman, the customers in the café, the tired pastries behind the glass panes of the front counter, the cars and pedestrians outside on Broadway—is a mere streak of blurred color.

As Jane reads the article that Nick Renfield wrote for the *Standard*, she doesn't hear Faith Trinkelman saying she hopes Jane doesn't feel she invited her here under false pretenses, or the man at the register telling her to stop because she never paid for her cappuccinos or her black-and-white.

Jane darts east across Broadway, then through the campus to Morningside Park; her sight is still blurred, her hearing dull, almost as if she is turning blind and deaf, almost as if she is suspended above the earth in a glass cube and cannot tell whether she is floating upward, standing still, or falling to the ground. Drizzle is falling upon her as she proceeds southeast to Central Park, reading and rereading the article, her life story returning to her, everything that has followed her, everything that she has tried to escape. Images strobe before her—a taxi crashing into a cement embankment; her parents in caskets, their faces dull, gray, empty; the rooms in her apartment so silent when everyone was gone and she could hear only her beating heart and ringing ears.

Jane walks through the mist and rain, madly flipping through the *Standard*, tearing out pages, crumpling them into balls, hurling them along the damp park paths. Tearing and crumpling, crumpling and flinging, she curves around the Great Hill, then speeds downward. She tears out the "Gossip" and "Parties" pages, throws them into the duck pond, flings the real estate feature and the paid advertising supplement about proper prostate care into a waterfall. She throws pages along the bridle path; at a white, hexagonal police booth; onto the baseball diamonds; into the Harlem Meer and the Untermyer Fountain of the Conservatory Garden. Nearing the eastern border of the park, Jane tears out the lone politics page and lobs it at the monument to J. Marion Sims, then balls up the "Books" pages, all of them devoted to Nick Renfield's article "Wizard Girl Revealed." Jane has been tearing and crumpling from back to front, but when she reaches the table of contents and the masthead, she stops. As she stands at the Woodman's Gate entrance to Central Park, the names of the publisher and editors seem to lift off the magazine, swirl, then float in midair, blocking her view of Fifth Avenue. Chloe Linton's name is on top; below her, that of senior editor Rebecca Sugarman.

Jane chucks the masthead out of the park, and as she crosses Fifth Avenue, letting the remaining pages of *The American Standard* drop into the gutter, everything returns to focus; every one of her senses is sharp again. She sees every crack in the sidewalk, feels every drop of rain. She remembers her first conversations with Darrell, remembers him incessantly complaining about his wife, Rebecca Sugarman. Somehow, Darrell is responsible for this article, she thinks, and as she walks past her sullen doorman, she can imagine how it might have happened. She can imagine Darrell exiting the East Asian Library one day, heading west toward Broadway after handing in his dissertation; he stops in the basement of Kim's Video. While choosing a celebratory DVD (say, *Conan the Destroyer*), he spots Rebecca hunched over the Jacques Demy disks. They talk over old times, order espressos at Oren's, pause at the window of Morningside Bookshop—a purple book is on display, a conversation ensues.

Or, Jane thinks as she rides up in the elevator, it might have happened this way: Darrell and Rebecca meet in their lawyer's uptown office, i.e., Starbucks, to discuss their divorce. Since Darrell is the son of comparatively impoverished academics, he says he feels entitled to a cash settlement. The lawyer asks if Darrell is living alone, at which point Rebecca hires a private dick, who tails him and discovers his lover's true identity. Or, Jane thinks as she walks out of the elevator, she can imagine the two of them planning the whole scenario; maybe Darrell knew exactly who she was on the day he approached her in the library. Jane takes out her keys. Her mind is exploding with swearwords, her fingers are tingling with the desire to grab dishware and fling it against walls.

As Jane enters, her apartment lights are off and Darrell's back is turned to her. He is gazing morosely out the window into the gray afternoon. The TV is on, tuned to a skin-care commercial on the Evangelical Shopping Network; Gil Scott-Heron is on the stereo ("Winter in America"); the laptop is playing some game by itself, emitting lonely *dink-dink-dinks*. Jane shuts down Darrell's computer, flips off the CD player and the TV, turns on a lamp, then asks if Darrell feels satisfied.

Darrell doesn't turn around; he continues staring out the window even when Jane repeats her question—is he satisfied?

Darrell shrugs and says he received some pretty harsh news today, so is not in any mood to talk.

That's good, says Jane, because she doesn't want to talk either. The less said the better. Now, is he leaving or what?

Darrell's voice remains distant, low, as if Jane's telling him to leave is akin to telling a man whose house has burned down with all his family inside that he's lost his car too. He says he doesn't want to argue; all he's been doing today is fighting and getting treated like crap. If Jane wants to treat him like crap too, fine. Declare a national fricking holiday—Treat Darrell Schiff Like Crap Day.

Jane holds out a hand; she asks for her keys. What the fuck, says Darrell. What does she mean, give up his keys? He lives here now, he's got no place else to go, he's like Floyd Ellis, man.

Well, says Jane, maybe he should have thought about that before talking to his ex-wife.

"Who?" Darrell asks.

Jane proceeds to enlighten Darrell on the topic of the *American Standard* article, pummels him with one theory after another in which Darrell and Rebecca conspire to humiliate her. Darrell registers the brunt of each theory with a squint and a shake of the head, as if someone is trying to cure him of a hangover by throttling him. Finally, Darrell says he can't deal with Jane's fantasies right now, can't deal with being accused of something he didn't do. Jesus, he says as he walks to the door, Jane still has one vivid fricking imagination.

"A what?" Jane asks.

But Darrell has already left.

Jane Earhart stands frozen. Darrell's departing phrase has stunned her—a vivid fricking imagination. It is the last thing that anyone would ever accuse her of having. A *vivid fricking imagination*. And yet, Darrell is clearly right. Not every scenario she has entertained regarding the article in *The American Standard* can be correct; she must have imagined all but one of them. And in this moment of recognition, a world that seemed black-and-white resolves itself into glorious Technicolor.

Jane now looks out her living room window down to Central Park, and before her eyes, the park is transmogrifying into an enchanted, imaginary kingdom. She can see the Untermyer Fountain and its three dancing maidens, with whom her heroine Iphigene frolics. She can see Cherry Hill—the mountain of cherries that Iphigene climbs. She can see one lone hot-dog cart become the Land of Rolling Frankfurters. She can see Strawberry Fields once again becoming the Land of Eternally Optimistic Song Lyrics. She can see the evil Sims imprisoning Iphigene, faithful Balto guiding her; can see the Turtle Pond and the Carousel where Iphigene hides; can see Mother Goose, Ludwig van Beethoven, Romeo, Juliet, and the marionettes, all protecting Iphigene. She can see winged horses, craters, cliffs, gulleys, Iphigene's Walk, along which her wizard girl dances. For years, Jane has wondered how she ever imagined the kingdom in her stories, and now, she can see it all. The entire city can be magical or mundane, she thinks, the entire world too—it depends only on how you choose to imagine it.

As Jane stands at her window, she can now think up dozens of other ways in which Nick Renfield's "Wizard Girl" story could have found its way into the pages of *The American Standard*. She can imagine Darrell telling Rebecca, Miles telling Rebecca, Carter Boldirev telling Rebecca, her parents' voices rising from the dead to tell Rebecca.

Jane can imagine fantastical scenarios involving psychics, sorcerers, hypnotists, incantations, spells, Ouija boards. But most important, at this moment, she no longer cares who revealed her secrets or why. The truth would surely be dull, like the stories she has been writing for eons, but the different and vivid permutations she is imagining fascinate her. She rushes out of her apartment to see if Darrell is still in the hallway, but the elevator has already come and gone. She looks out her window again and sees him walking north toward Woodman's Gate, his hands in his blue-jeans pockets, the collar of his Cobain shirt turned up against the rain. The city upon which she gazes is now filled with infinite possibilities, and she can imagine dozens of places Darrell might be going. When Miles Dimmelow arrives to suggest a new, tragic yet still somehow humorous conclusion for the musical *Ellington Boulevard* in which a broker is suffocated by a killer real estate bubble, Jane tells him he is too late; she has already imagined a better ending.

Darrell

At first, Darrell Schiff does not know where he is headed as he walks west into Central Park under ever-darkening skies through the rain. In the past, whenever he felt slighted, he has sought the company of any woman who might compensate for the slight. But today, he has no prospects— what's he supposed to do? Hit on his students like some raincoat-clad *wichser*? Troll "the piles" or the Hungarian Pastry Shop for Gertrude Mc-Fuzz, who sits in the front row of his Comp 101 class, intentionally mispronounces Kant, then winks at him. Most of the female grad students know Rebecca, and they all thought he was a *culo* even before he left her. He could head down to Times Square, reenact his moment of weakness in Piccadilly, but he doesn't have the cash, particularly if Jane is really kicking him out of her apartment, particularly if Bernard Ostrow won't back down from the position he took earlier today.

Proud as Darrell was of his dissertation ("Subtext Becomes Text: The Physical Nature of a Purportedly Intellectual Act in the Victorian Imagination"), he hadn't imagined that Ostrow would already have read the whole thing when they met this afternoon. Academics generally took six to eight months to respond to the twenty-page articles that he'd crap out in a day. But as he entered Ostrow's Philosophy Hall office, he was heartened to see "Subtext Becomes Text" atop Ostrow's in-box, heartened too that Ostrow was finally sitting here during his office hours; lately, when Darrell would stop by to see if the committee had formalized the renewal of his T.A.-ship, Ostrow would promise to meet with Darrell soon, but right now he was on his way to a squash lesson, he was meeting his daughter and her husband for lunch at their Harlem town house, he was off to the liquor store to pick up some hooch for a professor's retirement party on the Jersey shore.

Darrell had some trepidation about relying on a man whom just a few months earlier he had called "a useless man in an even more useless profession." But he now knew that his scholarship was so far beyond that of any other grad student here that Ostrow would be foolish and self-destructive to interfere with his research, for Darrell's dissertation would surely find a home at a major academic publisher, might even give him the rare distinction of producing a scholarly work that could cross over to the mainstream. Plus, Bernard Ostrow would surely be retiring soon and it was conceivable that he might want a young replacement whose research would revolutionize his discipline.

In Ostrow's office, Darrell apologized for having hounded the man so relentlessly. He said he knew from observing his parents that a professor's job involved so much more than teaching his students and counseling his advisees—as he spoke, he tried not to let his glance linger upon Ostrow's squash racket; when he became a tenured professor, he too would enjoy playing squash and creaming Noam Chomsky in straight sets. Darrell said he felt he was raising his scholarship "to the next level" and next fall would be taking a new approach to teaching; he didn't mention that this new approach would involve preparing for class and showing up for office hours rather than canceling them for fear that some black-clad prospective student would rightly accuse him of never having read the books he was purportedly teaching. He said he knew Ostrow probably hadn't had time to read his entire manuscript, but the introductory chapter, bibliography, and numerous anatomical diagrams would demonstrate the breadth of his research.

Bernard Ostrow picked up Darrell's dissertation and thumbed through it. Actually, he said, he had read all of it. Darrell noted that the first ten pages were marked up with black ink, but every subsequent page was pristine. Past page 10, Ostrow must have "really started getting into it," Darrell suggested, but Ostrow shut the manuscript. No, Ostrow said, at page 10, he simply realized there was "nothing here." He usually read Darrell's work with an open mind, in part because he always had a soft spot for Darrell's mother and in part because he didn't want anyone to misinterpret the department's decision. Contrary to what Darrell might have suspected, he didn't resent him for their differences; the discipline needed fewer *Speichelleckers* and more firebrands, fewer *jajis*, *culos*, and *mamsers*, and more whippersnappers, gadflies, and angry young men. But rebellion was useless for those who couldn't grasp what they were rebelling against. Oh, perhaps some institutions might be amused by Darrell's misreadings of literature, his single-focused misinterpretations of poems, his lewd articles and presentations that he himself sometimes recommended for inclusion in academic conferences to make them somewhat more spirited, but this dissertation didn't even have the advantage of ribald humor to compensate for its lack of intellectual rigor. Yes, some institutions might hire Darrell in the future, if only to ingratiate themselves with his mom, whose personal assurance had allowed Darrell to slide into Columbia to begin with. But not here, Ostrow said, not in the Ivy League.

Darrell longed to say something appropriate, but his mind was bereft of all witty comebacks and quotations; all he could manage was to ask Ostrow what sorts of institutions might be interested in his work. Bernard Ostrow leaned back in his chair.

"Have you ever heard of the Gauchos?" he asked.

Darrell Schiff exits Central Park at Strangers' Gate, then walks west through the rain to the Ding Dong Lounge. He peeks inside to see if any of his female students are here, but sees only his former real estate broker and his boyfriend, so Darrell keeps walking, still reliving his spat with

Bernie Ostrow. He insulted the man, then pleaded for another year of funding. Please, he said, he didn't want to go ABD, only fuck-ups and tards went ABD and he was never a tard and just recently he had decided to stop being a fuck-up. Ostrow said he had already discussed the decision with the rest of the committee and with Darrell's mom, who said she didn't want her son receiving special treatment anymore and was certain Darrell wouldn't want special treatment either. Well, Darrell said, that just showed how little his mother knew him—what kind of self-abnegating *Versager* didn't want special treatment?

Darrell left Ostrow's office in a daze. Before moving in with Jane, one of his many guilty pleasures had come from watching the tail ends of reality shows, where rich, well-scrubbed *culos* got fired, fashion ponces learned they weren't "in style," preening rock 'n' roll wannabes found out they were "just not right for our band." That's what entertainment had become—seeing who would get fired, who would get whacked, who was out of style, who was not right for our band, who would wind up ABD. Today, Darrell Shit was getting whacked. Before Jane entered and asked Darrell to return her keys, he had been Googling himself again; only seventeen entries remained—*Contemplate this on the tree of woe.*

Heading east on 106th Street, Darrell swears to himself as he passes the Ana Beauty Salon, whose caged parrot repeats Darrell's mantra ("*Culo, culo, culo, culo,*" says the parrot). Darrell just cannot allow himself to believe that Ostrow, a man the same age as his folks, would be so petty as to hold a few harsh words against him. At the same time, he finds even more improbable Ostrow's assertion that his work isn't up to snuff. *Quatsch!* If that's true, then everyone should be kicked out of the department, which probably wouldn't be the world's worst idea—boot out the grad students, close all the fricking universities, plow the fields, convert them into organic farms, put all the academics out to pasture, replace them with dairy cows, donate free milk to the world's starving children. But as long as universities are still functioning, as long as his fellow grad students are belching forth dissertations such as "The Ontological Presence of Absences in the Works of William Gass," then there has to be another reason Ostrow has dealt him the ass card. Still, Ostrow's true motives do not reveal themselves until Darrell is standing in front of the Roberto Clemente Building. That *vercockte mamser* is going to steal his thesis, he thinks—there can be no other explanation.

Nearing retirement, Bernard Ostrow, who has not had an original thought since the Ford administration, has little to show for his forty-odd years in academia. In the twilight of his career, a dissertation crosses his desk and he sees one last chance for the stardom that has eluded him. Such thievery has victimized Darrell before; he sent an article about George Meredith's shoe fetish to a refereed journal, anonymous reviewers took nine months to trash it, then what do you know, a different article about Meredith appeared in the very same journal the following year. Now Darrell understands everything. His only question is whether to confront Ostrow directly, file a grievance with the graduate student committee, or hook up with another institution to publish his work first. Any publisher will do—the Gaucho Press; S.S.O.W. Academic Publishers. He is relishing this thought when he rings the buzzer for #2B; the label reads, "Sugarman/Morphy."

Ostensibly, Darrell has come here to quiz Rebecca about the article in *The American Standard*, which has caused Jane's shit-fit. He is also here to see how Rebecca is faring. But most important, he is here because, despite all that has happened, Rebecca still might be the only woman aside from his mother who will talk to him, and during the week, his mom is usually too busy to return phone calls.

Rebecca doesn't ask who's at the door; she buzzes Darrell in. Obviously, she hasn't changed—the most trusting soul Darrell has ever met. She once invited a thief into their apartment, offered her coffee and a croissant, and didn't realize the woman was a criminal on the lam until the police busted in fifteen minutes later. The irony has never been lost on Darrell that Rebecca spends her life trusting people while he is naturally suspicious, yet he is the one who always gets macked. Gravity just doesn't work on the woman—when she falls, she only keeps going up. He, on the other hand, still has the reverse Midas touch—everything he touches turns to Darrell Shit.

Darrell enters the Roberto Clemente Building lobby. Only a few

months ago, it seemed as if "Schiff" would be printed on the mailbox label by now. By this time, he would have been attending meetings with the
condo board and with obstetricians, shopping for strollers, preparing to
climb these steps to the second floor wearing a BabyBjörn like some goof.
No way would he have finished his dissertation. And even if he had, no
way would it be as ass-kicking as the one he has written; to hell with
Bernard Ostrow—he'll get his work out before that lousy, thieving *boji*
anyway.

The door to 2B is half open when Darrell reaches the top of the stairs.
He doesn't know whether to knock or walk right in when Rebecca appears.
She is barefoot, in a loose white sleeveless top and black slacks, her hair in
a ponytail. A cordless phone is wedged between her ear and her shoulder.
As Darrell stands in Rebecca's doorway and his eyes meet his ex-wife's, he
can see an unfamiliar expression flash across her face—resentment, anger,
indifference, or some combination of the three, as if something elemental
about her has, in fact, changed; as if the intervening months have robbed
her of that disarmingly sweet, sympathetic, understanding gaze with which
she always regarded him, even when he was leaving their apartment for the
last time. He makes as if to step forward, but Rebecca holds up an index
finger—she'll speak to him when she has finished her phone conversation.

Rebecca takes her time on the telephone, while Darrell wanders into
her front hallway, then surveys the apartment, observing everything that
might have belonged but thankfully does not belong to him. $650,000 for
this, he thinks, for two bedrooms, a crapper, and a kitchen the size of an
elevator—for that money, he and Jane could own just about the ritziest
crib in all of Madison, Wisconsin. Why in the world do people bother?
What's here that they can't find in any other two-bit town? *$650,000?* How
many pizza slices could he buy with that? How many Quarter Pounders?
How many CDs? How many song and movie downloads? How many
books? How many nights in Piccadilly? Darrell enters the dim bedroom,
where a pair of pigeons still roosts on the air conditioner—still good candidates for an air rifle, he thinks. The place still needs a paint job; I'VE GOT
A GODDAMN LEASE! is still painted on the ceiling, and below it, two signatures. The only significant changes in the apartment involve Rebecca

herself. Her stomach looks even larger than the last time Darrell saw her, but at the same time, she no longer appears heavy. And as she continues to ignore him, she seems inexplicably cheerful. Her cheeks are flushed, she laughs frequently with a caustic tone Darrell does not recognize, makes unself-consciously sexy motions, acts in a flirtatious manner in which he never saw her behave toward anyone other than himself—she tosses her hair out of her eyes, throws her head back with a deep sigh as she speaks, stretches on her tippy-toes to take down a suitcase from the hall closet.

Darrell walks into the kitchen. On the refrigerator, he sees a business card: "Dr. Lisa Belfour, Obstetrics and Gynecology. WE DELIVER!!!" On the kitchen counter is a Kelly green plastic container of prenatal vitamins; next to it, a paperback copy of *Everybody's Making Love or Else Expecting*. And then there is the telephone conversation that Darrell has been trying to tune out—Rebecca's phone calls always seemed so distressingly wholesome that he learned to ignore them completely. Now, as he listens, he senses that she is talking to some guy, telling him how she'll soon be seeing him at her folks' house in Maine.

Oh my sweet fricking Lord, Darrell thinks—again she has bested him. He left her for another woman, left her for his one true love who has kicked him back out into the unforgiving city, treating him like fricking Marvin K. Mooney—*Will you please go now?* And here Rebecca is, apparently pregnant, cheeks glowing, eyes glistening, flirting on the telephone. "This mission is over, Rambo," Darrell tells himself. "This mission is over." Rebecca has to be the Obi-Wan Kenobi of women—*You can't win, Darth. If you strike me down, I shall become more powerful than you could possibly imagine.*

Darrell turns to walk out in defeat; Rebecca has always been superior to him in every way he could ever imagine. He can try to return to Jane, who is superior to him too, but for some reason either hasn't noticed this fact yet or hasn't held it against him. He must grovel until she takes him back. But the moment he is about to walk out the door, he hears Rebecca wrap up her phone conversation.

"Okay," Rebecca says. "Bye, Ike."

Darrell stops dead.

Bye, Ike?

He feels his cheeks flush.

Rebecca returns the phone to its cradle, but as she walks toward Darrell, her last two syllables are still echoing in his brain: *Bye, Ike*. Ike? Ike, the belligerent *clochard*? Ike, the towering, bald, bearded, black, bohemian *culo* who was paying three hundred fifty bones a month in rent and looked like he could barely afford that? Ike, the *salaud* who sprang his mad dog on Chloe Linton and a cop and was now apparently squatting in the Sugarman summerhouse? This is what has always killed him about Rebecca—such a poor judge of character. She fell in love with Darrell and even he left her—that was proof right there.

Rebecca asks Darrell what he is doing here. He begins to say he is sorry for intruding, but he can't take his eyes off of her belly. And though Rebecca remains expressionless, whatever affection she once had for him apparently long gone, he is stricken with an unfamiliar pang—conscience or guilt or regret; longing, perhaps, for something he cannot name. It would be typical of him to just escape at a moment like this one without doing or saying the right thing. He thinks of the words Rebecca said before hanging up; he now wonders if she might actually have intended for him to hear her say "Okay. Bye, Ike," as if she might actually have been issuing a cry for help, offering Darrell one last chance to save her. Why else would she be so thoughtless as to reveal that she knows where Ike Morphy is? He can't imagine any possible reason Rebecca would still be speaking to that man—except one.

Recalling the police car he saw on the evening of the closing, the dog's howls he heard, the postings he read on the Evening Noose about the dog that attacked Chloe Linton, Darrell tells Rebecca he has come here only to ask one thing. He gestures to her belly—"Was it consensual?" he asks.

Rebecca stares at her ex-husband. The color drains from her cheeks; her eyebrows fall. She stands up straight, Darrell's forehead only as high as her shoulders. Rebecca can remember the last time she and Darrell made love, can remember how soon thereafter he walked out. *Was it consensual?* "No," she says. "It wasn't."

Darrell begins to tell Rebecca that he knows how burdensome it must be for her to carry her secret, but Rebecca slams the door on him. And no matter how many times Darrell knocks, no matter how many times he says come on, Becca, he's here for her if she needs to talk, she does not open the door. So he walks downstairs, then back out into the rain, glad, he ultimately decides, to be walking away from the Roberto Clemente Building. But his pleasure is bittersweet; he does feel sorry for Rebecca, does feel he owes her something. At the corner of Columbus and 106th, he picks up the receiver of a pay phone, dials 911, and when the dispatcher answers, Darrell says he knows what happened to that man with the dog for whom they've been searching. And then he calls Jane, wondering if she's still angry with him, wondering if she'll still speak to him or if he'll have to book a plane ticket back to Madison. But when Jane hears his voice, she laughs. "Come on home, you fricking *culo*," she says.

Rebecca

Having resigned from her position as senior editor of *The American Standard*, Rebecca Sugarman, now six months pregnant, is driving fast through the night over the Triborough Bridge in a rented silver Volvo wagon, the Manhattan skyline shrinking in her rearview mirror, and her one wish is that it could shrink more quickly. Rebecca is bound for Maine, where she will see Ike Morphy and Herbie Mann for the first time since the pair escaped New York. Suitcases are piled on Rebecca's backseat and in the trunk. She has packed everything she needs for two weeks, maybe three. Immediately after Herbie Mann attacked Chloe, and Ike and the dog fled, she maintained her equilibrium by devoting herself unquestioningly to Chloe and the *Standard*, by attempting to block Ike and Herbie out of her mind and continuing to pretend that Ike had never contacted her and that she had no idea of his whereabouts. Now that she has switched her allegiance and quit her job and feels freer than she could ever have imagined, she is operating solely by instinct.

In the initial days following the incident, after Chloe regained consciousness and began to recover from her concussion, the clock radio would wake Rebecca at 6:15 a.m. She would take prenatal vitamins with grapefruit juice, throw on her gym togs, power walk to Inwood and perform

yoga exercises in Butterfly Meadow beside the tree trunk upon which Ike
had carved a message for her, if only to prove to herself that Ike no longer
had any power over her. She would return home in a taxi, shower, change,
read or edit on the C train to St. Luke's, then discuss editorial assignments
in Chloe's room. Afterward, Rebecca would walk to the *Standard* office
and lead meetings with a staff now composed almost exclusively of interns
and recent college grads, most as blindly enthusiastic as Rebecca had been
when she had arrived there.

Rebecca would work until 8:00 p.m., implementing Chloe's editorial
vision—"shit-canning" negative articles, rewriting columns that didn't contain a "call to action" and a "service component," assigning reviews of
books with titles such as *If Hitler Ran a Book Group and 99 Other Reasons
Why Democracy Works*, and allowing critics to assess these books on the
basis of the third paragraph of their sixty-seventh page. And even though
the magazine no longer contained any article Rebecca would ever read,
whenever the fulfillment house informed her that subscriptions were continuing to increase by a thousand per week, she was once again reminded
that her job was to help turn the *Standard* into a mainstream magazine,
and, apparently, her tastes had never been mainstream.

At the end of her workday, Rebecca would catch a cab home, change
into pajamas, plop into bed, and sleep. When she was living with Darrell,
then all too briefly with Ike, this was her most cherished time—she would
be nude; someone would be sleeping beside her; the whole apartment
would feel quiet, safe; she would turn on a night-light and read for hours.
Once, nearly any book could captivate her; now, none did.

Rebecca thought Chloe would be eager to leave St. Luke's, but the
woman showed no indication of wanting to go. Chloe seemed to enjoy being there, ordering out from her favorite restaurants; conducting long, un-
observed telephone conversations with other magazines that were wooing
her; charging her expenses to the company. The job Chloe would most
probably take, she told Rebecca, was publisher of *Chloe*, a new women's
lifestyle and sports magazine offering business acumen, motivational tips,
shopping suggestions, fashion and weight-loss advice, and NCAA basketball picks. The incident with Herbie Mann had raised her profile; her

recovery was the subject of articles in the *Post* and the *Daily News*, and eighteen snarky posts replete with dog puns on Nick Renfield's Evening Noose blog. Plus (again according to the Noose), her story would soon be fictionalized in a musical à clef coscripted by the anonymous author of the now-best-selling *Wizard Girl*.

Following the publication of Liz Fogelson's rave review of the aforementioned novel, Chloe had asked Rebecca to commission a feature story outing its author. Rebecca sought out Liz Fogelson for the job, but when Fogelson didn't return her calls, Rebecca stopped by her Upper West Side apartment building, in front of which the woman was struggling with four beige pet carriers. Liz explained that she had been planning to fly to Saskatchewan but worried about how her beagles would fare in the cargo hold; she and the dogs would be riding the bus instead. What was in Saskatchewan? Rebecca asked. Her new boyfriend, said Liz. Yes, perhaps it did seem absurd for a woman her age, who hadn't had any decent action in the past three decades, to leave just about the only home she'd ever known, traverse the country, and cross into Canada for a liaison with a high school dropout and car thief young enough to be her grandson. Quite possibly, she'd return to this city with her heart broken and her wallet stolen. But knowing she was finally living life to its fullest instead of merely reading or writing about it, which was all she'd ever done here, was most important.

Rebecca instead assigned the *Wizard Girl* exposé to Nick Renfield. Since Rebecca had last seen Nick, two other magazines had already fired him—one for blogging from work, one for blogging about work—but he was now making more money than ever, since the Evening Noose had been purchased by a major media conglomerate. The downside of this now-full-time job, which required him to do little more than sit in his boxers at his laptop and smoke pot while libeling celebrities and publishing types, he told Rebecca as he sat in her corner office, was that he had little to show for his j-school degree, for the college journalism award he once received for a series about meth, for the hard-hitting investigative career he'd come from Wichita to Manhattan to pursue. He was afraid he'd already lost his chops. Which was one of two reasons why he would accept

Rebecca's assignment. The second, he said, was that he was sentimental, and he found something historic about the prospect of contributing to what might well be the last issue of *The American Standard*.

Rebecca told Nick he was misinformed about the *Standard*; the magazine was in excellent financial shape. Nick observed that Rebecca was obviously not a regular reader of his blog; one of his most-linked features was "Magazine Dead Pool," which posted daily odds on the likelihood of various periodicals' imminent demise, and the *Standard* was usually atop the list. If Rebecca was telling the truth, then Chloe really was a "turnaround artist," he said. Still, he was dubious; recent issues showed all the signs of impending doom—flimsier paper, saddle-stitching, bartered ads, unknown freelance contributors. Friends were receiving free subscriptions and tossing the rag into the trash. He said he'd conduct some investigations once he was done writing the *Wizard Girl* article.

The story that Nick ultimately submitted to Rebecca, chronicling the solitary early life, even more solitary adolescence, and ultimate redemption of Jane Earhart, née Gigi Malinowski, did intrigue Rebecca, enough for her to convince Chloe to make it their lead feature story despite the fact that Nick's main source, Carter Boldirev, refused to go on the record. But the story was nowhere near as compelling to Rebecca as the one Nick Renfield had told her today about Chloe Linton and *The American Standard*.

This afternoon, Nick ambled into Rebecca's office, reeking of pot and carrying a thick binder, which he handed to Rebecca, who flipped through pages of Nick's notes, graphs, charts, and statistics from *The American Standard*'s fulfillment house. There were tables of subscription data for the *Standard* and for other periodicals for which Chloe had worked, such as the plus-sized-men's fashion magazine, *Clothes Horse*.

Nick said he had only started researching the *Standard*, but he'd already learned that what Rebecca had told him about the magazine's startling reversal of fortune was accurate. Subscriptions had been rising steadily; ad pages were up; payroll and other expenses had been cut. But despite all this seemingly good news, revenues had not increased significantly. Which would have seemed odd had Nick not also researched the other magazines Chloe "turned around." Journalists covering the publishing business attributed the increased subscription numbers and ad revenues, which always dropped significantly upon Chloe's departure, to the fact that her successors lacked her killer instinct. Maybe so, Nick said, but Chloe was "goosing subscriptions" too, using the money saved by cutting expenses to supply bulk subscriptions to organizations at a fraction of their cost. Copies were sent out like junk mail, dozens of copies to universities, hospitals, beauty salons, doctors' offices, senior centers, names randomly chosen from the phone book. All these copies counted as paid circulation, and the numbers lured advertisers, who assumed Chloe was responsible for the upward trend. Of course, Chloe's scam couldn't last; auditors would eventually come around asking questions. But by that time, as always, Chloe would be long gone, and she was good at covering her tracks.

Rebecca told Nick she could not accept the idea of her friend and boss engaging in such shady practices, but after Nick left, she borrowed Bella Ratny's key to Chloe's files, perused the business plan folders, and was surprised by how quickly she confirmed Nick's allegations. The piddling costs Nick listed for Chloe's junk-mail subscriptions were, if anything, too generous. And, as far as Nick's rough estimates of next year's payroll were concerned, he had accounted for nearly all Chloe's cuts save for Rebecca's salary, which she was stunned to see had been cut in half.

Confused, vaguely frightened, and suddenly riddled with new doubts about both herself and Chloe, Rebecca went directly to St. Luke's Hospital and reported Nick's story, hoping Chloe would provide some explanation. But Chloe only glanced briefly at the charts and graphs before admitting to everything. Seated in an armchair, one leg crossed over the other, a stack of old *Hockey Digest*s at her side, she dismissed Rebecca's concerns with carefree waves and laughter. *The American Standard* had been dying anyway, she said; it was little more than a petrified relic of a city that had disappeared years earlier. The only alternative to her approach would have been to fold the magazine immediately—at least this way, she had briefly saved some jobs and salaries. Of course the following year's budget for Rebecca's position had been cut—she hoped Rebecca would soon be joining her as co-editorial director of *Chloe* magazine. Rebecca would have no reason to stay with the *Standard* after Chloe left; and once they were gone, who really cared about its fate?

Rebecca stood with her arms folded, gazing down at Chloe, in her armchair, so blasé about everything for which Rebecca once cared so deeply, everything she had been trying to forget while working for the *Standard*. Well, Rebecca said, she imagined that Chloe would leave her behind too someday. She told Chloe not to protect her from the truth—if Chloe wouldn't really find a job for her after she left, she should tell Rebecca now so she could start making other plans. In three months, she would have a child to support and would need a secure job. What on earth made Rebecca think she would treat her so shabbily? asked Chloe. Rebecca said that if a venerable publication like *The American Standard* was expendable, then of course she was expendable too. Chloe touched Rebecca's knee. But how cynical Rebecca was becoming; yes, everyone in an organization was expendable, but true friends never were. She knew Rebecca might be angry with her, but she was still looking forward to their continuing to work together. If Rebecca wanted, Chloe would even be upstairs in the delivery room with her. She had always wanted a child and this was probably the closest she would ever come.

So why hadn't Chloe ever had that child? Rebecca asked—she had never received a satisfactory response to this question.

Chloe sighed. Here was the pathetic, miserable story, she said. She and "that Bradley person" to whom she had been married had made a deal. Though she married late, she always wanted a child but had never found the right time or partner; that Bradley person said he preferred dogs to children, but they compromised. After they had adopted a dog, they would start trying to have a child. But once that dog arrived—a stray black puppy that Bradley had found in Morningside Heights—suddenly, there was always some excuse: Bradley had drunk too much, he was coming down with the flu, there was a real estate convention he had to attend, a business function for which he'd have to get up early. He was always too tired or too stressed-out to perform.

For six months, Chloe put up with that dog Lucky chewing furniture, barking at the neighbors, crapping on the carpet, peeing on and in the tub. But when Bradley finally admitted that he no longer felt certain about having a child, Chloe understood that he had been leading her on all this while. Bradley told Chloe that he was having trouble imagining her as a mother, seeing how indifferently she behaved toward Lucky. But Chloe felt she knew the real story: Bradley was a salesman through and through; once he'd gotten what he wanted, he had no interest in holding up his end of the bargain. For Chloe, the worst part was not that Bradley had apparently been lying to her—given his line of work, she might have expected that—but that once she guessed the truth, she no longer wanted to have a child with anyone. The next morning, after Bradley left for work, she muzzled his animal, put the creature in the back of a taxi, rode to the animal shelter, and that was that.

But surely it wasn't the dog's fault, Rebecca said.

It was just a dog, said Chloe.

Rebecca's mind reeled back to her old Morningside Heights walk-up, where she saw Herbie Mann shredding Chloe's scarf; her mind spun forward to Herbie's look of terror when she and Chloe arrived in apartment 2B after the closing. She remembered the words Chloe uttered just before Herbie leapt at her—*Stop it, Lucky*. She remembered the nausea she felt whenever she discussed article assignments with Chloe over lunch, how she always assumed that she was naïve and Chloe must know best. So, Rebecca said now, so the dog was expendable too.

Chloe gazed at Rebecca—she now saw the shadows looming beneath those earnest green eyes, the unusually messy red hair, the pale skin. "You really still love that guy and his dog, don't you?" said Chloe. She smiled, but only for a moment, then told Rebecca that, earlier today, she had had her longest conversation with her ex-husband in half a decade. Bradley told her that the latest Labor Department figures and news from the Fed dictated that the time had come for them to sell their apartment, but he would agree to do so only on one condition—that she drop her charges against Ike Morphy and withdraw the reward she was offering for the capture of his dog. Chloe told Bradley his idea was absurd; one thing had nothing to do with the other. But now, she told Rebecca, she guessed that what she told her ex-husband would depend on whether Rebecca performed a favor for her.

What would that be? Rebecca asked. Chloe picked up the telephone, handed it to Rebecca and told her to call Nick Renfield. Rebecca should offer Nick whatever he wanted for his story about her, then kill it; afterward, she would call the police and do what Bradley had asked.

Clearly, what Chloe was suggesting was bribery, something of which Rebecca would never have thought herself capable half a year ago. Still, she barely even paused before calling Nick, who haggled briefly before agreeing to a price to destroy the research he had already gathered. And as she hung up, Rebecca felt no guilt, now knew she would have done far more for Ike and Herbie. Chloe had been wrong regarding just about everything, but not about how Rebecca felt about Ike and Herbie; she still did love that guy and his dog after all. She bounded out of Chloe's room and tossed Nick Renfield's folder into a hallway trash can. She returned home, started packing her bags, reserved a rental car, called Ike, kicked Darrell Schiff out of her apartment, then drove fast out of the city. She had no way of knowing that when Chloe finally would call the police to drop her charges, the dispatcher would say she was sorry but an officer was already on his way to apprehend the dog.

Rebecca is now speeding through the night on I-95. An early Funkshuns CD is playing on the stereo. The playful thumps and hiccups inside her keep time with the beats of the music that plays. She parks at a rest stop and makes a call from her cell phone, leaving a message for Ike that she will arrive in Croix-de-Mer by early morning. But when Rebecca gets to the house at the very edge of Maine, she sees a white Ford Crown Victoria parked in the driveway.

Ike & Herbie

For Ike Morphy, the previous evening had ended so perfectly—with Rebecca leaving a message telling him she would soon be on her way— that he is somehow not surprised when events take a sharp turn for the worse. On the answering machine, Rebecca's voice sounded soothing and familiar, also vaguely sad, like the tide coming in or Herbie whimpering in bed while dreaming of squirrels.

During his time in Croix-de-Mer, Ike has spoken to few people, only checkout workers at the IGA grocery store, farmers and fishermen at the Sunday market, and Phil Sugarman, who calls once a week to chat and to monitor Ike's progress but has made frustratingly evasive remarks whenever Ike has mentioned Rebecca. In Croix-de-Mer, the locals have taken little note of Ike or Herbie. And on their walks into town, the man and his dog catch only snippets of conversations. Whenever people are not discussing the small size of this year's crops or the day's measly take in the bay, the topic almost always concerns selling property, moving out, leaving town, making a fresh start somewhere else.

TheytellmeitsagoodpriceandIkeeploweringitbutstillnobodysevenmadean-offer, Herbie has heard one fisherman say.

When they walk home, the man and his dog follow a poorly paved two-lane road—wildflowers, tall grass, lilacs, and pussywillows lead down to the rocky beach and the still, gray water. On their walks, they pass weather-beaten homes with broken shingles, pale laundry hanging out to dry, rusted-out cars in driveways, howling dogs tied to trees, the owners nowhere in sight. FOR SALE signs are attached to stakes in nearly every front yard; it looks like Election Day—everyone's voting to sell and move.

As he and Herbie have walked, Ike has continued to develop the final passages of his Rhapsody in A-Flat, which has been approaching its coda with one solitary voice, seeming as if it will end much as it began—alone. Walking to and from town with Herbie, Ike has heard more sounds to incorporate into his piece. Turning his clarinet upside-down and breathing into its base creates a noise reminiscent of the ocean way off in the distance; putting his lips around the mouthpiece and blowing without forming the embouchure suggests a foghorn blaring. At the end of the piece, after he has performed it live, he will leave his B-flat Müller standing alone in a spotlight, and its keys will catch the light as if the clarinet itself is reflecting the town's unmanned lighthouse beacon.

Some time ago, living here might have been Ike's fantasy, a sort of self-imposed exile: talking to no one, hearing only his clarinet, his dog, birds, coyotes, and the bay; waking up to the sun rising over black water, walking through fields bordered with lilacs, watching fog rolling in and out, looking out to Canada, so very close that he could almost hit it with a stone. Of course, there would still be a touch of melancholy here, he knew that, but he would have expected some equilibrium, a bittersweet freedom, had not considered the memories that continued to swirl through him even as he rode here with Caleb Scheinblum, even as he walked down the road toward this house.

But yesterday, when Rebecca said she would arrive in Croix-de-Mer by early this morning, Ike could not contain his enthusiasm—he could no longer focus, could not sleep, could not play anything on his clarinet other than scales. His mother had been wrong, he told himself as he thought about Rebecca—maybe people weren't that disappointing after all. During the night, he tried to rouse Herbie for a walk, but since arriving here, Herbie has become increasingly skittish and he no longer likes taking walks in the dark: too many coyotes, too many wild dogs, better to rest in a safe, well-heated home and wait for sunrise. Ike tried to walk alone to the bay, but Herbie howled and wailed at the idea of his leaving before Ike had walked even fifty yards. Finally, Herbie at his feet, Ike sat by a window and waited—waited for the last muted white lights across the bay in Canada to go out; waited for the cries of coyotes to die down; waited until all he could hear was water and all he could see were stars and the lighthouse beacon; waited for fog to roll in, then out; waited for the sky and the bay to cycle through ever-lightening shades of gray; for rain to fall, then clear; for fishing boats to appear, then drift by; for Herbie to wake up, nose him in the stomach, lead the way out the back door, over the rocks, down to the water where they waited for Rebecca as the sun began to rise.

Ike is sitting on a rock, running scales on his clarinet, and Herbie is paddling in the water, chasing fish, when they hear a car rumbling toward the front of the house. "Come on, man," Ike tells Herbie, "Rebecca's here." At the sound of that name, Herbie scampers gleefully out of the water and up the beach, his black fur wet, tail at attention, mouth open in a smile, tongue lolling to one side. But Herbie stops at the side of the house. The dog peers out, and then his legs shake and his tail falls. He issues an alarmed bark and suddenly dashes back through the tall grass; he stops for a moment and barks at Ike as if beckoning him to follow before retreating farther toward the bay. "Come on, Herb," Ike says again, but when he reaches the driveway and sees the Crown Vic, his heart pounds. He sees the driver's-side door of the car open. Ike can hear Herbie wail the low A-flat he knows all too well as Officer Wayne Cahill walks toward him.

Once again, Ike's initial inclination is to run—to run fast down to the bay, run over the gritty black sand, dive into the blue-gray water, swim hard toward Canada, yell for Herbie to follow. But as the police officer approaches, hand on his holster, the trace of a smirk on his face as he asks what Ike is doing here, neighbor, Ike remains still. It seems to him as if he has spent his whole life running; in practically all his memories, he is hiding or running away from something—from people, from memories, from himself. Looking at Cahill, who stares straight back at him, Ike can see himself as a young man on South Colfax Avenue, can see his father dead on the kitchen floor, his mother with her head in her hands after Ruel tells her there had never been any love in her house. He can see himself grabbing his clarinet, knowing that soon he would have to run from this place. Ike can see himself walking away from Muriel, her face framed by the rear window of a black car stalled on Columbus Avenue. He can see himself driving east on I-80 from Chicago to New York; can see himself running away from Cahill in Central Park, then running down the steps at Strangers' Gate; can see himself running from the police station on 100th Street, up Broadway, through Riverside Park, up hills, over highways, to the very edge of Manhattan; he can see himself in Caleb Scheinblum's car speeding away from the city. And he can imagine himself now running for the water, swimming away from the house in Croix-de-Mer, reaching the Canadian shore, getting up, catching his breath before running even farther.

"What do you want from me, brother?" he asks Cahill. He lays his clarinet down at his side. No, he will not be running anymore.

Instead, it is Herbie Mann who is now running fast—through the grass, over seaweed and pebbles, back into the cold salt water. He no longer feels brave enough to protect Ike from the Crown Vic's driver. He hears Ike's voice and Cahill's too, knows he should move toward them, but he remembers the back of Cahill's squad car, remembers the muzzle, remembers Chloe Linton with blood oozing from the back of her head, remembers Rebecca's voice shouting—*GetawayJustgetaway*. He swims away fast, hoping Ike will follow. They have to swim; only if they swim will they be safe. Faster he swims, faster through the reeds and murky water, faster as he paddles across the bay, faster as he approaches the meadows of Canada.

When he reaches land on the other side, Herbie shakes himself off and turns around, panting as he looks across the water to the back of the house: one vehicle is moving toward it, but the other is driving away. The dog could have no possible idea of what Ike has said or done to make Wayne Cahill put his gun back in his holster and get into his car. He would have no concept of the fact that Ike has convinced Cahill to phone his station and make a false report, saying that Herbie Mann has been destroyed. He cannot know why Wayne Cahill is now driving fast back toward New York, would have no way of grasping the idea that a priceless B-flat Müller clarinet that over the course of two centuries traveled from France to Chicago to New York to Maine is now on the passenger seat of Cahill's car. But still, the dog can sense that a certain calm has returned.

Herbie Mann can see Rebecca step out of her car, can see Ike and Rebecca embrace, can see them walking down to the shore now, and he can hear them call across the bay: *ItssokayHerbyoucancomebacknow*. As he starts swimming back, the dog can hear the echoes of both voices, Ike's and Rebecca's running together, almost like a duet.

Mark & Allie

Autumn has arrived in Manhattan, and what will appear for a brief while to be one of the worst days of Mark Masler's life begins as one of the best. And though it seems unfair that bad news should arrive in this year when he has become a model citizen, when he attends shul every morning, routinely donates 10 percent of his income to charity, attends birthing classes with his newly pregnant wife and neither turns away during the videos nor leers during the breast-feeding demonstrations, still, he is strong enough to withstand some bad luck. Which song did his cantor used to sing in shul at Chanukah? "Who can retell the things that befell us? Who can count them?" What did Coach Hatfield say after he kicked Mark off his high school football team for the final time? "This too shall pass."

This was supposed to be a day of formalities—signatures, permits, handshakes. Mark's attorney Alan Ziegler had told him there was no reason to worry: Harvey Mankoff had accepted Mark's offer on the MTP building; the deal had long since closed; the trademark for Rolls Restaurant & Wash was secure; blueprints had been approved, construction permits procured, the menu finalized. Allie was negotiating good deals on napkin rings, goblets, fondue pots, pine-scented air freshener, and Turtle Wax. Marilyn Scheinblum—who had managed to convince her daughter and son-in-law that she had never been a thief and had been covering up all these years for Caleb, who was now living in Canada with his ancient lady friend—had taken a job as Mark and Allie's treasurer. Harvey Mankoff had banked his checks and moved to Spain. Josh Dybnick was leading negotiations with developers to build a high-rise condo with first-floor commercial space beside the restaurant/car wash, perfect for a bank or drugstore. Mark had even consulted with Dybnick about maintaining a small studio theater on the site to provide entertainment for his VIP customers who had finished their coffee and dessert but still had to wait another two hours for auto detailing. Dybnick had found a well-connected young actor with an enormous mailing list to run the theater.

Mark had been eagerly awaiting today's meeting at his lawyer's office; meetings with Alan Ziegler always brought back to mind his entire triumphant history—who he had been and who he had become. Ziegler had helped Mark beat half a dozen traffic tickets, plea-bargained a felony assault charge down to a misdemeanor disorderly conduct, and handled both of Mark's divorces, as well as the sales of all properties that Mark had inherited from his father. Mark loved being in Ziegler's presence, felt the two of them were kindred spirits. He loved Ziegler's expensive suits, his jewelry; loved how Ziegler called him "Markeleh"; loved how every time he presented a seemingly insoluble problem to Ziegler, the lawyer said, simply, "Done" or "Handled" or, in his more whimsical moods, "Okey-dokey, artichokey."

Which is why Mark was stunned when Ziegler led him into his office, shut the door, then said, "We've got big problems, Markeleh." Mark immediately knew he was in trouble; he asked if a lien had been placed on the property. But Ziegler said the truth was far worse than either of them could have imagined, then handed to Mark a faxed document on City of New York stationery signed both by the alcoholic beverage control board chairman and by city attorney Anthony Joseph Pools—Mark's application for a liquor license had been denied. They couldn't beat this, Ziegler said; even if they could pay someone off, there would still be too much liability. As it turned out, no one would insure a car wash that served liquor; the first DWI would put Mark out of business—didn't he have any sort of Plan B?

Mark wipes away tears as he rides in the backseat of a taxi speeding north on Central Park West toward home; he's wondering what he will do with his life now. He is a husband, soon to be a father. What would his son say if he could see him right now—that his father was a failure? Mark wonders if Hashem might be visiting retribution upon him for the life he led before meeting Allie, if Hashem is punishing him for having stuffed runts into lockers in high school even though he'd been wasted when he'd done it, for having spat and worse into the plates of customers who'd sent their food back to his kitchen, for having adorned the dishes of attractive female customers with phallic garnishes such as asparagus spears bulls-eyed through pineapple rings, for having cheated on Holly Kovacs and Tessa Minkoff.

Mark walks into his apartment, where Allie is lying on the water bed paging through restaurant-supply catalogs. Mark is afraid she will see he has been crying, then slap him in the face and snap, "Be a man!" Which is what probably should happen to him right now. Someone should slap him. Someone should say "Be a man!" Instead, Allie holds Mark in her arms, cradles his head against her breasts. She strokes his hair and his beard. But once Allie has finished drying Mark's eyes with a Kleenex, she says she doesn't understand why he is so upset. Without a liquor license, they're screwed, Mark explains.

No, they're not, Allie says, and when Mark asks her why, she raises her hands above her head, then draws them apart from each other as if describing the shape of a rainbow, or, in this case, a neon sign. "*Convertibles*," she says, then recites the motto she favors: "The Place Where Everyone Pulls Down Their Tops." With all-nude entertainment, Allie points out, one doesn't have to serve any alcohol at all.

At first, Mark shudders. Grim visions of the tit bars he used to frequent shimmy and twist around the dance pole of his brain. But then, the more he considers Allie's idea, the more he thinks she may be right. After all, a man must do everything he can to support his family; this is true. And once he has called Alan Ziegler to tell him the new plan, Mark Masler holds Allie in his arms. He looks out their window at the park and the city surrounding it. He never loved this view as much as he does now, he thinks; he will miss it when he and Allie move away from here.

A PROPERTY CHANGES HANDS

When I leave New York,
I'll be standing on my feet.

BOB DYLAN,
"Hard Times in New York Town"

THE VICE PRESIDENT & THE
UPTOWN MANAGER & THE NEW
OWNER & THE VICE PRESIDENT'S
EX-BOYFRIEND & THE VICE
PRESIDENT'S BOSS & THE
PRESIDENT'S EX-WIFE & THE
FORMER BUYER'S EX-HUSBAND
& THE FORMER BUYER'S
EX-HUSBAND'S FIANCÉE & THE
FORMER SELLER & THE FORMER
SELLER'S WIFE & THE PIGEONS ON
THE AIR CONDITIONER & JUST
ABOUT EVERYONE ELSE WHO HAS
EVER LIVED IN THE APARTMENT

or

ELLINGTON BOULEVARD:
THE MUSICAL
{Finale}

or

2B

It had always been an apartment much like any other in a building with little to distinguish it from the dozen other five-story tenements that went up in the late-nineteenth and early-twentieth centuries on West 106th Street in the neighborhood of Manhattan Valley. The apartment, 2B, might have had a few more square feet than 2A next door, might have received more daylight than 2C and 2D across that hall. Still, it was rarely anyone's final destination. Too small and inconveniently located to raise a family in for any great period of time, it was an in-between sort of place, a way station for Manhattan's newest arrivals, not nearly as indicative of its tenants' lot in life as where they went after they left.

For nearly fifteen years, 2B was the residence of the Treusch family—Franz, a barber who had left Alfdorf, Germany, with his wife, Mary, and their son, Gerhard. When Franz and Mary were no longer able to climb the steps to the second floor and decided to return to Alfdorf, Gerhard took over their lease. But he lived here for less than a year before he married an actress named Peggy Hopkins, with whom he moved west, opening his own barbershop in Las Vegas, where Peggy gave up her dreams of acting, choosing to raise a family instead.

In the building's first decades, its residents were largely tradesmen and laborers who worked long hours to ensure that their children would be able to lead lives more lavish than the ones they led at 64 West 106th: 2B was home to Billy Tracy, a plumber; his wife, Susanna, a stenographer; and their three children; to Viktor Baitz, a butcher from Hungary; his wife, Henrietta, a homemaker; and their four children. Then there were Bernard Ryan, John Higgins, Patrick Doyle, Jim Cahill, and Michael Gilmartin—a toolmaker, a postal clerk, a steamfitter, a brakeman on the Ninth Avenue Elevated Railway line, and a night watchman. They had all come from Ireland with their wives and children. The kids played kick-the-can and stickball on the street, their pockets full of penny candy from Clem's a block and a half west on 106th. The air was awash in the yeasty aroma of the Lion Brewery on Columbus Avenue.

During the Depression, the building's owner, Sol Cohn, declared bankruptcy, and 64 West 106th Street became the property of Relief for Poor Widows with Small Children; during those years, 2B was occupied by up to a dozen individuals at any one time—the building's din was audible to passersby at nearly all hours, and refuse piled up on the sidewalk out front. In 1934, the building was sold to the Lynch Dwelling Corporation for $52,000, and though the corporation performed some minor renovations, the building still showed the wear of its previous occupants. Nevertheless, with the preponderance of artists and musicians moving into Manhattan Valley, 2B became home to a motley group: Osbert Krause, who played saxophone in Harlem cabarets; then Liane Cardinella, who taught tap dancing lessons at home, much to the chagrin of her downstairs neighbors. Later it was home to Mildred Gerstein, who was deported back to her native Russia after being investigated for her secretarial work for the Communist Party.

In the late 1950s and early 1960s, as the neighborhood became seedier— it did not benefit from any of the federal government's urban renewal programs—the turnover in the building accelerated. The owners were a shady lot, families of slumlords operating under shell corporations, refusing to provide basic maintenance while milking the rent roll for all they could. Their tenants were mostly poorly paid downtown garment workers, until the city condemned the building in 1969. Soon, the only occupants were squatters who included struggling actors; a sculptor; a counterfeiter; a pair of adventurous political science graduate students from Columbia University who, while drunk one night, painted the Cuban flag in the stairwell; and a radical fugitive who stored nitroglycerine in the building's basement, where he produced crude leaflets for an offshoot group of Students for a Democratic Society.

In the autumn of 1977, Tommy Reyes lived in a sleeping bag on the floor of 2B for three weeks. He had left the Dominican Republic for New York with dreams of becoming a flyweight boxing champ, but managed to fight in only one Golden Gloves match before he died, along with two families, in the arson fire that nearly destroyed the entire building. The building remained unoccupied save for the occasional drug dealer or prostitute until Jerry Masler bought the building.

Still, even after 64 West 106th Street became the Roberto Clemente Building, a condominium, it represented less an ultimate destination than a midway point, its apartments parcels to be sold at a profit before the occupant moved on to the next step—the safer neighborhood, the larger space. Upon his arrival at 2B, Ike Morphy saw the apartment as a symbol of his escape, a step from the city he left to the artist he would become here. For Rebecca Sugarman, 2B was where she and Darrell Schiff would begin to raise their family before they too would move onward.

But after Rebecca had spent more than a year away from Manhattan with Ike and Herbie and, later, her daughter, Ella Mae, in Croix-de-Mer, she saw no need to return to the city in the foreseeable future or to keep making monthly mortgage and maintenance payments. She asked Josh Dybnick to put the apartment back on the market. Josh's first open house yielded a passel of potential buyers, none of whom seemed on the way to doing anything else; they were all established in their careers or had retired from them altogether. The interested parties included couples who had lived out in Westchester or on Long Island for the past two decades and were now looking forward to enjoying their retirement in the city; bankers from the Far East who needed a safe place to stay while doing business in New York, since boutique hotel prices had become exorbitant; white-collar couples who were still planning to move out of the city but wanted a cozy spot for weekend getaways. Even a former beat cop who had recently come into a small fortune and retired from the force attended the open house. Ultimately, though, Josh Dybnick, vice president and associate broker for the Overman Group and manager of Overman's uptown offices, found a buyer willing to outbid them all; tomorrow, apartment 2B in the Roberto Clemente Building will belong to him.

SHORTLY AFTER THE final curtain call of a matinee preview performance of the musical *Ellington Boulevard*, Josh Dybnick, now thirty years old, is quickly exiting the brand-new Mark Masler Studio Theater, located in the basement of Convertibles Car Wash & Gentlemen's Club. He is heading toward 64 West Duke Ellington Boulevard, where he will carry out the final walk-through of the apartment on which he will be closing at Gotham Mortgage tomorrow at noon. He had wanted to see 2B with good, natural light, but the musical ran long; now, the sun has nearly set, and he will have to make do with the overheads that remain.

Josh had attended the musical as the guest of his ex-boyfriend Miles Dimmelow, the Masler Studio Theater's general manager, who plays several supporting roles in the show, and Gigi Malinowski, author of the musical's book. Gigi will soon be moving to the West Coast to begin work on a new collection of stories, tentatively entitled *Iphigene's Return (or Whatever I Feel Like Writing About)*, while her fiancé, Darrell, completes his doctorate at a university for which a South American cowboy serves as mascot.

Josh hadn't seen a play in more than a year, and spent much of Acts I and II of *Ellington Boulevard* checking his watch, wondering why theaters couldn't institute industry-wide standards—no more than one intermission, no more than forty-five minutes per act. The only reason it might have been worth his while to attend was to distribute business cards to potential clients at the postshow party, but the audience was stacked with actors and hangers-on, all friends of the cast and crew, none of whom could buy any of the apartments Josh was representing.

Josh spent the major part of Act III, which took place in a Maine coastal village that was purely the product of Gigi Malinowski's now exceedingly vivid and surprisingly accurate imagination, in the lobby talking on his cell phone with clients and checking messages. He erased all the messages, including the ones from his father, who had called to ask why Josh had donated $500 to Nelson Frederick Twyne, the Republican candidate opposing his bid for Congress; and from Bradley Overman, who, now that he had moved into a new building, once again thanked Josh for having handled the closing of his and ex-wife Chloe Linton's apartment so smoothly. Linton, publisher of the start-up magazine *Chloe*, had moved to a house in Pound Ridge, while Bradley had bought a town house on 139th Street, where he was now living with Megan Yu and their dog Lucky Two on the top floor while Megan's family, who had grudgingly accepted their daughter's recent engagement, lived below.

When Josh finished listening to his messages, he made as if to return to his seat to watch the rest of Act III, but he no longer enjoyed sitting inside cramped theaters. He walked outside for a breath of air and stood on Broadway beneath Convertibles' brand-new pink neon sign. Behind fifteen-foot-high windows, workmen were buffing out SUVs and sports cars as men in suits watched from behind a red velvet rope, debating whether to enjoy the food and entertainment inside or supervise the waxing of their vehicles. He could hear the music blaring out of Convertibles' sound system, a new ballad by the Funkshuns: "This Funk's for Muriel (Not for You)." Josh spent his time surveying the avenue, picking out the high-rises in which he had recently sold apartments—there over Commerce Bank, there above Washington Mutual, there across from Citibank, there beside Garden of Eden.

All over America, air seemed to be seeping out of the real estate balloon. Potential buyers were taking themselves out of the market, vowing to rent for a year or two and see whether prices dropped. Forecasters were predicting recession. Customers who had speculated by taking short-term adjustable-rate mortgages were already taking a beating. The subprime loan industry was imploding, and foreclosures were going way up. There was a glut of new brokers in the industry; the number in the city had increased by 400 percent in the last six years even though new For Sale by Owner websites were rendering many of them obsolete. But Josh Dybnick was doing just fine. True, this business was being bled, but as manager of the Overman Group's uptown offices, Josh was performing a good deal of that bleeding. Every day, clients would ask Josh whether this was a buyer's market or a seller's market, but the truth was that, for him, it was neither; what mattered was that it was Josh Dybnick's market—a broker who knew what he was doing could always make a good living.

Josh timed his return to the Masler Studio Theater perfectly, walking in moments before the end of *Ellington Boulevard*'s Act III. Miles and the cast sang the show's finale, "Bing Bang Bust," then gathered for the curtain call. Josh politely applauded before the audience filed out. In the lobby, he shook hands with Mark Masler, who told him he was sorry he couldn't stick around to talk; he would have invited Josh for a drink in Convertibles' VIP room after the show, but he had to return to Allie, who was home in Westchester with their son, Bruno, whom they had named after Bruce Springsteen and Bono.

Josh was heading out of the lobby, trying to make a quick getaway en route to the Roberto Clemente Building, when he felt someone poking his shoulder. "Hey, Joshua," Miles Dimmelow said. "It's Josh," Dybnick corrected. Miles was still wearing his stage makeup as he gave his ex-boyfriend a handshake and a kiss on the cheek, while Josh offered some generic words of congratulation. Miles said that a cast party was being held tonight at the Ding Dong Lounge and Joshua was welcome to come; there would be lots of people he might want to meet. But Josh smiled and shook his head; he was on his way to his new apartment and no longer had time to meet Miles's friends. Besides, he said as he exited the theater, he didn't go out with actors anymore; the unctuous schnorrers never bought their own drinks.

Josh Dybnick walks down Broadway whistling Leonard Bernstein, then turns the corner at Duke Ellington Boulevard—he loves the sound of that name, so evocative of a rich artistic history, so full of rhythm and music and promise, so much the city that he had left Ohio to discover and that he has finally found. To the untrained observer, the boulevard looks much the same as when Josh first started selling apartments here. And although some of the neighborhood groceries have changed hands or been forced out due to high rents and increased competition, at first glance the buildings do not look much different either; nearly all the changes are occurring inside.

Entering the Roberto Clemente Building, Josh again notes that improvements are still being made—an elevator under construction, upgraded mailboxes, a four-camera video security system. Posted to the bulletin board is a job notice for a twenty-four-hour doorman. Never mind any talk of a real estate slowdown, this will be a good place to invest. Josh climbs the stairs, then opens the door to 2B and turns on the overhead lights. As per his requests, the floors have been waxed, the walls and ceiling repainted; no evidence remains of the message Ike Morphy once wrote on the ceiling. Josh carefully studies each room, even though he has already memorized every square foot of the apartment. He may no longer have any interest in set design, but he certainly knows how he will rehab this place. He can see pendant lights, an island kitchen, aqua tile in the bathroom, a granite sink, a silver tub. First thing he'll do, he'll take down these walls.

Josh is inspecting the front hallway closets when he hears a strange noise coming from the bedroom. He turns on the overhead light in that room and steps inside. Something is warbling outside the air-conditioner window. Josh pulls up the blinds; the window is spattered with dung and he can't make out anything beyond it. But once Josh focuses, he can see the air conditioner's newest pair of pigeons, who are cooing as they sit in a nest made of twigs and strips of the final issue of *The American Standard*. He watches the pigeons for a few moments. Although the apartment will not officially be his until tomorrow, he can make at least one improvement now.

Josh holds the air conditioner in place with a forearm, then pulls up the window. The pigeons' cooing becomes louder; a strong wind is now audible too. Josh can hear traffic on Duke Ellington Boulevard and he can see the colors on the pigeons' bodies—black, purple, just a trace of iridescent green. Then he shoves the nest—pigeons, eggs, and all—off the air conditioner and down the shaft from which, just before he shuts the window, he hears a flutter of wings, a thud, and the hint of a bird's alarmed cry.

Josh rinses his hands, then extinguishes all the lights in the apartment, locks the front door, skips quickly down the stairs, and steps out onto Duke Ellington Boulevard, heading past the Ana Beauty Salon, where a parrot is whistling "Conquering the City." Josh Dybnick continues walking quickly west, bound for Broadway.

THE FAMILY OF MANN

On the day before Rebecca Sugarman's daughter Ella Mae will celebrate her first birthday, Herbie Mann has been digging up the front lawn of the house in Croix-de-Mer to find some sweet-smelling dirt. But now his ears perk up. Dusk has fallen again, and Herbie has enjoyed another satisfying day—a swim in the ice-cold bay, a walk through a muddy forest, a bowl of fresh turkey gizzards for brunch. Ike is in town buying groceries, and soon Herbie will eat a late dinner consisting of plain, whole-fat yogurt mixed with kelp, and then, weather permitting, he will take a walk along the rocky beach with Ike, Rebecca, and Ella Mae. Tomorrow, he and Ike may walk into town with Ella Mae while Rebecca works at home on "Something of Great Constancy," the dissertation about Shakespeare's representations of love that she once thought she would never complete. Someday soon, they all may return to Manhattan, but for the time being, their home is here.

During the days, when Ike, Rebecca, and Ella are inside the house, Herbie has the run of their property. He swims. He chases fish. He smells the earth. He chases bobcats, runs from coyotes, barks for no apparent reason except perhaps to hear his barks cross the bay to Canada and return to him. He digs up soil, rolls in the dirt. He lies on his back and gazes up at the sky. He sleeps. He dreams of squirrels. Mostly, he remembers; he has not evolved sufficiently to have developed the capacity or even the desire to forget, and he remembers all that he has ever seen and felt. The dog cannot sense true distance—every place he has traveled seems to lie just outside his field of vision. If he ran fast enough, he could find the patch of dirt behind the Cathedral of St. John the Divine where he was born, could find Bradley and Chloe's old Riverside Drive apartment, the shelter, the Roberto Clemente Building, Mrs. Morphy's house on the South Side of Chicago, Rainbow Beach, the back of Ike's pickup truck, Wayne Cahill's squad car, the town of Croix-de-Mer. He does not understand the idea of moving to one place and leaving another behind; he can remember every place he has ever slept, and every one of them is still his home.

Herbie does not fully sense the passage of time—to him, it seems to be almost all one moment of running and standing still, of swimming and dreaming, of happiness and despair. He is a puppy and he is growing old. Ike is here and he is not. Part of Herbie is still swimming toward Canada, part of him never escaped the shelter, part of him is still in Chicago, part of him is digging in front of a house in Croix-de-Mer, part of him has only just been born. He smells the present and the past—he smells the meadows and his mother's breath, smells Chloe Linton's perfume and Ike's shirt, smells Lake Michigan, the grass in Central Park, and the steps at Strangers' Gate that once led down to West 106th Street and now lead to Duke Ellington Boulevard.

Herbie's hearing is sharp—he can hear the sound of footsteps approaching the house, but he can hear every other sound as well. He can hear his mother's distant heartbeat, can hear Ike's footsteps on a cold cement floor, can hear the B-flat Müller clarinet that Ike gave away to save him, can hear the Rhapsody in A-flat that Ike has completed on the new clarinet he has bought, can hear the symphony that Ike has only just started to write, can hear the snap of garden shears when Ike works in the garden; Herbie can hear the bay, can hear the tide coming in and going out, can hear Ike and Rebecca kiss, can hear little Ella Mae breathe while she sleeps, can hear the words Ike and Rebecca say to each other every night before they go to bed, hear them as a single thought, one single sphere of sound without beginning or end, words that always sound to him like *GoodnightRebecca**GoodnightIke**GoodnightEllaMae**Iloveyou**Iloveyou-too**Goodnight**Goodnight*.

Inside, Rebecca is putting Ella Mae to sleep, but outside, Herbie is standing at attention. His tail stands straight up. And as the footsteps approaching the driveway of the house grow louder, Herbie Mann starts running fast—Ike is coming home.

SONGS FROM
ELLINGTON BOULEVARD

By

*Miles Dimmelow and Gigi Malinowski**

(I'VE GOT) A PERFECT
SPACE FOR YOU

*An up-tempo number sung by The Broker to a Husband and Wife who
have come to his office in search of an apartment*

I've got a perfect space for you
A kitchen, a bath, a room with no view
No elevator; walking's good for you
I've got a perfect space for you

I've got a perfect space for you
Far from the subway, but close to the zoo
The plumbing's a mess, so you'll have to make do
I've got a perfect space for you

Who cares about doormen
You don't really need them
Who cares about pigeons
You don't have to feed them
Who cares for perfection
Perfection's a bore
If you want perfection
Don't move to New Yooooooooooork

I've got a perfect space for you
The ceiling is leaking; the floors are askew
The monthlies are high, but it's still quite a coup
I've got a perfect space for you

Who cares about laundry
The sink's big enough
Who cares about storage
Get rid of some stuff

Who cares for perfection
Perfection costs more
If you want perfection
Don't move to New Yoooooooooork

I've got a perfect space for you
A kitchen, a bath, a room with no view
No elevator; walking's good for you
I've got a perfect space for you

TOO MANY BOOKS
(The Song of the Jaded Literary Critic)

A romping Broadway patter song sung by The Literary Critic to The Buyer during their first interview at the offices of a New York–based literary magazine

Intro dialogue:
The Buyer: I envy you; you have the best job in the world—reading books all day long.
The Literary Critic: You think so?
The Buyer: Of course. Don't you agree?
The Literary Critic: Well . . .

(A PIANO FLOURISH IS HEARD)

Song:
I am the literary critic
For a well-known magazine
The perfect sort of job
For a gal who likes to read
But one thing I know now
It's not as easy as it looks
Because the fact of the matter is
There are just too many books

(Chorus)
Books! Books! Books!
There are just too many books!
Books! Books! Books!
There are just too many books!
I have no space to write
I have no time to read
There are just too many books . . . indeed!

There's too much David Baldacci
And there's just too much Maeve Binchy
Too many biographies of Liberace
Too many books about da Vinci
There's just too much James Patterson
And much too much Terry Brooks
That's the thing that I know now
There are just too many books!

Dialogue:
Literary Critic: You don't mean to tell me you actually like authors?
The Buyer: I've never met one. Are they wonderful?
Literary Critic: Well . . .

(THE CRITIC CONTINUES HER SONG)

I've met a lot of poets
I just don't like their style
I've met plenty of novelists
They sure like to take a while
I knew a guy who wrote sci-fi
I didn't like his looks
And the worst thing I'll say about him:
He wrote too many books

(Chorus)

(THE BUYER JOINS IN THE SONG)

The Buyer: But what about Singer?
Literary Critic: He wrote too much Yiddish.
The Buyer: But what about Rowling?
Literary Critic: Who cares about Quidditch?

The Buyer: Don't you love Roth? Don't you love Foer?
Literary Critic: Phil is a pill and Foer is a bore.
The Buyer: Surely some poet? Gwendolyn Brooks?
Literary Critic: I know who you mean; she wrote too many books!
The Buyer: That's so sad. Have you always felt this way?
The Critic: No. Not always.

Once I loved everything I read
I loved *Don Quixote*
I loved *The Naked and the Dead*
I loved Truman Capote
But Coleridge was my albatross
And Kafka was a trial
Now I have hard times reading Dickens
Even *Lyle, Lyle, Crocodile*
Bibliophilia is the disease
That I finally shook
And here's the way I cured it
I read too many books

(Chorus)

BING BANG BOOM!

The showstopper sung by all the brokers in The Realtor's office discussing the recent New York real estate boom; concludes with a group tap dance

Intro dialogue:
Customer: So, what's the real estate market been like? How are prices?
Broker: Well, let me tell you . . .

Song:
First they went SPLAT
Then they went BING
Then they went BOOM!

The market looked FLAT
Then it went SCHWING
Now watch it go ZOOM

If you have an interest in low interest
No need to forage for a mortgage
First you go BING, then you go BANG, then you go BOOM!

Customer: (spoken) Can you tell me about this apartment we're going
    to see?
Broker: (spoken) Sure . . .

First it looked UGH!
Then it looked FAB!
Now it looks WOW!

Man, there were BUGS
Then they REHABBED
Now it's worth SIX HUNDRED THOU!
You may not know the truth, so I'll be first to say it:

Don't worry 'bout your principal; you'll never have to pay it
First you go BING, then you go BANG, then you go BOOM!

Customer: (spoken) And what about the neighborhood? Is it safe?
Broker: (spoken) Well . . .

There were guns that went BANG!
Drugs that went PUFF
Bad folks all AROUND!

Once there were GANGS
Yeah, they were TOUGH
But they all moved UPTOWN

I don't want to pressure you; in fact I'd never try it
But if you don't make an offer, someone else will buy it
First they'll go BING, then they'll go BANG, then they'll go BOOM

Customer: (spoken) So, you don't think prices will go down.
Broker: (spoken) Well, as I said . . .

First they went SPLAT
Then they went BING
Then they went BOOM!

The market looked FLAT
Then it went SCHWING
Now watch it go ZOOM

If you have an interest in low interest
No need to forage for a mortgage
First you go BING, then you go BANG, then everybody goes BOOM-
    BOOM-BOOM-BA-BOOM-BOOP-BOOP-BOOP-DEE-DOOP-
    BOOM-BOOM-BOOM-BA-BOOM-BOOOOOOM!!

CLOUD ON MY TITLE

A soul-searching number sung by The Broker who has succeeded in business but failed in love

Intro dialogue:
Broker: *What's the matter, Josh?*
Josh: *Nothing. I'm just thinking.*
Broker: *Are you sure you're okay? Come on—you can tell me . . .*
Josh: *Well . . .*

Song:
I'm so single
I can't commingle
I have no covenant or trust
Is there no one I can lien on
If this boom goes bust?

There is a cloud on my title
I'm a-loan with no security
If you have no interest and no principal
You can't find partners with maturity

There's a cloud on my title
I need a brand-new start
Won't somebody repair
This broker's broken heart?

Broker: (spoken) *That's so sad. I never knew you felt that way.*
Josh: (spoken) *Wait, there's more.*

Seems like every decision
Leads to a rescission
I just want a partner who's preferred

What good's fiduciary friendship
When my deal's always deferred

There is a cloud on my title
I'm so filled with strife
Should I cease and desist
Or find a new lease on life?

There is a cloud on my title
It's not free and clear
I've done all my due diligence
So why am I still here?

Josh: (spoken) *You know, I always felt a certain attraction to you.*
Broker: (spoken) *Really? I never imagined.*

I'm so single
I can't commingle
I have no covenant or trust
Is there no one I can lien on
If this boom goes bust?

There is a cloud on my title
I'm a-loan with no security
If you have no interest and no principal
You can't find partners with maturity

There's a cloud on my title
I need a brand-new start
Won't somebody repair
This broker's broken heart?

Josh: (spoken) *So, what do you say? Do you want to see a show tonight?*
Broker: (spoken) *I'm busy tonight, Josh. In fact, I'm busy for the rest of
the year.*

WILL YOU LOVE ME WHEN THE BOOM IS OVER (THE MORTGAGE BROKER'S PLEA)

A searching love song sung by The Mortgage Broker to her lover as she contemplates recent, not-particularly-encouraging developments in the real estate business

Will you love me when the boom is over?
Will you love me when my debts accrue?
Will you love me when the prices fall?
Will you be there for me at all?
Will you love me when the boom is through?

I never thought I'd feel this way
I thought the boom was here to stay
What will happen when all these loans come due?
Will you love me when the boom is through?

Will you love me when the boom is over?
Will you love me or will you say adieu?
Will you love me when the prime rates rise?
Will you love me when no one's left to buy?
Will you love me when the boom is through?

I thought I heard a market crash
I dreamt last night I lost my cash
I dreamt that all my clients chose to sue
Will you love me when the boom is through?

Boomtime is over
Our honeymoon is dead
Boomtime is over
The market's in the red
Boomtime is over

I saw it on the news
So will you love me when the boom is through?

Will you love me when the boom is over?
Will you love me when the forecasts are proved true?
Will you love me when you fear the worst?
Will you love me when the bubble bursts?
Will you love me when the boom is through?

Boomtime is over
I can see the prices drop
Boomtime is over
I thought I heard a pop
Boomtime is over
This bomb won't be defused
So will you love me when the boom is through?

ACKNOWLEDGMENTS

Many many thanks to: Marly Rusoff for her unwavering support; Cindy Spiegel for taking me with her and continuing to offer her always invaluable and refreshingly blunt editorial guidance; Perry Payne, my not-so-secret informant who has helped me to navigate the world of real estate, and Bill Lychack who led me to her; Jerome Kramer for suggesting the novel's first joke; Evaristo Urbaez and family, Jose Valerio, Jackie Wildau, Steven and Adrianne Roderick, for their insights into the pregentrification world of Manhattan Valley; Yebio, Ethiopis, Imnet, the Sherman family, Norma Hernandez, Glenn Kubota, and everyone else in the Diego Rivera Building for representing a true sense of community on Duke Ellington Boulevard; Doug Lynch and Neri de Kramer for inspiration; Joe Feyjo for perhaps unintended inspiration; Kris Kruse of Halstead Realty, Peter Rodis of Brown Harris Stevens, Ariel Cohen of the Shvo Group, Kate Steffes, Edward Smolka, Michael Calica, and the New York Real Estate Institute for additional real estate insights; Gil Scott-Heron and Chris Connelly for musical inspiration; Mark J. Gleason for imparting his knowledge of the magazine world; Gretchen Koss and Meghan Walker for their early enthusiasm; Jennifer Gilmore, Bradley Langer, and Esther Langer for editorial feedback; the staff at the New-York Historical Society Library for always cheerful assistance; and for a variety of reasons, my thanks as well to Rich Aloia, André Bernard, Beth Blickers, Matt Carney, Christopher Cartmill, Robin Chaplik, Bryson Engelen, Jane Gennaro, Margaret Groarke, Barbara Hammond, Mary Herczog, George Howe, Melanie Kent, Michael Kerker, Hana Landes, Frances Limoncelli, Jeff Lodin, Dylan Lower, Ciara McLaughlin, Katie McLean, Dorothy Milne, Jordan Moss, PBC, Stephanie Rogers, Anjali Singh, Colin Smith, Andras Szanto, and Amy Topel. Thanks as always to Nora Langer Sissenich and Beate Sissenich for reasons too numerous to mention here. And one final thank-you to my father, Seymour Sidney Langer, who passed away at the age of eighty while I was writing *Ellington Boulevard* (I'll have more to say about him in my next book).

ABOUT THE AUTHOR

ADAM LANGER, the author of *Crossing California* and its sequel *The Washington Story*, earned his brokerage certification while writing *Ellington Boulevard*. Born in Chicago, he now lives on Manhattan's Duke Ellington Boulevard with his wife, daughter, dog, and a pair of pigeons who roost on his air conditioner.